THE RUSSLÄNDER

BOOKS BY SANDRA BIRDSELL

NOVELS
The Missing Child (1989)
The Chrome Suite (1992)
The R[u]ssländer (2001)

SHORT FICTION
Night Travellers (1982) and *Ladies of the House* (1984),
reissued in one volume entitled *Agassiz Stories* (1987)
The Two-Headed Calf (1997)

SANDRA

BIRDSELL

THE *R*USSLÄNDER

National Library of Canada Cataloguing in Publication Data

Birdsell, Sandra, 1942–
The russlander

ISBN 0-7710-1450-3

I. Title.

PS8553.I76R88 2001   C813'.54   C2001-901030-3
PR9199.3.B47R88 2001

We acknowledge the financial support of the Government of Canada through the Book Publishing Industry Development Program for our publishing activities. We further acknowledge the support of the Canada Council for the Arts and the Ontario Arts Council for our publishing program.

The author wishes to acknowledge the assistance of The Canada Council, The Saskatchewan Arts Board, The Regina Public Library, and McMaster University, during the writing of this work.

The epigraph from "Requiem: Epigraph" on page vi is taken from *Poems of Akhmatova* by Anna Akhmatova, translated by Stanley Kunitz and Max Hayward (Boston: Houghton Mifflin). Reprinted by permission of Darhansoff & Verrill Literary Agency, New York.

This is a work of fiction. Names, characters, and incidents either are the products of the author's imagination or are used fictitiously.

Typeset in Sabon by M&S, Toronto
–   Printed and bound in Canada

McClelland & Stewart Ltd.
The Canadian Publishers
481 University Ave.
Toronto, Ontario
M5G 2E9
www.mcclelland.com

1 2 3 4 5   05 04 03 02 01

For my mother,
Louise Schroeder Bartlette
and
in memory of
Judy Scott

No foreign sky protected me,

no stranger's wing shielded my face,

I stand a witness to the common lot,

survivor of that time, that place.

— ANNA AKHMATOVA

Massacre at Privol'noye

Eleven people were piteously slain by bandits at the Abram Jacob Sudermann estate of Privol'noye on November 11.

The dead are:		
Abram Sudermann	57
Aganetha Thiessen Sudermann	55
Peter Vogt	38
Marie Schroeder Vogt	37
Margareta Vogt	18
Gerhard Vogt	13
Johann Vogt	7
Peter Vogt	5
Daniel Vogt	3
Mary Wiebe	42
Martha Wiebe	43

Ältester Wiebe (no relation to the Wiebe sisters) brought news of the massacre to Nikolaifeld church members on November 13. Kornelius Isaac Heinrichs of Arbusovka happened upon the murders late in the day of November 11. All who were slain were found outside on the yard, with the exception of the young Gerhard Vogt, who was found slain on a field near a haystack, where it is believed the bandits caught up with him as he attempted to escape. The victims had either been shot, or had had their throats cut. Abram Sudermann's head had been severed, and lay some distance from his body. Kornelius Heinrichs heard a noise coming from inside the house and looked through a window where he saw a baby crawling around on the floor amid broken glass, its nightclothes bloodied. There are three other survivors who managed to hide, and escaped with their lives.

I

IN GREEN PASTURES

And they shall say, This land that was

desolate is become like the garden of Eden . . .

– EZEKIEL 36:35

She would always remember the awe, the swelling in her breastbone when she'd first seen her name written, Lydia guiding her hand across a slate. When she had learned to make her name she began to put herself forward, traced K.V. in lemon polish on a chair back, through frost on a window, icing on a cookie. K.V. Which meant: Me, I. Which was: Her. A high-minded child, body small for her age, and so alive. She had come to realize that she'd been small from the size of her own children and grandchildren. She'd been a tiny yeasty and doughy person going to and fro with a huff and a puff, as though the day was all she had, and at the same time, thinking the day would go on for good. As though she were living in eternity.

More than likely she had been born near-sighted, and her nest of yellow hair grew long and wispy, too fine for anything but a single plait that her mother intertwined with spun wool so the braid would not curl like a pig's tail and expose the nape of her neck to the chill of a witch's kiss. Being near-sighted was not a hindrance. She learned this from early on, through inference and the attitudes of people around her. What went on beyond the borders of her Russian Mennonite oasis was not worth noticing.

Because she was born female she could expect to dwell safely within the circumference of her privileged world. Her time would be consumed by the close-up busyness of a girl learning to be like the virtuous woman of Proverbs, by the work of becoming a ruby. Young girl busyness, such as noticing that the sun had overheated the classroom in which she sat, a corner room of the east wing of the Big House. Potted geraniums on the sills had begun to exude their distinct odour, and a Swiss clock hanging on a wall between two windows ticked unobtrusively. She was Katherine Vogt, the second-born daughter of the overseer of the Abram Sudermann estate, Privol'noye. Daughter of Peter Vogt and Marie Schroeder Vogt; Katya, her parents called her, the diminutive an expression of their affection.

While Abram Sudermann and his brothers Isaac, Jakob and David held their annual business meeting in an office at the front of the Big House, Katya supposed that her father, Peter, was impatient for their meeting to end and for his anticipated visit with David Sudermann to begin. She didn't know that her father's anticipation was for more than a visit, that he waited to hear whether or not the brothers had decided to fulfill his longed-for dream to farm his own land. She didn't know that the outcome of their meeting would set her father planning a future that wouldn't come to pass. But this was not the only story about to be interrupted. She was seated with children at a table in the classroom, studying a blank sheet of paper her tutor had given her and rehearsing silently what she was expected to recite at a Christmas Tree program that evening. *Ihr Kinderlein kommet, o come one and all, to Bethlehem haste to the manger so small.*

"Dear children, listen to me," their tutor, the spinster Helena Sudermann, said. Her voice rose effortlessly above the give and take of the children's conversation that had turned sleepy-sounding in the heat of the sun.

"*Ja*, I'm listening," Katya was quick to assure her tutor, and remembered not to rattle the bells that were strung through the laces on her boots and further annoy Helena Sudermann.

Katya's older sister, Margareta, was there, too. Greta, she was called. She and Lydia Sudermann, Abram's daughter, were joined at the head, and they sat now on the same chair, each with a behind cheek planted firmly on it. They had tied their braids together with a ribbon to demonstrate to Lydia's girl cousins, who were visiting over

Christmas, just how close they were. The cousins were daughters of Jakob Sudermann who, like his brothers, came to Abram's estate at Christmas when an accounting of their various enterprises took place. Lydia and Greta had tied a braid together to remind the sister cousins that they were best friends, and the cousins were not to try and come between them. It was 1910; Katya Vogt was eight years old. Her sister Greta and Lydia Sudermann were eleven, Lydia the oldest by ten days: twins, one light and one dark.

"We're listening, also," Greta and Lydia said, their eyes lifting from the pictures they had already begun to draw. Greta's eyes were the colour of hazelnut; Lydia's, a field of flax blooming beyond the meadow in summer.

"I generally pay attention when someone speaks. But usually that someone has something worthwhile to say," Dietrich Sudermann intoned in his new voice, causing Katya's little brother, Gerhard, to chortle. Gerhard was as sturdy as the oak-plank table in the kitchen of the Big House. Like the table, the Big House, the workers' houses lining the roadside of the compound, like the barns, sheds, and equipment buildings, her brother Gerhard had been built to last. He shared a bench with Dietrich, who was home from school for the Christmas holiday, and whose presence made Gerhard act older than six years.

"I want you to think of an oasis," Helena Sudermann said.

The odour of pipe smoke drifted into the room, and they heard a woman begin to cough. A door closed loudly, muting what had been a brood of women clucking. *Ja, ja. What do you think, Jakob says, even though Abram* – their conversation had spilled out into the hall outside the classroom all afternoon.

Beyond the window Katya could see the parade barn, and a boy, one of the coachman's sons, coming past the barn, leading a team of ponies hitched to the *kindersleigh*. White smoke streamed from the animals' nostrils and hung in a cloud for a moment before drifting away, and so she knew that while there was a wind, it wasn't a strong one, and so it shouldn't be too cold to go skating.

"Now, you all go on little trips, yes? With your papa, isn't that so?" Helena Sudermann was saying, hoping to snare their attention with questions.

7

"*Ja*, Papa took me along on a trip before Christmas. We went to Lubitskoye, and this is what came of it," Katya said and swung her feet, making the bells on her boots tinkle.

"Of course we go on trips," Dietrich said, the tone of his adolescent voice conveying to his spinster aunt that he wasn't going to be taken in by her questions. Besides, she knew very well that he went on trips. He had gone as far away as America, and could remember touring the Pillsbury flour mill in Minneapolis with his father.

"Yes, we do too. We go on trips, too," Greta and Lydia said. They were like two bells; one person with two heads, Greta's being shiny black, and Lydia's white gold.

"*Ja, ja.* Everyone here around goes on little trips," Helena conceded, relieved to have gained their attention. And the next time they went on a trip they were to be sure and notice how green the steppe was around the Mennonite villages in the colony of Yazykovo, in comparison to the land owned by Russians, proof of how God had blessed them.

They should notice how the glorious colours of spring burst forth so suddenly, and then from the month of June and throughout the summer, the sun scorched the land, an iron left standing on an ironing pad and turning it the drab colour of sand. However. A person needed only to travel a few *versts* in any direction from the Chortitza road, and they would soon notice that Mennonite land stayed green all year round, she went on to say to her overheated and lethargic charges as they sketched and coloured and waited for Sophie Karpenko to return from Ox Lake and announce, "The fire is lit, the skating hut will soon be warm. They can come now."

"Wait a minute. When we came here for Christmas, we didn't see any such thing," one of Lydia's cousins droned. She was drowsy-eyed, and her mouth hung open as though she didn't posses the energy to close it.

"We only saw snow," her sister concluded in a tone that suggested she couldn't understand why that should be. The girl cousins wore identical wine-red velveteen dresses with scalloped linen collars which had become palettes stained with Christmas food and drink.

They only saw snow, Lydia whispered to Greta, who rolled her eyes, and they broke into giggling. They only saw snow, Katya said, and laughed, too, while the sister cousins made pickle faces. As if on cue Greta and Lydia stopped laughing. Monkey see, Lydia said, monkey do, Greta finished, although she'd never been anywhere near a zoo and seen the mimicking antics of such an animal.

Helena Sudermann ignored them as she went on to say that the fields owned by Mennonites were oases of green in a semi-arid Russian land. Half black, half chestnut soil; the same sun, snow, rain; but God had chosen to bless the Mennonite farmer, including her brother, Abram, owner of the estate of Privol'noye and the chairs they sat on, the pails of *lebkuchen* and *gruznikie* – honey cookies and peppermint cookies – they had consumed over Christmas, the cocoa milk they would later drink when they went skating. God blessed the Mennonite farmer who prayed and gave credit, in godsholyname, amen. And that was what they had to be thankful for at Christmas, she concluded.

"Give credit?" Dietrich asked. He was the second youngest of Abram and Aganetha Sudermann's children, Lydia being the youngest. They had two older married sons living in Ekaterinoslav, and a daughter, Justina. Dietrich wasn't bothered that his hair covered his eyes. It came forward from the crown and at the sides, and when he was at home he was a blond sheepdog. But once he returned to the *Zentralschule* in the town of Chortitza, he wore his hair slicked back, a high-buttoned tunic belted at the waist. He resembled a well-to-do Russian, and not a Mennonite farmer's son. A *gutsbesitzer*'s son.

"Who does the Mennonite farmer give credit to?" he now asked his aunt.

"To God, of course."

"And at what interest does the Mennonite farmer give credit?" he asked, his eyes wide with a feigned innocence.

Helena's hand came up to hide her irritation, and to stroke a silky fringe of hair that grew above her lips and which she kept trimmed evenly with embroidery scissors. They sometimes called Helena "Moustache," *Schnurrbart-Len*, when they thought she couldn't hear. She now pretended not to have heard Dietrich.

"What picture will you make, Katya?" Helena asked, having noticed that the girl's paper remained untouched.

"I don't know. It's so terribly hard," she said with genuine anguish. She feared spoiling the sheet of paper, and at the same time, not being able to imagine what to draw, she feared betraying more than a weakness of her eyes.

"What have we been talking about so far?" Helena asked.

"Oases."

"Being thankful for God's blessings, yes? God sent his son at Christmas, did he not? To save us. And so the greatest blessing of all is Christmas."

"I would think Easter was the greatest," Dietrich said.

"Well, yes. Easter. But Jesus had to come first, did he not? He had to be born as a man and live among us, isn't that so?"

"Being born wasn't as difficult for Jesus as being crucified, was it," Dietrich countered.

"I'm sure that's so. But think of it. Knowing. Having to leave heaven, knowing what was in store for him. Having to leave his father," Helena said, with strained patience.

"Yes, but when he was a baby, when he was born, he wouldn't remember that, would he? And so the actual birth, Christmas –" Dietrich was not allowed to finish.

"That's not what I was talking about. I was talking about God's greatest blessing," Helena said.

"Yes, but . . ."

While the aunt and nephew sparred, Katya thought of the recitation she was expected to deliver later that evening at the Christmas Tree, grateful when the word *manger* sparked her imagination, and she began to draw.

Now male voices rolled down the parquet hall floor from the front of the house as the Sudermann brothers ended their annual business meeting and Abram, no doubt, brought out a bottle of good Mennonite brandy to toast their decision. All right, then. So be it. Abram had likely concluded that this was the third year he'd prevailed on his overseer, Peter Vogt, to be patient. In all fairness, a promise had been made before God, and it should now come to pass. The youngest Sudermann brother, David, must have declined the ceremonial drink, choosing instead to go and find Katya's father and bring him the good news. He came to the classroom door and stood for a moment looking in at them, a man the same age as her father, but his slight frame, and his face, untouched by the weather, made him appear younger.

From the kitchen came soft murmurs, bubbles of laughter as the servants, the Wiebe sisters, went about preparing the evening meal. The voices of small children rang out from an upstairs room where they played under the watchful eye of their *nianka*. They were the children of Jakob and David Sudermann. David's daughters had just come through whooping cough and were still pale to the point of being transparent. They had not been allowed to join in the play in the classroom, and for that, Katya was relieved, as they made her feel as though she were a gust of wind they had to protect themselves against.

She had decided to draw the scene of the nativity, the Christ child in a manger beneath two palm trees. She would suspend the Bethlehem star between the trees, and the entire scene would happen on an oasis, and therefore she would set the manger on grass, and not desert sand. I was born on an oasis, she thought as she tucked her chin into her neck and licked salt from her skin.

Finally Sophie Karpenko appeared. "The hut is warm, and the ponies are hitched to the sleigh. They can come now," she announced from the doorway of the classroom. She loosened her headscarf and shook it onto her shoulders, where it lay across her sheepskin coat, a splash of red colour, as red as her wind-chapped cheeks.

"Manya is waiting outside. She says her toothache is stronger," Sophie said to Helena.

"Still? *Liebe* Greta, you're a good girl. Go and tell Mary to make some clove-wax for Manya," Helena said.

Greta got up quickly, forgetting that she was still attached to Lydia.

"Ow, ow, ow. Let Sophie go and do it," Lydia said hotly, and held onto her braid to keep it from being yanked from her head.

"I can tell Mary, it's easy enough," Sophie said with a shrug.

"Did I say so? Did I say, Sophie go and tell Mary? No, I did not," Helena said, but before she could finish, Dietrich finished for her.

"The gypsy queen is supposed to go," he said.

"*Ja*, that's what I said. Greta should go," Helena said, her voice rising in annoyance.

"Oy, oy. This is a story," Sophie said as Greta and Lydia, their braids still tied together, manoeuvred their way across the room to the door. "Are you girls going to go skating like that?"

The bells fastened to the laces of Katya's boots jingled as she left the table, the sound making her think of muscular hares bouncing across a horse's path, their hind feet kicking up licks of snow. The bells said, I am coming, here I am, I am going. When she reached the hall she went off in one direction, while Dietrich nonchalantly strolled down the hall in the other, following the sound of a metronome and piano music coming from the parlour. Justina, playing a choppy rendition of the "Blue Danube Waltz," and faster than it was meant to be.

"Don't worry. Greta's coming with toothache wax," Katya consoled a forlorn-looking Manya, who stood shivering outside the back door, her jaw lopsided with a swelling.

She turned and went down the steps, savouring the bright clash of the bells as she followed a well-trodden path through the snow, going home before skating to make sure that her mother was there, her little sister Sara, and Johann the baby asleep in his cradle, as usual. The path home was one spoke in a giant wheel that circled the Big House, other paths leading off it across the compound. Smoke trailed above the roof of the summer kitchen and washhouse, the buildings blind to winter with their shutters fastened down tightly. The smoke came from the greenhouse chimney, she saw now. The building's sloped glass roof and windows ran with water, and although she could only see the blurred shapes of two people moving among the greenery, she knew from the breadth of shoulders and tumble of auburn hair that her father was one of them. The other, a thin shaving of blond wood, was David Sudermann. Her father and David were inside Eden, where mist watered the earth, the flats of peat moss set out on tables in preparation for tomato seeding. The two men had been friends since their *Gymnasium* years, when her father studied Agriculture in a technical institute in Alexandrovsk, and David, Russian. Whenever David visited his brother's estate he'd spend most of his time with his old school friend rather than Abram.

"We live on an oasis," she told them, even before the greenhouse door had closed behind her.

"*Hots-ducent!* An oasis, yet. So then where are the camels and fig trees?" her father said, his laughter vigorous and deep. She made two fists, and her father cupped them in his hands, her stiff arms vibrating with his happiness as he lifted her and set her onto the table that ran the length of the greenhouse. Then he stood back, crossed his arms, his teasing nature shining in his green eyes. "Go ahead, show Teacher Sudermann here what you can do. Emperor and Autocrat of all the Russias, Tsar of Moscow," he said, challenging her to recite the names of the tsar.

"Tsar of Kiev, Vladimir, Novgorod, Kazan', Astrakhan," she recited without the shyness that ordinarily would have tripped her tongue, but David Sudermann was her father's friend, and although they weren't related, he was like an uncle to her, more so than her real uncles, whom she seldom saw because she didn't live in one of the many towns and villages in the colonies, but here at Privol'noye, which was far out on the flat palm of the steppe.

"Of Poland, of Siberia, of Tauric Chersonese," her father prompted.

"Prince of Estonia, Livonia," she said, and gulped the moist air, felt her expanding lungs push against her ribs.

"Whoa," David said and laughed. "Isn't Tsar of Georgia in there somewhere?"

"Your head is on Christmas holiday, yes?" her father said. "That's what comes from eating so many honey cookies. You also missed Tsar of Lithuania, among others." He poked her in the stomach before lifting her down from the table.

"And what about King of Kings and Lord of Lords," David said.

The titles of the tsar were framed and hung beneath the monarch's portrait in the classroom, and although she couldn't read Cyrillic yet, she had heard Dietrich rhyme off the twenty or so titles enough times to have remembered almost half of them, and she couldn't remember having heard of King of Kings and Lord of Lords. When she said this, the two men laughed.

"Some people might also want to call him Blood-Sucker," David said.

Her father's laughter died and his eyelashes flickered as he looked out through the misted windows. "I've heard that very thing said several times now. In reference to us. Just the other day. I went for a load of coal in Nikolaifeld, and a man made a point of saying rather loudly that foreign blood-suckers ought to be made to pay twice as much."

"He was likely feeling his drink," David said.

"Even so, usually they don't speak so openly. We're to blame for everything, it seems. From bad weather to the taxes St. Petersburg puts on kerosene and vodka. Why they want to blame us is beyond me," her father said.

"Because it's convenient. Because the Russian peasants see what we have in comparison to what little they possess, the poor souls, and that's all they see. However, we Mennonites could set an example by paying higher wages. Make more of our schooling available to them," David said.

"Yes, not less," her father said with a hint of sarcasm. Katya knew that as Abram's overseer, he wouldn't say more. He'd voiced his disapproval loudly at home when Abram discontinued school lessons for the workers' children.

"Count Leo Tolstoy, champion of the peasant, that's my brother Abram," David said with a bemused look. "They're going to come in the hundreds to sing at his funeral, too."

"Funeral?" her father said in surprise. He hadn't heard that the writer had died.

"Last month. The newspapers were full of reports. The so-called enemy of the autocracy has gone to claim his reward," David said.

He went on to say that Tolstoy had been travelling when he'd become ill, and was taken off the train at a station called Astapovo. "Once the news spread that he was dying, the peasants came in crowds to say farewell. They were forbidden to sing hymns on threat of arrest," he said. He shook his head as though he couldn't believe his own words.

Beyond the steamed windows Katya saw the indistinct shapes of

Greta and Dietrich going to the carriage house where the ponies and *kindersleigh* stood waiting.

"In any case, I don't think a person should give too much credence to what those Lubitskoye loaf-abouts say," David said. "Blame the Jews, blame us. The peasant will spout the jingoism of whoever will promise him cheaper vodka."

"The talk's becoming too big for small ears. If you're going skating, girl, you'd better be off," her father said. "*Schnell.*"

She made her way through the unheated potting shed and its dampness, its spiders' webs shredded silk hanging from windows and rafters, mulling over the words *foreign* and *blood-sucker*.

Loaf-abouts, the loaf-abouts, she practised saying as she walked down the path towards home. Lubitskoye loaf-abouts, she said as she touched her mother's skirts in passing before scurrying up the ladder to her attic room to fetch warmer clothing. Touched her mother in the way her own children would one day touch her, a soft pressure, long enough for them to feel her warmth and be assured that the world was real.

She walked gingerly towards the centre of the lake to a patch of untouched snow, the bells on her boots tinkling, the sky high and farther away than a summer sky. The cold air was a hand pushing against her breastbone, her breath a white cloud in front of her face, her scarf matted with crystals and rough against her chin. Her father had once shown her the thickness of the ice when he'd gone to harvest their winter supply of water. Thick enough to support the weight of Percherons and a wagon.

The workers' children had beat them to the ice, had already cleared their spot across the lake before she'd arrived with the others in the *kindersleigh*. Over a dozen children, their twittering voices like wrens, probably carrying as far as Siberia. No, not Siberia, she thought, because the wind was from the north. Not Siberia, where some of their own had gone for land, and had lived on potatoes in a hole in the ground for an entire winter.

She could see Kolya playing with the children today, Kolya the furnace keeper, who was the same age as Dietrich, and the oldest among them. His barklike voice carried across the lake. Kolya the yell-throat, informing the entire world of his presence.

Greta and Lydia came skating past her, their arms linked, their skate blades inscribing the ice with their synchronized push and glide, while the sister cousins struggled to catch up. The cousins had kept them waiting while they'd changed their velveteen dresses for skating clothes, emerging from the Big House in rabbit-trimmed wool skirts and matching muffs. It was what they wore when they went skating in Einlage, they'd explained primly. Einlage being the town where they lived, and where their father, Jakob Sudermann, owned a wagon factory. Katya had heard that he walked the streets in a black homburg and mohair coat to distinguish himself, an industrialist, from the farmers. As though that was something to be proud of. There once was a time when a man would be ashamed to admit that he was anything but a farmer. But that was long ago, and now many had become other than what God intended, storekeepers and factory owners, buyers and sellers of goods who travelled between countries as frequently as they did the colonies.

Dietrich skated around the perimeter of their patch of ice, hands clasped against the small of his back, his legs scissoring in easy strokes, while Gerhard took running slides in his felt boots, which carried him far across the shining surface.

"Where are you making?" Gerhard asked Katya as he glided to a stop beside her, his arms extended like wings, cheeks reddened, eyes lit up like candles.

"I'm going where I'm going," she told him. Wait and see, and soon you'll know. She hoped he wouldn't want to follow.

His arms came down and across his brown wool chest. "Anyway, it's more fun here," he said.

She approached the stretch of snow. Beyond it was the patch of cleared ice where the workers' children played. The snow was laced with the three-toed prints of birds, and the footprints of rabbits. A lapwing flittered by, startling her for a moment with its giddy and erratic flight, a male in his winter attire, a green metal spoon stirring the air.

She stepped onto the snow, satisfied that it was loose, and as light as flour. She began to stamp out the initials of her name, while beyond, the workers' children ran screaming in a game of crack-the-whip, their voices overlapping, waves of sound echoing amid the frozen hillocks.

When she had formed her initials, she retraced the letters, keeping her feet together, shuffling up the lines to broaden them. *K* for Katherine, her father's mother, who had died before she was born. Known for having a green thumb, and for cutwork embroidery. She had been trampled to death by a runaway horse on a day when plans had been made to have a family portrait taken. They went on with it, let the photographer come, and her father's mother, held upright by her sons, was included in the photograph. A wide-awake-looking person, but who seemed flat, as though she were a picture of a picture.

She grew aware of the absence of voices, saw that the workers' children had lined up like fence posts and were turned towards the Chortitza road, where a vehicle was approaching. If it proved to be the Orlovs' rickety omnibus, then it would go on past the gates of Privol'noye to the Orlov estate. But as it drew nearer, she realized it was too small to be the omnibus. A visitor was coming to Privol'noye. The *droschke* slowed as it approached the service road leading to the barns and provision house, and then, as the driver apparently became aware of the main entrance beyond, the *droschke* went on past the service road to the stone gate posts, and an avenue of chestnut trees leading to the front of the Big House.

Their curiosity satisfied, the workers' children returned to their play, running and sliding across the ice and falling, the little ones scrambling after the big ones to catch a ride on their coattails. If there should be any cocoa milk left when she and the others were finished having *faspa* in the skating hut, Manya of the lopsided jaw would go across the lake and bring it to them. The children would clamour for a gulp, wipe their runny noses on their coatsleeves when they were done, then see who would fart the loudest. They were rough and stubborn children, unrestrained, heading for the door as soon as they could walk, as though they knew how soon they would be harnessed for work. A child shouted, and then another began to cry as Kolya's voice rose in anger.

"Little shit-puddle," Kolya shouted. "I'll trounce you to paradise. I'll teach you not to fool with me." He was kneeling on the ice beside one of the boys and hitting him about the shoulders and head.

Katya turned to the other shore and called for Dietrich, and when he continued his long and lazy gliding stroke around the perimeter of the ice, she knew that her voice was too thin and high to carry. Other children came running to the rescue of the smaller child, tried to jump on Kolya's back, yanked at his arms, but he flung them aside as though they were nothing more than a nuisance.

"You little chicken-fuckers, piss-pot lickers," Kolya shouted.

Her chest ached at the unfairness. Kolya was picking on such a small boy, and on Christmas holidays, yet. He set a bad example with his fighting, which the others were eager to take up, choosing sides, those who were for and those who were against Kolya, the big against the small, raising their fists and spitting at one another.

"You there, stop fighting." Don't swear, don't cry, don't pound at one another, rub faces in snow, tear at each other's hair. Their cries, snot-noses running, mouths contorted in hurt feelings and anger, disturbed God's air, the high clear sky given to them for the day. No one paid attention to her, and so she ran towards them, obliterating the letters she had tramped out in the snow. She would make her presence known, light into Kolya. She would pull his hair, pinch an ear, make him stop trouncing the little ones.

"Katya, Katya," Greta and Lydia called.

"Katherinaaaa," the girl cousins called, their young voices warbling like old women's.

"Katya, you come here. Right now," Dietrich called.

She was relieved that Dietrich was at last paying attention, was skating towards the patch of snow at the centre of the lake, and she turned and went to meet him. He would make Kolya stop acting as though he were a dog that had gone mad. She saw Sophie and Manya coming along the ridge of the pipeline path, carrying a pail between them, and baskets which held their *faspa* – buns, cheese, and jam – she knew. Jars of sugared cocoa to mix with heated milk. Kolya shouldn't be given any of the leftover cocoa.

"What were you going to do?" Dietrich asked.

"Make them stop," she said, her lungs burning from running and inhaling cold air. The children's voices had subsided, the skirmish over with.

"And how were you going to do that?" he asked.

She was glad for the diversion as Greta came skating over. Her answer to Dietrich's question wouldn't have been the honest one: I was going to talk with them. I was going to make them reason.

"You lost your temper," Greta said.

No, she hadn't, she explained. She'd held onto it. It was in her pocket, balled inside her fist.

"Well, show me, then," Greta said.

She opened her hand to reveal a crumpled soft square of sheepskin that her father had given to her and named Temper. She was to hold it and recite a psalm until her anger subsided. She hadn't lost it, she said, meaning she had called, and asked for help. Which she would not have had to do in the first place if the yell-throat hadn't started fighting.

❚❘❚❘

After supper her mother heated water and brought the bathing tub out from the pantry. She set it on the floor in the family room, arranged chairs around it which she draped with towels. Because they would attend the Sudermann's annual Christmas Tree gathering at the Big House, this was their second bath this week. Greta had been invited to play crokinole at the Big House, and stay for supper. It was understood that Katya didn't play board games, not until she could lose without anger, without sending game pieces flying. She sat now, enclosed in moist air that held the familiar odour of their evening meal of fried potatoes and onions, absorbed in the sight of her wet skin, the dimple of her navel. Her body was an oasis in the tub of water, and everything came to it, the soap bubbles, a cloth she had used to wash. She had bathed Sara, and then it was Gerhard's turn, but her brother had begun to object to being scrubbed by his sisters and so he'd been left, as her father would be, to her mother's hands.

After they had all bathed, tension began to permeate the house as her mother fretted over loose threads, a spot of chicken gravy on a pair of trousers which required sponging. While her mother rushed about, Katya stood on a stool and recited the two verses of *Ihr Kinderlein, Kommet* to the room.

"*Sehr gut,*" her mother said when she finished reciting. The only thing she needed to remember was not to tuck her chin into her neck and pinch off her voice.

She went with her family across the compound, the bells on her shoes jingling musically amid the sound of voices, as other people came from the workers' houses, people whose feet were familiar with the pathways that eventually connected to a single lane of packed snow leading to the back door of the Big House.

She wanted to widen the distance between herself and her family, and hurried on ahead. As she passed the stairwell of the Big House cellar, she sensed a presence. Then the darkness below was pricked with a sudden glow of light, and her legs went stiff. It was Kolya, she knew, the coachman's son and keeper of the furnace. *For thou art with me*, she thought as she stuck her hand in her dress pocket and held the square of sheepskin, not because she was in danger of losing her temper, but for uneasiness. Kolya exuded an energy that made her wary. His bark is bigger than his bite, her father had said, and praised Kolya for being strong and willing to do the work of two men. He kept the Big House warm in winter, slept on a mattress in the furnace room, made trips across the yard with a wheelbarrow to a stack of manure bricks which he piled at the cellar door, a supply that kept the house heated throughout the night. He emerged from the dark stairwell, and she was relieved when he greeted her with a nod, drew on his cigarette and blew the smoke heavenward.

Beyond her, the snow at the side of the house was lit up from the kitchen windows, and she passed through the light as quickly as she could, and then the light from the servants' quarters, and her parents still hadn't noticed the distance opening between them. She wanted to enter the house from the front door, to see the land beyond turned to silver by the winter moon. The windows in Helena's, and in Abram and Aganetha's room, were in darkness, and so the remainder of the way to the front of the house stretched before her dark with navy-blue shadows.

She reached the front of the Big House, where halos of soft lamp-light illuminated the entrance way, and stone steps, cleared of snow and sprinkled with salt crystals, led to a vestibule. She was about to go up the steps when her mother called. She hesitated, and when her mother called again, she returned to the corner of the house and stood where they could see her, and she them. More workers and their families had begun to arrive, and several were gathered in a dark cluster near the platform at the back door. She waited for her father to say that she should come and go into the Big House through the back door with them, and when he didn't, she waved and returned to the front entrance.

She wanted to see the spectacle that could be viewed from the front door: sleigh-runner tracks along the avenue; chestnut trees spreading their spindly shadows across the yard. Beyond the Chortitza road lay the meadow, a stretch of radiant snow edged by the trees of Abram Sudermann's forest. The brittle tree branches along the avenue rattled and clicked, and she listened, not wanting to hear anything other than frozen branches, not wanting to hear a baby crying in the forest, the cackling of Baba Yaga as she came flying in her mortar bowl, banging her pestle against its side as she hurried through the winter night with some evil intent. She didn't believe in fairy tales, and so she didn't want to hear Baba Yaga coming to pinch her arm to see if she would make a lean or fat meal.

She believed that Cain had slain Abel, that an angel had protected Daniel against the lions, that Jonah had lived for a time in the belly of a behemoth. She believed the stories told by people around her. Stories which, on a dismal blustery day in the distant future and in another place, she would suddenly be asked to tell. An earnest, friendly young man with a tape machine would come knocking on her door, some-one's grandchild on a journey into the past. Wanting her to tell the stories of the people she had sat next to in church – yes, we went as often as we could, when the weather permitted us to go, she would tell him. It wasn't always easy. Too cold or too wet. Too much snow. She and the man were in some way related; his grandparents had lived in the same colony she'd been born into. A colony of believers called to live in the world, but to remain separate from it, peace lovers, non-resisters who believed in turning the other cheek.

Katya entered the vestibule, the bells jingling softly as she removed her boots and set them on a sisal mat already lined with boots of various sizes. She entered the front hall and the house surrounded her with its warmth, its cooking odours, the sound of laughter.

Justina Sudermann stood in the doorway of the parlour, a slender young woman in a blue wool dress trimmed with pleated taffeta at the cuffs and yoke. Her hair was bound up at the back of her head like a skein of wool, a blond knot that shone whenever she moved. She was an older version of Lydia, a student in her third year in a *Mädchenschule* in Rosenthal. When Justina noticed Katya, she turned and beckoned to someone in the parlour. A stranger came to her side, a young man wearing a black Sunday coat, his Adam's apple protruding sharply overtop his shirt collar. A fox, Katya thought as he took her in with his small red-rimmed eyes.

"Is this one of them?" she heard him ask Justina, not taking his eyes off Katya.

"Katya, come over here and greet Franz Pauls. He's going to be your new tutor," Justina said.

She was struck silent by the news.

"Oh ho. So this is Katya. I saw the picture you made. It has lots of colour, doesn't it?" Franz Pauls said.

Did he mean too much colour? Had she put herself forward with too much colour?

"Do you like to sing?" Franz asked, bending slightly at the waist as he spoke.

There were voices and movement down the far end of the hall. Katya's parents were the first to enter, her father carrying baby Johann, with Sara in hand. She was about to go to them when Franz Pauls said, "I'm sure you do like to sing. I think we could have quite a nice choir, don't you think?"

She didn't know what to think. He had asked three questions, and so fast, she hadn't had time to come up with an answer for the first one. Gerhard came behind her mother, and was the last to disappear into the dining room, a room halfway down the length of the hall.

Dietrich was at the piano, no longer looking like a sheepdog with his slicked-back hair and his trousers tucked into his knee-high boots. Only Greta, Lydia, and she took school in the classroom now that Dietrich went to *Zentralschule* in Chortitza town. There would be four of them once Gerhard began. Do four people make a good choir, she wanted to ask him, but he was leafing through a music book on the piano as though he could read the notes flying up and down its pages, trying to look loose, like a high-school student. Beyond him, on a settee beneath a window, was Helena, fanning her face with a handkerchief.

Abram's coachman was the next to come, wearing his uniform, his scarlet cap held against his chest. With him was his wife in a blue striped dress of cotton madras, her head bound in a scarf and decorated with paper flowers. Their six children followed single-file, with Kolya, the oldest, in the lead. They were hushed and solemn, each one pausing before entering the dining room to peer up at the electric lamps lighting the hall, both mesmerized and confounded by the sight.

"And those children?" Franz Pauls asked.

Justina shook her head. "Some of them go to school in Lubitskoye. My father provides a man to take them, and a wagon. Those who aren't inclined don't attend, which is most of them." She spoke curtly, as though the question had rankled her.

The coachman was followed by the blacksmith, his eyes owlish, the skin around them, compared to his smoke-tinged complexion, startlingly white. His wife walked with him, a child in her arms, and behind them came another eight children, shuffling along in their sock feet, their hair shining as though wet.

The gardener and his family came down the hall next, and then the locksmith, who was keeper of the provision house and granaries, followed by Abram's head groom, an old bachelor, with two unmarried assistants. Last of all came the outside women, looking freshly scrubbed and wearing embroidered holiday blouses and red skirts. Manya was among them, the skin of her jaw stretched taut and shining with its swelling. Unlike the others, the outside women looked down at the floor, shy, and too overwhelmed to take in the sweep of lilies and ferns on the wallpaper, the electric sconces on the walls shedding their pale orange light. The Wiebe sisters and Sophie made their entrance behind the outside women, flushed and self-conscious in the frilly white caps and aprons they were required to wear with dark flannel dresses on special occasions.

Helena Sudermann got up from the settee and came over to Katya, extending her hand. "I can see you're surprised to have a new tutor," she said. "Everything in this life comes to an end, but something new begins, yes?" Katya took Helena's hand, feeling the scratch of thick calluses against her palm, and they went down the hall to the dining room where everyone had gathered.

Helena must have been in a woman's time of night-sweating and heat when she'd asked Abram to hire a tutor to replace her. There was much about Helena Katya didn't know and would only learn years later, when Helena's life was unravelled by others in another country, an old sweater taken apart piece by piece and knit into something that bore little resemblance to the person Katya remembered.

"Now let's go and sing our very best, *ja*? Let's go and make those little bells ring," Helena Sudermann said.

After much tugging and whispering by Helena, Katya lined up with the other children in front of the Christmas tree. The smallest – David Sudermann's children and her sister Sara – made up the front row, while she stood between Greta and Gerhard in the middle. The Sudermann sister cousins and Lydia, being the tallest, formed the back row of their choir.

The reflection of lit candles on the Christmas tree quavered in the glass front of a cabinet across the room. Shelves inside the honey-coloured cabinet were laden with Aganetha and Abram's wedding china, pieces which Katya had held to admire, how each rose pattern was slightly different, the gold inscription of their names, and date of marriage. Behind locked doors, shelves held chests of silverware, boxes of candles wrapped in tissue, silver candle holders, mono-grammed napkins and table linens that smelled of lavender. Linens such as the damask cloth that covered the dining table in the centre of the room, a table which was usually spread with a velvet cloth. On the table were small wooden plates, each holding an orange, a scattering of mints, and a chocolate. Silver coins for the adults, spin tops, tiny mirrors, mittens, and stockings for the children.

"All together, pay attention. Watch me," Helena Sudermann

whispered. She raised her arm, the fabric darkened at the armpit by a circle of sweat. She waited for their attention to turn from the people in the room, from the wooden plates, from the toes of their stocking feet, to her face, which strained with expectancy. If we're going to do this, then we'll do it right, yes?

Kling Glöckchen – klinge linge ling, Ring, little bells, ring, everyone around Katya sang, while she thought that perhaps she was partly to blame that they faced the uncertainty of a new teacher and his ways. She, along with everyone else, should not have called Helena Moustache-Len. Now they were paying for it. Time would tell how much. In the front row, Sara lifted the hem of her dress and flapped it in time to their music, making the adults smile. *Lasst mich ein, ihr Kinder*, is so cold the winter. *Öffnet mir die Turen*, don't let me freeze to death. Ring, little bells, ring, they sang as *Lehrer* Pauls stood in the doorway listening, as if undecided whether or not he should come into the dining room.

"Look, there's our new teacher," she whispered to Greta, who nodded as she sang; yes, she knew.

His reddish-blond hair and sharp features were what had reminded her of a fox. He was wary and anxious looking, and moved aside quickly whenever the Wiebe sisters and Sophie entered the room with platters of cookies and left again. Fearing that he was in the way, she knew. But as they sang he turned an ear to listen, nodding as though counting beats, already becoming their tutor.

While they'd lined up to sing, Abram Sudermann had entered the room in a bustle with his brothers, each one wearing a dark vested suit and a cowboy hat, bringing with them the smell of tobacco and a rich odour of fermented cherries. He had taken his chair at the head of the table, set his hat on the floor beside it, his brothers sitting on either side of him doing the same. David had come without a jacket, and with the sleeves of his shirt rolled to the elbows. He'd chosen not to wear his cowboy hat, but carried it with him. He'd also chosen not to sit with his brothers at the table, but had found Katya's father and gone to stand with him and the other workers, those who lived at Privol'noye and didn't return to their homes in nearby villages at the end of a work day, or for holidays.

The workers and their children stood on two sides of the room, their feet barely touching the fringed border of the blue and gold Persian carpet, the children's eyes reflecting the lights of the chandelier hanging above the table. Although her parents were not standing with the Sudermanns, Katya didn't think of them as being among the workers, either. Her mother had parted her light brown hair at the centre and gathered it at the back of her head with ivory combs. She held her chin high, her graceful neck framed by the lace collar of a messaline blouse the colour of cream, which made her skin glow.

Katya would one day learn how her father and David became friends, brought together during their student years in Alexandrovsk, when they'd spent hours at the beginning and end of every day waiting in a station for a train to take them across the Dnieper. David Sudermann had studied Russian History, Language, and Literature to qualify him to teach, and her father had studied Agriculture. She would hear that when he came to ask her mother to marry him, his Adam's apple was chafed raw from his collar, and bobbed as he struggled to say the word, *yes*. Yes, he promised Oma and Opa Schroeder, he wouldn't take their only daughter far from her family home in Rosenthal. There was no available land in either the Chortitza or the Second Colony, but instead in Arkadak, or in Ufa, which was near to the Ural mountains. Young men such as her father had gone to Omsk, parts of Kazakhstan, the Crimea and Georgia, and to the Caspian Sea for farmland, which was too far for the promise he'd made to the Schroeder grandparents. And so he went to work as overseer for Abram Sudermann, with the agreement that after ten years, Abram would sell him a parcel of land. Thirteen years had passed, David Sudermann had reminded his brothers during their meeting that morning. He'd found her father in the greenhouse and broke the good news. This year, Peta, my friend, you shall be your own man. In the coming months the brothers would decide which piece of land to sell to him.

By the time their carol had ended, the Wiebe sisters and Sophie were done fetching and carrying, and stood at attention in front of the sideboard, which was now laden with platters of cookies and jugs of *kvass*.

Everyone was now quiet as, from the youngest to the oldest, the children began to recite. Gerhard had memorized a long poem which he recited in a voice that would never be soft – the voice of a drunken sailor, someone had once joked. But in spite of the loudness of her brother's voice, Abram's head, which had begun to bob the moment he'd settled in his chair, dropped to his chest and remained there.

When Gerhard finished reciting there were smiles all around the room, and then a silence. Helena nodded at Katya. You may begin. Katya took a deep breath. "O come all ye children," she began, and then realized that Mr. Red-Eyes – *Lehrer* Pauls, she corrected herself – was staring at her from the doorway. Did he question why she'd given Joseph a striped coat of many colours, mistaken her whim to be an error? Were there too many tulips growing around the manger?

The lights of the candles flickered in the cabinet doors across the room and in the glass front of a wall clock whose brass pendulum swung across a brocade wall. Abram Sudermann's goat head rested on his chest; his hands, clasped across his immense stomach, were obscured by his grizzled beard. His snores filled the silence. She felt her mother's eyes urging her to recite, Greta's arm nudge her shoulder.

"O come all ye children," she began again, and then stopped.

Justina glanced at her mother, Aganetha nodding, giving Justina permission to tap Abram on a shoulder and wake him.

"*Ja, ja,*" he said roughly as his head reared up, a hand batting the air as though he'd been disturbed by a fly. "Let's get on with the parade."

"O come one and all," Gerhard said impatiently, and everyone smiled. In the silence that followed, one of the sister cousins laughed.

Across the room, someone began to recite in Katya's stead. She looked up and saw that it was Sophie, reciting in German, and so quickly that she hardly stopped to breathe. When she finished, astonishment bristled in the room, while Katya felt the heat of shame burning in her face.

Sophie stepped back and crossed her arms against her chest as though she expected to be buffeted by wind.

"Who is next?" Abram asked, breaking the silence, the only one in the room not to be astonished. While some of the Russian workers could speak a word or two of Plautdietsch, Sophie had recited in High German, the Mennonites' formal church and school language.

By the time they arrived at the part of the program when Abram and his brothers presented everyone with a Christmas plate, the sting of Katya's failure had subsided. Now, as she lined up once again with the other children, this time to receive a saucer of cookies and a glass of *kvass*, given the amount of jostling and excitement, she was sure everyone had forgotten. As she stepped up to the buffet, her eyes met Sophie's.

"It's wrong for someone to laugh," Sophie muttered.

Aganetha clapped her hands for attention as she rose from her chair. Her taffeta skirts whispered loudly as she went over to the table and, except for the wavering flames of the candles clipped onto the evergreen tree, the room fell into darkness. Katya heard the collective intake of breath, felt the intense stillness radiating from the perimeter of the room, where the workers and children stood.

"And now, on again," Aganetha sang as the chandelier above the table jumped with light. "And off," she said, her cheeks flushed, a strand of pewter hair falling over one ear, plastered now against her slick face. "Off, *ja?*" she said with a childlike giggle, her bright eyes scanning the workers, who were trying not to be taken in by the electric lights as their children were, by the switch Aganetha held, which was on the end of the cord hanging from the chandelier.

"Enough is enough," Abram grumbled.

"Once more," Aganetha said.

The room went dark once again, then lit up again, the objects on the wooden plates disappearing and, much to the relief of the children, reappearing.

The clock had struck the hour, its pendulum sliding across the brocade wall; the candles on the tree had burned down to their holders when Abram wished everyone a good year and God's blessings. Katya went out into the vestibule, its windows fuzzy now with the velour of frost. She felt the satisfying heaviness of an orange and a box of crayons knocking against her thigh as she wedged her feet into her boots and tied the laces. Salt crystals shattered underfoot as she went down the stone steps. The excitement of the evening left her unmindful of the immediate contrast of the heat of the house, and the frigid air. *Ihr Kinderlein, kommet*, she recited, the words tumbling out unbidden, the entire two verses of the song.

When she reached the back of the house where her family waited, they turned all at once, and together they went through the darkness. Her father's reassuring clasp and then pat on her shoulder was what she needed to know, that her loss of memory was not taken as a failure.

As they passed through the shadows cast by the summer kitchen and washhouse, the inverted V-shaped hood of the butter well, the other workers returned to their identical brick houses which stood in a row near a stone fence and the Chortitza road.

Her family's house was on the opposite side of the compound where, in warm months of the year, yoked oxen went through a gate two by two onto the fields, and where a buried pipe entered the compound from Ox Lake, bringing water into an engine shed. Katya's house had been the house of Abram's parents, built when they'd first arrived from Prussia, with a trunk of gold, some people said. How else could Abram's father have managed to immediately buy up so much land from a Count Ignatieff? Abram had built the Big House while his parents were still alive, and they had chosen not to live in it, ending their days in what was now Katya's house, and had been for as long as she could remember hearing the rattling of its shutters in a high gale, the creak of a floorboard underfoot, seeing the sun shining through an open door turning the polished floor the colour of butter.

She knew each scuffed door sill, the dent in a door frame made by a hammer her father had thrown across the room in a fit of unaccustomed anger. He'd chosen not to mend the gouged wood; it served as a reminder of a time when he'd been too hotheaded, and not what he had become, a willow bending over a creek bed, giving into the wind and not breaking; a soft man with a hushed voice that made people stop and listen, a smile sometimes pulling his face lopsided over an inner picture that had arisen. Katya knew there was a mouse hole in the pantry behind a bottom drawer, a drawer that held cooking utensils, a soup ladle whose ivory handle had turned brown when her mother had absentmindedly set it on the stove the day Gerhard was born. Everything in the house reminded her of something, a moment; a shaft of light moving with particles of dust brought to mind a time when she had sat on her mother's lap, when all around her had been new and unfamiliar.

Tonight when she looked out the back window of her little attic room, she would see the steppe moving with light. From the front window she would watch the lights in the windows of the workers' houses dim and extinguish. Look how one candle illuminates a window, a single lamp an entire room, and how the darkness is softened and made easier because of the light, her father had said. So let your light shine, and the world will be better for it. *And God saw the light, that it was good: and divided the light from darkness.* The crescent moon was bright and high, and tonight from the front attic window she might see beyond the forest to the Orlov estate, a dim suggestion of light from lanterns that were sometimes left burning all night in the sheep barns. She felt the orange knocking against her thigh and anticipated peeling it then scattering the pieces of rind on the windowsill to dry. Later she would put them into a drawer, the scent of Christmas lingering for months.

They were almost home when Katya suddenly realized something was wrong. She had the vague sense that she had forgotten something. When they had almost reached their gate she realized what it was. She dropped onto her haunches, her breath snatched away. The four little brass bells, two on each boot, were gone. She was eight years old and knew that thunder followed lightning, that if a sow had more piglets than she had teats, the smallest piglets would starve, that a hand held too close to a flame would soon feel its heat. But she had never known loss, and to lose something was incomprehensible. Oh, for the goodness of love, she cried out, bringing Gerhard to his knees beside her.

Peace be unto you, my dear friend Peter Vogt,

It was good to have fellowship with you during Christmas and to see how your blessed family has grown, and continues to grow. Your dear Marie must have passed the recipe on to my Auguste during the season, as we just recently discovered that we're once again about to be blessed in a similar way.

Further to our conversation around Tolstoy. This is bound to tickle your ear as it did mine. I was in the *volost* office when I overheard our favourite preacher say that he felt sorry for Tolstoy's family as all he'd left behind were the books he had written, which, in the preacher's humble opinion, wasn't much to show for a man's life. This is the same person who opposed the need for a Teachers' Seminary. He fears too much education will ruin a person for life. It is my experience from living in the centre of our thriving burg, that the less informed a man is, the larger and louder his opinions.

Thank you for sending me a copy of the inventory, which should prove useful when it comes time to advising Abram on which twenty-three *desiatini* he should part with. I say this because I noticed that three hundred *desiatini* my brother recently acquired is not included in the records, which, in my opinion, it should be. The absence of this recent acquisition in the inventory is good reason for me to bring it to Abram's mind when next we meet. Although I realize you would prefer the parcel of land near to Franzfeld and Cow Puddle Lake, I think Abram would be more open to giving up a piece of this newest purchase, which hasn't yet felt his plough and oxen.

Auguste sends her greetings, and wishes you continued blessings, as do I, as always.

Your friend,
David Sudermann

On the final day of school the tall grass went running before them in the wind, the unbroken land around and beyond Ox Lake becoming like water, and the plumage of the grass like a silver mist rolling across it. She would say to the young man who, in another time and place would want her to tell old-country stories, that in spring the steppe smelled like licorice. It was the perfume of the wild iris; and then there was also the sweet smell of hyacinth which always made her think of Easter – had he noticed that on Good Friday the sky was often grey with clouds? In Russia the sky was cloudy too. Nature did that. Nature paid homage to the one who had willingly gone into the tomb. She imagined that the scent of hyacinth was like the scent of the oil the women had used to prepare the Saviour's body.

But on that last day of school when she was young – her legs sometimes carrying her too fast, and she'd go rolling like a tumbleweed across the ground – she thought, such a waste, the iris and hyacinth blossoms shrivel so quickly and turn the colour of rust. You had to go slowly, search for them growing near to the ground among the steppe grass. She wondered if that was why they looked and smelled so extravagant, so they'd be noticed, even for a short time. The sight of spring wildflowers lifted a sadness she'd felt throughout the winter whenever she thought of the missing bells. She had expected she might yet find them when the snow had melted, but that was not to be.

Lydia called, and pointed out a steppe eagle riding the air currents far above them, and soon after they heard a grebe call out a warning from among the reed beds. They went round Ox Lake, the wind sweeping through the reeds, the sound a church of whispering, a dryness soon to be filled with green shoots and birdsong. In a field beyond the lake Greta startled a nest of newly hatched larks. She bent, hands on knees as she peered at them, the wind tearing her hair loose from its braids and whipping about her head. Look, when she moved, the birds opened their beaks. They became three apricot-coloured flutes as wide around as their bodies. If she should go close enough, why, she'd be able to see right through to their feet, yes? Let's not, Katya told her; the sight of near-naked birds always made her shiver. They must remember what they'd seen, as their parents would want to know.

We saw baby larks in a nest.

We heard a water fowl of some kind.

We saw an eagle.

When we went close by the baby larks, we looked inside their beaks and saw a pile of wriggling worms.

Earlier in the day she had gone to the road with Lydia and Greta, had chased after a carriage taking Helena Sudermann to the train station at Ekaterinoslav. Their former tutor was off on a journey and would be gone for the entire summer. Who was going to yammer at them for bringing mud into the kitchen? Not Sophie. The Wiebe sisters perhaps, but they were so mild they couldn't scold without weeping. Like Helena Sudermann, the Wiebe sisters hadn't married and borne children. While the absence of such joy had made Helena as gritty and bitter as a grape seed, the Wiebe sisters were as malleable as butter.

Now they went far away from Privol'noye and the Chortitza road, the meadow and forest beyond it. They went away from the Orlov estate, which they were not to explore as they had once done, had gone near to its wooden Great House stained charcoal by the elements, its roof carpeted with moss and peppered with the growth of mushrooms. They had taken turns standing on an upended pail and looking in a window to see a dwarflike man dressed all in black, poking at a fire. Then they had peered in a front window to see a long table spread for Easter with two-foot-high *paska* breads and bowls of coloured eggs. They had been surprised to find the familiar, and wondered how the Russians had come to know their custom.

Greta and Lydia began to run, their gingham backs becoming a flutter of pink and blue amid the rolling plumage of grass. Katya, watching them move away from her, would see them that way when her hair had turned white, moving away from her like that, their arms swimming to part the air and grass before their faces, the clouds racing before them as the clouds beyond their classroom windows had all morning on their final day of school. Windows which looked out east and south, and on clear mornings Franz Pauls, whose red-rimmed eyes were sensitive to light, would draw the blinds against the sun. Draw the blinds to blind him to what was going on in the compound beyond. Especially at the parade barn, where Abram, if he had a visitor, would bring his prized red stallion out into the yard and put it through its paces.

"Ecclesiastes, Song of Solomon, Isaiah, Jeremiah, Lamentations," Greta and Lydia had chanted as Franz Pauls's slender frame passed in front of a window. He had the mincing and calculating step of a rooster; he would stretch his neck suddenly and poke his head in this and that direction, as though amazed at something he'd just seen. Katya's earlier recitation of the Twenty-third Psalm had been almost perfect, and now Lydia and Greta were reciting the books of the Bible for the final test of the year. Lydia's fingernails grew white half-moon spots as she gripped the back of her chair, standing shoulder to shoulder with Greta, whose dark eyes shone with concentration.

Franz Pauls raised a ruler as though he might stop them, but his attention had been drawn by the sight of Dietrich coming across the compound. Dietrich had returned home for the summer, which meant that his older sister, Justina, must have too. Katya guessed this was what occupied their tutor's mind, from the way he began preening his rooster feathers, grooming the moustache he'd sprouted since coming to Privol'noye, smoothing it, twirling its waxed ends that curved so proudly up to his ears.

From the way Franz Pauls paced, only half listening to Greta and Lydia's recitation, Katya guessed that their tutor was as impatient as they were for school to be over. A guitar rested against the wall beneath a window; he'd brought it with him intending to play it as accompaniment for his proposed choir. But they hadn't done much choir-singing, after all. Instead, Franz Pauls frequently gazed out a window while he plucked the guitar, thinking of his town of Rosenthal, she supposed. Thinking of his pals at the high school he'd left a year early, going out into the wilderness to teach children who did not necessarily want to be taught. Thinking of the red stallion Abram, in a fit of good nature, had promised he would ride. Franz Pauls had bought new leather riding breeches which he wore on Sundays and holidays no doubt to remind Abram of his promise, but to no avail.

The sun came out from behind clouds, beaming full strength, and instantly the classroom was warmer. Brass chains looped against a wall brightened to the colour of gold. The chains were attached to the Swiss clock whose works were so efficient, she couldn't hear the clock ticking above Lydia and Greta's recitation. Beneath the face of the clock was an alpine house with two doors. A boy in blue trousers stood in one of the doorways, as though he couldn't decide whether to come out and predict rain, or go back inside and let his red-frocked sister come out of her door to give them a day of sunshine. The light was reflected in the picture glass of a photograph of the tsar hanging on a wall opposite the windows, highlighting a diorama, a picture they'd painted depicting the zones of plant and animal life of a eutrophic lake.

A silence followed when Greta and Lydia finished reciting. Franz Pauls's moustache went flying up as he smiled. "Very good, girls," he said, and their last day of school was over. Katya heard a hollow click, like a key being turned in a lock. The boy in blue had gone back inside the house, and the red-frocked girl had come out. The remainder of the day was going to be a fine one to go roaming.

They had wandered only for a short time when the wind rose suddenly, pressing the purple globes of wild onion flat against the grass, its plumage becoming stiff brushes which chafed their skin. Soon they had to shout to be heard, and by the time they'd reached the pipeline path and were racing to the compound, Katya was soaked to her skin and had nothing to gain by running.

By summer, the larks they had come upon in the nest were fledglings, and Katya couldn't tell them apart from their parents. When they perched on a marmot's hill and sang, they too stretched their crested heads and dipped their tails when they trilled.

How do you know those are the same birds? Gerhard asked, his voice full and rough-sounding. Her brother was eager to know what Katya knew, and more, his shoulders already squared in anticipation of gaining a seat on a bench in the classroom following the harvest.

Greta said she couldn't be sure it was the same nest, but Katya recognized the indentation of the earth where it sat.

"Yes, it's possible to know," her father said.

He had something to tell them, and so he'd come walking with them, his long legs pulling him through the weeds, a wide-shouldered, sinewy and work-fit man with a pie-shaped and flat face, a fringe of brown beard decorating its edge. You wait, they'll be back soon, he'd called to Lydia, who'd stood on the road watching them go. Just his own this time, he told her without explaining why.

He took them out into a field, where they startled a flock of birds, hundreds of starlings rising up at once, twittering, their wing pinions squeaking. As the birds flew off, they became a broad ribbon wavering above the steppe. The ribbon began rising at each end, the ends finally meeting at centre sky and forming a circle. It brought to mind Jeremiah's chariot, her father said as they watched the birds wheel from one end of the horizon to the other.

He said they should notice how certain plants turned the edges of their broad leaves to the sun, rotating as the sun travelled from east to west. They did so to preserve precious moisture. Notice the downy stem hairs, which drew in what moisture there was from the air. The plants' thirsty roots spread deep into the soil under their feet. Which was what he wanted for them, he said. He wanted his sons to put their roots down into their own soil. For his daughters to learn how weeds in a vegetable garden disguised themselves in similar-looking foliage, mingled with the food plants in order to escape the eye of a gardener. He wanted them to take lessons from the garden, to become good stewards of their future husbands' efforts, to become precious rubies. He wanted them to know that the next harvest he brought in would be their own. Over here, there, or there, he told them, gesturing with a wide sweep of his arm, west, east, south, their harvest brought in from whatever land Abram and his brothers saw fit to sell to him. Beyond them the grass lay flattened in a swirl, as though crushed by the body of a huge sleeping animal.

On the same day in late summer that Helena Sudermann returned home, the harvest workers arrived, all at once, over a hundred and fifty men. Katya was in the summer kitchen with the Wiebe sisters when they heard them coming down the road. They went to the stone fence to watch as the workers came four abreast, singing. They had just brought in the Orlov harvest, and were coming now to do the same at Privol'noye.

Their harmonious song rolled across the land as they streamed onto the compound along the service road, Little Russians, Tartars wearing astrakhan hats, Rumanians and Bulgarians. Men who would one day all look alike in grey army uniforms. Her father would sit next to such men on a bench in an inductee centre, but they would go to war carrying guns while her father would never even know the weight of a gun carried for shooting another human being. Instead, her father would wear the uniform of a Red Cross *Sanitäter*, and be trained as a nurse, and would know how to turn their bodies in a bed without causing needless pain, to change their bed linens and the dressings on their wounds.

The harvesters were met at the provision house by her father and Dmitri, the gardener's assistant, who recorded the workers' names and gave each one a mattress tick to fill at the straw pile, and a tin basin holding a rolled-up towel and a cube of soap. There were women among them, stubby and tanned, their faces lined and mouths chapped from the sun. They were field workers, and cooks whose cart was drawn by two lean cows and filled with bundles and pots and an icon which the women would set up on a shelf in their kitchen. When the workers had filled their ticks with straw, chosen their bunks, stowed what musical instruments they had brought with them, they formed a line again, this time at a shed, where Dmitri distributed tools.

In the days that followed, the men rolled a shed on wheels across a field, freeing the harvesting machine inside it. They dug an ash pit beside the harvester, and shovelled the wagonloads of coal until it towered in a glistening black mountain beside the machine. They sang as they unloaded barrels of water hauled from the lake. As Katya watched from her attic window, the oxen, looking like miniature wood carvings, went out into the fields at the break of day. They were hitched to cutters, whose blades carved a swathe through the gold carpet and threw it off in rows for the women to gather and tie into stooks. Throughout the days of the harvest the air in the compound was saturated with spicy cooking odours, the smell of straw firing the bake ovens, of freshly baked rye bread.

Katya's father was gone from the house long before sunrise, and returned only after the sun had set. He became one of the workers, unrecognizable, his face caked with the dust of chafe, the shape of his body emerging in the creases and folds of his dusty clothing. She lay awake in the thick heat of the attic room beside Greta, listening for him to return, listening as the house stilled and the clock's tick in the *grossestube* downstairs took over. During the day she watched over Sara and baby Johann, while Greta helped her mother harvest their own vegetable garden, the two of them picking it clean, hovering over the heat of a stove in the summer kitchen as they set jars of vegetables to cook in a boiler.

The day came when, for the last time, the women greased their hands and faces with fat to protect their already cracked and bleeding skin against the bite of wheat chafe and straw. At the end of the day when the harvester was shut down for the last time, the silence seemed deeper, and more complete. That evening the fires outside the workers' quarters were smaller; the songs the men sang quavered with melancholy, sighs and longing.

In the morning the workers lined up at the provision house, bundles and instruments slung from their backs, waiting for Katya's father to pay them.

When they left, he slept for half a day on a bench in the summer room, overcome finally by exhaustion and the silence in the compound beyond, lulled by the sound of baby Johann as he crawled about the floor. When he awoke, he hitched up his suspenders and went to see Abram. Today was the day he would talk to him about the land.

They were going to have a house in a village and land nearby where her father would go out and work with his own hired men, the village community pastures becoming home to their German red cows, watched over by a herder and shepherd dogs. Katya went through the rooms of the Big House looking to tell someone who did not already know, and found Mary and Martha Wiebe in the kitchen. The sisters were daughters of a drink-bump, a man who loved his brandy more than life, she'd heard, and they had been sent away to work at an early age to keep the family going. They were ordinary-looking women, Martha being heavy-set and brown-haired, Mary lighter-coloured and lighter of nature, too, more apt to laugh, while her sister looked for the dark side of things. *Ja, ja*, Katya, we know, the Wiebe sisters said, their soft sadness emanating from them like a night vapour.

She found Aganetha mending in the sewing room. Aganetha looked out overtop her glasses and her great bosom heaved when she sighed, and she said it would be terribly hard to get used to a new family living across the backyard. Someone else sleeping in the attic room, Katya thought, her room with its two views of the world.

Yes, I know you're going away, but you won't be going far, will you? Helena said. They would be nearby in the village of Franzfeld, or Hochfeld, perhaps, and Helena would often see them at church. The window in Helena's bed-sitting room looked out across the yard to the west garden wall, the flower gardens beyond it, and the orchards. Patches of colour moved among the fruit trees, workers picking in the pear orchard. Above the window was a shelf holding ivy plants, and an old birdcage whose presence had gone unexplained. Whenever they asked, Helena pretended not to hear, or said that some things were private and would remain that way. She now said that Katya and her family would not be going as far away as she wanted to go. Since she had returned from Germany she was softer, would sometimes nod and smile to herself as though she nursed a pleasant secret.

Sophie was in the washhouse, having finished cooking up a batch of soap. She was the last to know that the next harvest Katya's father brought in would be from his own land. Oy, Sophie said, my eyes will hurt not to see you. My heart will burn. My toes will curl up and fall off. Katya was grateful, and eager to help Sophie loosen the soap from the moulds, freeing the thick opaque slabs that always looked good enough to eat. And not only that, Sophie said, as though picking up on an argument she'd been having before Katya arrived. And not only that, now she had to wash the mattress ticks the workers had used, which were lying in a heap outside the door. Then she was expected to go and help Manya scrub the quarters, count the tin spoons fastened to the tables by chains, straighten the bent ones; she was being made to do the work of outside help. God, God, she muttered. She would need to fire up the stove in the bathhouse later to heat water, get rid of the tiny beasts that, no doubt, were living in the mattress ticks and wouldn't miss the chance to hitch a ride on her clothing, a bite of her tender skin. Outside is outside, she said. Inside is in.

She went over to the door of the washhouse and pulled her headscarf free. Then she sucked in her breath and her hands flew up and covered her eyes. Katya came to the door and saw what it was Sophie didn't want to see. There was Manya, carrying a bundle, running off down the Chortitza road. Oy, Sophie said, now my eyes really do hurt.

Photographs of the tsar and tsarina hung near the ceiling of Abram Sudermann's office, and Katya felt watched as she waited for Dietrich to show her and Gerhard what the imperial seal on land documents looked like. Her father would come to own such a document, he said. A Wells Fargo safe sat under a table in the office; a vise was clamped to the table and held a half-finished carving of a horse; a bottle of peach schnapps stood near the vise, and a glass clouded with fingerprints. The room held the conflicting smells of newly carved wood and a heavy body odour emanating from a chair whose back and arms were stained with perspiration. A smaller chair sat across from it, and she wondered if that was where her father sat when, throughout the years, he had come for his meetings with Abram. If that was where he'd sat when he'd come to remind Abram that it was understood and had been agreed. The time had arrived for the brothers to determine which parcel of their almost twenty thousand *desiatini* of land they would sell to him.

The office had two doors, and one was always closed. She knew from overhearing Aganetha's complaints about having to go through her husband's messy office at the start and end of every day that their bedroom lay beyond the closed door.

Abram's office was in disarray; piles of magazines were stacked around his chair, which sat at an angle near two tall windows. Their sills were deeply grooved with burns the length and width of her finger. She imagined Abram in his chair at the window, watching for incompetence and sloth, for *nekhai* – don't bother, it's good enough – the prevailing attitude of a Russian worker, he said. When Abram had grown too heavy for horse riding, he conducted his business from the overstuffed armchair, her father explained, and relied on him to be where his eyes and ears couldn't reach. Whoever would become Abram's extra pair of hands now in place of her father, would live in her house?

Dietrich found the combination to the Wells Fargo safe in the toe of an old boot lying to one side of it, and she was relieved when at last, after much fiddling, the door opened, and Dietrich put the slip of paper put back into its hiding place. Just then Lydia came down the hall and stood in the doorway, startling Dietrich, who then grinned sheepishly. You should have had someone keep watch, she said. You should start using your brains. You watch, he told her as he slid documents from a leather portfolio and began unfolding them. Katya went to look. The papers were stiff with age, and crackled. She peered over his shoulder with Gerhard, as awed by the sight of the official papers as her brother was. She touched the embossed double-headed eagle pressed into wax.

The document proved that his father had purchased the forest land from the Orlov family, Dietrich said. As he put the papers away, Katya turned back to the room and the shelves lining the wall above Abram's workbench, which were littered with an assortment of cobbler's tools, a bottle of horse liniment, a bronze statue of a bull.

Scraps of papers were tacked to the edge of a shelf, lists of supplies to be bought, the names of horse dealers and grain handlers, Scripture verses to remind Abram that the meek would inherit the earth, to render unto God, and unto Caesar; Christ's instruction on how to pray, in secret, and to begin, *Our Father which art in heaven*. She noticed the inevitable presence of a sack of roasted *knacksot* on a shelf, and beside it, a silver cup. A cup with two ear-shaped handles.

"That used to be yours," she said to Lydia, surprised that she had remembered, and to find the cup in Abram's study.

Lydia followed Katya's gaze as she came over and took the cup down from the shelf. She held it up to the light in the window. The silver had tarnished, which accentuated the relief pattern of vine leaves rimming the bottom of the cup, and its engraved letters, LS.

"It made my teeth hurt when I drank from it," Lydia said as she put the cup back onto the shelf.

Katya remembered the cup being pushed across a table towards her, how much cooler milk seemed to be when drunk from it. She remembered her tongue tracing the grooves of the engraved initials on its side.

"The best there is, Wells Fargo," Dietrich said as the safe door closed with a thud, as if to remind Katya and Gerhard that he'd been to America, and how much he savoured the English words, *Wells Fargo*.

Just then the closed door across the room suddenly opened, startling them. Abram stood on the threshold scowling, his bushy grizzled beard almost covering his entire chest. His bare feet were puddles of flesh on the dark floorboards.

"We didn't know you were there," Dietrich said lamely.

He had already got up from the floor and moved away from the safe when his father surprised them. Now he went over to the table and touched the half-carved horse, as though to imply to his father that he had brought them to the office to admire this latest carving.

"That, I don't question. Lydia, be useful. Come and help your Papa, yes?" Abram said as he held up a pair of socks. Lydia hurried to comply, waited for her father to settle in his chair before lifting his feet onto a hassock.

"Go tell Mama to bring my boots," Abram called after Dietrich as he made his hasty retreat.

While Lydia struggled to pull on and garter her father's socks, he studied Katya and Gerhard, his eyes half shut. "What makes you happy these days?" he asked, his voice rumbling with phlegm.

"We – we – we –" Gerhard stuttered.

"What does he want to say?" Abram asked.

"We like to go exploring," Katya said.

"It seems that everyone these days wants to go exploring," Abram said, as if referring to her father's desire to be his own man. He was going to do as promised. He was going to Ekaterinoslav, where he would meet with his brothers and discuss the sale of the land. Be still for the next few days, their mother had told them. Your father is anxious.

As she, her brother, and Lydia joined up with Greta at the rondel, horses whinnied in the carriage house, and then its doors flew open, letting out a team of chestnut bays hitched to a *federwoage*. The coachman sent the team galloping about the yard, testing the harnesses and hitches before he would drive to the front entrance and wait for Abram.

Everyone wants to go exploring, Abram had said, in such a way to imply he scorned such a desire. Forgetting that he'd taken his family to America during the time when Russia's navy was being humiliated in the Strait of Tsushima. They'd toured a soap factory and the Pillsbury flour mill in Minneapolis. Travelled south on a train to see cotton fields, and ranch lands, and had eaten watermelons that were oblong and not round, and weren't nearly as sweet as what they were used to.

Abram returned with an appreciation of the size of the Pillsbury mill, and its efficiency at moving grain and flour in and out on railway cars. He brought home the wide-brimmed Stetson hats worn by the cowboys, and as they had at the Christmas gathering, the brothers wore the hats when they met to report on their various business endeavours. The English, however, were ahead of the Americans when it came to steam engines, and so on the return trip, Abram had stopped in Ipswich, England to visit the gentlemen at Namsons, Sims & Head, and purchased one of their engines for his brother's flour mill in Ekaterinoslav.

It was years later that Katya learned the stories behind the Sudermanns' long absence during the war with Japan. She and her sister had been sent away: her father left in charge of Privol'noye to fight off the Red Cock while the Sudermann brothers visited the royal palace in Berlin. From there they went off to America, where people gathered at a train station in Kansas expecting to find them wearing rags, while "the truth be known," Aganetha had said, "we were dressed much better than they." Katya and Greta had been sent to the safety of their grandparents' village, Rosenthal, where Katya acquired a sweet tooth. She became so plump that even the rolls of fat on her legs had rolls, her father teased. And yet she returned with the notion that she'd grown smaller while she was away, and was relieved to see, once again, her reflection in her parents' eyes.

Now, as they went through the orchard, they came upon fruit pickers, women and children, working up on ladders. "We're going to explore the forest," Gerhard called, his chest suddenly becoming barrel shaped. One of the women pickers beckoned for him to come over.

"Take some," she said, indicating the sling of pears at her hip. Their journey would be more pleasant with a full stomach. As Gerhard scooped up a pear, she urged him to take several more.

"We could take them all, if we wanted. They're our pears," Lydia said.

"For sure, go ahead. Take all of them. Eat as many as your little stomach has room for, but you'll fill your underpants tomorrow," the woman said to Lydia. Then she laughed at her own humour, her face crinkling like a walnut.

The children around the fruit picker burst into laughter, their shaved heads bobbing. On the ground near the tree where she worked, a baby lay asleep on a shawl. The laughter had awakened the child, and the woman's attention was taken by its fussing, and she came down the ladder to tend to the infant.

They went across the meadow of wild thyme, grasshoppers clicking and springing up before their feet while Dietrich, mounted on his palomino, went riding down the road. Off to see Michael Orlov, Lydia said and pulled a face. Dietrich had become such a gadabout since he'd gone to *Zentralschule*. Her white-blond plaits were wound about her head, making her neck appear long and stemlike. She was either puffed up with excitement, or let down, and seldom in between. She had travelled to America and had seen more than her little eyes could take in. She had stretched her eyes, and now they needed to be filled with something new all the time, or she would put on a big lip, and sigh like an old woman who had known better days. Katya and Greta were dressed alike that day, in percale print smocks and wide white collars, black socks rolled to their ankles. Greta's sandal strap had broken earlier in the day and flapped as she walked, completing her fly-away and loose look, a collar button undone and her collar askew, hair rising from her head like tendrils of dark smoke.

Katya watched her shadow travel alongside her, felt her breath jolting in her chest with each hard step, arms swinging with an enthusiasm she didn't feel as her father began to sing, the sound coming from near the ox barns, his round baritone voice singing *Praise God, from whom all blessings flow. Praise him, all creatures here below, Praise him above, ye heavenly host, praise Father, Son, and Holy Ghost.* In summers past they had picknicked in the meadow but had never ventured into the forest, a dark band of trees that seemed to finger the land, as though the meadow was a tablecloth the forest would draw into its lap.

There was a clearing deep inside the forest, beyond the path, filled with mottled light. Two columns stood in the clearing, a set of steps leading up to a platform on which they stood, Corinthian columns, their stone rough and porous looking, and tinged halfway up with moss. High above, the leafy crowns of linden trees swayed in a gusting wind, opening up holes of light, the light warming the air where Katya had stepped from the path; like Greta, her mouth hung open as she gaped.

The forest had once been a park with formal gardens and an orchard, and the mausoleum had held the remains of members of the Orlov family, Lydia said. Its crypt had been moved to a cemetery in Odessa long before her father had bought the land. A growth of weeds marked the cracks in the steps, weeds that were all of the same height, as though they'd been shorn with cutters. Dried leaves had been swept into piles along the perimeter of the clearing. Beyond the clearing were dead and falling-down apple trees, the giant lindens, all of them planted years ago by the Orlovs.

Katya sat with the others on the steps, feeling the chill of stone, listening as a carriage went by on the Chortitza road. Abram, on his way to Ekaterinoslav. A dog barked in the distance as the carriage passed, and was joined by another, their voices rising and falling away.

She thought of her father singing "Praise God, from Whom All Blessings Flow," thankful in advance for his piece of land; his back young-man straight, as though he were wearing a new pair of shoes and trying not to notice. She thought of the stone they'd come upon near the entrance to the forest, a large smooth stone the colour of wet sheepskin. Around Privol'noye the stones the plough turned up were small, about the size of sugar melons. She'd heard of large stones far out on the steppe, as large as the one near the entrance into the forest, stone people with sledgehammer jaws, their hands holding up their protruding stomachs. Baba stones.

Her grandfather had told her about the Baba stones, about a storekeeper in one of the colonies who'd brought in such a stone from the land, and put it outside his store for the elderly to lean on when they used the mud-scraper. He'd also told her about a time when there hadn't been as many trees. No Lombardy poplars, no slender women waltzing along town and village streets, no acacia, mulberry, chestnut, and walnut trees, all of which had been planted by Mennonites.

They, the first Mennonite settlers, had come to an almost treeless land, and spent their first winter of 1789 in the north, at Dubrovno, a Potemkin estate. They believed they would farm near to Berislav, where the soil was a rich loam, and not as arid as that where they eventually wound up. The oldest villages in the Chortitza Colony, Chortitza and Rosenthal, were surrounded by a plateau of sandy soil, and grew up among hills and ravines, and among the giants who populated them. Giants who carried watermelons around in their wide trouser legs. Trousers that were made with enough fabric to sail a ship. What a comical sight those giant men must have been, swinging their legs as they walked, and the melons rolling around inside their trousers. But those men in the wide pantaloons had the last laugh. When the settlers went to the dock on the Dnieper to claim their trunks, they found them to be either half-empty, or emptied and refilled with melons.

"I spy," Gerhard said as the sound of the dogs' baying grew louder; a pack of hounds seemed to be nearing the forest. He made binoculars of his hands and scanned the treetops.

"Something blue that is the sky, yes?" Lydia said.

"I spy something that is red," Gerhard said and pointed to a piece of fabric snagged onto the lower branches of a tree.

Gerhard brought the piece of cloth to them. Lydia recognized her own embroidery, a chain of yellow daisies, the scarf the usual birthday gift given to the women workers, made by Aganetha from leftover scraps.

Abram Sudermann's forest wasn't really a forest, but three *desiatini* of overgrown parkland that he'd purchased, thinking it would be an inviting place for his family to spend a late Sunday afternoon. Just as Katya hadn't known about the presence of the mausoleum, she hadn't known that occasionally a gypsy caravan would camp there. That the sounds she sometimes heard weren't the witch Baba Yaga banging her pestle against the mortar, but tree poachers axing down trees in the night, which they left lying to infuriate Abram with the evidence of their thievery and waste. She didn't know that women went into the ruined garden to meet their working men in its gloam and shadows. She would be surprised to discover that people who had never been to Privol'noye would know such things, that the stories would travel wide and far and into the future.

She didn't know what Helena Sudermann knew, that Abram would sometimes follow a woman into the forest. His aging legs and girth no longer allowed for a chase, and so he was known to wheedle, and threaten, and to offer a ruble. She would remember finding the headscarf and imagine Abram had followed Manya into the forest and come upon her sitting on the steps of the mausoleum, her skirts up about her thighs to cool herself, and had taken it to be an invitation.

Lydia suddenly came to life. What they should do was play hide-and-seek, she said, and began to pace out the boundaries for their game. They wouldn't go any farther than the mausoleum, a gooseberry bush, a particular birch whose bark was scoured and peeling. Then she put her forehead against a column, and began to count.

Katya saw a fallen tree and ran to it, Gerhard behind her, the two of them dropping onto their stomachs on the ground beside it, while Greta ran first in one direction, and then another, as Lydia counted. And then her voice seemed to come from a greater distance than the pillars, but Katya didn't dare lift her head to see if Lydia had moved. A magpie settled in a tree beside her hiding place and began screeching, as if to boss them away, and then the sound of dogs barking grew louder, while Lydia's voice grew faint.

"Ready," Greta called out from where she'd at last settled.

Katya could no longer hear Lydia counting. A second magpie joined the one in the tree above her, and their scolding became intense. Then the baying of dogs suddenly grew closer, and the magpies flew away, a flitter of white and black darting among the trees. Gerhard sucked air and slapped his arm. *Mensch*, he said. The ants were stinging. Moments later they heard the snap of twigs and rustle of underbrush as Greta emerged from her hiding place.

Katya and Gerhard approached the steps where Greta sat, looking down-hearted. White fluff clung to her dark hair, seeds that had hitched a ride, and Gerhard pulled them out and blew them off the palm of his hand. This wasn't the first time Lydia had played a trick on them. Lydia, pretending to be surprised when they found her in the Big House playing the piano, asking, What? Were you still hiding? The sound of the dogs grew faint again, and a silence moved in. The air around the mausoleum smelled like a closet of mice, Katya thought. The stillness made her feel she was being watched. They began to hear a mewing sound, like a cat.

They crept back along the path through wild rhubarb and fern, the sound growing louder, the mewing turning into an angry cry that rose to a howl. Greta stood still on the path, and then she suddenly hugged herself. "Oh no," she said. There, lying on a shawl near the rock at the entrance to the forest, was a baby, its fists beating the air. Lydia had stolen the fruit picker's baby.

They began to hear the woman call, her voice on edge, and rising above the baying of the dogs. "My Ivanoushka, poor Ivanoushka,

Mother's coming," she called as she came running through the meadow.

Katya braced herself against the woman's anger, as she thought it was the woman who was now scuttling through the underbrush towards them, and not a small animal on the run from the dogs. She heard the boom of a gun, and the air reverberated with the sound, and the sudden ferocious noise of the dogs, the woman's cries. Greta scooped the baby up, and then hunters, Dietrich, the elder Orlov and his son Michael came crashing into the underbrush in search of a rabbit they were sure they had killed.

▮▮▮▮

Katya went across country with her father and Greta. Grass swept against the wagon bed, its wheels banging against a corrugation of furrows, jolting the air from her chest. Then the mares found their stride, pricked their ears as killdeers cried out while racing across the sky. The ride grew less unpredictable, the bumps even and quick, making her bones chatter. Her father's sharp knees jutted out from the bench, his hands clenching the reins and resting on his thighs, his knuckles white, and she knew he was still angry. They would need to apologize to the fruit-picker woman for taking her baby, he'd said.

"*Na*, girls, what's to be done with you?" He ended the silence which had come between them since he'd turned the horses from the road for open country. Katya knew he didn't expect an answer.

The sun travelled alongside the wagon, a fiery apricot about ready to drop into a yellow sea of grass. Her father turned his face to it for a moment, its warmth at sundown a caress, its slanted light making the curvature of the earth more apparent, making a person realize how the earth was a sphere that rotated as it moved through the heavens, the miracle being that, somehow, they didn't fall off. She often wondered if the earth might one day become too heavy to float, because each year plants grew and died, leaves fell, people died too and became dirt, which all added to the weight of the world. Her father's eyes became slits and his sun-browned face wrinkled, giving her a picture, she thought, of what he might look like when he grew old.

He turned away from the sun and lifted his hands from his thighs, allowed slack in the reins, and the whiteness of his knuckles began to fade. He said he thought he'd made it clear, long ago, that they were not to borrow any more babies.

Whether or not they improved the babies was beside the point, he had told them. A bath in a basin of water in the summer kitchen and a set of clothes which Lydia would smuggle from the Big House weren't improvements that the baby's parents necessarily appreciated. A child feeling lost and wanting its mother wasn't comforted by their cuddling, their songs and chanted nursery rhymes, or a curl stiffened with spit to stand up on top of the baby's head. *Jump, billy goat, jump, over the garden fence, here comes an old gypsy to pull your beard.* They gave up teaching babies, then, for teaching Sophie; Greta and Lydia coached her to learn the German Christmas carol she had recited so well that Christmas. They had not taken a baby in years.

"Unless you're a parent, you can't understand how a mother feels to find her baby gone," her father said.

"But it wasn't us. It wasn't us who took the baby," Greta said in a burst, her voice betraying how close she was to crying.

"Birds of a feather," her father said, meaning that they, being with Lydia, became guilty of her action.

They were going across country to Lubitskoye, a village they travelled through when they went to church in Nikolaifeld, a Russian village of thatch-roof cottages and small gardens set behind wattle fences lining a single dusty street. Katya wondered now if the women she had seen working in the gardens blamed her father for the high cost of kerosene and matches.

When they reached the outskirts of Lubitskoye, a cottage suddenly appeared. Children of varying ages sat on their haunches near to its door, playing a throwing game with pig-knuckle bones. Katya had seen the children of the workers on the estate play this game. When they saw the wagon, they gathered up their bones and drew together, becoming silent and watchful. Her father drove the team onto the yard, a piece of earth marked by its flattened grass, and scattered a flock of russet-coloured chickens. Several more children came running from the back of the cottage, followed by a man who must be their father, she thought. The man took off his cap and she saw it was Dmitri Karpenko, Sophie's father and the gardener's assistant.

Her father got down from the wagon and went over to Dmitri, and the children, seeing that their father knew him, gathered around the two men as they stood talking. Then a girl who looked to be Katya's age left the others and came over to the wagon, where she stood and stared at Katya. Cat's eyes, which were hard to turn away from. Sophie's eyes.

When Greta climbed down from the wagon the girl's gaze shifted to her, the girl watching her every movement as though she'd never seen anyone get down from a wagon before. Just then a yellow dog came loping round a corner of the house raising a hullabaloo, running towards Greta, who stopped to let the animal come to her, extending her palm to its inquiring nose. The dog wagged its tail and Greta scratched it behind the ears before joining her father. She had a way with animals and with people, Katya thought. Strangers smiled when they looked at Greta. Gypsy Queen, Dietrich called her, because of her brown eyes and wavy dark hair.

"You there, hello. I'm Vera," the girl beside the wagon said in Russian. Katya turned to meet Vera's intense stare, her hand opening to reveal a spin top. Vera was inviting her to come down from the wagon and Katya hesitated; the yard was carpeted with chalky curlicues of chicken dirt which would stick to her shoes, and she would drag it into the house when she got home.

"*Nyet*," she said.

Vera's features twisted with a frown and she ran off, went scooting round the side of the house, startling the chickens, their useless wings flapping and raising dust.

Dmitri called in the direction of the house, and its door opened. The fruit-picker woman emerged, her baby cradled in the crook of her arms.

"You have something to say, don't you," Katya's father said in Low German, reminding her of their mission, and then, in Russian, repeated what he'd said to the woman, who dipped her head and smiled shyly, beckoning to Katya that she should come inside.

The odours of the Karpenko house clung to her clothing, the black fumes of kerosene, tobacco drying in the rafters and the dankness of its earth floor. The yellow dog had parked itself under the table and whenever Katya moved it growled, which made the children laugh. They'd sat on benches along the walls, the bigger ones holding little ones on their knees, their eyes constantly on her as though she were a strange creature. The girl, Vera, wasn't among them. Now and then someone rapped on a window, the door, which brought more laughter. Vera had stayed outside, and when Katya thought of Vera's frown, the way she had gone running off when Katya refused to come down from the wagon and play, she concluded that Vera was making fun of her.

Dmitri's wife lost her shyness and spoke to them in Russian, asked them how many sisters and brothers they had, and their names, and they replied in Russian, which they studied in school, but which, except for talking Russian to Sophie, they seldom had the opportunity to practise. Unlike their father, who spoke Russian most of his working day. An old oma perched on the stove, the baby's cradle suspended from the ceiling above it.

That Sophie's home was such a damp and smelly place grew large in Katya's mind as they rode away from it. They were not returning to Privol'noye, as she'd expected they would, but going away from it. She was surprised, but neither she nor Greta asked why. Dmitri's wife had served them sweet tea and hard-boiled eggs after they had apologized to her for the worry they had caused, even though they had not caused it. Never mind, the woman had said, her face becoming young when she smiled. She likely knew who was responsible for making her worry. But their apology had not eased the moodiness Katya had felt gathering in her father for weeks. He sat now with back too straight, eyes fixed above the horses' heads, and unswerving. Moths fluttered about the lanterns hanging on each side of the wagon, keeping up with them as they travelled towards a thin rim of watery light on the horizon.

"*Ja, ja*, you're just going to have to wait and see," her father said suddenly, and then, realizing he had spoken aloud, he grinned at them, looking sheepish, his shoulders relaxing into a slouch. He reached behind him in the wagon for woollen shawls, which he dropped into Greta's lap and hers. As Katya huddled into her shawl, its scent brought to mind the bright clean rooms of her house, and she thought of Sophie, sleeping on a bench, or the floor, along with all the others, including a goat and pig in winter.

"Open your hand," her father said to Greta as he fished about in the pocket on the bib of his overall. He dropped an object the size of a thimble into it. Greta held it near to the lantern's light, and Katya saw the glint of gold. Greta gave the object to Katya, a tiny head of a woman, a sharp-featured woman whose hair was braided and hung in loops at the sides of a crown.

"I found it over there," her father said. He pointed to a dark loaf of land where the ground dipped into a gully overgrown with stunted trees and shrubs, and then headed towards it. When they had come as close to the mound as the growth would allow, he stopped the team. The silence filled with chirping crickets, a vibrating hum of insects, a hum that seemed to come from beneath the earth.

"I was kneeling one day to take a stone from a horse's shoe, and I saw something shining on the ground. There it was," her father said. "I thought this would be a good chance to bring it back."

He took a lantern and went round to the back of the wagon for a spade. He chopped at the hard earth again and again, but failed to break it. Then he tried cutting through the grass with the spade, stepping on it with his whole weight, finally throwing the spade aside, and gathering the long grass in his arms, grunting as he wrestled the roots from the ground. Almost brought to cursing, Katya thought as her father began to dig furiously, the earth flying from his shovel.

He held up his hand to receive the figure and she gave it to him, its presence lingering in the heat it left on her skin as he went to the shallow hole he'd dug and put the figure gently down, covering it with earth.

When they got back onto the wagon, the night closed in and the lanterns seemed to eat up the darkness, but when she turned, she saw the darkness behind them, a black smudge hanging above the trail.

They came near to the sprawl of buildings that made up Privol'noye, the rhythmic clop of the horses' hooves along the road growing faster as the animals anticipated the gates and horse barns beyond.

"What the devil," her father said. The presence of light in Abram's office brought him out of his slouch. He urged the horses into a gallop, but as they came near to the service road he slowed the team, as though needing time to think. Then they went past the service road and turned at the avenue of chestnuts towards the house, the wagon wheels throwing off sparks against the cobblestone drive. There was movement at a window in Abram's office, a shadow, and moments later light spilled out from the vestibule door and onto the steps as Abram came outside.

The wagon came to a standstill beside the rondel, whose clipped symmetrical hedges appeared to have been carved from stone. At the centre of the rondel was a fountain, made up of tiers of bowl-shaped marble, cascading water, which meant that the master of the house was home. In the dusky light, the water looked like silvery banners of silk. When Abram went away Aganetha had the gardener turn off the fountain to save on water, not believing what the gardener had told her, that the same water was used over and over, and except for a bit of evaporation caused by sun and wind, the birds coming to drink, no water was lost.

Greta climbed down from the wagon and hurried away, going to look for Dietrich and Lydia, Katya knew, while her father reached for her and swung her to the ground, saying, Hup! as he did so, becoming suddenly filled with energy, swinging her so hard so that her legs and skirts went flying, and she felt giddy when her feet met the ground.

"Go tell Mama where I've stayed," he said without turning, as he went to meet Abram, following him up the steps and disappearing into the vestibule.

She went along the side of the Big House and saw that Helena Sudermann's room was lit, saw Helena beyond the window at a table and the Wiebe sisters with her, listening as Helena read to them. Greta had already disappeared into the shadows of the west garden, wanting to find Lydia and Dietrich in the vine arbour where they had begun to go since the evenings had grown cool. A rustle of cloth came from beside the back door, Sophie on a bench, brushing her hair.

"Hsst. You there, come here," Sophie called in a whisper.

"I can't. I'm supposed to tell Mama where my papa is," Katya said.

"She already knows," Sophie said. She had seen Aganetha Sudermann going over to Katya's house. It was unusual for Aganetha to visit her mother, and the news made Katya want to rush home, but Sophie drew her into her lap.

Sophie's chin poked into Katya's shoulder as they watched lights moving in the orchard; the harvest was over, and the seasonal workers free to glean grain on the fields, fruit in the orchard, as they were now doing. They were free to pick through the gardens for potatoes and other vegetables the diggers' forks had missed. They had the right to some of the produce of their labour, what wheat there might be lying on a field, scraps of fat from the fall killing, the feet of butchered chickens. The gardener had set out paper sacks of flower seeds in the greenhouse and the workers were encouraged to take what they wanted to brighten their own yards, a sapling to provide a legacy of shade for their children, to break the wind and snow, a swaying green crown to rest the eye, weary of the flat bleakness of the steppe. They weren't free, however, to roam about the pastures, where villagers drove their cows to graze until Abram fenced the pasture lands and hired several Cossacks to ride the steppe, both day and night. And they weren't free to help themselves to the timber growing in Abram Sudermann's forest, although some of them protested that they had the right to do so, and to prove their point would drag a felled tree out onto the meadow and light it on fire.

"So you didn't come and tell me about your trip to the forest," Sophie said with mock petulance. "Next time you ask for a story, I'll think twice. Guns going off, you girls could have been mistaken for a rabbit. And my baby brother, too. I heard all about it from my father."

"We didn't do it. We didn't take your brother," Katya said.

"Good thing, or I would have bitten off your ear." Sophie laughed and nibbled at Katya's earlobe, her breath warm and smelling of garlic and onions.

"And you didn't tell me about this, either," Sophie continued, pulling the headscarf from her apron pocket. Lydia had brought it to her, she said.

"When you were on the road, did you see Manya anywhere along the way?" Sophie asked. "This is her headscarf."

Katya looked across the yard at the women's quarters, where the windows were always the first to go dark. The women would be up and about before daybreak, when she would sometimes hear the clink of their milk pails, a faint rising din of the cows bawling for relief as the women entered the barns.

"I don't think she's going to come back," Sophie said. "She's a Pravda, and most of them have no pride. They're known to kiss the hand of a person who kicks them around. But that's not Manya."

Katya thought of Sophie's cottage, its one crowded room, the dirt floor, and that Manya likely came from a similar place. "But why would Manya want to leave?"

"If I were God, I'd be able to tell you," Sophie said.

With Manya gone, Sophie wouldn't have anyone of her age and kind to meet with at the bathhouse on Sundays and complain to about the knotholes, which, although they were frequently stuffed with sod, were always unplugged. Sophie would have no one to grumble with about aching muscles, that her ears were full up from listening to Helena, who sometimes acted as though she had a ram in her skirt. Let her chew on her own moustache, not mine, Katya had overheard Sophie saying to Manya. Sophie would plug the knotholes, bathe, and say nothing, except she would tell the other outside women that Manya had been complaining about there being a fox prowling about their quarters, a fox had followed her into the forest.

One by one the lights left the orchard. Horses whinnied in a field beyond the fruit trees, and wagon trusses began to jingle. The peasants would likely sleep on straw beside the road, as once the harvest was over, the doors on the seasonal workers' quarters were padlocked. The sky was clear and bright with stars and a quarter moon whose light was strong. Look how the darkness is made less dark by the moon's reflection on the water in the rain barrel, how everything, even a spider's web, is turned to silver by its light.

"Do you believe in God?" Katya asked Sophie. She was thinking of the Red Corner in the one-room cottage where Sophie had lived.

She was thinking of its saint-picture, the candles placed before it, thou shalt not worship idols or any graven image.

"What kind of question are you asking? Of course. Everyone believes in God."

"And God's son in the New Testament?"

"Oh, that book. Helena reads it to them every night," Sophie said with a scornful snort. "It's better not to believe in that book. When the priests come round with their Pope sacks, they expect you to give them twice as much. For the son, and for the ghost. If you only believe in God, then they don't come as often," she said.

"Sophie, it's time Katya went home, and for you to come inside," Helena said from the doorway.

Sophie started, and released Katya from her lap.

"Yes, Mistress, I'm coming," she said.

Sophie hesitated before going into the house, and turned to Katya. "When you were at my house, did you see my sister Vera?"

"*Ja.*" And she was rough-looking and too bold.

"I miss that little *suslik* so much, sometimes my stomach hurts," Sophie said. She sighed deeply and the screen door closed with a gentle clap.

Katya was drawn through the dark gulf between the lit windows of the Big House, towards a warm glow of lamplight in the open doorway and windows of her own house. Acacia trees, their crowns the breadth of the roof, were guardians leaning over, listening, she thought, to her mother and Aganetha's visiting outside on the platform.

"You'd think that woman would have had more sense than to buy meat from a Russian," Aganetha Sudermann was saying as Katya came up the steps.

Her mother had dragged their one good chair from the parlour outside, and Aganetha sat in it, overflowed the chair on all sides, her plump arms resting on the shelf of her bosom, while Katya's mother sat on a bench leaning against the house.

"So, Katherine, you had a nice trip with your papa, yes?" Aganetha said to acknowledge her presence.

Before Katya could answer, Aganetha turned to Katya's mother, who leaned against the house, her face patterned with diamond shapes of light and shadows cast by lamplight through a trellis beside the door, her hands folded across her lap as though not itching to scrub the cucumbers afloat in the washtub at her feet. Katya realized that Aganetha's visit had not been expected.

"She was grinding meat in the summer kitchen," Katya's mother said to remind Aganetha where she'd left off in the story. She glanced at the tub of water, a scrub brush floating on its surface, then across the yard at the Big House, her eyes coming to rest on Katya's face and asking, Do you have any idea why your father is taking so long?

"Yes, she was grinding meat in the summer kitchen, and she called across the yard to one of her help, who was carrying the milk too carelessly and slopping it over the sides of the pail. I was telling your mama about a Mrs. Krahn. Mrs. Willy Krahn from Arbusovka," Aganetha said to Katya. "She passed away, and her funeral is on Saturday. The woman had bought a butchered lamb from a Russian who came knocking at her door. When she was grinding the meat and calling out to the girl who was slopping the milk, the meat grinder came loose and fell. It landed on her foot and split open her big toe. The meat was bad, and so she was poisoned," Aganetha said.

I'm so hungry for company, Katya's mother often said. Sometimes she sang a ditty about a bird that came carrying a letter in its beak. A letter from a mother in Rosenthal. The tips of her mother's shoes barely touched the platform as she sat on the bench, which made her look like a child. She motioned to Katya that she should take up scrubbing the cucumbers.

Katya cleaned the cucumbers, hearing Lydia and Greta's voices rise from the arbour in the west garden, and then the sound of a mandolin as Dietrich began to play. A balalaika took up the song, its music coming from the field beyond the orchard where the light of the gleaners' bonfire glimmered through the trees. A man began singing – *Odnozvuchno zvenit kalakol'chik* – his voice, honey sweetening the night. A door closed, and moments later Franz Pauls came across the yard, drawn by the magnet of song through the garden gate and the orchard, singing in his thin tenor voice as he went into the field to join the workers at their fire. A breeze wafted across the compound from the outer edges of their oasis, flipping the leaves of the acacia guardians behind her house, bringing with it the smell of manure which had been spread on the fields. When enough time had passed, and an ocean distanced her from the place where she had been born, she would recall this moment as proof that she had once lived in paradise.

Aganetha sighed. "I'll be so glad when Lydia goes off to *Mädchenschule*. There's just not enough for that girl to do out here. She's too old be playing with babies. When our Justina went, we saw such a difference," she said.

Just after Dietrich came home in spring, Justina returned from the Girls' School, but left to holiday in Simferopol in the middle of summer. It seemed that once her children got an appetite for travel they wouldn't stay put. The same thing had happened with her married sons, Aganetha said.

Katya had been relieved when Justina went away. She tried to avoid Justina, whose mouth uttered sweetness while her eyes said something else.

"Yes, soon Lydia will go off to the *Mädchenschule*," Katya's mother said as a spark of laughter rose from the gazebo. "I wish Greta were able to go, too."

"Well," Aganetha Sudermann said, and appeared as though she wanted to say more but was restraining herself.

"Mrs. Krahn's kitchen girl went out and collected herbs to make a poultice for her injured toe," Aganetha said, taking up the story again. "She also came back with mushrooms. Frau Krahn fed those mushrooms to the pigs later on. She didn't want to cause hurt feelings, and so, when the girl's back was turned, she hobbled barefoot to the pigpen and threw the mushrooms to the sows. By then, her toe was too swollen for a shoe, but she wasn't worried about it. The next morning, however, it had become worse. She had a black streak going up the inside of her calf. When she started to feel dizzy, Willy Krahn sent one of his men to Chortitza for the doctor. By the time Dr. Warkentine came, she was sweating so much they had to change her bedding on the hour. Not even a week later, she was dead," Aganetha said.

Katya set a cucumber on top of a pile in a basket and it started a slide. Cucumbers tumbled down and rolled across the platform.

Aganetha nudged a cucumber with the toe of her shoe. "Some people call this clean?" she said.

Katya's mother bristled, and then swallowed whatever was on her tongue.

"All I can say is, that's what happens when you buy meat from a Russian who comes knocking at the door," Aganetha said.

"It's more than likely germs got into the wound from the pigsty," her mother said. Her voice trailed off as though she regretted having spoken.

Katya's mother stood up and massaged a spot near her lower back, her eyes drawn to the Big House. As her mother stretched, Aganetha stared at her stomach long and hard, her eyes veering away when her mother noticed and blushed.

"Dr. Warkentine said the meat was spoiled. The woman handled the meat when she was grinding it, and then she handled her injured foot. That's how the poison must have got in," Aganetha said.

"Yes, that's likely what happened," her mother said, as though wanting to drop the topic. "Will Abram be home for a while now, or will he be off on business again?" she asked.

"He's going to Simferopol soon to get Justina and take her back to school," Aganetha said.

"Then we won't get to see her before she goes."

"I thought it was best Abram took her right to school. Keep her away from Mr. Cow-Eyes," Aganetha said cryptically, and then, in a whisper, "From Mr. New-Riding-Breeches. Mr. Trying-to-Grow-a-Moustache."

"Mr. Rained-on Rooster," Katya's mother said, and for a moment the two women laughed as though they were girls sitting on a step, trying to outdo one another. Katya stopped scrubbing, amazed to think that her mother would say such a thing, that she would hear her own opinion of Franz Pauls coming from her. The kitchen door at the Big House opened and Helena emerged. Her long white apron glowed as she went along a stone path and into the gardens where she had begun to go at the end of a day to say her prayers. She wanted to be close to nature, and to make sure that the garden paths had been raked.

"East India, yet," Aganetha muttered as they watched the woman disappear into the shadows.

Her mother's face closed, and she remained silent.

They heard the horses and wagon before they saw them emerge from the half-circle drive at the front of the Big House, her father going with the team to the wagon house.

Aganetha put her hands on her knees in preparation to leave, as though this action would somehow assist her in heaving her bulk up from the chair. "Do you know what Mrs. Krahn's last words to her family were?" she asked as she got up and shook creases from her skirt. A smile strayed across her face.

"No, I don't," Katya's mother said, surprised the conversation had turned back to this.

"She told them to be sure and scrub the meat grinder before they put it away."

Her mother stifled a burst of laughter, the tension relieved as Katya's father came across the compound.

"You may remember what the woman was like," Aganetha continued. "She was always, Do this, do that. But I suppose she had to be. Willy isn't known to be overly energetic. I'm sure it won't be long before he finds someone else. Those kind always do."

"Yes, some poor young girl who needs a place to go. Someone who doesn't have much say in the matter," her mother said.

"Never mind that." Aganetha's voice became soft. "I came over here because I wanted to say something."

As Katya's father drew nearer, she saw Aganetha's quick nervous glance in his direction. She knew his presence had stopped Aganetha from finishing what she'd wanted to say to her mother, and wondered why. If she had been older and more experienced in the ways of women's talk, she would have known that Aganetha had something on her mind that made her feel guilty.

"The prime minister has been killed. Stolypin. I think that's who Abram said it was. He was shot," Aganetha said.

"How could that have happened?" her mother exclaimed.

"In Kiev. In the opera house. And in the presence of the tsar, too. Had Chaliapin been singing? Of course, Abram couldn't say. I wondered, though, because I once read in the *Odessaer Zietung* that Chaliapin had agreed to sing in Kiev," she said, the sentence trailing off as she realized how foolish she sounded. There she was going on about an opera singer she had once heard sing and was eager to remind people of at any appropriate gathering, when the prime minister had been assassinated. A man whose name she couldn't remember.

A name that would come back to Katya when, years later, she saw a photograph in a book, a dacha wall blown to bits, timber tossed about a yard like sticks of kindling, Stolypin's summer home bombed during a first attempt on his life. She would read somewhere that the death of the prime minister in the opera house had ended what chance there'd been to turn aside the runaway horses of revolution, and would remember that a woman in Arbusovka had died when a meat grinder fell on her foot.

"What I really came to say is, I'm sorry," Aganetha said, and fled as quickly as her jiggling girth would allow.

As Katya's father came up the steps, her mother rose to greet him. "I heard about the prime minister. Is that what brought Abram back so soon?"

"Well, yes. He came with news," her father said, his eyes flaring with a sudden hardness, and his jaw working.

"Peta, tell me." Her mother took his arm and led him to the bench.

Her father leaned forward and dangled his cap between his knees, breathing deeply, his mouth twisted to one side as though to prevent him from speaking.

"Yes, it's true," he said at last, and tossed his cap across the platform. "Stolypin has been assassinated, which likely means the end to land reforms. Some people are breathing a little easier over that." His voice held more than a touch of bitterness.

"What other news?" her mother asked. When she put her hand on his arm, he drew away from her touch. She glanced at him with worry, at Katya, and began bouncing her knee. Katya felt the platform jiggle as she sat at the water-filled tub, her stomach gathering into knots.

What other news? he repeated. Abram and Jakob had been elected to a committee which would plan a celebration to mark the three hundredth anniversary of the Romanov dynasty. A pharmacy in Chortitza had been robbed twice. Workers in Isaac Sudermann's factory in Ekaterinoslav had threatened to strike, but Isaac averted the strike by scattering coins about the factory yard.

"And so?"

"Do you need to ask?" The words were a fist against a table. Then his shoulders slumped and he buried his face in his hands, his fingers curling to grasp at his skull. "It's not to be," he said, the words muffled.

"Not? Why not?" Her mother's voice was accusing.

"Because it's not to be." He left her side to pick up his cap and returned to the bench. "Because we couldn't agree on the price. The brothers believed I should pay today's prices for the land, not the price the land stood at when Abram and I made our agreement years ago, which was understood at the time. All except David wanted more. But when I reminded Abram, he said I was mistaken, he couldn't remember agreeing to any such thing. It was not written down that the price would be the same, but it was understood. It was understood. Before God it was understood." His voice had risen and then dropped, all his energy suddenly gone.

"But how much more?" her mother asked.

"Over three times more. Marie, it's not to be, not now, likely, not ever." The light in the doorway showed the sudden weariness on his face.

Katya felt her mother's deep sigh in her own chest. It was as though her mother had been holding her breath, had feared this disappointment might be in store. "I don't know if I'll ever want to forgive them," she said.

Katya's anger rose with her mother's bitter-sounding words. If she had had a stick, she would have hit something. The stairs, the railing. Blood-sucker, blood-sucker, she thought, repeating what she'd overheard in winter, without knowing the meaning behind it. She had taken the words to be an expression of anger, and now used them because she didn't have any curse words of her own. She threw the scrub brush into the pail of water and her father started at the sound, seemed almost surprised to find her crouching on the platform.

"Go and see where the others are keeping, Katya," her mother said. Go and leave us alone, her eyes said.

Her father's feeble smile gnawed at her stomach as she went to the arbour, where light was shining out through the vines. As she stepped inside she saw that Dietrich, Lydia, and Greta were gone. They had left a lantern burning on a table and, beside the lantern, the scooped-out remains of an unripe watermelon, the tabletop scattered with its pale seeds. And there, on a bench, was Lydia's silver cup she'd seen that morning in Abram's office; Lydia must have decided to use it.

The sight of the cup, which had been polished, made her suddenly furious at Lydia for having forgotten to take it in. A silver cup wasn't something to be left out in the damp air. Nor should a lantern burn for no reason. The square of sheepskin lay folded in her apron pocket, but there was no need to clutch it and recite a psalm. Lydia's voice came from the front of the Big House where she, Greta, and Dietrich were likely sitting on the edge of the fountain, trailing their feet in it.

She snuffed the flame and took the cup with her as she left the arbour, intending to go to them and point out that they had wasted kerosene. She went along the path in a grainy darkness hearing her parents' voices, their long silences taken over by the sound of rustling leaves of the acacia trees. Her father's grief eclipsed any joy she might have had at the prospect of not having to leave the estate. The intent of Aganetha's uncommon visit was now clear.

She approached the summer kitchen and the butter well just beyond, its roof a silhouette in the faint remnant of light. She was going to go to the front of the house, point out to Lydia and the blond sheepdog that they had wasted fuel, that Lydia had left behind her cup, which, in the dampness, would become tarnished again. A waste of polish. But her parents' hushed and hesitant voices, their sentences all turning up at the ends in a question, the sight of the Big House, its windows bold with light, diverted her from the path.

Before she knew it, she had gone to the butter well. She stepped up onto a log which Greta stood on when she drew the butter box up from the depths. She set Lydia's drinking cup on the brick wall enclosing the well and leaned over the wall, immediately feeling a chilly dampness emanating from the water below. The reflection of her head on the black surface blotted out what light there was from the moon.

Then someone called her name. She would remember for the rest of her days that someone had called, and would hear the voice among other voices in a crowded restaurant, coming to her on a lake shore while she watched over grandchildren at play, the voice would travel across the water, clear and distinct, *Katya*. If only she had answered, Yes, I'm here. But she hadn't. No, instead she had picked up Lydia's cup and held it over that chasm of damp darkness, and thrown it in. She had willfully thrown Lydia's cup into the butter well.

*T*hey arrived in Rosenthal during night, when it was too dark to see much of anything, certainly not the storks nesting on the *Zentralschule*, which Greta had written Katya she should be sure and look for. She would likely hear the clacking of the birds' beaks before she saw them, Greta said. They had started out for Rosenthal in the morning, and had stopped only once, to eat and to rest the horses. Katya's arms ached from holding her brother, Peter, on her lap. He'd been asleep for several hours and now she was clammy from his heat, her feet chilled from not being able to move. A light shone from a ridge of hills beyond the town, someone walking with a lantern, she thought, and when she pointed it out, her mother said it was the silver dome of an Orthodox church.

They passed a lone man, a watchman going along a sidewalk shaking a rattle, and he tipped his hat to them as they went by. Lanterns hanging from lampposts were welcoming circles of light illuminating the *volost* building, a store, a pharmacy. She was relieved when at last she saw a light glowing in a window and knew it was her grandparents' house. As they came to a stop in front of the gate, her Oma Schroeder came running from the house and down the steps in her slippers.

"Where's that girl of mine?" her grandmother called, and a dog in a neighbouring yard began to bark.

Oma gathered their mother and baby Daniel in an embrace, then took Daniel and unwrapped him there in the street, anxious to see how much he'd grown since she'd come to attend his birth in winter. When Daniel awoke with a shiver and smiled, Oma shouted to a woman across the street who had come out to watch. "Look at this one. This one is just like Kornie's Wilhelm's Jasch. Kornie's Wilhelm's Jasch would give you such a smile even when he was wet and hungry," her grandmother said.

They had all come to Rosenthal to fetch Greta at the end of the school year, as Lydia was not returning home but going off on holiday to the Azov Sea, and Greta was not allowed to travel alone. Abram had lent them the use of a *federwoage*, and its cushioned seats and strong springs made the trip seem shorter than usual.

"Welcome, welcome," her grandfather sang out as he came through the garden. When Katya embraced him she felt his fingers press a coin into her palm. Greta came from the house behind him, anxious for a greeting, and when Katya hugged her, she realized her sister had grown. Gerhard, eager to prove his strength, rushed between the house and the carriage, carrying several bundles at once. He would have carried his sister Sara too, but for their Uncle Bernhard, who came from his house at the back of their grandparents' yard and scooped Sara from his arms.

Within moments they were drinking tea and crunching *rollkuchen* dripping with watermelon syrup, her grandmother hovering over the table refilling empty glasses, touching Katya's shoulder, Gerhard's head, in passing. Their grandfather's eyes went from one to another while he plied her father for news, how much land had he seeded, how many lambs and calves had been dropped this spring. Greta came with towels and a large bucket of water; she wanted to wash Katya's and Gerhard's feet, as she had already done for Sara and her little brothers, who were now tucked in bed. Katya stood in the bucket up to her shins in soapy water, her feet warmed instantly, this nightly ritual of foot cleansing always making her feel that the day had been a good one, making her suddenly need to pee.

That night she lay awake between Sara and Greta, the excitement of having arrived still too strong to allow sleep. Her father, Uncle

Bernhard, and her grandfather talked in the parlour over the heavy ticking of a Kroeger clock. She felt watched over by the portraits of Schroeder ancestors, men whose images were set in matching oval frames which hung on a wall beside the bed.

The portrait nearest to the door was the oldest, a painting of Wilhelm Schroeder, whose ancestors had suffered persecution in the seventeenth century. One of the Flanders Schroeders had a white-hot bolt pushed through his tongue for having publicly testified to his faith. The bolt had been passed on from one generation to the next, but where it was now, her opa couldn't say. His family story was a common one; most Mennonite families had similar stories, an ancestor who had sung hymns while burning on a pyre, another who was thrown into a river to be drowned, a woman who was lashed to death by a whip, stories that had either been passed down from generation to generation, or recorded in a book of Mennonite martyrs.

The Schroeders eventually wound up in the Vistula Delta south of Danzig, in time to help drain the marshlands, where over half of them died of swamp fever. The place Wilhelm Schroeder lived was called Krebeswalde, south of Elbing. It was there that Plautdietsch, a language adopted from the Western Prussians, became the common language of Mennonites. The colonists lived behind the dikes and canals they laboured over, praying that the waterwheels they built would drain the fields in time for spring planting. Wilhelm left Krebeswalde at a time when, out of fear and envy, the Mennonites' right to purchase land was being threatened. A man named George von Trappe came calling, sent by Catherine the Great to convince the Plautdietsch speakers to settle in Little Russia. Wilhelm was among the first to go. He was the one who had first told the story about giant men whose wide trousers were used for storing watermelons, which eventually was told to Katya's grandfather, who had passed it on to her.

Wilhelm Schroeder didn't look like an adventurer. He had a soft look. His eyes were turned away from the portrait painter as though he were shy, or didn't want to be thought proud. His beard was illuminated and made his face seem blurred round the edges, and his expression indecisive. Or perhaps here was a man whose kindness would prompt him to say the soup was tasty when the cook had forgotten to salt it.

The middle picture was a photograph of a man named Johann Schroeder, the son of Wilhelm. Unlike his father, Johann's features were crisp and clearly defined. He looked directly at the camera, appearing confident without being taken with himself. His small compressed mouth was set in such a way that implied a forced sternness, such as would be required of a teacher, which was what he'd been. He left Rosenthal for the Mariopol district north of the Azov Sea when there came a need for a teacher. The land in the new daughter colony, Bergthal, was fertile and promising. It also had a high outcrop of rock, which proved to be a valuable source of stone for the foundations of their house, and for object lessons in religion studies: *You are my rock and my fortress. A man builds upon a solid foundation, which is Jesus Christ our Lord.*

Bergthal was where Katya's grandfather had been born, he being the subject of the third portrait. Her opa had a similar softness as his grandfather, and a long, white, flowing beard. He was a young man in the 1870s, when most of the people in Bergthal, fearing their rights were about to be taken away by the tsar, packed up and went to Canada. She'd heard the story often, that his father wanted to go to Canada too, but he had promised his wife's parents he wouldn't take their daughter far away. He never mentioned that he had extracted a similar promise from Katya's father. Then, soon after the villagers left Bergthal for Canada, the village burned down, and Opa's father returned to Rosenthal. He bought the farm of someone who also wanted to emigrate to Manitoba, a place where land had been designated for Mennonites on the east and west sides of a river. A river that often flooded, Opa had heard; a hard and frozen place, the soil was black, but the growing season shorter, so that winter wheat didn't produce nearly as well as it did in Russia. Opa's father had built the house at the front of the property, in the style of the houses in the Vistula, L-shaped, with the barn attached, and Katya's grandfather had inherited it, a house built to last more than a hundred years.

Whenever her grandfather told the stories behind the three portraits, Katya was reminded of a chapter in Genesis: And these are the generations of Noah . . . Shem, Ham, and Japheth. In church tomorrow she would come together with her even larger family and be made to stand still, to turn, to feel hands under her chin drawing her to face the inquisitor. This one looks like Tooth-Puller Jakob's daughter, a man known to yank out his own teeth when they offended him, sparing the expense of a dentist. They would ask if she had a way with her hands, as her namesake did, her father's mother who had died on a picture-taking day.

These are the generations of the Schroeders: Wilhelm, Johann, Gerhard, she recited, the last thought she had before drifting into sleep.

The towns of Rosenthal and Chortitza spread halfway up the sides of a valley, red and umber brick houses graced with trellises of ivy, their shiny windowpanes mirrors reflecting light. Coal piles glistened in yards of factories, chimney stacks trailed smoke, a factory door was open and its dark interior alive with the chuffing sound of a machine building steam, a clatter and whirr of wheels and belts. In the town, when they walked down the street, men came over to their gates to greet her father, and she felt taller as she walked beside him, made so by his easy friendliness and people's apparent respect for him. She noticed, too, that after the initial greeting and talk, there came the usual sideways questions about Privol'noye, which her father dealt with in his usual way, evading, or pretending not to hear.

One day she and Gerhard went with their father on foot from Rosenthal to David Sudermann's house on New Row Street in Chortitza. The main street of Rosenthal merged with Chortitza's New and Old Row Streets, Old Row being a broad street paved with cobblestone, the oldest street in the oldest Mennonite settlement in Russia. The street became a carriage road, led to outlying villages such as Arbusovka, a settlement that once boasted a silkworm factory, until other countries began producing machine-spun silk. In the east, Old Row Street led to the town of Einlage, known for its wagon makers – such as Jakob Sudermann – and then across the Dnieper via the Einlage bridge, to the city of Alexandrovsk. Although the city was only an hour away, Katya had never been there. She had stood on the banks of the Dnieper watching the steamboat *Leonid* cross the river below the rapids, ploughing towards Alexandrovsk, a collection of buff-coloured buildings, a smudge of dark smoke staining the sky above them.

She knew they were near David Sudermann's house when she saw his three blond daughters playing on a veranda with other children. Their large flat eyes turned on her as she went by, and she felt David's daughters were questioning what right she had to be there. David Sudermann was expecting her father, had been watching for them, and now came to greet him, sprinting down the sidewalk the last of the way. Her father grinned and readied himself to receive David's enthusiastic embrace, but Katya saw a distance in her father's eyes, a slight turning-away.

The windows in David Sudermann's summer room fronted New Row Street, a street busy with the coming and going of *podvodchiki* hauling goods from factories to railway-yards, and between the many villages in the colony of Chortitza, the colony named after the oldest town. For well onto an hour Katya was content to sit and watch the teamsters pass by the window while David and her father visited, their conversation an equal exchange of give and take until the subject turned to theology, and then David did most of the talking.

"If you ask me, the real reason why we hold onto our creed of non-resistance is because it gives us privileges other people don't have," David said in reply to something her father had said.

"Some of us still believe we're to be messengers of peace," her father said.

"Sure, yes. But messengers are supposed to deliver messages, are they not? Our wily ancestors agreed not to. They promised not to preach to the Orthodox. Why risk offending the hand that gave us such a generous start?" David said.

"A man's life is a message, for good and for bad. You know as much. So then, are you becoming an evangelical like your dear sister Helena?" her father asked, his smile a gentle teasing.

A chorus of voices arose in the street beyond the window, and their conversation broke off while a dozen or so boys went riding by on bicycles, with them several men, teachers, Katya supposed, and from the satchels they carried on their backs, she gathered they were on a school outing, a celebration, perhaps, to mark the end of the school year.

"Look at that. There's not a Russian among them," David said. "In my class I've only got one, and one Jew. That's all we let in this year. I pity the poor Russian."

Katya's father glanced at David sharply, his face working as though he had something he wanted to say, and then his features softened and he shrugged. "Yes, the poor Russian, what's to be done," he said.

"Far be it from me to say we should preach to the Orthodox – the heathen, as my dear sister might put it," David said, continuing where he had left off before the boys had come riding by. "That's not the point I wanted to make. Take a look at our privileges. Autocracy, Orthodoxy, Nationality," he said, ticking the three words off on his fingers. "That's the tsarist philosophy regarding the Russification of the people in the domain. That's what it boils down to, yes? All right, we pray for the monarch, and sing 'God Save the Tsar,' and every now and then donate a sizable amount of shekels to one of their causes. Orthodoxy? We're free to worship how we please, as long as we don't proselytize. Nationality? Now that's a strange one. We're Russian Germans. Baltic Germans, some claim, which gives us pretty high status, don't you think? And our religious belief conveniently affords us the privilege to be consumed with our own interests, mostly financial. We have come to think that being separate from the world means we can ignore the plight of the people who are not of our kind."

Her father was about to protest when Auguste Sudermann entered the room with a tray of tea and apple juice. David peered up at his wife, clearly irritated by the interruption.

How is your mother? Auguste asked, but Katya didn't know what to say. Should she say that her mother was tired often? That the new baby, Daniel, kept her awake most of the night with his fussing until Oma rubbed brandy into the soles of his feet? That Peter, whom Auguste had last seen as an infant, was now two years old, and Johann three? The little ones were almost more than her mother could keep up with in a day, but she refused to hire a girl as a nursemaid, even though most women did. Katya had told Auguste her mother was fine, thank you, as she knew this was the answer the woman expected.

She couldn't tell Auguste that her mother's chin had grown sharper, that when a batch of bread didn't rise as high as usual, she blamed it on her children for having been too noisy. She blamed the weather for their quarrels, for their father's headaches, which had begun to seize him from time to time, ever since Abram had broken his promise. He would need to lie down in a darkened room with wet towels on his forehead. Her father didn't have a taste for bitterness. He never spoke again of how Abram had broken his promise. Outwardly he seemed to be the same person, so much so that for months on end Katya would forget what had happened until one day he would come home, pale-faced and clenching his teeth.

Katya took a glass of juice from Auguste, who said that, since Greta began attending the *Mädchenschule*, she saw her often. And when would Katya enter the Girls' School?

When she told Auguste she would be attending the following autumn, the woman seemed surprised and said she had taken Katya to be younger. She'd brought a kaleidoscope for Gerhard to entertain himself with. She had also brought a book, an illustrated *Grimm's Fairy Tales*, and when she gave it to Katya, she did so with an apology for having remembered her as being younger.

"If you ask me, we're proud of our separateness. We've become architects of separateness," David Sudermann said to her father, continuing the conversation when Auguste left the room. "Wherever our people have gone in this world, wherever we continue to go, we demand special privileges. And when those demands are met, it reaffirms how we view ourselves. We're superior. Some even think we're chosen. Don't say that's not a conceit."

"Some people died for our beliefs," her father reminded him.

"Yes, as recently as the seventeenth century," David said with a sharp laugh.

Whenever either of them spoke, Gerhard moved the kaleidoscope from one face to the other as though spying on them, experimenting, wanting to see the difference the shades of light would make, Katya knew. David sat near to the window, his features were fair, while her father's were tanned by the sun.

"Martyrdom's a conceit too. I've come to think a person's willingness to die for a belief is in itself a vanity," David said.

Her father smiled and shook his head. "If that's so, then I pray you and I will never be guilty of committing such an act. Sometimes I think you enjoy making things more complicated than they need to be."

"Now there's a man who keeps life simple," David said. He drew aside the curtain as a grain wagon went by in the street, a lone man stooped over the reins. "Bull-Headed is the most uncomplicated person I know. He decides there is no God, and so there isn't. No discussion. Nothing to ponder. That's top-quality grain he's taking to the mill. The wicked seem to prosper, too, and they get a good night's sleep while they're doing so, I might add."

"Are you sure that's what the man thinks, or is that what people say he thinks?" her father asked.

"Well, he still refuses to darken the door of the church."

"That's another thing altogether."

David didn't respond, but went over to a desk in the corner of the room and returned with a brief letter, which he gave to her father to read.

When he finished reading, he returned it to David with a question in his eyes.

"I was sure you didn't know," David said. "I could refuse to give him a recommendation, but that wouldn't change the fact that he's made up his mind to leave. I spoke to my dear brother about it, but it seems Abram isn't inclined to replace Franz Pauls now that his children have outgrown the need for a tutor," he said.

The news made her father go quiet, his eyes coming to rest on Katya and Gerhard. "Nikolaifeld is too far for them to go to school. They'd have to board with someone; I can't afford that. And there are still three more at home," he said quietly.

So Franz Pauls wanted to leave Privol'noye. She wasn't surprised. Last spring when Justina Sudermann married, Franz Pauls wore a sour-pot face to the wedding and held back his good wishes, looking throughout all the celebrations as though he'd bitten into a pickle gone soft.

"Look. Look who's coming. The *barashku*," David said as Greta, Lydia, and the sister cousins, Barbara and Mariechen Sudermann, came hurrying along the street. With them were two other students.

Katya went to meet the girls as they came pounding up the steps looking self-conscious in their identical heavy capes, stiff white collars, black stockings and shoes. The day when her father learned that his dream of owning land would not come true, the Sudermann brothers scattered a few coins in his direction, in the way Isaac had done to avert a strike at his factory. They had volunteered to provide tuition for Greta and then Katya to attend the *Mädchenschule* in Chortitza.

Lydia introduced Katya to the two students: Olga, whose father owned a store, and Nela Siemens, whom Katya had already met, as Nela lived just across the road from her grandparents in Rosenthal. She was a tall and bony young woman whose thin hair didn't completely conceal her scalp. Katya was mesmerized the first time she'd discovered that Nela Siemens's nose was so thin, sunlight shone through the tip of it. When Nela felt herself being scrutinized she smiled and said, "You look terribly nice today."

"So you've been out exploring with your papa, yes?" Barbara Sudermann asked Katya.

"Yes," she said because she wanted to be agreeable. But no, they hadn't gone exploring. She and Gerhard had walked the two miles with her father from the Schroeder house in Rosenthal to David's house in Chortitza, which, in her mind, wasn't exploring. But when she was in town, her tongue became too stiff for detailed explanations.

Auguste had been busy at needlework when they came into the family room, and she set it aside now and began filling glasses with grape juice from a pitcher resting on a side table. The girls brought their autograph books to show Auguste the verses and messages their friends had written bidding them, and the school year, farewell.

Greta had changed. She seemed quieter and more self-assured. Katya noticed too that Auguste's eyes would come to rest on Greta, and the woman paid careful attention whenever she spoke.

Did Katya want to come with them for a walk around the town? Lydia asked. They would acquaint her with what lay in store down the road.

Her father stood in the doorway for a moment, looking at her and Greta as though measuring them against the other girls, and then feeling satisfied. He said he knew that the five-kopeck coin Opa gave Katya the night before was singeing the pocket of her apron and he gave his permission for her to go with Lydia and Greta and the other girls.

As they walked, Lydia explained that they were going to a special store, not the one owned by Olga's father, but a different store, owned by a Jew who sometimes had quite unusual things in comparison to what could be found in a Mennonite store. They passed through the spotted shade of Lombardy poplars, beneath the canopies of mulberry trees sprawling across fences, the air immediately cooler there. Fruit and nut trees crowded platforms and verandas, their trunks sometimes painted white and shining starkly among shade gardens overgrown with ferns and wild strawberries.

When they approached a machine shop, she saw workers standing out in a yard smoking, their faces blackened with coal. They were gathered around the grain wagon of the man David had pointed out to her father earlier, the man he'd called Bull-Headed. As they passed by, the man stood up in the wagon and doffed his cap, and she saw that he was young, that his straw-coloured hair lay like thick ropes, and touched his shoulders. He bowed as they went by, his hair sweeping forward and narrowing his face. "Girls, girls, and more girls," he said in a lazy-sounding voice.

The girls became stiff-legged and silent and looked down at their feet, except for Lydia, who squared her shoulders and lifted her chin. "*Dommkopp*," she muttered, causing Greta to giggle. Then they began jostling one another, Olga bumping Greta with her hip and sending her lurching from the sidewalk into the street.

"He's nothing but a cheese-head, a pimple, a pig's squeak," they said one after another, while Nela remained silent, her cheeks flaring with colour.

"They call him Bull-Headed," Nela said. "Don't you think that's enough?"

"Oh, don't be such an old nose," Lydia said.

Katya took it all in, feeling as though the girls had moved far away, were years ahead of her, and in an unfamiliar land that she didn't think she would want to visit.

A bell jangled above a doorway as they entered a small store, and a man came out from a room behind the counter, his eyeglasses pushed up onto his head. The shelf behind him was stacked with bolts of bright fabric, the casing filled with a display of the usual remedies and dry goods. She was disappointed to find that there wasn't much that was different from a Mennonite store, after all.

Then she saw a small purse with a chain. Among its embroidered flowers of glass beads were tiny mirrors reflecting light. Lydia waited near the door with the others as Greta pointed out a comb with a grosgrain bow. *Nein*, not that, she thought. What she wanted was the purse, with its delicate decoration of beaded flowers and mirrors, the brass chain looped against the dark wood on the display shelf. Her mouth filled with saliva, and her hands itched to feel the pebbly beads, the weight of the purse lying in her hand.

"You're such a turtle," Lydia said.

Her parents would not approve, she knew. The purse wasn't something she could use for anything. She would keep it in a drawer and take it out now and then. As the man slid open the door of the showcase, she noticed a stack of notebooks on top of the counter, and reached for one.

"That? That's what you want?" Greta asked.

No, not that, she thought. But they were waiting for her to decide, the man too, his stained fingers already hovering over the items in the case, demanding that she point to what she wanted.

The notebook was an ordinary notebook, and when she opened it, she could smell a clean smell. She liked the cream-coloured paper lined faintly with black. What would she do with a beaded purse, except try not to treasure it too much?

"I guess everyone has her own taste," Lydia said.

Yes, she did have her own taste. "I'll take the notebook," Katya said, and as she spoke the words, it suddenly became what she did want, and most of all.

"I think you made a good choice," Nela said to Katya as they continued on down the street.

Soon they came to a quiet stream, next to which goats on tethers were grazing. Lydia pointed out a pair of swans that were coming into view round a small island in the centre of the stream. The girls went onto a footbridge and waited for the swans to reach them, stood in a row at its railing, looking down, their faces given back to them in the sepia-coloured water; the stream a shallow one, Katya noticed. Water plants swayed gently beneath the surface among stones the size of her fist. She held the notebook against her chest, fearing she might drop it, listened as children playing near the water called to one another, a fish, a fish, they had just seen a fish. A woman pushing a baby buggy hurried to them and stooped over the water to look.

"I wish you would change your mind and come to the Azov Sea with us," Olga said to Greta moments later, and Katya was surprised to learn that Greta had been invited.

Greta smiled enigmatically and didn't reply, and Nela for some reason sent Olga a dark look over Greta's head. The swans glided towards them, seemingly without effort, as though drawn along by strings. But when the birds came near to the bridge, she saw the ripples radiating out around them, their paddling feet disturbing the water. The girls' features wavered and came apart, the white circles of their faces disappearing.

When she looked up, the children and woman were gone, Greta, Lydia, and the girls were not on the bridge, and for a moment the silence held her in place, and her legs began to tremble; it was as though everyone, the town itself, had vanished. The sound of laughter brought her back, and she saw that the girls had gone down to the bank of the stream on the other side of the footbridge. They were taking off their shoes and socks, and the swans were slowly drifting towards them.

Dear Greta, our gypsy queen,

Although I'm coming near to the end of the year it still seems strange that days can pass before I speak a word of German. If it weren't for our exchange of letters, my Chortitza friends would have reason to call me *verrusst*. There is no danger I'll ever be taken for Russian at the *Gymnasium*, however. Although my benchmate calls me Sudermannchenko, he's also pleased to remind me on a daily basis what I am. He calls me *poganiy niemets*, and although he means it in fun, there are others who would agree with him behind my back. *Poganiy*, by the way, not only means dirty, but some Orthodox take it to mean heathen.

Katchenko, the Cossack, continues to talk about nothing but his ancestry – when he's not challenging everyone with his strength, that is. He reminds me so much of Papa's Cossacks. Full of dash and high spirits, with a wonderful singing voice. The Moldavian also continues to borrow heavily from me, but what should I do? Even for his long hair, he's a good friend. I suspect he spends much of what I lend him in cafés and taverns.

In your previous letter you asked me to comment on your ambitious plans to attend the Teachers' Seminary when you finish *Mädchenschule*. I don't know what to say, as it came as a complete surprise. I didn't realize you were thinking along this way. However, I wasn't surprised to learn that my Aunt Auguste is encouraging you to go, as she has written letters of recommendation for other girls in the past. The thought just came to me: Aren't you at all afraid that people will start calling you a know-it-all – as they call my Aunt Auguste, who so aptly serves the affairs of the

Girls' School, but can't make a pot of edible soup (I'm sure you recognize my usual teasing when I say this). My first reaction was that if you should go on to the Seminary, well, Chortitza is rather far from Ekaterinoslav, and we wouldn't get to visit very often, would we? While I've come to appreciate and look forward to your letters, they've made me realize how much more I'd sooner hear your voice. I am anxious to know what your parents decide.

Last Sunday I was invited to the home of Millionaire Toews for a social evening. Everyone was in high spirits. We played games and sang well into the hours and I'm afraid that I wasn't in the best of condition for the gymnastics club the following day.

Write to me soon. I always look forward to hearing what you girls are up to at the school. Rempel's photograph of the three of you taken in his studio was overly romantic, I thought. But you stand out, as usual, as the brightest of all.

Your dear friend,
Dietrich Sudermannchenko

*W*ithin weeks of Katya's returning home from Rosenthal, the weather turned as hot as summer and the tulips and irises flowered at the same time, a profusion of colour in the west garden happening all at once, not a gradual unfolding that made a person anticipate which beds would be the next to bloom. There was almost too much colour to take in, Katya thought as she went walking along the sand paths with Greta and Dietrich, the evening air still warm and saturated with the scent of lilacs. Dietrich had returned home shortly after they had, having completed his first year of Commerce Studies at a *Gymnasium* in Ekaterinoslav. She thought he had become puffed up and full of himself, and sounded much like his uncle David had during their recent visit in Chortitza. She didn't care to listen, and didn't mind when the two of them went on ahead where the white path curved round a grove of lilacs. But moments later when she rounded the curve, she was startled when a bough suddenly bent, and then swished back, stinging her face. Dietrich had twisted a cluster of pink lilacs from it, and was poking them into Greta's hair.

Katya awakened the following morning with a band of tightness in her abdomen, her tongue thick and tasting of metal. The air in their attic room was close and warm, and when she arose, the bedding held the shape of her body and rust-coloured spots of blood. It happens to all girls eventually, her mother explained when she demonstrated how Katya should fold the strips of cotton and pin them into place. She was not to worry about it but accept it for what it was, a nuisance to be endured. The washing and hanging of the banners of cotton must be done at night when the boys were asleep, and hung to dry on bushes behind the house. Her mother's hushed tone didn't suggest that Katya ought to be ashamed of the bleeding, but rather that it was a mystery, and one day she would understand. Katya guessed it had something to do with becoming a woman and having children, but what, and how, she couldn't imagine.

She helped Greta strip the bed and soak the stains. "Yes, it happens to me, too," Greta said, sensing Katya's question. But she'd spoken in such a way to imply that was all she wanted to say.

Then Lydia must bleed, too, Katya thought. The girls she had gone walking with in Rosenthal. Her mother. Helena. Mary and Martha Wiebe, Oma. All of them knowing the secret and, like her, going about their day with a wad of cloth between their legs, and she had never suspected. The bulky cloth was awkward, and she was afraid it made her bow-legged and was grateful for the length of her skirt.

Later in the day a carriage came onto the compound with three men in it, looking for Abram. They were dressed in black Sunday frock coats and wore bowler hats, and she knew from their sombre demeanour that their visit was significant. When she went to the carriage house where Abram had gone with her father, she walked more slowly than she had ever walked, aware of the cloth chafing her skin, thinking that if she rushed, the pad would come apart, or give off an odour they might notice. Years later when her own daughters began the nuisance, she would explain what it meant, and not leave them wondering. She would give them pamphlets ordered from a company that sold the supplies they needed each month. She would remember her first time, remember the men who had come looking for Abram, and realize that the news they had brought to Privol'noye that day meant the everyday lives of the Mennonites in Russia were about to become extraordinary, and the extraordinary, commonplace.

"People who know better than I seem to think there could be a war," her father said at supper.

Katya went around the table, stacking dishes into a pan while her mother struggled with little Peter, attempting to tip a spoonful of warm oil into his ear. Katya may have moved a step closer to becoming a woman, but life continued as though it hadn't happened, and she was left wondering what the connection was between her discomfort and the description of a good wife in Scripture: *She seeketh wool, and flax, and worketh willingly with her hands, she riseth also while it is yet night and giveth meat to her household.*

The Archduke Ferdinand had been killed in Sarajevo, her father announced. Meetings were held throughout the colonies, and Abram had been voted to represent the colony of Yazykovo and head a delegation, which would go to St. Petersburg within days, to determine whether the threat of war was real, and to remind their one member in the Duma of the colonists' utmost loyalty.

"A war? With who?" her mother asked now, her face reddened with frustration as Peter twisted and thrashed.

"With Germany," her father said, as though he was surprised that she'd had to ask.

"But not a war with us," her mother said. "Come and help," she said to Katya.

Katya held her little brother's head while her mother put the oil in his ear, stuffed it with wool and released him to go running after his brothers.

"Of course with us. One way or another, it means us," her father said.

Katya saw the fear in her mother's face. "But not fighting," she said, her eyes coming to rest on her sons as they went out the door to have a last hour of play.

Her father shook his head.

"Go and see where Greta and Dietrich are," she said to Katya, a frown creasing the skin between her eyes.

As Katya went across the meadow, Greta and Dietrich were standing near the edge of the forest, and when they saw her Dietrich beckoned, then set his finger to his lips. She followed them into the forest, going along the path towards the sound of an axe ringing. When they came near to the site of the mausoleum, Dietrich stopped suddenly. "Devil, I don't want to see this," he muttered, turned away, and went quickly down the path. Dmitri Karpenko, Sophie's father, was cutting down a tree.

With Dmitri was his daughter, Vera. Perspiration dripped off the end of his nose as the axe bit into a tree trunk. Vera turned, saw them, and tugged at her father's trouser leg. Dmitri's old grey face twisted in surprise, but as he realized Katya and Greta were alone, he spat into the palm of his hand and resumed hacking at the tree.

"Go on, Vera. Go with the girls, and you'll save me a trip," Dmitri said between blows to the tree, his voice coming out in grunts.

When Vera wouldn't move, he set the axe aside and wiped his brow on his shirt sleeve. "What are you waiting for, you lump of goat manure? Go on. And remember, if you get into trouble over there, you'll be in trouble at home. She's starting work tomorrow," he said to the air above Greta's head, his explanation that they were to take Vera to Privol'noye.

Vera went with them across the meadow and didn't look back, seemingly unconcerned about her father's gruff send-off.

Dietrich stood waiting for them at the Chortitza road, looking troubled. He questioned the presence of Vera, whose eyes grew wary at the mention of her name. Dmitri, assistant to the gardener, had been at Privol'noye for as long as they could remember; the miniature farm he'd carved for them from wood one Christmas still occupied a corner of the vegetable garden – barns, a Mennonite wagon painted green with red trim, draft horses and cows. He was assistant to the gardener, but his skill with woodworking had been put to use in the building of storage chests and tables, which both Aganetha and Katya's mother prized. Dmitri, despite his swearing, more than earned his pay, her father said. Dietrich puzzled aloud that he couldn't understand why Dmitri would poach a tree. He spoke to Katya and Greta over Vera's head in German, with an authority he hadn't possessed before. They shouldn't mention it to their father, he said. When his own father returned from St. Petersburg, he would decide when was the right time to tell him. Dmitri was too good a man to lose, he said.

Somehow Sophie had known Vera was coming. And she waited for them beside the Big House, her face flushed and anxious. Just then Helena Sudermann emerged from the summer kitchen, stopping Vera in her tracks. Helena grimaced as she took in Vera's dirt-smeared face and uncombed hair, the hem of her greasy tunic hanging loose on one side, the grime on her bare feet.

Mary and Martha Wiebe had been watching at a kitchen window and now came round the side of the house, Martha wiping her hands across her apron.

"What have we here, look Mary, a little girl, isn't that so?" Martha said. Her eyes misted with sympathy over the scruffy look of Vera.

"She can sleep with me," Sophie said to Helena, sounding defensive.

"We were just recently saying how nice it would be to have a little girl in our room," Mary said, and Katya realized – and was certain Helena did too – that the Wiebe sisters and Sophie had already discussed where Vera should sleep.

It was well known that the only Russians Abram would allow in the Big House were Sophie, and the furnace keeper, Kolya. Vera was being hired as an outside worker. She would milk the cows and work in the gardens, feed and butcher chickens, tend the lambs and calves. And she would take her meals and sleep with the half-dozen female workers in the women's quarters.

"Outside is outside," Helena said, and then more softly, almost apologetic, "You know my brother's rule."

❚❙❚❙❚

Years later, Katya would tell her grandchildren how, in the late summer of 1914, a fever had spread like wildfire. Abram went with the delegation on a train to St. Petersburg, and Aganetha, feeling the need to be near men, took Helena and Dietrich to Ekaterinoslav to stay in the house of one of her married sons until Abram returned. During that time, the devil had been cast down onto the earth, Katya wanted to say to her grandchildren, but they were educated modern people and didn't believe in the Evil One, and so she told them a fever for war had broken out.

The train to St. Petersburg was packed to overflowing, she would say, as though she had been there and was not repeating what she'd heard. Soldiers rode on the tops of coaches and on the steps, hanging from the train for hours until others took their place. There had been such a high pitch of activity in St. Petersburg, carriages and motor vehicles going to and fro, crowds of people gathering at the Winter Palace, cannons and cases of ammunition lining the streets, ready to be shipped should they be needed. At Privol'noye, a tension pervaded their lives. She remembered clearly there being a tension, as though rock plates in the earth were about to shift.

Her father surprised them by announcing they would have a holiday, an afternoon picnicking beside Ox Lake. For him to take time off was unusual, but when they overcame their astonishment, her mother made them pack up a supper, fill a wheelbarrow with straw, some wood for a fire, a rug for sitting on, quickly, quickly, she said, before your father changes his mind. She was as excited as they were, her cheeks gone rosy for a change. Go and invite the Wiebe sisters to come join us at suppertime, she told Greta, and Sophie, too. Greta should leave washing up the dinner dishes for later, just clear the table and stack the dishes in a pan and put it out of sight under a bed.

Then off they went, going single file, her father leading the way. They went along the elevated path that, each autumn, was blanketed with fresh straw which they were not to trample down, or else in winter the water would freeze in the pipes. The marmots had made the ground around the pipeline their home, and they stood at attention now and whistled as Katya and her family came walking along the ridge of earth covering the water pipe, the rodents so chubby that the fat hung from their little bodies, furry skirts covering their feet.

When it came near the time for cooking supper, Gerhard built a fire and let it burn down, kicked aside the embers and then emptied his pockets of potatoes. The embers flared, the light reflecting in her father's eyes as he sat on his haunches, an arm clamped around Johann's middle lest the boy become too interested in the bonfire. But Johann's attention was turned outward, to the edges of their picnic site, where dragonflies skimmed the tall grass and the surface of Ox Lake.

Within days of being home from *Mädchenschule*, Greta had found her place in the household routine, busy now, her nimble fingers shiny with fat as she speared sausages and slid them onto a sharpened stick for Katya to place on the spit. Greta wore her hair parted at the centre, rolled up, and fastened with combs. But, as usual, spirals of hair had worked loose and rimmed her forehead, and she blew at them to clear her eyes as she worked. A good girl, Oma had said of Greta when they were about to leave for home, and had pinched her cheeks. The word *good* resounding in Katya's mind, making her feel as though her shoes were in need of shining.

Johann turned in the circle of his father's arm, following the flight of the dragonflies, whose wings snapped as they fixed to glide, their legs crooked, becoming baskets to scoop insects from the air. Warblers chortled deep in their breasts as a harrier swept across the reed beds. The water was alive with darting lines, ripples and dimples of movement as the dragonflies' younger and still wingless cousins skated across the elastic surface, voraciously feeding.

Sara went over to a boat on the shore and began pulling fish flies from its hull. She'd snagged her dress on a nail and its hem trailed against the backs of her muddied legs, and she looked as untidy and rough as Vera had when Katya and Greta came upon her and Dmitri in the forest.

Her mother lay on a blanket, baby Daniel cradled at her side, a straw hat covering her face. Years later someone would tell Katya that her mother had been fond of hats. Even as a young girl she wore hats, and sometimes the hat was too large and the brim concealed her eyes, but always her grin was in place, displaying a fetching space between her front teeth. She was known to have a good singing voice, sweet and clear. To be swift and light on her feet. Katya's own clearest memories of her mother were of her cradling a baby on her arm in a tub, laughing as she trickled water from a cloth over its stomach, or sitting with her feet hooked through the rungs of a chair as she took time to have *faspa*, gnawing on a piece of hard bun, dunking it in coffee to soften it, sometimes humming a tune, sometimes gazing across the room, lost in her thoughts. She remembered how the house was transformed to order and cleanliness under her touch. All these memories, but she would not be able to describe, more than anyone else could, what was in her mother's heart.

"What time is it getting to be?" her mother called from the blanket where she lay, a straw hat covering her face, and baby Daniel cradled at her side.

"Why don't you children see if you can tell what time it is from nature," her father said. "Take a look around."

"The sun?" Gerhard said, disappointed that their father's challenge would be such an easy one.

"The water," her father said, and indicated Ox Lake, out beyond the parsnips and rushes, where the water lilies grew.

Sara jumped up and down to be able to see farther out. "There's nothing to see," she complained.

As Greta turned sausages on the spit, grease dripped and sizzled, sending up a column of smoke and an appetite-rousing odour, which Katya suspected would travel as far away as Lubitskoye.

She went to help Sara look for a sign that would tell them the hour, but all she saw were water spiders and midges swarming above a rippling wake where a fish had just jumped.

"What about the water lilies, are the flowers opened or closed?" her father asked.

Earlier, they had gone rowing among the lily pads to admire their blossoms, yellow teacups set on green saucers. Now, the teacups were tapers standing on a green tapestry of shadow and light.

"They're closed," Sara reported.

"Well then, it must be five o'clock," her father said. He took out his pocket watch. "And so it is. They're right on time."

"Here come the Wiebe sisters," Greta called.

The women no doubt had smelled the sausages cooking and knew it was time for supper, Martha carrying her guitar on her back, Mary a basket, which more than likely was filled with something she had just baked.

"Look," Sara shouted. There were little brown tubes among the lily pads, poking through the water and moving in circles.

"Six of them," Gerhard said as their father came to them, Johann riding on his shoulders.

"Be still, listen. There's a mother hen nearby, can you hear her?" her father asked.

Katya heard the hollow sound of a hen calling from among the rushes.

"Come away, let's see what happens," her father said, fiery-eyed with excitement.

They stood back from the shore, listening as the hen's call became a rapid clucking. The bobbing tubes proved to be beaks as, one by one, the hen's chicks bobbed to the surface among the lily pads. They shook beads of water from their backs and paddled in a line towards the mother hen, who was hidden among the striped shadows of the reeds.

Her father shook his head in silent amazement. He had heard of a kind of moor hen whose chicks would do this, but had never seen it for himself. Ox Lake, which had been formed when Abram's father dammed a small creek, attracted many different water fowl to the area, including storks that visited in early evening, picking their tentative and stiff-legged way through the reeds.

"We must have frightened the mother hen with our noise; she called to her chicks and they dove out of sight. When we moved away and stayed quiet, she told them that it was safe to come," he explained.

The Wiebe sisters had arrived, their voices high and youthful sounding with the excitement of an unexpected holiday. Martha scooped up Daniel, while Mary added the contents of the basket she'd brought to the food Katya's mother was spreading out on a cloth.

Katya's father lowered Johann to the ground and he ran off, yelling, Me too, me too, the dragonflies seemingly forgotten now that his brothers Daniel and Peter were garnering all the attention. Katya saw Sophie and Vera coming along the ridge clutching their skirts against tick burrs.

Sophie had braided Vera's hair, and had wound the plaits around her head, woven flowers and ribbons through it, which lifted and trailed out behind her as she came along the path. They were wearing holiday clothes, embroidered sateen blouses and skirts whose red fabric fell in soft folds from their slender waists. Sara went running to meet them and, after being introduced, took Vera by the hand and brought her over to the lake's shore.

When Katya greeted Vera, the girl's eyes slid briefly across her face, and went flat. Gerhard became awkward in Vera's presence and would not look at her directly, as though he needed time to decide if he should welcome her or not.

Just then the hen and chicks emerged from the reeds. Sara asked her father if she could show Vera what the chicks could do, oblivious to the girl's cold expression, the chill she gave off.

What did Sara have in mind, her father wanted to know. She would clap to make a noise, she said, and her father assented. Sara instructed Vera to watch what would happen, speaking awkwardly in Russian for her benefit. When the hen and her chicks had almost reached the edge of the lily pads, Sara clapped, and the mother called out. Instantly the chicks dove all at once, leaving behind a wake which the mother hurried away from, going swiftly back the way she had come, to disappear among the vegetation. Moments later, one by one, their beaks poked through the water, moving in circles as the submerged chicks paddled. Katya's father stood watching, crossed his arms, his smile fading as he fell deep into thought.

Katya held her breath while the chicks stayed under the water waiting for their mother's call. She wondered how long they could do that, if eventually their tiny webbed feet might tire, if a fish might come to bother them. She was awed by nature, how marmots whistled an alert, cows on a pasture kept their young inside the herd, how the chicks waited for a signal.

She hadn't seen Vera go over to the wheelbarrow and pick up a piece of firewood, and was startled when it went flying across the water to land near the submerged chicks. "*Ach Mensch,*" Gerhard exclaimed in disgust, and like Sara and Katya, he stared at the spot where the tubes had been, and where a piece of wood now floated among the lily pads.

"Well, well. Now you see just how smart they are," Katya's father said in Russian, and after a moment of silence. The chicks hadn't surfaced, but look, he said, although their beaks had momentarily disappeared, there they were, a little farther away, their tiny brown pipes bobbing and circling.

Katya had expected her father would say something against what Vera had done, and apparently Vera had too, as her expression had implied that she was strong enough to take whatever the consequence might be. But at his words she grew unsure and stepped away from him, glanced at Sophie, who was busy helping Katya's mother put out food and hadn't seen what had happened.

"Even though the chicks are likely frightened, they won't show themselves until their mother says so. I sometimes think animals are smarter than human beings. Come away now, let's let them be," he said.

Her father offered Vera his hand, and after a moment of hesitation she took it. As they went to join the women, Vera sent her a triumphant glance. *Haulftän*, Katya thought. Vera was a grudge-bearer. After so many years she was still getting back at her for not agreeing to play with the spin top. She'd heard of people like that, but until now, she hadn't met one.

After supper, the water still and reflecting a bank of cumulus clouds that had risen as the sun began its descent, Katya's family began to sing, Martha accompanying them on her guitar. Vera had to go and help with the milking, Sophie reminded her, and as they headed back to the compound, the others grew silent, not wanting the day to end. They listened to the stillness and watched the zig-zag flight of dragonflies among the wisps of smoke hanging above the lake, a stillness that stretched far across the land as far west as Poland, Katya thought, north to Moscow, and in the east, Arkadak, which was where the real Russian forests began.

Suddenly Gerhard disturbed the silence when he called attention to the Chortitza road, where two of Abram's Cossack guards were riding hard. The horses left the road, dipped down into a shallow ditch and across land, coming towards the lake. Katya's father rose and went to meet the men.

"What is it?" her mother asked when he returned, beginning to scatter the embers of their fire.

"They came from the west pastures," he said.

"And so?" her mother prompted.

"They found several cows injured and had to destroy them," he said. "Go and get water and finish this off," he said to Gerhard.

"Injured? How?" her mother asked.

"Butchered," he said, as quietly as he could.

"Who did so?" Gerhard demanded.

Her father turned on Gerhard in a sudden flare of heat. "Don't you use that bossy voice on me. A person gets to hear it often enough and shouldn't have to listen to it coming from his own son. Now go, take your brothers and get some water to put out the fire."

Katya went with Gerhard and the little ones and, seeing that he was close to tears, touched his shoulder.

▮▮▮▮

There is no herb for dying, she wrote in her notebook that night. She'd got the saying from Martha Wiebe on the way home from their picnic, when she'd told them about a *Gutsbesitzer* who'd succumbed to tuberculosis after travelling to various spas in Europe in search of a cure. As she wrote, a minuscule paprika-coloured spider raced across the page in front of her pencil.

A spoon or two of brandy added to the rollkuchen batter improves its flavour.

Brandy rubbed on the stomach and soles of a baby's feet eases its colic.

Lilac tea for stomach ache.

She was of the age to begin collecting recipes and household hints her mother and other women would pass on. But since she'd begun writing in the notebook, she'd couldn't resist entering other, less useful, notes, such as the tip Sophie had given to her: *Throw a piece of bread in the well to keep the witch from going among the cattle.* She had written, *Papa and Mama are waiting for Abram to return. They want to know what he plans to do about Franz Pauls's leaving. Vera doesn't like me.* The line came unbidden, her hand penning the words without her having consciously thought them. As she looked at the sentence, she realized it was true. Vera didn't like her.

She lay in bed thinking of the black kite she'd seen at the picnic, gliding in sideways across osiers and purple loosestrife. An umber shadow passing over her in church in Rosenthal when the *Ältester* had read the Scripture: *Blessed are the pure in heart*. She thought of Lydia's silver cup and felt the stone of regret settle on her breastbone. She wished she had answered when someone called her name. But she hadn't. Nor had she given into the heat of the sheepskin square against her thigh and recited a psalm, *For Thou art with me. Surely goodness and mercy*, until the urge to throw the cup into the well passed. When she closed her eyes she could see the dragonflies darting to and fro above the lake. Darning needles stitching the sky closed for night.

S he awoke in the morning to the sound of rapping on the door downstairs. Greta was already up and gone, and her nightgown hung from a clothes hanger on the cupboard door as though floating in mid-air. Her scuffs sat pigeon-toed on the floor beneath it, and Katya stopped breathing remembering the moment on the footbridge in Rosenthal when she'd thought all had disappeared. Greta, lifted from the slippers and nightdress and taken to heaven. The murmur of her father's voice reached her, and then a woman's voice, and Gerhard's, and the rising fear that everyone had been taken to heaven evaporated. She went to the window and saw that Lydia had come home, she was hurrying along the path towards the house and Greta was coming to meet her, the two of them embracing. When she went downstairs, Mary Wiebe was standing in the doorway to the outer room.

The Sudermann women and Dietrich had returned from Ekaterinoslav late in the night, bringing Lydia home with them, Mary said. Aganetha Sudermann wanted Peter Vogt to know there was going to be a Faith Conference at Privol'noye. When Mary said *Faith Conference*, she wrinkled her nose. They all knew how Abram brought together a select group of people to admire one of his recent acquisitions, a thresher, an Arabian stallion. Abram called his gatherings Faith

Conferences, invited church elders and ministers, and set aside half a day for sermons.

Staring at her feet and blushing slightly, Mary Wiebe delivered her message. She said she'd been sent to inform Katya's father that within ten days near to a hundred people would attend Abram's gathering, and he was to select three sheep for butchering.

Mary returned to the Big House, and soon Katya saw there were wagons in the yard, covered with tarps. She learned that Aganetha had not only come home with news of the pending conference, but also with a contingent of painters, upholsterers, and furnishings. Abram had sent Aganetha a telegraph from St. Petersburg saying there should be a gathering of people so the delegation could deliver its report, and Aganetha had got it in her head to refurbish his office in time for that gathering.

Throughout the following days Katya would see Vera doggedly plodding between the pig barns and dairy barns, her narrow face hooded by a red headscarf as though she wanted to restrict her vision to what lay in her immediate path. From a distance, the sight of Vera brought to mind an awkward fledgling, the skirts she wore either too long or too short, her shoulders sagging, and her step unsteady beneath the weight of a burden. Katya noticed Sophie's affection towards Vera, the occasional acts of tenderness, a braid tidied, a pat on the rear in passing. Their quiet, almost secretive talks in the evenings when Sophie went to sit on the steps of the women's quarters. Katya felt excluded, that Vera's presence had changed Sophie. She missed Sophie's attention as much as she did her stories, was put off by her preoccupation, how she was forever stopping what she was doing to gaze across the com-pound, saying God, God, hoping to catch sight of Vera, to place her, learn where she was, before continuing on her way.

A pile of rubble grew in the yard as the renovations to Abram's office proceeded. The workers' wives would come to investigate, and salvage a bit of cloth, carpet that had been cut into strips, nails that they would straighten. So as to not cause them shame, Katya pre-tended not to notice them, and told this to her mother one evening as they sat together out on the steps shelling peas.

"What do they have to be ashamed about? They'll make good use of whatever they find," her mother said.

The great bustards sauntered slowly through the meadow beyond, their size and colour making them look like sheep grazing. They were shy birds, and hard to get close to. Greta and Dietrich came into sight along the road, Lydia behind them, and one of the great birds raised its head, all the others then doing the same. Birds of a feather, Katya thought, the saying taking on new meaning. The birds began to run, long, loping steps, their broad wings moving slowly and their bodies looking too heavy for flight. When the bustards took off, the three stopped to watch until the birds had flown out of sight beyond the forest. Then Dietrich linked his arm through Greta's and drew her to his side as they resumed walking, Lydia staying back and looking on for a moment as the couple ambled along the roadside, their heads almost touching, their voices a quiet rising and falling.

Katya watched her mother watch them, her pea-stained fingers moving in her lap as though shaping a ball of dough. Then Katya saw Greta go over to the roadside and begin to gather wildflowers, while Dietrich stood waiting, hands in his pockets as he gazed at the sunset, his face and hair turned red-gold. Lydia's voice rose briefly, and then she turned and started walking back towards the avenue of chestnuts. Greta called after her, but Lydia kept on going, Dietrich and Greta watching her go.

"Oh, why don't those two come back already," her mother muttered, suddenly active, scooping up unshelled peas and dumping them in Katya's lap.

Days later, the bustle of activity at the Big House had ceased. The rubble had been carted away and dumped behind a small Sudermann family cemetery near to the back of the estate. That evening, Katya went across the compound to the women's quarters and sat on the step. Although there were no clouds, the air felt like rain. She knew Vera would soon arrive for supper. When Vera did come across the compound, it was with her usual plodding doggedness, as though eating supper were another chore she had yet to complete. The front of her grey dress was wet; she had likely washed up at the water pump. As Vera saw Katya, she stopped, annoyed at having been taken by surprise. Then she left the path, as if the women's quarters hadn't been her destination.

"Vera, come. I would like us to be friends," Katya called out in Russian.

Vera slowed, then returned, pulling at her scarf so that it fell onto her shoulders, her chin lifted.

"Sophie's my friend, and we could be friends too, yes?" Katya felt herself blush with the insincerity of her words. She wanted Vera to like her, more than she wanted her for a friend. Vera stood at the bottom of the steps squinting up at her, and Katya knew she wouldn't want to hold hands with her and go walking at the end of the day. Vera wasn't Sophie. Vera looked like a sharp-eyed animal that would bite the fingers of a person offering it food.

Vera swiped at her nose with the back of her hand, her scowl fixed as she came up the steps, and Katya smelled the day in her skirts, barn smells, the chicken coop, the rooting of pigs, felt Vera's boot bump her elbow as Vera stepped around her and went inside.

Katya thought about how, on days when the air was thin and clear, she could see the village of Lubitskoye rippling on the horizon beyond her house. She imagined the river Dnieper to the south, alive with light, its rapids thundering; she'd heard from Lydia, whose arms were freckled from her summer holiday spent there, about the Azov Sea, and the boats of fishermen hugging its shore. As she worked with Vera Karpenko in a field beside the orchard, scrubbing a canopy that was to be erected for the Faith Conference, she thought of St. Petersburg, the city Abram had gone to with the delegation, and since returned from in a gruff mood. A city that had been built on water, she'd been told. At a cost of thousands of lives. She thought of the places she had learned about in geography lessons so she wouldn't think about being here, on her hands and knees scrubbing a mildewed canvas canopy with Vera, an outside worker who was so much more agile and quick than she was. She thought of mountain ranges on ocean floors, of floating ice seas, a circle of ice and snow capping and cupping the world, continents adrift on the earth's desperately thin crust, North America, East India, where Helena Sudermann was bound to go, even though her four brothers were against it. Her knees grew raw from the canvas, and stung, while Vera, her skirt knotted about her thighs, made energetic little soap swirls with her brush.

"Tell me what colour I'm thinking of," Vera said suddenly.

A game. As Vera rose to her knees and put aside her scrub brush, Katya vowed that this time, she wouldn't decline to take part.

"Blue?" she asked, as Vera's skirt was blue.

"*Nyet*," Vera said.

"Red?"

Vera nodded and her face broadened with a grin, revealing a mouth of crooked teeth pitted with decay. She unwrapped a tiny bundle she'd taken from her pocket; inside it was a candied cherry. She bit it in two and offered Katya half.

Katya hesitated, thinking of Vera's spotted teeth, but knew she must accept the offering. As she chewed the sticky confection, the thought occurred, where had Vera got it?

Their attention was taken as a *droschke* came along the road and approached the chestnut-lined avenue. Then Lydia emerged from the Big House, came down the steps, and stood waiting as her sister Justina and her husband arrived at Privol'noye, home for the upcoming party. Justina was dressed like a queen, as usual, and Katya watched as her husband helped her down, the skirts of a white dress flaring out around her as she hurried to embrace Lydia, and then they went up the steps to the vestibule where Aganetha and Abram stood waiting on the threshold.

She could imagine Aganetha Sudermann was anxious for Justina to voice her approval of Abram's new study. His gruff disposition had become even blacker when he'd learned of the slaughtering of six cows, and more so when he saw the refurbished room. Everyone on the estate became aware of his displeasure. He could be heard shouting at Aganetha. How was a man supposed to think in such a stink of turpentine and wallpaper paste? He hated the window drapery and door curtain. But eventually he stopped shouting to admire a lacquered cabinet built around the safe. He demanded that his chair and the gramophone be brought to the vine arbour, where a man could breathe. And so, late into the night, they were treated to the music of Caruso. A sobbing aria of *Pagliacci*, and then "Nessun Dorma," played again and again, Enrico Caruso's voice floating out and across the meadow where the great bustards had begun to flock; the birds not sleeping either, Katya's father had said.

A red plush sofa scattered with small cushions covered in the same fabric as the window drapery now stood where Abram's work table had been. Matching plush chairs were arranged around an oval table of cherrywood. When Katya's mother and father returned from a meeting with Abram, her mother said she didn't know if the chairs were hard or soft. She supposed they were for looking at, as she hadn't been invited to sit.

Katya's parents were relieved and then discomfited that Abram had, indeed, been thinking about the education of their children. He'd gone so far as to pray about the matter, and had received an answer. He would replace the tutor, Franz Pauls. But in return, the children should be made available to do chores. Her parents agreed, but when, hours later, a list of chores came sliding under the door, they were quietly astounded.

Which was why Katya now found herself scrubbing a canopy with Vera, who was watching her, just as Katya had been watching Justina and Lydia.

"You people. You think we're no better than the oxen," Vera said, and shifted her gaze to the Big House as the door closed behind the Sudermann family.

Katya knew Vera had thrown out a line to see what she might catch, and yet the words stung. "I'm not one of them," she said.

"Then show me," Vera said.

Katya waited behind the cow barn for Vera to return from the chicken coop, where she had gone without explaining why. A wire was strung between trees, and hanging from it were plucked and gutted chickens.

There was a fire whose embers flared under a cauldron of water, and flies crawling over a plank table where the chickens had obviously been cleaned. Moments later Vera returned, struggling with a hen which she held to her side tightly to keep its wings from flapping. As she took the chicken to a tree stump, Katya understood what test Vera had in store.

"You should know how meat gets into your soup," Vera said.

She knew how meat got into her soup. She'd often gone with the Wiebe sisters to the storage cellar to collect the family's Sunday chicken, cooling on a hook along with all the other Sunday chickens. She had chanced upon the outside women butchering the hens, and been present on killing day, when the pigs went into the slaughtering shed squealing, and wound up hanging from the rafters, their bodies cracked open at the ribs.

Vera stroked the chicken's neck and its clucking grew less frantic. Then she pinched its beak and stretched its neck across the block. The mesmerized hen lay motionless, its eye turned to the sky.

From the Big House came the sound of piano music; Katya recognized the piece, *Liebestraum*, which Lydia had taught herself to play, and more than likely wanted Justina to hear. Wedged in the ground beside the chopping stump was a hatchet which Vera pulled free.

"You say you're not like them," Vera said, and motioned for Katya to take it.

The piano music unfurled, distinct in its sound of longing; Katya imagined Lydia curled over the keys, minding its signature with her swaying body, nodding when it came time to turn a page of music – yes, now. Count the beats, the rests, watch how the notes go up and down on the page, Lydia would say, even if you can't read, you can follow, turn now.

"You are so like them. You sound like a bear but act like a mouse," Vera said.

The hatchet felt different than one used for splintering wood into kindling. It was heavier, and seemed to hum with meaning. The hen's neck was no thicker than a stalk of rhubarb, she could do it quickly, without thinking, both hands, one swift chop. No, she was not *you people*. Justina, nose in the air, Aganetha, reminding the world that she had once been to an opera house and heard Chaliapin sing. She was not Lydia home from a holiday summer at the Azov Sea. Even her young brother Gerhard knew that the pears in the orchard didn't belong to them, nor did the house they lived in, the furnishings in the parlour; the soup ladle in the pantry drawer, with its scorched ivory handle, was one of Aganetha Sudermann's cast-offs. But she was not like Vera, either, and taking up the dare would somehow put her on the same side.

"*Nyet*," she said.

Vera laughed, grabbed the hatchet from her hand, and with one swift movement severed the hen's neck. Katya saw the crimson spurt, felt the heat of blood against her arm. The chicken's head lay on the block, its opaque eye blinking, body convulsing in Vera's grip.

"You shit-hole of a pig, that's how meat gets into the soup," Vera said. And then she glanced around as though suddenly frightened. "You won't tell anyone, will you?"

The sound of hammering rose above the music, Katya's father in the carpentry shop repairing benches for the gathering at Privol'noye. She felt giddy with relief that she hadn't given in to the dare, and disappointed him.

The coolness of the shaded north wall of the potting shed, the familiar odours emanating from the manure and soil banked up its sides in bins, had always been comforting. This was where Katya used to come to play as a child, had spooned soil into pots, discovered the pale mushroom knuckles pushing through the earth. She had finished scrubbing the canopy, then she rinsed her blood-spattered apron, put on a clean one and returned several flowerpots to the potting shed.

There were three jars sitting on the windowsill in the shed holding leeches, *Hirudo medicinalis*, blood-suckers that left purple marks on a person's skin when they were pulled off. The leeches were lying curled in a mucousy sediment at the bottoms of their jars.

When Katya had pointed out the faulty barometer of their classroom clock to Franz Pauls, he'd said they should make one of their own, so she and Gerhard had gone with him to collect the leeches from Ox Lake. What they made was called a "Tempest Prognosticator," which Franz Pauls had learned about in a magazine showing pictures of exhibitions at a world's fair in Paris. He'd cut out drawings of the invention, which resembled a large cruet, and they'd copied the illustrations, which depicted the different behaviours of the *Hirudo medicinalis*, noting what kind of weather each behaviour indicated. When a storm was brewing, the leeches darted about the bottles and caused a bell in the handle of the cruet to ring. Today, their crescent-shaped stillness promised more of the same good weather, heat, and calmness for the upcoming gathering at Privol'noye.

All the previous autumn, winter, and spring, the live barometers had consistently forecast the coming of blizzards, wind, and lightning storms, calm and clear skies. When school ended, their Tempest Prognosticator had been moved to the potting shed.

The mouldering and dark interior of the building gave way to the greenhouse, a long narrow room filled with light; in summer it was cobwebbed and piled high with overturned flats; watering cans and tools hung from rows of hooks beneath the windows. A glass room ready for the season when plants would be brought in before frost, a season when she loved to go in and feel the heat of the sun and breathe in the moist air. During all the years that would come to pass, she would always associate greenhouses more with darkness than with light.

It's good you didn't take on Vera's dare, her mother had said. Leaving a chore unfinished is enough to do wrong in a day. One bad choice is like a single thread, which is easy enough to break, wound around your body. But one leads to another, and then a person becomes bound and can't break loose no matter how hard they try. And soon, if a person tells you to lie, or steal, you will do it.

Of course she wouldn't. She would not steal. Unlike Vera, if she happened upon a jar of candied cherries, she wouldn't think to take one. She hadn't mentioned the cherry, although she was certain this was how Vera had come by it. She knew she wouldn't steal, and yet she had taken Lydia's cup and thrown it in the butter well. She felt the familiar wash of shame whenever the cup came to mind. *Na*, Katya, what's to be done with you? First chore on the list, and you leave it half done. And Vera? Poor Vera. When Dmitri found out his pay would be reduced by the cost of cutting down a tree, and now for the extra chicken Vera butchered as well, poor Vera would feel the brunt of his anger.

When she came out of the shed, she heard the Wiebe sisters chattering in the summer kitchen, her mother calling after Sara. As she crossed the compound, she was met by Kolya, who had come up from the cellar stairwell balancing a table on his back. He carried the table through the garden and into the orchard, where another table had already been put down under the trees. She went to the summer kitchen – Sara, Sophie, and the Wiebe sisters sounding like a bush of sparrows before a rainfall – glad that she'd put on an apron trimmed with embroidery. That she had taken the time to fix her hair, as usually *faspa* eaten in the orchard meant there would be something special, sliced melons, freshly baked *schnetje* to dip in jam and honey, and not the everyday *faspa* of buns and cheese. Sara had come offering to help Mary and Martha make *plautz*, but she was eating more than helping, Martha said, greeting Katya with a soft smile. The smell of the sugared fruit and pastry was exciting the flies, which were thick and knocking against the window screens.

"Mama is asking, where is Greta?" Gerhard called as he came across the yard leading the goats Sheba and Solomon, who were hitched to a cart.

"If you want to know where the goose is, go looking for the gander," Sophie said, and Katya saw the Wiebe sisters exchange glances.

"*Nanu*," Mary said, to change the direction of the conversation. "Now you have Katya you can manage without us."

Katya thought of Greta, who had gone for a walk to the forest early that morning, running back through the meadow, her straw hat in hand like a bird flying alongside her. She saw Greta come from the back door of the Big House now, carrying two pails, which she took through the garden and into the orchard, where Kolya had set up the tables. Helena had found another chore for Greta, and one that wasn't on the list.

"What goose, what gander? What kind of story were you saying?" Sara asked and wrinkled her nose.

"You want a real story? Then I'll tell you one," Sophie said. "Guess what? The witch has left the forest."

Katya saw how Sara's eyes had grown, and so she held her tongue.

"Someone recently saw her in Lubitskoye," Sophie said.

"What does she look like?" Sara asked.

Sophie set a pinch of flour on Sara's palm, and blew it away. "Like that," she said.

"How did they know they were seeing a witch?" Sara asked.

"When a person sees a witch, they know they've seen one, and won't easily forget it," Sophie said. She put on her storytelling voice, became the old Sophie, the swan girl, yellow hair streaming out behind her as she flew across a dark sky, strings of rain falling from her apron.

Gerhard tethered the goats and unloaded the straw he'd brought for the oven. Then he sat on his haunches near the door to listen.

"A widow in Lubitskoye saw the witch looking through her window," Sophie said. "That night, the woman had a most terrible dream. She dreamed of a giant grasshopper coming near to her house. The grasshopper made a noise like thunder, and lightning spurted from its head. When her seven sons came running to see the insect, its lightning struck each of them dead. She woke up from her dream when it was still dark outside, but she went into the yard and built a kneading trough. She wanted to make the largest *paska* that had ever been made in the village of Lubitskoye," Sophie said.

"Why would she do that? It's not Easter," Gerhard said.

"Because she heard the voice of God telling her to do so," Sophie said. "If the woman made the largest and most perfect *paska*, then her dream wouldn't come true. When she finished building the kneading trough, she mixed the bread. She worked the dough from the time the cock crowed until the sun reached the centre of the sky. She grew very tired, and so she went to the tavern where her seven sons spent most of their waking and sleeping hours, and she called them out, and said they should come home. She made them wash their feet and take turns tromping on the dough."

"With their feet," Sara said in disapproval.

Gerhard laughed with relief, convinced now that Sophie's story was not real.

You have to take what a Russian says, divide it by ten and subtract it by two thirds of its sum, sprinkle it with salt, and somewhere near to the middle, you may or may not find the truth, their father liked to joke.

Katya judged by Sophie's eyes. When their pupils became small, she knew Sophie was holding something back or not telling the truth. But as Sophie told the story of the woman and her *paska*, her eyes were wide and clear.

"At last the time came for the woman to set the bread to rise. While it rose, she lit candles and prayed. 'Oh Lord most high. Here I am, an entirely miserable creature not worthy of Your kingdom. I beg You, O Almighty One, look upon my *paska* with favour. Most Holy of the Highest! Redeemer of the Lowest!'"

The woman prayed with much groaning and rolling of eyes, according to Sophie's enactment.

"'Grant to this humble and undeserving servant, one who is the lowest among the lowly, that in Your infinite wisdom and mercy You may see fit to spare my seven worthless sons,' the woman prayed."

The secret to a perfect *paska* were the words *Bogu na pomoshch*, Sophie stopped to explain, and made Sara repeat after her, *Bogu na pomoshch*.

"The woman chanted 'God help me,' and crossed herself many times over until the *paska* had at last risen high enough and was ready for the oven. The fire roared in the chimney and her face shone from the heat of it. She cut willow branches and dipped them in water and sprinkled the oven until the temperature fell just so. As the *paska* bread baked, she chanted and sang so loudly that the villagers grew curious and gathered around her gate. The woman believed that if her *paska* baked high and perfectly round, God had hearkened to her prayers, and would spare her seven sons."

Sophie leaned towards them as she told the story, gestured with her hands, crept low to the ground to the left, and to the right.

"Finally, the bread was ready to come out of the oven. But as the widow opened the door, she was amazed to find that the *paska* had risen so tall, it couldn't come out.

"What would she do with a *paska* bread too big to come out of the oven? the villagers wondered, and crowded into the yard to watch.

When the oven cooled, the woman began knocking away its clay covering. Brick by brick, she dismantled her *pech'* until, at last, there stood the bread, bigger around than a wagon wheel, and just as tall. People sighed in amazement as they made room for the woman's sons to carry the *paska* through the garden, and up and over its gate to the street, where they set it on a wagon. The woman brought her best shawls and tied them together and put them around the *paska*. Then she sent one of her sons for the priest to come and bless it."

"And so now she doesn't have to worry about her dream coming true," Sara said.

"I wish that were so," Sophie said. "But there is some doubt, because of the eggshells." She didn't wait for the questions tumbling behind Sara's face to surface, but continued telling the story.

"As the widow sat on a chair beside the wagon, waiting for the priest to come, the villagers began to wonder aloud. How much flour had she used, lemons, sugar and butter? The woman smiled at each of their questions, and replied that the answer was a secret between her and the Most Holy One.

"By and by, someone began to guess at how many eggs she'd used. Twelve dozen, they supposed, and when everyone agreed yes, it must have been twelve dozen, the woman set aside her willow switch. She got up from her chair, and went into the house. Soon after, she returned wearing a necklace of eggshells. She looped the garland of shells around an olive hedge growing near her door, and returned to her throne beside the wagon and *paska* bread.

" 'One hundred and sixty-five eggs,' " a woman declared when she had finished counting the shells on the bush and divided the sum by two. There came a great sigh from all the women. Never before had one hundred and sixty-five eggs gone into making *paska*."

"Not here, either," Sara announced, and Sophie rewarded her with a look of gratification.

"Where did she get so many eggs?" Gerhard interrupted.

"From here and there. She must have borrowed them," Sophie explained.

"But you said it was dark when she made the dough. Everyone would still be sleeping," he persisted.

"She likely had hens. And that was likely why she stayed up late in the night and saw the witch looking in the window. She was washing eggs. She was going to take them to the bazaar at sunrise," Sophie explained.

"You didn't say at first that this was a bazaar day," Gerhard said.

"Well, I'm saying so now. Should I finish the story, or not?" Sophie asked.

Gerhard blushed and nodded.

"All right. Here's the end of the story." Sophie took a deep breath. "And God said to Zinfonia – which was her name, I forgot to say – Zinfonia Golubonski. God said, 'Oh, thou lowest among the lowly. This was supposed to stay between you and me.' And Zinfonia said, 'As I stand here and breathe, it is between You and me.' God said, 'That's not the truth. Look at what you've done with the eggshells. Can you say you haven't made the *paska* the entire world's business? Because of the eggshells, I must now think over our arrangement.'"

"Because of the eggshells?" Sara asked, puzzled by the ending of Sophie's story.

"I know. Because she made a show of them, yes? She was boasting over how many eggs she used." Gerhard said.

"Yes, and God doesn't like boasting," Sara said, pleased that she at last understood.

At that moment Mary and Martha came from the back door of the Big House, followed by Helena, carrying baskets which, Katya knew, held *faspa*. And then Aganetha Sudermann came from the front of the Big House across the grass, her billowing taffeta skirts a dove-coloured fabric which became pale blue and then slate grey as she moved through sunlight and shadow. Justina came behind her mother on her husband's arm, her husband a tall, quiet man wearing a white linen suit, followed by Lydia.

"Zinfonia Golubonski was showing off with the eggshells," Gerhard said, reluctant to let the story come to an end.

"Yes, she was showing off in the same way some people like to show off with their big fat stomachs," Sophie said.

Abram came last of all, round and dark, rolling from side to side as he poked the ground with his walking stick. Then they all stood still and watched as a carriage turned in at the gate posts.

Sara whooped and took off on a run, but Katya hesitated. As the carriage emerged from the front of the Big House and came to a stop at the parade barn, she realized that Dietrich had brought Michael Orlov for *faspa*. The two young men doffed their caps and bowed dramatically, and the ensuing laughter somehow made the distance between them and Katya seem greater than it was. A small man dressed all in black got down from the carriage. She knew he was Konrad, the man they had once seen tending the fire when they'd looked through a window at the Orlov house. He scurried to unload Michael's camera equipment, a tripod and a scrim which Michael then directed him to set up near to the garden wall. The dwarfish man had been part-time tutor to the workers' children until Abram put a stop to it. He was also the Orlov's confectioner, whose only tasks in their household – other than making pastries, sweets, and cakes for special occasions – were burning incense on a shovel in the fireplace, and trimming and cleaning the lamps.

Katya joined Sara, who stood apart from the group, balancing on one foot as though, with this trick, she hoped to gain their attention. Konrad finished setting up the scrim and returned to the carriage, taking from it two chairs, which he set in front of the scrim. Then he went to the carriage to fetch a cake, presenting it to Abram with a little bow and a flourish.

"*Abba*, Mama. Come and see what this man has brought for *faspa*," Abram called loudly. Everyone went to admire Konrad's cake, Mary finally taking it from him and into the orchard, where she set it on the table.

"Oh ho! Look at this. Lots of money, cost lots of money," Abram said as he shook his walking stick at the camera and scrim.

Michael Orlov began to arrange the Sudermanns for the photograph; Abram and Aganetha were to sit on the chairs, their children to gather around them. When the grouping was as he wanted it, Michael Orlov crouched behind the camera. He was about to take their picture when Dietrich suddenly broke away and looked around the yard. Michael groaned and raised his hands in mock impatience.

"What's the delay?" Abram called, twisting awkwardly in his chair to glare at his son.

"Where's Greta?" Dietrich asked Sara, who pointed to the orchard where Greta stood in the shadows, watching.

"Come and be in the picture," Dietrich called.

"Yes, yes, Greta, come, hurry. Come be in the picture," Lydia said. "What are you doing, hiding there? Don't be so suddenly shy."

"All, or none at all," Dietrich proclaimed, which Sara took to mean her and Katya as well, and she began tugging at Katya's hand. They should wait for Greta, Katya said. But for some reason Greta wouldn't come, and so Dietrich went to get her. Moments later they emerged through the garden gate, his arm wound about Greta's waist, and Justina glanced at her mother, at the sky, at her feet.

They were all looking at Greta and Dietrich, Katya and Sara obviously forgotten, and so Katya held Sara back, saying, "They just want grown-ups."

"There's room for Greta beside me," Lydia called.

"She can stand between us," Dietrich said.

Aganetha Sudermann fussed with her skirt, her smile fading and her eyes half closing as she frowned.

"Stand wherever you want. Just stand still," Michael Orlov said. His mock despair dissipated as he hunched over the camera.

In the photograph Dietrich would look tentative, and even though the round face of his boyhood had given way to that of a young man, had become angular, with a strong jaw and deep-set eyes, he would look too young to be in love. Katya would come to think that most people ventured into love far too soon, her own children, their children, and she would always be a little afraid for them, afraid that they would put so much trust in another at such a young age, risk failing, risk the injury of accidents. Love hadn't come to her until she was near to twenty-two, old for those times, almost of an age where marriage would likely not happen at all. In the photograph taken that day, Lydia had chosen to stand sideways to the camera; Justina leaned into her young husband, looking as though she would like to have his arm around her. Greta faced the camera squarely. Her white blouse, dark pinafore and vivid colouring were in high contrast to the other women, whose fairness and light-coloured clothing caused them to look faded in comparison.

She would later see the photograph published in a historical account of Mennonites in Russia, the young man who came with his machine, asking her to tell stories, bringing it with him. Beneath the photograph the names were given, except for Greta, whose identity was stated as "unknown." Greta's vivid beauty returned to her across the time, and by then she had a word, *vivacious*, to describe her. She would tell him, regarding the unknown: That vivacious young woman was Greta Vogt, my dear sister. She would show him a photograph of Greta, Lydia, and the Sudermann sister cousins, students in their school uniforms grouped around a pedestal on which lay an open book. She'd once owned a photograph of herself at three years old sitting on that same pedestal in the photographer's atelier in Rosenthal, taken during the time the Sudermanns had toured America. There was a blurred spot at the end of one of her chubby legs – she'd moved – and Greta had a fistful of her dress to keep her from rolling off the pedestal, she was so plump. She remembered a photograph she'd had of her parents on their wedding day, her mother wearing the traditional black dress, her father too thin, his beard spindly, his large hands splayed across his knees; remembered a group portrait of the Schroeder family where she was a child held in her father's arms. Photographs she had brought to the new country, and which were taken from her, one by one. By offspring of her children suddenly wanting to know their heritage, wanting to be more than Canadian-born fair-skinned people, potato eaters; some of them remaining Mennonites, others, not. They wanted to be more exotic, like the people they lived alongside in their modern world, a multitude of different peoples, tongues, and cultures. The photographs she had brought to Canada were proof that they were offspring of the oasis-dwellers who had lived within the country of tsars.

When Katya came into the orchard everyone was milling about the put-together tables, gawking and then moving away, impatient for Abram to take his place, impatient to stand with their hands folded against the chair backs and sing "Praise God, from Whom All Blessings Flow."

Konrad's cake was set at the centre of the table, a two-tiered confection covered in frothed cream and dotted with candied cherries. Katya recognized the cherries with a shock, remembering the cherry Vera had shared with her earlier in the day. She recalled her own spying through a window at the Orlov house, and she wondered if Vera had gone spying, too, and if she'd been so daring as to go inside.

She felt Greta's eyes on her, a message she didn't understand. Then Sara made the situation clear, as she went around the table counting, and noted in a puzzled voice that there weren't enough plates.

Abram seated himself at the head of the table and hungrily eyed the cake, while Dietrich mentally counted the chairs and told his mother more were needed.

Katya saw the look which passed between Aganetha and Justina, a look that said they already knew about the lack of chairs.

"Martha, go and get more chairs and more settings," Dietrich ordered.

"Yes, go and get more chairs so we can be one big happy family, as usual," Justina said with crisp sarcasm.

"There are exactly as many as there need to be," Aganetha said.

*T*he equipment shed had been turned into a prayer hall, the doors standing open, a square of light framing a picture of a grooved path worn into the earth by wagon wheels, the stone fence meeting the gate posts at the avenue beyond, where Katya and Nela Siemens had set pails of flowers. This was the day of the Faith Conference, not yet noon, and already the heat inside the shed was sweltering. Katya's father and David Sudermann sat near to the open doors. Tables had been set up for tea beside the doors, and the inevitable five-pound sacks of sunflower seeds. Katya waited at the tea table, ready to pour for those who preferred heat as a means to cool down.

The trains were packed to overflowing with soldiers, Abram Sudermann reported on behalf of the delegation who'd gone to St. Petersburg to meet with a Mennonite member of the Duma. He gave the report standing at the front row of benches, his breath laboured and perspiration running down his face, which he kept swiping at with a balled-up handkerchief. Behind him, sitting on chairs, were six ministers from nearby villages sat on chairs facing the congregation. The members of the delegation had been impatient for the formal part of the service to end, what had been a time of silent and spoken prayers, hymn singing, and greetings from each of the ministers, who now looked haggard and wrung out. During the service a woman was overcome by the heat and fainted, and the other women, grateful for the opportunity to escape the stifling air, had gone with her to the shade of the canopy, where they now visited with each other.

Earlier that morning, while a blue mist still hung in the gardens, Katya had gone to cut flowers. She had seen Nela watching from an upstairs window, and was surprised when, moments later, she joined her in the garden. As they crept among the beds in search of perfect blossoms, the cool morning air set them shivering. Nela's teeth were chattering, her hair still wound up in rag curls. A mouth-watering smell wafted across the compound from the summer kitchen, where pans of cherry and plum *plautz* cooled on tables. Pitchers of coffee were being kept warm for those who had arrived the previous night. Among them was the woman who had fainted during the service, a shy woman who tried to be inconspicuous in the way she tiptoed to the summer kitchen for breakfast. But no sooner had she gone inside, than she came rushing out and into the garden, clutching her stomach.

Abram said the delegation had volunteered their first-class passage to the soldiers, and spent the entire trip in the heating compartments of two railway cars, taking turns sitting on the floor and on the stove, while the others stood back to back in a space that amounted to the width of a corridor, trying to see something of the countryside through grimy windows.

At every station, the train was met by wagons filled with soldiers waiting to board, their women and children with them, dwarfed by huge baskets of provisions. Imperial banners were to be seen in more than the usual number, and priests holding aloft icons of Christ, St. Nicholas, and every possible saint. Bands played marches while church bells pealed incessantly. Women and children wailed whenever the train departed a station and, all together, it was almost too much for a person to bear.

As Abram related this, Willy Krahn, the man from Arbusovka whose wife had died of poisoning when the meat grinder fell on her foot, pulled a handkerchief from a pocket and blew his nose. Katya's mother had pointed him out during the service, a man slumped on the bench, chin on his chest as though asleep.

"It's the opinion of our Duma member that the possibility of war is very real," Abram said. A silence descended in the equipment shed, all movement suspended.

"Once war is declared, the call for our men could come at any time," he continued. The call would come for alternate service. To work in the forests and on the roads, with *zemstvos* and institutions such as the Red Cross. They would be required to work as *Sanitäters* on hospital trains and ships, in administration offices in Russian cities; so many men would have to leave the colonies and the influence of their own people.

"How many?" Willy Krahn called out.

"In all, there are about twelve thousand between the age of twenty and forty-five," Abram said. "The mobilization of the reserves will take most of our Russian workers. Which is going to make it difficult for the harvest. And should our own be called? Getting the harvest in will be near to impossible. We'll have to hire women and children," Abram said.

"I wanted to know how many to pray for," Willy replied.

Abram seemed startled by this thought, and then continued with his report, saying that the delegation arrived in St. Petersburg somewhat the worse for wear. Their clothing was rumpled and stained with coal dust. They were shocked by the sight of cannons, and boxes of ammunition stacked in the streets. And once again when the hotel manager came to them in the dining room and asked them to refrain from speaking German, saying he'd received complaints, and several lodgers threatened to leave. When they themselves left the hotel, a man spat at them and called them *Germanzi*. If there should be a war, and if that war were to go badly, then the old canard *Beat the Jew and save Russia* would no longer suffice to save the skins of those in power.

"We could become the new scapegoat," Abram said.

"We already are," David said softly to Katya's father.

"Let's not exaggerate," her father replied.

In the silence that followed, birds could be heard singing from the briar hedges that grew alongside the equipment shed. The woman who had fainted was Willy Krahn's new wife, Frieda. She'd afforded the women the opportunity not only to escape the heat but, as well,

Abram's report. Helena Sudermann had sent Sophie and Greta to the storehouse to get refreshments for the women and they were returning now, pulling wagons filled with pails of sliced watermelon and bottles of *kvass*. The bottles tinkled noisily as they came past the shed, drawing longing glances from the men inside. The trill of women's laughter rose above the sound of tinkling bottles on the wagon, above the voices of small children playing in the shade of the vine arbour, entertained there by Lydia and her friends.

"*Na ja*. Those who have much to lose also have much to fear," one of the ministers said.

"The more a person fears, the more he looks to God for help," another man countered.

"Yes, and he looks to his Cossacks, too," a man sitting beside Willy said, and laughed to temper his words. But most knew he wasn't joking, as there had been criticism levelled at Abram when he'd hired Cossacks to guard his pastures and fields.

"We're not German. This is our fatherland. We're as much Russian as anyone," Isaac Sudermann stood up to say.

"Whichever the way the wind blows, you're sure to find good old Isaac," David said to Katya's father, loud enough that others heard, and nodded in agreement.

When Isaac sat down, David Sudermann got up, causing a stir around him.

"Some of us think we should talk about our pacifist principle. While I may believe that its our duty to try and uphold that principle, others may disagree. Intolerance isn't the Christian way. Different views should be allowed and debated, and we should begin to do so, today." David's voice was strong and confident, the voice of a man accustomed to speaking in public.

"Why today?" a man asked.

"Well, that should be apparent," David replied.

"This is not the time, nor will there ever be a time for such talk. As Christians we will not depart from the belief of pacifism. It was the practice of Christ, and it's what Christ demands of his followers." When the *Ältester* spoke, his voice quavered with emotion.

"I'm speaking about self-protection," David said. "There's a callous disregard for the law everywhere. Just recently six of my brother's cows were butchered on the pasture, and in broad daylight. If there's a war, and if, as my brother says, it goes badly, we could find ourselves without protection. We should begin to talk about what to do if that should happen."

"The tsar is our protector," the man sitting beside Willy Krahn replied. "We have his word. We're Russian citizens and entitled to protection against our enemies."

"How can we expect the tsar to protect us when we're not willing to protect the tsar?" David asked.

"This talk must stop," a minister said.

The shed erupted with voices, men rising to argue all at once.

Late in the afternoon the Wiebe sisters came with baskets of food, and Katya helped load the baskets onto the wagon. Then she and Mary noticed at the same time the hunting guns lying on sacks. There was a crate holding brandy and schnapps already on the wagon. Faith Conference, Mary said wryly. When Michael Orlov rode in moments later with a greyhound tethered to his saddle and three more dogs running behind, it became clear what Abram had in store.

Franz Pauls and Dietrich went to meet Michael, Franz wearing leather riding breeches which revealed his spindly legs. Although this was the first time he'd seen Abram's refurbished study, he'd offered to show it to several men, acting as though he were one of the hosts and not an unexpected guest. They should see the fine craftsmanship of the lacquered cabinet which had been built around the Wells Fargo safe, or the new painting Aganetha had purchased, a painting of hounds and red-coated horsemen. He had surprised the Sudermanns with his presence, arriving in time for the noon meal – which was convenient, Helena had said, but one more person wouldn't matter; she'd given the platters heaped with lamb and slabs of ham, the pots filled to brimming with *varenyky* in sour-cream gravy. He'd been in Ekaterinoslav, and thought, why not drop in before returning to Rosenthal, he'd told Helena, his eyes roaming among the young women, flickering with hurt as he glanced at Justina on the arm of her new husband.

Katya's father and David Sudermann decided against going hunting and rounded up those who wanted to go for a walk, and although Greta was kept busy helping Sophie in the kitchen, Katya was free to go with them. As they crossed the meadow, Lydia and her friends hurried to catch up. When it became apparent that another man would ride Abram's prized red stallion, Franz Pauls decided against going hunting and called from the road that they should wait for him too. Lydia groaned and went off in a huff, and except for Nela Siemens, those with her turned back. Nela's father was one of the ministers from Rosenthal attending the gathering, a stout elderly man who hadn't joined in the noisy discussion which broke out following Abram's report. Katya had seen him ambling in the west garden as though deep in thought.

Now as they went walking in the forest, Franz Pauls, who had received news that he'd passed entrance examinations to a teachers' college, gave Katya's father and David an account of the exam questions. He walked in front of Katya and her father, alongside David, his hands clasped at his back as though already a learned teacher, and not a prospective and awkward-looking student stumbling over tree roots. They were followed by a squirrel that leapt from tree to tree, and stopped to peer at them with its beady eyes. During the time he'd been in Ekaterinoslav writing the exams, there had been a students' strike at the Institute of Geology, Franz went on to say. However, it had been quickly brought under control by the police.

"A few students have made it bad for everyone, and now a person can be arrested just for going for a walk," Franz said. "I didn't dare speak German. My Mennonite colleagues and I spoke Russian, even while travelling between our lodgings and the college," he said, sounding suddenly world-wise, although everyone knew that this had been his first trip to the city. "We'd be smart to stop speaking German in public."

Just then the squirrel leapt to a tree beyond the path and came halfway down its trunk to chatter at them.

"And who will you report us to, eh?" David said to the squirrel. "Look, Franz. Already there are language spies behind every tree.

You'd better speak Russian here and now, or that little fellow will see to it that you enjoy the enchanting sights of Siberia.

"Come now, surely a man as well travelled as you can endure a little teasing," David said, when it was apparent Franz took offence.

"Did you hear anything in your travels about the proposed law to liquidate land owned by Germans?" her father asked, and Katya knew he had done so to steer the conversation away from Franz's discomfort.

David's young daughters and Sara had run on ahead, Sara anxious to show them the mausoleum. Franz and David were walking abreast, and Katya at her father's side. Nela and Gerhard came behind them, and Katya was amused to see that Nela had taken Gerhard by the hand. Although his ears had turned red over being treated like a child, he was politely attentive while Nela pointed out the various wildflowers growing in the dense vegetation along the way.

"Yes," Franz said, eagerly taking up the topic. There were two laws proposed, apparently, one to prevent ownership of land by certain categories of Russian subjects, including German, and another to confiscate land presently owned and tenured by Germans.

"Don't you agree that the point should be made to the authorities that we're Russian, and not German?" Franz asked, phrasing his opinion in a question to avoid appearing disrespectful of the older men.

"Perhaps we should make the point that we're Dutch," David said. "Because it would be difficult to convince them we're Russian when we don't want to be treated as Russians."

"But we are, in every way," Franz said.

"Not so. For example, only recently I came upon the brother of one of my Russian university companions. He looked rather down-hearted when he told me of having to leave his engineering studies a year before completion. He was wearing the uniform of an ordinary foot soldier and earning a ruble a month."

"And you know how highly regarded a soldier is," Katya's father said to Franz. "He's held in such esteem that there are signs in civic parks warning *Dogs and Soldiers Forbidden*." Katya heard the old energy in his voice, what was there when David used to visit.

"I didn't go to any parks," Franz said lamely, by way of explanation.

"A soldier who fails to greet a superior in the proper way will be made to feel the butt of a rifle. In the face," David said. Meanwhile, Mennonite men drew lots to see who would go off to alternate service in forestry camps run by co-religionists instead of having to go into the army. And if he could prove a hardship would be created by his absence, or if there should be a need for teachers, physicians and mill bosses which he might fill, the man could well find providence at his elbow, and not have to go to forestry camp.

"A well-placed payment of money can assure that a son will stay home," David said.

An awkward moment of silence followed, in which Franz Pauls tugged at the collar of his shirt. No, he hadn't heard, he allowed. Then he sidestepped the issue and went on with what he did know, what he'd just experienced first-hand during his trip to the city.

"Most of the students involved in the strike at the Institute of Geology were Decembrists, likely," Franz said.

"I take it that you're in no danger of becoming caught up in any uprising," David said jovially, and clapped a hand on the young man's shoulder.

Katya was glad to see the smile pulling at a corner of her father's mouth. The tips of his boots were scuffed, and his trouser bottoms frayed. He hadn't worn his best for the conference, and had chosen not to eat with the other men at the noon meal, but at their own table. He took Katya by the hand now, and adjusted his stride to match her own.

"For sure, not. I know what I believe and stand for," Franz said.

"And what is that?" David asked. He had tipped his hat to the back of his head, opened his collar and rolled his shirt sleeves, and looked as though he had never hurried for anything or anyone in his entire life.

The question startled Franz. "I stand for the monarchy, of course." His voice trailed away, and then he added, "For what my father has taught me. As well as our church," he said, as though for good measure.

"Good, good. Of course. Pacifism," David said. "By arriving late you missed out on a lively discussion on that very topic."

Her father laughed. "We all missed out on a lively discussion. I'd hardly call that brawl a discussion."

"How can a person be for the monarchy, and at the same time not be willing to stand up for the monarchy?" David asked. "I know, of course, we pray for them, yes?" he said, answering his own question. "We give money to their war efforts, grow food, and make a good profit along the way, I might add. We build *podvods* for them to haul their weapons and the wounded, as we did in the Crimea. The monarchy is of the kingdom of this earth, I understand that. And we're about the business of the heavenly kingdom; at least, that's what we profess. We're only pilgrims on our way to our real home, aren't we? Russian pilgrims who sing 'God Save Our Tsar' along with everyone else. It seems to me that, for pilgrims, some of us have become pretty set on staying here. We've acquired so many possessions along the way that there aren't enough wagons and horses to carry all of them. We may as well own up to it and stop thinking of ourselves as being strangers travelling in a strange land as we make our way to our heavenly home. We're here, but we keep saying we're not. It's a convenience, if you ask me." He had stopped speaking to Franz, and seemed to be arguing with himself.

In the following silence, Katya's father released her hand. His eyelashes fluttered as he gazed at the back of David's head. When her father's patience was tried, he could speak with a bluntness. "No one is asking anyone to carry the millstone. If the weight of a person's earthly possessions is felt so strongly, then why doesn't a man just give away everything he owns, and make his load lighter? If a man's conscience bothers him, he should just come out and say so, and not paint everyone with the same brush so as not to confront his own feelings of guilt," her father said.

"I wish it were that simple." David laughed, and Katya thought he'd somehow become smaller. He'd become a small man with a big hat tipped to the back of his head.

"Behind every tree there's a complication," her father said, and Katya could tell that he wanted to say more, but there was Franz Pauls to consider, his neck poking out from his collar like a rooster's, eyes opened wide, as he took it in.

The silence was filled with the noisy tramping of feet, Gerhard breaking free of Nela's sisterly grasp and running on ahead. Katya was caught by a stiffness in Franz's voice as he asked, "So, Mr. Sudermann. May I ask then, what about you? Do you plan to take up a gun and fight for the fatherland if need be?"

David Sudermann's eyes followed his children running among the trees. "No, I do not. But I'm not going to cloak my decision in the high-minded language of religion. I'll call it what it is. Cowardliness. And what's more – you may as well know this, Peter," he said. "If need be, I'll use what influence my brothers have in order to keep from being sent to work on a Red Cross train or ship. As far away from disease and danger as possible. There you have it. My confession."

"If there should be a war, then I, for one, will be among the first to volunteer," Franz's voice was loud with self-importance. "I'll willingly go wherever I'm sent and do what I'm given to do."

Katya's father raised his eyebrows, but remained silent.

"You, Peter, you should stay as close to home as possible," David said.

"Yes, of course. Someone would have to keep an eye out for Privol'noye." Her father had spoken with an unaccustomed brittleness.

"I didn't mean it that way," David said quietly. "So then, Franz, as a true pacifist you wouldn't protect your mother, say, or your sisters, if the need for it arose? Because if there's a war it could spill right into our laps. We'd have to decide whether or not to resist."

"We're here now," her father said, quickly pointing out that Gerhard and David's girls had already reached the site of the mausoleum.

The hunters returned midway through the afternoon with their trophy, a badly mangled fox, and an inebriated Abram Sudermann. Abram's brothers assisted him to the house as quickly and discreetly as possible, undressed him and put him in a nightshirt, and then must have propped him in his chair in front of the window in the study where he could watch the comings and goings, as, from time to time, he would call out. Aganetha indicated he was to be ignored. Yes, yes. See who's going to come running, she muttered. The ministers and *Ältester*, anxious to pass on news to their congregations of there being a strong possibility of war, had left after the noon meal. Others left soon after the hunting party returned.

Someone among the conference attendees was a thief, Helena grimly and privately reported to Aganetha, who quickly spread the news. Whoever had taken the six long-handled dessert spoons, a tray belonging to a sugar and cream set, a butter knife, must have done so early in the morning, Aganetha said. Martha had cleaned and counted the silverware last thing at night. When it looked as though they would be short of spoons for the noon meal that day, she went to get some of the less valuable pieces, and noticed that the silverware was missing. The thief must have entered the house while they were still sleeping.

Katya's mother wanted to know, had Katya seen anyone when she and Nela were cutting flowers in the garden early in the morning. They'd only seen Frieda Krahn going off into the garden after breakfast to retch into a bush. This was while they were arranging the flowers in pails of water, Katya told her. Then they had taken the pails and set them at the bases of the chestnut trees along the avenue. So much fuss over a few spoons, her mother said with a certain haughtiness Katya had not seen in her mother before.

Her mother had been kept busy with the little ones until several daughters of guests had come asking if they could watch the little ones for her, and so she was free now to join the women visiting together under the canopy. She had knotted her hair and fastened it on the top of her head, which made her neck seem longer, and her eyes larger. She was dressed better, more fashionably, than many of the women present, Katya realized as her mother went to join the women, her back straight and skirt swishing with the movement of her slender hips.

After supper, lanterns were lit and hung from the canopy. The children, worn by the sun and play, lay curled on rugs beneath it or asleep in women's laps. Dietrich and other young men had entertained them all day with games of horseshoe throw, tug-of-war and races, and now it was time for them to be bathed and tucked into camp cots and trundle beds. These were children of a chosen few who were staying another night. The sons and daughters of other estate owners, teachers, proprietors of stores, and, like Willy Krahn, owners of full farms.

Katya had noticed differences between the *gutsbesitzers* – estate owners – and the others. The estate owners, like the Sudermann brothers, weren't hunched and stiff looking, or overly friendly, either. Nor did they square shoulders before going across the yard. But the extent of the real differences between the estate owners and farmers would only become apparent years later when she would hear how one family's Big House had frescoes on the ceiling of its hall, the work of an Italian painter. Another house, a bowling lane. Another was decorated in Victorian style, its salon furnished entirely with black lacquered furniture and gold velvet. Then there was the one with an arboretum on its second floor that held full-size lemon trees and had an aquarium, alive with water plants and tropical fish, suspended from its glass ceiling.

Can you describe the Privol'noye mansion, the young man would one day ask. She would say that the Privol'noye Big House was neither a mansion, nor was it palatial, as she'd heard someone describe it. It was a cumbersome-looking two-storey affair built in a combination of styles. Designed by Aganetha Sudermann, daughter of a half-farmer who had married into wealth. While travelling in European cities Aganetha had sketched whatever caught her unpractised eye, an entrance, a window, a parapet. It had been said by those who knew, by a teacher of art who had once brought his students on a trip to see their house, that it possessed a canal-house entrance, but a parapet along the east wall was neo-Renaissance. Its gables were decorated in Jugendstil, a more recent style and one picked up in newer Mennonites schools and institutes. It was a big house, she would tell him. With a front and back door. An addition on one side which they called the east wing. The house was made of stone. "Where they got the stones, I don't know."

Faith Conferences, such as the one Abram held, had been opportunities for the offspring of people with the same size purses to meet, for marriages to be hatched, for cousins to marry cousins, half-sisters to marry half-brothers, as many children of the wealthy did in order to combine family fortunes. A Mennonite aristocracy, complete with albino offspring, children with bleeding and sight problems, those who were sickly and sometimes not altogether too bright.

Willy Krahn's wife had brought a bandura with her, and she came alive now as she plucked the instrument and sang in a sweet voice a ballad about the steppe. Gradually the men joined the women under the canopy in the field, everyone made weary by the heat of the day and giving into contentment as they reclined on rugs.

The sun waned, and a coolness drifted in off the land. The sky was made to seem darker by the light of the lanterns hung along the perimeter of the canopy. Katya sat on a rug beside her mother's chair, hugging her knees, Greta on the other side of it, her head resting against her mother's thigh. Lydia sat on a cane chair at the edge of the canopy, her hair turned to silver in a halo of lantern light. Throughout the evening she had seemed restless, and kept trying out different chairs, or a space on the ground whenever someone got up and left. It was as though she were trying out who she wanted close by her. As though she were trying to become familiar with being farther away from Greta, until, at last, near the end of the evening, she was sitting apart from everyone, having inched her chair beyond the halo of light and into the semi-darkness, her leg crossed, a foot swinging.

The murmur of voices, the men's laughter as they teased their women and one another, making fun at their own expense, was like the sound of the bandura, like the soft plucking of a harp. And then Katya heard another kind of music, and as her eyes grew accustomed to the dusk beyond the lamplights, she saw a cart coming along the road, and what she'd heard was an accordion being played. As the cart drew near, Frieda Krahn broke off playing, and the lively accordion music took over.

"It's Sen'ka Pravda, that good-for-nothing louse," someone said.

"It's Manya's brother," Helena exclaimed, and rose from her chair.

A mongrel came up from a ditch and over to the donkey cart, barking timidly as several of the men left the canopy, and went over to the side of the road.

Manya's brother resembled an ordinary peasant fallen on bad times. He was deeply sunburned from living outdoors, and wore what looked like homespun clothing. His hair reached his shoulders, Katya noticed when he took off his cap and bowed.

"May the devil ignore your oxen," he called.

"Simeon, what shakes you loose? And where did you get such a fine animal?" Willy Krahn called out.

Simeon Pravda squinted to see who had called and, recognizing Willy, answered, "From the Wild One."

Willy climbed up the ditch and onto the road to admire the donkey. Pravda, being true to his name, had spoken the truth, he said. He recognized the donkey as having belonged to Bull-Headed Heinrichs, he called to them in German. Bull-Headed had become a horse dealer, among other things, he said.

"A good little animal," he complimented Pravda in Russian.

"What brings you here?" one of the men asked.

"The road, the donkey," Pravda said, and laughed heartily. He set the accordion aside and went to get down from the cart. He swung his shoulders to move his body, and lowered himself to the ground. Katya saw that he was half the size of a grown man, that his legs were cut off at the thighs and he walked on the stumps.

"Father, how about a few kopecks," he asked Willy Krahn.

"A man like you, with such a fine animal," Willy scolded.

Pravda shrugged dramatically, as if to say, Who knows how that happens, but his eyes in the meantime surveyed each of the men, appraising, sweeping across the people beneath the canopy, lighting on Helena Sudermann.

"Manya said that if I should ever see you, I should tell you that she has done better than she's doing right now," he called. "And to also wish you God's favour." Then he took a bottle from his tunic and drank deeply from it, and raised it. "To freedom. It kills the pain." He patted a thigh to indicate what he meant.

"Where is Manya?" Helena called across the ditch. "We didn't hear anything from her after she went away."

After she ran away, Katya thought.

Pravda scowled and waved, as though in disgust. "Why don't you go and see for yourself how Manya is, and her little German bastard. Be our guest," he called to Helena, gesturing with his bottle towards the horizon, and the village of Lubitskoye. He returned to the cart and drove off, his dog loping behind.

"Who was that?" one of the women asked when the men had returned.

"Sen'ka Pravda," Willy Krahn said. "Simeon Panteleimon Pravda." The man had once been a miner in the Don coal basin.

Another man said he'd heard Pravda had drunk too much vodka one day and, under its influence, tried to hitch a ride on a train and fell under its wheels. The storyteller and several of the men present had seen him before, in Ekaterinoslav. A woman, his mother more than likely, had used him for begging. She pulled him through the streets in a wagon, calling out for pity.

"*Domma-bädel*," someone said. Bowing and scraping, and laughing up his sleeve the whole time. Helena's expression discouraged questions anyone might have had about Manya, and although the light had long ago been too dim for needlework, she picked up her embroidery and bent over it.

The field where they gathered beneath the canopy sizzled with insects, a sound which drew Katya's attention to the steppe and far beyond, where the earth curved at the horizon. The sizzling made her think of the night her father buried the gold head beside the loaf of land. The insects spoke of lives that had already been lived; the invisible kingdom of believers her father often spoke about; the Baba stones whose shadowed features guided travellers across the faceless steppe. Under their lumpy stone bodies lay other bodies perhaps, of Turks, Tartars; a nomad who had been stopped by a lance, a fall from a horse.

The time had come for sleep, someone suggested, and everyone agreed and got up at once. Katya was taken by Willy's gentleness as he helped Frieda to her feet and offered her his arm. When Helena came near to them, Willy stopped her to ask if she might know of a girl who would come and stay at their place. He wanted Frieda to have help immediately, he said.

Aganetha, overhearing him, came bustling over. "You don't need to look far," she said. She motioned towards Greta, who was collecting the pillows from the chairs, and gathering up glasses and half-emptied bottles of *kvass* and schnapps.

"There's Margareta. She's old enough to start earning her way. Her mama and papa have a whole house full of little ones who will need a teacher. I'm sure Margareta would welcome the chance to help," Aganetha said.

"Mama," Lydia said, the word a groan which Aganetha pointedly ignored. Katya saw the disbelief in her mother's face, her agitation as what Aganetha said became clear. Greta pleaded silently for Auguste to intervene, but David's wife appeared flustered, as though she didn't understand what had transpired, or chose not to, and continued with packing her violin. Lydia quickly left, her bright hair and white shoulders moving swiftly away through the garden.

$\mathcal{K}$atya would remember that clouds driven by the wind had cast shadows on the shorn fields on either side of the road, making the fields appear incandescent as patches of earth brightened to a yellow-gold and faded to the usual monochromatic beige of autumn. All around her the land glowed and dimmed; it was a remarkable thing to see how a landscape shadowed with running clouds seemed to turn itself on and off, and she stood very still, her slate-grey eyes taking it in, wanting to remember the day her father went to serve in the war.

She watched with Gerhard and Sara as the *droschke* taking her parents to Ekaterinoslav reached the vanishing point and disappeared, and then they returned to the gate posts where Oma Schroeder waited with baby Daniel clinging to her neck, Johann and Peter to her apron. Because the air was cool, she knew not to expect that her parents would be given back to them in an image projected above the road. She wouldn't see the usual wobbling amoeba go floating across the land when, miles away, the carriage turned onto the Colony highway, went northeast to the pink- and peach-coloured city of Ekaterinoslav, where, her father had explained, hundreds of men would soon camp on the platform of a train station and wait to board a train for Moscow. Abram Sudermann had predicted that their father would likely be home from the war by Christmas. Most people thought the same, that the men wouldn't be away for more than five months.

Her mother had never been to Ekaterinoslav, a city named after the great empress. She went for the first time, wanting to shorten, by a few days at least, the separation from her husband, just as many other women had done. But their encounter with the Russian city, and life beyond their Mennonite oasis, would make them anxious about their husbands and sons. They didn't fear the painted birds, the whores moving among the men at the station, their seduction garish and as plain to see as the day. Rather, they feared the fair and rosy-cheeked Russian nurses their men would work alongside in field hospitals, ships, and trains. Sisters of mercy, who, it was rumoured, could be entirely too merciful.

Katya's parents had been treated by Abram Sudermann to a stay at an ostentatious hotel in Ekaterinoslav, and the painted birds were even there, her mother told Oma when she returned. Abram was acquainted with the manager, whose quick movements and glibness made her mother suspect he was afraid his true self would be revealed if ever he slowed down. He offered her parents a key to a private steam bath, which they declined. What with the presence of the painted birds, her mother was reluctant to sit where they might have sat. But they did accept the man's invitation to take supper in the hotel's elegant dining room; they refrained from speaking German, and were treated to the music of a string ensemble of women musicians.

The second night, they lodged in Isaac Sudermann's factory quarters, a suite that was made available to out-of-town business acquaintances in a three-storey building across a courtyard from his tractor factory. The building where they stayed also housed several of Isaac Sudermann's factory workers and their families, those workers who had shown industry and promise and proven themselves to be worthy of a higher education, which he provided for them in a classroom after work. Because of the impending war the students' benches now stood empty. Isaac's factory was running at half its productivity, he complained to them as he took them on a tour. He would need to hire women, he said. If the war went on longer than Christmas, it was likely he would be required to manufacture cannons and shell casings.

We're so rich, Mama, Katya's mother said to Oma when she returned, meaning that Mennonites had become rich. The extent of some people's wealth had been brought home to her. She wrung her hands and paced, made anxious by what she'd seen in the city, Isaac's factory, his flour mill. The ornate and luxurious house Abram's married sons lived in, the servants all in uniforms. She had seen a mansion owned by a Mennonite, a man whom people weren't ashamed to call Millionaire Toews, that occupied a full city block. There would be a price to pay for all of this, she predicted, and quoted a biblical list of what could be bought in the world marketplace, gold and silver, pearls, fine linen, silk, vessels of ivory, brass, ointments, wine, beasts, horses and chariots, and slaves, and the souls of men.

Years later Katya would hear the stories, relive the scene through the eyes of people who had been there: the platform shaking as locomotives drew in and out beneath the vaulted ceiling of the station, steam, thick as wool in the chilly air, and obliterating the crowds that gathered across the tracks. Beyond the crowd was a broad tree-lined avenue where omnibuses and carriages and automobiles went to and fro. The avenue opened to a central square, a statue of Pushkin, and gilt-trimmed and pastel-coloured apartment buildings.

She would remember the moment the *droschke* carrying her father and mother passed through the gates of Privol'noye, the clouds casting their shadows, the incandescent earth. The parlour clock ticked as usual, but its sound now became accentuated, became a counterpoint to the rhythm of her mother's footsteps when she returned, moving through the house in the months that followed as though feeling her way in the dark. Greta's departure for Arbusovka to keep house for Willy and Frieda Krahn, and their father's departure for three months' medical training in Moscow, had left an aching silence.

She would read, years later, about that particular autumn when her father had gone away, about the crowds that had gathered in parks in Odessa to listen to military bands while enjoying ice cream on balmy summerlike evenings. People strolling in parks, wheeling baby carriages, their voices blending as they called for war. In Berlin, Paris, and London, there were similar parks, and choirs whose thundering recitative had all been the same.

II

IN THE PRESENCE OF ENEMIES

Whence then cometh wisdom?

and where is the place of understanding?

— JOB 28:20

Dear Greta,

You'll be happy to know that village life suits us well. Within the first week our Sara won everyone over with her sunny disposition, judging from the fact that there's hardly a day when she isn't invited onto someone's yard for a visit. I'm sure she knows the inside of almost every house here around. She's also become such a *Niescheaje-op*, always wanting to know why this, why that. Our tongues are sore from answering her questions, which only bring more questions. Gerhard seems determined to grow up quickly and helps Opa and Uncle Bernhard every way he can. Once school begins, I'm sure he and Sara will fit right in.

I'm glad we moved closer to Papa, but we had to get used to not being able to see him whenever we wanted. Even Mama would find a reason to go walking near the Seminary in hopes of having a short visit with him. When he comes home, it's usually only for a day or two, and then Opa and Uncle Bernhard find something to keep him occupied in the barn and on the fields, which is good medicine, according to Mama. Papa is made for the outdoors, but he works hard at the Seminary to prove his loyalty.

Mama says I'm to thank you for your long letter, which she will sit down and answer this coming Sunday. Arbusovka may be a small village but it sounds as though there are many interesting people, including Willy Krahn. We hope to surprise you one day with a Sunday visit.

Lovingly,
your sister Katherine

September 20, 1915

Dear Katya,

I'm sorry that this must be a short note, but Dietrich is waiting as I write. He has agreed to deliver this parcel to you. We were surprised and happy to see him, and welcomed his brief visit. Tell Sara to be careful with the buttons on the tunic, as there aren't any spare ones. They are such special buttons, and should she lose one, then all of them would have to be replaced. Frieda Krahn has been good to show me how to use the machine, and as you can see, I'm making progress.

I will write a longer letter at another time. Needless to say, I think of you all every day, and you are in my prayers.

Margareta

Dear Greta,

Another quiet Sunday, while across the street, the Siemens'
veranda and garden are overcome with visitors. Even though Opa
and Oma have one of the largest houses in town, they don't receive
many Sunday callers, and I'm beginning to wonder if it's because
we're living with them. In my walks about town, I've come to
notice that full farmers visit with other full farmers, just as the
owners of half-farmers stick to their own, and so, even though
Opa is a full farmer, the other owners of full farms don't often
come to visit, and I'm thinking that perhaps it's because they don't
want to be seen mixing with us, who have no land at all.

Today in church the minister's sermon was based on Scripture
that says those who are last on earth will be first in heaven, and those
who are first will be last. Therefore, people who live the farthest
away from the centre of the village should one day occupy the
centre of heaven, yes? Or are there other ways of being first and
last that have nothing to do with the size or place of a person's
dwelling? If so, I would like to hear what those might be.

This afternoon while Mama and the boys slept, I sat out with
Opa and Oma on the steps and, when no one came calling, Nela
invited us over. She has invited me several times now. She introduced me to an old lady, Tante Anna, who in spring came to board
in their little house at the back of the orchard. For all her seventy-
eight years, she's as spry as can be, and full of good humour. Nela
said that at first, their student borders weren't happy with the
thought of sharing the little house, but they have grown quite fond
of her. Nela has been good to come and help with the pickling.

Did you know that if you pierce an overly large cucumber with a knitting needle, it won't go hollow inside? Also, a layer of oak or grape leaves makes the cukes stay green longer. Horseradish keeps them firm. Nela sends her regards.

You have likely already heard of our fires. The two barn-burnings in Chortitza. One barn was saved, and has almost been rebuilt. A straw pile standing too near to it caught fire and the fire spread. It's being said that both fires were purposely set by jealous peasants. I can't imagine a person being so wicked. We had to close all the windows and could smell the smoke for days.

Sometimes I dream that we are all back at home, as I'm sure you do, too. Papa was home for three days recently and spent most of the time suffering with a headache, but he was happy to be with us, and by the time he left, he looked more like his old self.

Lovingly,
your sister Katherine

*T*he day had been long and hot, and a shortage of draft animals made the harvest slow. Her uncle Bernhard's black disposition was on the verge of erupting when voluminous rain clouds appeared, rimming the edge of the valley. He was anxious for the herdsman to bring the cows home, as he wanted to go up the hill for an hour's work before it began to rain. Katya waited at the barn gate with Gerhard watching for the cows and thought about her father.

She imagined him tending the soldiers whose litters and cots filled the classrooms and the auditorium of the Teachers' Seminary only minutes away in Chortitza. When she thought of the last days they'd had as a family at Privol'noye, she recalled their picnic beside Ox Lake, the walk in the forest the day of the gathering. Of the three men who'd gone walking, only her father had ended up nursing the wounded. Years later, she would read David Sudermann's letters to her father, which were filled with accounts of street riots in Odessa, of the burning-out of Jewish shops, and mob killings. He served with the Red Cross as an executive secretary for medical personnel in a finance office. He had written to her father with his usual sideways humour, "As you can imagine, my position has created genuine friendship towards me, as it is my signature that is required on requisitions of the medical personnel before the cashiers will hand over the money."

She'd heard that Franz Pauls was a bookkeeper in a Red Cross administration office on train number 159, a train that went to the front to collect the severely wounded and bring them back to the interior. There were thirteen Mennonite *Sanitäters* assigned to number 159, most of them from the colony of Chortitza. Franz Pauls's letters to his parents would one day be published in a Mennonite journal along with other men's letters, memoirs, a record of their non-military service in the Great War. He would describe the administration coach where he worked, its desks bolted to the floor. A pharmacy coach separated the administration coach from the surgery, and so the fumes of ether and the sound of bones being sawed didn't reach him, but the odour of blood did. It seemed to have permeated all the coaches on the Red Cross train, even where he slept. He received first-hand the accounts of the soldier's wounds and their suffering. His being able to smell blood everywhere was his imagination playing tricks, they told him, as they, too, smelled blood, even when they were off the train and walking in the countryside.

Her father, following three months in Moscow, had been sent to work in the town of Chortitza, in the Teachers' Seminary, which had been turned into a *Lazarett*. In her family, as in most, it was taken for granted that the mothers cared for the ill; now her father was changing soiled diapers of Russian men and washing their stitched-together bodies. He spoon-fed them *kasha* and soup, comforted and prayed over them; he described the heat pouring from their lungs as though they were being consumed inside by fire.

The many times she went to the post office and passed by the *Lazarett*, she'd see the open doors and imagine how the fresh air must lift the men's spirits. She once saw her father sitting outside on a chair, looking up at trees on the slope of the valley where something seemed to have caught his attention, and it took her a moment to recognize him. That her father had a life separate from theirs made him seem a stranger, and the days when he was on leave there was an awkwardness until he shed his uniform and emerged from the summer room freshly bathed and wearing his farm clothes.

A fog of yellow dust hung above the crest of the hill, and she knew the cows would soon appear. She saw Nela come out of the house across the street and onto the veranda. When she saw Katya, she hurried down a set of stone steps leading through the garden, and came over to her gate. The book circle was meeting tonight at Auguste Sudermann's house in Chortitza, Nela called. Would she be able to come?

I'll see, Katya said, which was what she'd said both times Nela had invited her, declining, at the last moment, to go.

"What is there to see?" Nela asked in a teasing voice.

"I haven't read the book," she said.

"Many don't. Olga, for example. She comes for the gossip and the eats," Nela said. "Auguste and Lydia said I should issue a special invitation."

"I'll see," Katya repeated.

"When you see what there is to see, let me know if that means whether or not you're able to come," Nela said, and laughed.

Within moments they heard the sound of the herder's horn, and then, up and down the street, people opened their barn gates. The cows drew nearer, each one knowing which gate to enter. Gerhard rode their gate open, and the animals entered the barnyard, their bodies streaked with sweat and dust.

When her uncle and grandfather brought the team and wagon through the gate, she and Gerhard went with them to help with the weed cutting, riding on the back of the wagon, their legs dangling.

Dear Greta, Katya thought, composing a letter she would later write.

Dear Greta,

I have news. I believe that the stork is going to visit us again, judging by what's behind Mama's apron. Daniel won't be happy to give up his place in her lap. For my mind, I hope this time the stork brings us a sister. Then we will be four and four.

Dear Greta,

Abram Sudermann came to see Papa when last time he was home. According to Mr. Sudermann, it would be a simple thing for Papa to obtain a three-month medical leave. David Sudermann has made a friend of a chief physician in Odessa who says arranging a leave for medical reasons wouldn't be too difficult. Mr. Sudermann said it was highly unlikely that, once the leave was up, anyone would come looking for Papa to return.

Of course, our dear Papa has refused.

The rain would hold off, don't worry, her grandfather predicted. Wait and see. She heard a faint rumble of thunder as though the earth had been lifted and shaken. Her uncle Bernhard chewed on a piece of straw and, as usual, let her grandfather do most of the talking. Uncle Bernhard wore his cap low to his forehead, which made him look like an animal peering out from a burrow. When he did speak, he would noisily clear his throat before, and after. Her mother's oldest brother had been born with one leg shorter than the other, which had made him exempt from military service.

The road out of the village was lined with houses; they passed by the colony's gardens and, beyond the gardens, the watermelon patch, at its centre a cone-shaped twig hut where an old man stayed the night to guard the melons whose syrup would be a valued source of sweetener if sugar proved costly or scarce. They crossed a bridge at Kanserovka Creek, the creek bed almost dry in autumn except for a narrow stream of wet trickling down the centre, colouring the stones a brighter grey.

Then they were mounting a hill, and as the wagon reached its crest it seemed as though the town had disappeared. Always, the wind was different on the plateau, it held smells and sounds that didn't reach town. The weather was different, too, warmer or colder, and up there, the land was hooked onto the edge of the world and the sky more generous.

Today the rain clouds had gathered, but were not pressing against the earth as they appeared to be in town. Today the land rattled with clusters of black seed-pods that grew near the tops of weeds as tall as her uncle. Last year the field had raised emmer, but there was a short-age of draft animals, and so the field was one of several that had been given over to the weeds which, because of a scarcity of straw, they would burn in the stove for winter.

Without speaking, her uncle Bernhard strode off into the field, his scythe in motion, a giant cutting down a forest as the scythe cleared a broad path. Gerhard took up a ball of twine, ran to keep up with him.

"*Na*, then, girl. You stay a good distance from my blade. I don't want to have to think about you being too close behind me," her grandfather warned. "Don't try and make the bundles too large. They only come loose in the end."

She followed him into the field and went to work, listening to the rhythmic sweep of his scythe, watching his body pulling it through thick stalks without hesitation; a sweep, and a step forward, and another sweep. The seed-pods rattled loudly in a rift of sudden wind, and behind the wind came a shake of thunder. But she trusted what her grandfather said, that the rain would wait, and as she gathered the cut weeds into bundles and tied them, the air became thick with dust that stung the membranes of her nose.

Since the decision had been made to move to Rosenthal so that they might be near to her father, she hadn't yet visited with Lydia, who, during school months, stayed in Chortitza with her aunt Auguste on New Row Street, and the remainder of the time with her sister Justina in Berdiansk. Lydia lived a world away, in a language learned at the Girls' School. Katya had seen her walking across the street with the students who boarded at the Siemens', heard them singing in harmony a song they had just learned in Music. Their classroom windows faced a courtyard, and at one end of the courtyard were the teachers' residences and gardens where Katya had once been sent on an errand. She had smelled the bread baking in an outdoor oven, heard the girls' voices as they conjugated Russian verbs in unison, imagined them struggling with geometry, algebra, and cross-stitch embroidery. If the day was a Monday, they'd study Religion, Russian reading and poetry, German reading, Arithmetic, and Music. The girls who went to the book circle had been Greta's school friends, Lydia and the Sudermann cousins, who made her aware that the gap between them was more than a difference in age.

She noticed that the light around her had changed, and that it had been a while since she'd last heard the sweep of her grandfather's scythe. When she turned around, she saw that she had wandered from the cleared path, and the weeds she'd bundled were not to be seen. She was lost, suddenly, in a forest of weeds, not knowing which way to go. She heard a train whistle, its echo returning across the land. A train was arriving at the station on the outskirts of Chortitza, or departing, she thought, and as the whistle came again, she made her way through the weeds towards the sound. She battered at the thick dried stalks, her hands out before her to protect her face, until suddenly her hands met air, and there in a clearing on the ground before her lay a man.

She must have startled him as much as his presence startled her, as he sat up quickly, looking as though he were in the wrong, and then he snatched up a jacket he'd been using as a pillow as though fearing she might steal it. A broad scar ran along one side of his nose and pulled up a corner of his mouth, revealing purple and swollen-looking gums.

"Close the door, you booby," he said. His voice came out full of breath and hollow-sounding. She wheeled around and went crashing through the weeds in the opposite direction, feeling the plants scratching her arms and not caring. She ran without thinking where she was going, only knowing that she had to get away. She stumbled into a ditch alongside the road. Beside the road in the distance stood the wagon, and she ran to it, climbed onto it, and onto its bench, from where she could see. Her uncle, her grandfather and brother were standing on a large burial mound, looking towards the cluster of buildings and sheds that was the train station. When she called, Gerhard turned and waved, motioning that she should come. She followed the path her uncle had cut through the weeds, which took her directly to them.

They'd been watching the train come into the station on the edge of town, and a yard beyond the tracks where the teamsters were gathered with their horses and wagons. Dust rose from the road going into Chortitza, and what looked to be a grey banner moved along it. Soldiers, she realized. A black dog dodged among them; here and there metal glinted, a sabre, a gun.

"They don't have the heart to fight any more," her grandfather said, his pale eyes looking beyond the scene, looking into his thoughts, she knew, as he shook his head and turned away. "That's war. It takes the strong and leaves the old, like me. And those who return are maimed in one way or another."

As they came across the Kanserovka bridge, she saw the man she had stumbled across in the field, coming over the crest of the hill. His short bowed legs propelled him down the grade faster than his body wanted to go. Her grandfather said that he'd seen him before. The man went from door to door, looking for chores in return for food. He'd shown up in town one day, from where, no one knew. A stranger who didn't have a place to lay his head, like so many others who came to town. He went by the name of Trifon.

The thunderclouds had circled around the valley and emptied out far beyond the town, and Main Street was lit by twilight, pink light trimming rooftops and chimneys. People sat out on their platforms, verandas, and steps, and as their wagon passed by a yard, the pungent aroma of tobacco would sometimes come wafting across a garden amid laughter, and a woman's voice as she called for her children to come inside.

Later that evening she stood waiting at the gate for Nela, knowing that her grandmother and mother were at a window. She'd felt their satisfaction when she'd given in to their prodding to go with Nela to the book circle meeting.

Nela's house was set back from the street and on an incline, and the entire front of it was enclosed in a veranda whose walls were covered in clematis vines. Stone steps ascended through a garden that throughout the summer was tall with delphinium, monkshood and hollyhocks. It was one of the most beautiful houses and yards on the street. Behind the house stood an orchard, and beyond it, the small house where the Siemens boarded Tante Anna and the students. She often watched the students coming and going in their school uniforms. Aganetha had stolen Greta's dream, and without needing to ask why, Katya understood she herself would not attend *Mädchenschule*.

Her day began with the appearance of the students coming through the Siemens' garden, looking bright-faced with anticipation as they went off to school amid the humming sound of cream separators, the slosh, kerplunk of butter churns, and she didn't regret not being with them. She knew from having visited them that a china dish on a bureau held their combs, odd buttons, and safety pins; their shoes were lined up on a shelf in a wardrobe; three beds had been pushed together to make room for a long table and benches. One of the girls had lavender oil, which she'd purchased in the Crimea when her class went there on a spring outing. She gave Katya a dab to rub on her temples to experience the scent's soothing qualities. She claimed the smell reminded her of Greek ruins she'd visited at Chersonesus, where Christ's message had come ashore from Constantinople. The lavender reminded her of Lavadia, she said, where they had gone walking, hoping to come upon the tsarinas doing the same, in a park.

Tante Anna, a spinster, occupied a smaller room in the two-room house where the students boarded. Katya had been there one evening, and learned that the students would pile onto the woman's canopied bed and listen as she told them stories of the olden days, which they heard many times over. A mirror, whose frame was a carving of grey-hounds bounding up to its centre, gave them their reflection as they reclined on the woman's bed, and always under the soft and remote gaze of a young tsar and tsarina.

Tante Anna's presence in the house ensured that the students never became rambunctious, that they faithfully attended to their lessons before going to bed. But it was more that the girls attended to the elderly woman, Nela had said. Before they went to school they laid out the woman's clothes and made sure she had an adequate supply of handkerchiefs, as she'd had a mild stroke which had left her with a drool. When, in the evening, Tante Anna finished telling them an old-time story, they lowered the curtains around her bed, rinsed out her handkerchiefs and hung them to dry.

Katya had seen this happen, she'd been invited to come and hear Tante Anna tell a favourite story, and had felt the girls' reverence, their sincerity and earnestness. How dear the spinster was to them. Which made Katya think of Helena Sudermann, and her own sometimes less-than-favourable thoughts about the woman.

A sparrow hawk followed her and Nela down the street, lighting in a tree beyond them and screeching as they went by. They came near to a crossroads, the boundary between Rosenthal and Chortitza. Had they gone west, they would've come to the *Lazarett*, the brown brick building where her father stayed. They went beyond the crossroads and passed by the *Mädchenschule*. The three-storey red-brick school towered over the street, its canal-house front upheld with arches and pillars in contrasting white brick.

Auguste Sudermann came to meet them at the gate, and Katya was surprised by the heat of her arm against her own, as her narrow body didn't suggest warmth. Both Auguste and Nela wore similar wire-rimmed glasses that gave them a studious look. Nela's sharp nose and her thin hair made her look needy, newly-hatched and wingless. As they came up the steps, Katya heard a noise inside the house, and was surprised when Dietrich appeared in the doorway with one of Auguste's girls straddling his shoulders.

"Hello, Katherine Vogt. I'm Dee Dee the horse. And so I'm sorry, but I can't stop to visit. Unless you have a carrot in your pocket, that is," Dietrich said.

"She doesn't have anything in her pocket," the girl shouted and thumped Dietrich's chest with her heels to make him go.

"Goodness, Tante Auguste, what are you raising here?" Dietrich asked. Then he whinnied and went galloping down the stairs and into the yard, the girl screaming with joy.

"It's like that every time he visits," Auguste complained, shaking her head in mock dismay. Another of Auguste's girls stood watching at the door as her sister and Dietrich went galloping down the street. A woman came to her gate to investigate the commotion, and began calling that Dietrich should go faster. What was he, a horse or a lazy camel? she called.

"Me, me. My turn," the girl at the door whimpered, her bottom lip quivering.

Nela laughed and dashed up the steps and into the house. She scooped the girl into her arms and nuzzled her neck, while the child squirmed to be free.

"Tien, Tien. No hugs for Nela? What's poor Nela going to do for hugs if you don't give them to her?" Nela asked as she set the child down.

"You'll have to get your own girl," the child said and Auguste laughed, her eyes touching on her daughter with fondness, not seeing that Nela had turned away quickly, not seeing the hurt in her eyes.

"Sasha will never get them settled for bed now," Auguste chided as Dietrich returned from giving the first girl a ride, and swung her down from his shoulders.

The book they would discuss that evening was a collection of essays by Ufer Hold, *Quiet Women, Powerful Women*. Katya shouldn't be concerned about not having read it, Auguste said.

But Katya had read the book, and had concluded after reading it that her moodiness was a weakness that needed to be overcome. She was someone who took herself too seriously. In her room, hanging above a washstand, was a calendar whose squares she coloured in according to her different moods: yellow for the days she felt like whistling, purple when she felt as though she was ploughing thigh-deep through water, blue for a sinking feeling she sometimes got in her stomach that something was about to go wrong.

Another of Auguste's girls came over to Dietrich and held up her arms. He obliged by swinging her onto his shoulders. "So Katya, how's life treating you in the big town?" he asked.

"It's altogether different," she told him.

"Of course," he said, and nodded as though what she'd said was significant and had started him off on a train of thought. "Tante Lena says the bustards have begun to venture across the road. It seems they've developed a taste for apples," he continued cheerfully. "Who knows, maybe we'll all be home again, soon." His aunt Helena and the Wiebe sisters were looking forward to his parents returning. The Big House had been too quiet since the war.

"It sounds as though you've gained an appreciation for Privol'noye," Auguste said.

Annoyance flickered in Dietrich's face, which Auguste didn't seem to notice.

"When your father returns, I'm sure he'll put a stop to the tent meetings," Auguste said, more to herself than to Dietrich.

"Not necessarily," Dietrich said rather curtly. Then spots of colour rose in his narrow cheeks. "Not many people have been attending anyway," he said, softening his tone.

Helena had invited Baptist preachers to use the meadow at

Privol'noye to set up their tent and all summer long they had been conducting religious services, Dietrich went on to explain to Katya.

"Oh look, the girls are here," he said, obviously relieved to see Lydia, the sister cousins, and Olga Penner coming through the gate, followed by another girl Katya hadn't met.

When Lydia saw Katya, her face worked with a variety of emotions, and then she collected herself and became Lydia the student, slightly aloof.

"What have you heard from Greta?" Lydia asked when they embraced.

"She's joined a choir, and likes it very much," Dietrich said, jumping in to answer the question himself. "We exchange letters often," he said in reply to his aunt's quizzical look. Then he left the room to give his niece the longed-for ride.

"Everyone hears from Greta," Lydia said, her tone implying that she didn't.

"Sometimes a person has to write letters in order to receive them," Auguste said as she steered her daughter towards a doorway and called for a woman named Sasha to come and get the girl washed up for bed.

"Margareta's an example of a person who does whatever she's called to do, and with a cheerfulness," Auguste said. "Which is a good way to begin our discussion."

"Oh, are we going to go ahead with it?" Olga asked. She had gone over to a bookshelf and was scanning the titles. The other girl who arrived with them had been introduced to Katya as Agnes Friesen.

"Yes, of course, would you rather we didn't?" Auguste asked.

"Well, I thought . . . because we have company . . ." Olga said.

The girls exchanged glances, half-smiles of acknowledgement that more than likely Olga hadn't, as usual, read the book.

The discussion that followed didn't seem to be a discussion but a rewording of the author's essays, each of the girls struggling to find a different way to say the same thing, Katya not contributing, grateful that they seemed not to expect that she would. When they ran out of things to say, Auguste brought the discussion to a close with a quick summation, and then said it was time to remember a blessing they had experienced during the week. "Let's go around the room and share something," she said.

From the way Auguste looked at her, Katya realized she was expected to contribute, and her face grew stiff. She knew she was thankful for her grandparents' house, especially the large corner summer room whose windows let in the morning sun, and had a view of the street and Nela's house. She watched the students arriving and leaving, Tante Anna working in the garden stooped and slow, enjoyed the symmetry of the white picket fences enclosing the houses and yards. The fences were a pleasant geometry of definition and division, she would come to think when enough time had passed and picket fences were no longer in style. Now, as the young women spoke, she was overcome by her rushing thoughts. What should she tell them?

When it came time for Katya to speak she didn't tell them that she liked the way the town of Chortitza began where Rosenthal left off, that she felt sheltered by the valley; its arms of rose bushes and trees made her patient to wait for the war to end, to be reunited as a family and returned to the steppe, where there was nothing between the eye and the horizon but a sea of grass. Instead, she told them she was blessed by her grandparents' house, without explaining why, and knew they'd been puzzled and had likely attributed her vagueness to her young age.

Nela's old father came to get them, and Katya waited in the carriage with Nela while he stood at the gate talking with Dietrich. Ohm Siemens was a secretary at the Chortitza *volost*, and one of the church's eight ministers. He was a cheerful man, and well liked. He was known to cut a hole in the ice on the creek in winter, strip to his combinations, and lower himself into it while singing "Gott ist die Liebe." The stars are bright, yes? Nela said. She was blessed every day by nature, Nela had told the girls. The previous night she'd heard an owl hooting behind the little house, which had put her to sleep.

As Katya rode home with Nela and her father, the moon lighting the hilltops, the roofs, the silver dome of the Orthodox church, she wondered if there would ever come a time when she didn't feel disappointed in herself.

*T*he winter came early and all at once, the shortened days and the extreme cold keeping the little ones underfoot. Katya's mother became too quick to scold, which bothered Katya's grandfather, but he kept silent and began to spend more time in the barn. Her mother often seemed not to notice when there was work to be done, and increasingly Katya's grandmother took over caring for the small children. It was February when Katya was awakened to the darkness of early morning, grateful for the sound of her grandfather's coughing in the room next to the one she shared with Sara. The sound had pulled her out of a dream. She'd been in a courtyard, and standing before her was what looked to be a millstone. There were names engraved on the stone radiating out from its hub, and she'd heard a voice saying that if her name was on the stone, she would be allowed to enter heaven. She awoke damp with perspiration.

Floorboards creaked as her grandfather got up and went across the room. When he took the lid off the chamber pot it clanked, just as it did when he set it back on. He made as much noise as possible, as it was a cue for Peter, their very own *vorsänger*, to call out from the boys' room.

"Opa, hurry and make a fire. Won't you please make a fire, make a fire, make a fire," Peter, their song leader, obliged, Johann then adding his voice to the chant.

"*Ja, ja.* You boys hold your horses in there. Opa's going to make a fire yet," her grandfather called.

"Make-a-fire, make-a-fire, make-a-fire," her brothers chanted, Gerhard adding his voice to theirs, sure-sounding and clear.

Katya heard her grandfather go out into the kitchen, through a hall and into the barn, and her brothers stopped calling. Moments later there was a washing sound against the walls and floor as he returned with a bundle of weeds.

There wasn't an apron wide enough to conceal how high her mother's stomach had risen, and so Katya had taken her place on the milking stool. She didn't mind getting up before the others as it gave her time go roaming in her thoughts. Beyond the window, the barn cast its shadow across the snowy yard. A lantern moved through the darkness as her uncle Bernhard came from his house at the back of the property.

While the image of the millstone had faded, the fear of not knowing if her name was written on it remained strong as she went into the family room, bits of dried weeds crunching underfoot. Opa knelt in front of the oven, raking ashes from its chamber.

"You slept well?" he asked.

"Yes, soundly." Until the dream, she thought.

"Then it should be a good day, snow or shine," he said.

She took her father's barn jacket from a hook in the hall and went out into the equipment shed, following a path down its centre that was kept clear. At the end of the path the darkness gave way to sepia light shed by the lantern her uncle had hung near to the stalls. As she came into the barn, the air was warmer and moist, full with the sounds of lowing, a swish of tail and thump of hoof against the earthen floor.

The outside barn door opened a crack, and her uncle Bernhard's wife Susa slipped through it, bringing a bluster of icy wind that billowed up Katya's skirt.

"You should be glad you don't have to go out in the cold first thing in the morning," her aunt said as she closed the door behind her.

Her aunt Susa came with more than the hump of early-morning discontent on her back. Her youngest child, Ernest, was huddled under her shawls, his hands folded against his mother's neck. He wormed his way up through the layers of wool and peered at Katya, his eyes lighting with a grin.

"Hello little Omtje," she said to Ernest. "You don't have Zhinka this morning?" she asked her aunt.

Her aunt shrugged in resignation. A kerchief hid her red hair, which she was known for, with a complement of cinnamon freckles and eyes of amber.

"Zhinka's brothers came in the evening and took her home. Your uncle wanted to know why, but they wouldn't say why. This time they couldn't even bother to make up a story," she said. She seemed about to say more, but for some reason decided not to.

Whatever her aunt left unsaid would eventually come out, Katya knew. She took down her milking stool and went over to Reddish-Brown's stall, a gentle slow-moving animal who lifted her head from the manger to greet her. Katya blew on her hands to warm them, and then went to work, the creaking and breathing barn punctuated by a tinny, syncopated music as the strings of milk hit the bottoms of the pails. She listened for the sound to soften, for whose music would be the first to change. Usually it was her aunt's, but her son was a burden that made her slower this morning, and she kept adjusting him with a heavy sigh. A tabby cat leapt down from the loft and sauntered towards Katya, its tail hooked in a friendly greeting.

She leaned her forehead into Reddish-Brown and closed her eyes, lulled by the animal's warmth and the rhythmic sound of their milking. At Privol'noye, the outside women gave their favourite cows names that expressed their affection, such as Honey, Lovely, and Darling. Naming an animal after its colour seemed less than practical. It seemed to come from a lack of trying, and a lack of caring for the animal. The cat rubbed against her thigh and meowed, expecting to be offered a lick of foam skimmed from the pail.

The boy poked his head out from his mother's shawl and called for the cat, which went running over to him. His mother shifted him farther up her back and shooed the animal away. Katya knew she blamed it for her children's frequent bouts of ringworm. A sleigh went by in the street beyond the barn, the sound of harness bells echoing intermittently as it passed by open spaces between buildings. The sleigh could be bringing the mail, Katya thought, and wondered if in the mailman's sack there might be a letter from Greta. Greta had entertained them at Christmas with stories about Willy Krahn, who proved to be an unusual man. He sometimes painted pictures on the window curtains – geometric borders, flowers, an outdoor scene.

"Your uncle Bernhard told the brothers that if they thought he was going to pay Zhinka more wages to get her back, they were in for a disappointment. Not with the way things are going. Those men were already halfway to the road when, this one, he comes back. The middle one. The one who used to go to school with the Koop boys. The boy the Koops took in and gave board to, in exchange for chores. He did so very well in school, until his father came and said it wasn't right for his son to know more than him, and took him home. That one," Susa said, forgetting that Katya hadn't lived in Rosenthal all her life.

"You may remember he was the one who got so angry when the Koops' pup chased him and grabbed hold of the seat of his trousers, and tore a hole in them. He lit into the dog so hard that eventually it died. Mrs. Koop saw it happen, and that night, the baby she was carrying started to come. She had such a terrible and long time of it. The midwife said it hadn't been good for her to have witnessed such a scene, and that was why the baby was born with a flat nose. Her nose got better, later. It got some bone, later on. But the girl's nostrils are still fairly wide open, you can almost see right up into her head.

"It was that boy who got so upset over his trousers being torn, he was the one who came back to the house and said to your uncle Bernhard, high and mighty, 'We don't want your money. Keep it, because one day soon, everything you own will belong to us,'" her aunt said, finishing the story she had begun earlier.

Katya heard a noise and froze, her eyes locking with her aunt's as they listened. There had been a recent episode of a man in the Second Colony who, one day, called across the yard in German for his hired man to come to the house for dinner. An informer reported him to the police as having said *Long live the Kaiser*. Without a trial, he'd been sent to Siberia.

The barn door opened, and although it was unlikely to be anyone else but her uncle, she was still relieved to see him. She expected he would take up a shovel and begin cleaning out the stalls, but he went into the equipment shed instead.

"What's he up to now, I wonder?" her aunt said, switching to Russian.

He returned draped with harnesses, and the news that Nela Siemens had seen him out in the yard and come over to tell him that Tante Anna was leaving that day. That she'd been invited to go and live with relatives in a village in the Second Colony. There were other people travelling to a village nearby Tante Anna's destination and Nela had arranged for the spinster to travel on the train with them. Bernhard would take Tante Anna to the station.

In autumn a government school inspector had padlocked and sealed the doors to the *Zentralschule* and the *Mädchenschule* without a warning or an explanation. With the boarding students gone, the days became too long and lonely for Tante Anna. Winter was taking its time ending, and the town looked dismal, dark tree branches set against a grey woollen sky, the street deeply rutted and icy, wooden sidewalks criss-crossed with the slushy footprints, mostly small ones of the children who had gone to school earlier.

As Katya went through the orchard at the back of Siemens' yard she saw a sandpit beyond the small house, a shallow bowl of land that, except for a trail of footprints across it, was a clean expanse of snow. The sound of someone chipping at ice came from a shed on Teacher Friesen's yard, beyond the sandpit. She thought it was the teacher in the ice shed, and was startled to see the man, Trifon, emerge from the shed, carrying a chunk of ice which he dropped into a water barrel beside the door of the house.

He clapped as though applauding his achievement, and when he returned to the ice shed, he saw her and stopped to stare. The man she had stumbled upon in the fields after harvest wore whatever warm clothing people gave him, and his jacket was too large, and hung on him like a blanket. She pitied rather than feared him. Where did he come across such a fancy scarf, people wondered about the yellow silk knotted at his neck. Town boys began to call him *Dommajon* Trifon, simpleton, because of his scarred face and the blackness of his confused eyes. When Trifon went back inside the shed, she searched the windows of Tante Anna's little house, thinking the old woman would be watching for her, but the curtains were drawn and the house looked abandoned.

She entered a front hall; to one side of it a door opened to what had been the boarding students' room, used for storage now, trunks and crates piled at its centre. Hanging from the ceiling on hooks were bunches of dillweed, horseradish roots, and clumps of summer savory, their dried purple flowers looking like knots of embroidery.

She entered Tante Anna's room, and the old woman greeted her with a smile. She was perched on the edge of a rocking chair, wearing a Sunday *haube* and a black travelling coat buttoned to the neck. She looked as though she had been ready and waiting for hours, the way people who fear they're a burden are apt to do. "I have something I want to tell you," Tante Anna said and beckoned for her to come close. Katya greeted Tante Anna with a kiss, but she frowned and then shook her head in dismay. "Oh, that's me. One minute I have something to say, and the next, I don't."

Katya was surprised to see that Tante Anna's bed was already stripped to its feather-mattress tick, and that the crimson bed-curtains, always such an onslaught of colour in the otherwise plain room, had been taken down, and lay folded across a table beside the bed. The oval mirror rested against a wall, giving her a reflection of her skirt and black-stockinged ankles. Leaning beside the mirror was the woman's wall sampler with the saying *Be not dismayed if sorrow enters; better days will follow.*

Tante Anna followed her gaze about the room and, seeing her attention come to rest on the wall sampler, she said, "I always went by that. But this time I'm not sure tomorrow will be better."

Her pessimism was surprising, as she was known to be a dear-heart, a person who usually turned disappointment to its bright side. The woman gave into the chair and rocked, having forgotten that she couldn't remember what it was she wanted to tell Katya.

"Now as I'm waiting for Nela to come and take me to the train, the time goes so slowly. And yet, where has seventy-nine years gone? I feel as though I've only just got started," Tante Anna said in a small voice. She always held her eyes so wide open, as though she thought she might be seeing the world for the last time, as though she was constantly surprised to find herself aged, a wrinkled potato, her chin made shiny and raw from saliva, which she kept dabbing at with a hanky.

Katya sat down on the bed to wait for Nela, thinking that the room held the odour of ammonia, and something else which she'd never been able to identify. She noticed a scrap of paper lying on top of the folded bed curtains, and the words *The dream. The cheese* written on it in the woman's script.

"*Na ja*. It comes down to this. Eleven children, and it comes down to Anna being left. Eleven little ones, and my mother never raised her voice against us. Not once. She was the soul of the family, and he must have been able to see it," she said.

"The tsar saw it," Katya said to prompt the woman to tell her favourite story.

"*Ja*, the tsar. That's what he said to us at the end of his visit. He said, 'The man is the brain of a family, the woman its soul.'" She was quoting a proverb Tsar Nicholas had bestowed on her mother the day he stopped by to visit while on his way to the Crimea.

"I was only four years old, but I remember seeing in his face, his eyes especially, that he was a strong man. I was afraid to look straight at him. He came with so many others, and all of them, the brass buttons on their uniforms so highly polished, it was hard to look at them without blinking. Row upon row of gold braid and medals hanging from their chests, from this war, and that one. How many hours went into polishing those buttons and medals every day, I wonder? Of course, they themselves didn't do the polishing."

Katya only half listened as Tante Anna began to tell her story of the day Tsar Nicholas came to visit. Perhaps Tante Anna had collected the herbs and hung them to dry in the unoccupied room. She wondered if she should take down a string of the parsnip and tuck it into the woman's satchel. Come spring, Tante Anna might want to make a pot of *postanacksupp*, Katya thought as the woman went on to say that her father invited Tsar Nicholas to stay for dinner.

Her mother hadn't fussed, but served the tsar what she made for her own family: cottage-cheese *varenyky* with sour-cream gravy, fried ham and rye bread. Meanwhile, up and down the village street, in neighbouring gardens, the tsar's entourage was being treated to similar meals. Tante Anna would recite the grace which her father had prayed, and then would come the moment when the tsar would present her mother with the gift of a diamond ring. But Tante Anna was only midway through telling the tale when she stopped. She put a finger to her lips and listened for a moment.

"Some people think I've made up the story," she said. "They think I might have overheard a similar story, and my old woman's mind took it as being my own. That it's a way for a woman who's never married to make herself seem important." As Tante Anna fell silent, Katya wondered if she was remembering the long-ago suitor Nela once alluded to. Someone she'd set her heart on, but who chose a younger sister instead.

"*Nanu*, it's coming to me now. Now I remember what I wanted to tell you. I had a dream about your papa," Tante Anna said.

Katya looked down at the scrap of paper and the words Tante Anna had written, *The dream. The cheese.* Obviously she'd written them to remind herself what she wanted to say, and had likely forgotten where she'd set the paper down.

"Why I should dream about your papa, who I hardly know and have seldom seen, is strange. That's likely why I remembered the dream when I woke up. Your papa was coming down a road past my childhood home. He had his hands in his pockets and was whistling such a happy tune. As he came near to me, he said, 'Well, hello there, Anna Rempel. Isn't life wonderful? It's just as they say, life is like a bowl of cherries.' I asked him where he was going in such a hurry, and he said, 'At last, Anna, I'm going home.' When I woke up, I said to myself, you must remember to tell this to Katya, as I know how much you've been missing your papa.

"Good," she said, congratulating herself for having remembered what she wanted to say.

She began to rummage through a satchel resting on the floor beside her chair, and took out a leather box. "Now come and see if my story is true, or not," she said.

She held a brown leather ring box in the palm of her hand, then she fumbled with its clasp and the lid sprung open to reveal an indentation in the ivory satin lining where a ring had once been.

"I haven't shown anyone for a long time. Not even the girls." She pointed to the indentation. "My mother kept it locked away in a cupboard and would take it out when a visitor would sometimes ask to see it. But then my father sold the ring to buy more land. When she died, he gave the box to me."

There was the sound of footsteps outside on the snowy path as someone came towards the house, then the door opened and Nela called out from the hall. Tante Anna quickly closed the ring box and put it back into the satchel. "It's for our eyes only," she said conspiratorially as Nela stamped snow from her shoes before entering the room.

"You haven't left anything for me to do," Nela said when she saw the stripped bed, the mirror and wall sampler leaning against a wall, a commode basin and pitcher on the floor beside the door.

"There's still something for you to do yet," Tante Anna said. She pointed to the doorsill over Nela's head.

Nela understood, and dragged a chair to the door and climbed onto it. When she stepped down, her hands were filled with cubes wrapped in cheesecloth.

The odour that Katya had always wondered about now filled the room. It was the smell of old cheese. As Nela put the cheese into the woman's lap, Tante Anna selected a bundle for each of them; a parting gift, she said.

Nela locked the door behind them and was about to cross the hall, close and lock the door of what had been the students' room, but Tante Anna stopped her. She wanted one last look, she said. "I hope those girls remember what I told them when they came to say goodbye," she said.

"What did you tell them, Tante Anna?" Nela asked.

"I told them about eating ice cream bought on the street," she said, her voice dropping to a whisper.

Nela coloured. "I'm sure they'll remember." Bernhard was already at the gate, she said. Katya watched Nela go off down the path through the orchard, carrying the woman's satchel, and was curious. Obviously Nela knew what Tante Anna was going to say.

"I'll tell you, also," Tante Anna said, and took Katya by the arm. "You should know about this. Katya, if you're ever in a city, and someone is selling ice cream on the street, be sure not to buy it. They make the ice cream they sell on the street from leftover milk. Milk that actresses have bathed in."

They went through the frozen orchard, Tante Anna leaning heavily on Katya's arm. "Why would someone want to bathe in milk?" Katya asked.

"I don't know, Katya. But I do know that one day they'll have to answer to God for it," Tante Anna said. "I suppose we'll all have things to answer for one day," she added, her indignation evaporating.

They waited on the platform at the train station waiting for Tante Anna's travelling companions to arrive. Snow fell all around them, large flakes that felt good as they melted on Katya's face. The woman's gift of cheese was a pungent lump in her coat pocket, and she'd been relieved when they'd left the stifling heat of the waiting room, as people had begun to question the source of the odour. Her uncle had gone to talk to several men gathered in the railway-yard. Men who hoped to receive a delivery of coal, the supplies they ordered, but which seldom arrived.

Nela fussed over Tante Anna, tucking a loose strand of hair into her black bonnet. The elderly woman looked frailer out in the open. She stared straight ahead, her chin high, ancient and dignified in the falling snow. Tante Anna had allowed herself to be led here and there and, at last, to be planted in this spot to wait to be taken away to live in a strange household, gloved hands clasped against her stomach, satchel at her feet.

A wagon rumbled towards the railway-yard, and although years had passed since the first time Katya had seen the man in it, she recognized him as Bull-Headed Heinrichs. He glanced in their direction with curiosity, his eyes going from one to the other, and then coming to rest on her. He lifted his cap, and she saw that his straw-coloured hair was not as long as before, but still looked as though he had never pulled a brush or comb through it.

Nela saw Katya looking at the guns in the wagon, three barrels filled with guns, their muzzles pointed at a sky heavy with snow clouds.

"He buys them from the soldiers for wheat. There's talk about what he does with them, who he sells them to. Talk from men who wish they'd thought to do the same, and denounce him now because they didn't," Nela said.

Katya was surprised to hear such a speech coming from Nela, her defence of a person it seemed she hardly knew. Snowflakes melted on her eyelashes, and for a moment, Bull-Headed became a blur. She blinked, and he became clear again. He was still looking at her, and this was not the curious glance of a man wondering what family she came from. This was not a teacher's look, a question, a greeting, patience, impatience. He was trying to pull something out of her. He smiled, and she felt heat rise in her neck. And then he wasn't smiling any more, but astonished and looking beyond her. In an instant he had jumped from the wagon and came running towards her, his jacket open and flapping.

What happened next happened in an instant.

"What is it?" Nela asked, and then she was pitched forward onto the platform, her hat flying across it and onto the tracks.

Katya could feel someone standing immediately behind her, she could hear movement, and then suddenly Tante Anna was thrown into her side, hard, the force sending her down onto the platform with Tante Anna on top of her. The boards shook with the pounding of feet as someone ran away, and Bull-Headed leapt onto the platform. She heard him shout for help as he went chasing after the fleeing person. She saw Nela rise to her knees, people moving towards them, felt Tante Anna's weight against her body as the woman sighed and relaxed, lay still, a child going to sleep.

The *Ältester* decided the funeral for Tante Anna should be held in Chortitza church to accommodate the number of people who wished to attend, who wanted to hear what had happened, to speak to those who had been bystanders to the tragedy, and to point out the survivors, Nela and herself, as though she and Nela had come near to God, had been brushed against by the angel coming for the old woman. After the funeral, Tante Anna was buried in the cemetery beyond the Orthodox church and the men returned to the church for a meeting that went on past supper, and passersby could hear a loud debate going on inside.

The debate had degenerated into a shouting duel between two groups, her grandfather said when he returned with her father, who had been granted a day's leave to attend the funeral. With them was Abram Sudermann. He had come to Chortitza on business, and in hopes of speaking to her father. A small number of men had overcome the majority with their voices and threats, as the subject of the debate had escalated from whether or not to arm the town watchmen, to whether or not it was time to do as the *Gemeinde* in the Second Colony had done, and form a self-defence unit.

There was no reason to hold such a discussion, her father said. The death of the woman had nothing to do with hatred against Mennonites, but was the act of a madman. Tante Anna had died from shock, and thanks to the heaviness of Nela's coat, the ice chisel had not gone through it, so her wound was not a wound, but a contusion. A half-quart of Red Head vodka was behind Trifon's act, and not hatred towards Mennonites.

"I agree with you. But it doesn't change the circumstances. Your girl could have been hurt too, or worse, if Heinrichs hadn't been there. If he hadn't chased that hooligan off, he might have taken the time to come back at them again," Abram Sudermann said. He sat in the parlour, his knees spread; on his lap rested the pumpkin that was his stomach.

He had come to urge her father to reconsider an early release from service. He'd hired more Cossacks; there had been no trouble at Privol'noye, except for the usual thieving and beggars coming by on the road. The estate was suffering. The barns and building roofs needed repair. What horses hadn't been requisitioned were neglected and in poor condition. Many *gutsbesitzers* had left their homes, and were hiding in the villages for the sake of safety, but someone had to take a stand.

"In any case, you see what can happen in a village where it's supposed to be safe. Peter, let David arrange things," Abram said.

The day was dismal with wet slush and the biting cold of February. On a similar day a man would come knocking on her door wanting her to speak stories into a small microphone he held, his knuckles chapped from the cold, his trousers damp around the cuffs. Bringing the wet smell of the outside with him.

She told him that although she hadn't been present during Abram Sudermann's visit, she later heard how her father had hitched up his shoulders and taken a deep breath before speaking. He would agree to apply for an early medical leave and return to Privol'noye as overseer on the condition that Abram give him ten *desiatini* of land. Her grandmother enjoyed retelling the story, how Abram had sputtered and begun to perspire. Now, Peta, listen here, be reasonable. How could you oversee and, at the same time, farm? Yes, her father had said, I am a reasonable man. And, in turn, Abram should also be reasonable. Abram must give him the meadow land, he bargained in the end, and reluctantly, Abram gave in.

And that was how, and when, and why they had returned to Privol'noye. Her father's fate, their fate, sealed by a promise her grandparents had extracted from him, oh so many years ago, that he wouldn't go and take their only daughter far away in his search for land.

Katya had been to funerals in the past, of children and the elderly taken by illness, a young man who'd been struck by a falling tree. She had seen the photograph of her dead grandmother held upright by her sons, and a son of the photographer, unseen, crouching behind her with his back set against hers. But she hadn't been present at the moment of a person's last breath until Tante Anna, whose passing she'd felt in a weight on her chest. When she couldn't sleep, her mother invited her into her bed as she had every night since the day of Trifon's attack at the train station. Now as she lay beside her mother in the dark, the clock in the parlour struck the ninth hour, and the portraits of the Schroeder ancestors kept their watch. She knew she'd always been moving towards this moment.

With each passing second – the clock's striking finished, and the house settling once again into a deep silence – she realized she'd known this time would come. She might hear a voice calling, such as the voice she'd heard at the butter well, or perhaps a circumstance would arise: one minute Tante Anna had been sitting in a rocking chair telling her of the dream, and the next, she was in heaven and able to read all of their lives from the beginning to the end, Katya's life, her misdeeds, unkind thoughts. She couldn't sleep, not because the need for sleep wasn't present, but because she was afraid she would dream and find herself once again in the courtyard, and in the presence of the millstone carved with names.

She thought of Lydia's silver cup and the jealousy, the anger that had caused her to drop it down the well. There was tension in her mother's curled body, her breathing shallow, and Katya knew she wasn't asleep.

"Mama," she said. She had waited too long, she had carried around the weight of the secret for too many years. Her mother lifted her head so as to listen with both ears.

"Do you remember Lydia had a silver cup?"

"What cup?" her mother asked.

"The silver cup with two handles." She couldn't imagine how her mother wouldn't remember. Everyone had gone looking for it, including her mother. "I threw the cup in the butter well."

When she'd finished telling the story, her mother sighed and rolled onto her back, her hand coming to rest on Katya's stomach.

"But why? Why would you do such a thing?"

She recalled the impulse, but no longer remembered the reason behind it. She remembered the initials she had stamped out on the lake melting as the snow had melted, initials being wiped from a windowpane in spring, initials she'd stitched into the corner of a handkerchief becoming frayed with each washing. She remembered thinking that Lydia's initials on the cup would last forever, for as long as a name chiselled in stone.

"I never suspected you would have had anything to do with it. Well, what's done can't be undone. You'll have to tell Lydia, and ask for her forgiveness."

But what was done *had* been undone. It was over, finished. She'd grabbed hold of the moment.

"However much the cup was worth, we'll find a way for you to pay for it," her mother said. With difficulty and groaning she rolled onto her side and pulled her knees up to cradle her pregnant belly. "It's good for everyone that you confessed. But most of all, it's good for you," she said.

A spot of warmth centred on Katya's forehead and spread into her neck and shoulders. She was being infused with a light that made her limbs weightless, her new breasts jelly sliding off her ribcage, and she could breathe more deeply now, draw in more air. Although at fifteen years old she was almost a woman, she had a child's faith in the existence of angels, and a God who would arrange this day, the dream she'd had early that morning, in order to bring her into His courtyard.

My dear Dietrich,

I apologize in advance if this sounds like a lecture, but I have been forming what I want to say for so long, and I can't think of another way to put it.

I believe that friendship is of higher value than marriage, because God intended that the first man and woman were to be helpers to one another. It was only after the serpent accomplished what he set out to do that marriage came about. God intended Adam and Eve to be friends, and forever innocent. I know we aren't living in the Garden of Eden and that God's original intention for mankind had to change.

However, for us, friendship seems to be our future. We're privileged that this should be the case. As my friend you may expect my utmost loyalty, honesty, and love. You cannot, however, expect me to kiss you. Please stop asking. If you continue to ask for a kiss, our friendship must end. What a terrible loss that would be. It's good that you're back at Privol'noye, and that I remained here. (Although I'm going to miss your surprise visits very much.)

My dear friend, do you think it's wise to make Michael Orlov your close companion? His ways are not our ways. I know how difficult it is for you, being so far from like-minded people. Try and go to Nikolaifeld church as often as you can, even if the sermons put you to sleep. You need the fellowship.

Please think about what I've said. Why a kiss? This intimacy would only lead to something else and destroy our friendship along the way. You know as well as I that the something else isn't possible. If either of our parents refused their blessing, then most certainly we can't count on God's approval. You also know as well as I that when it comes to your father and mother, disapproval would most certainly be the case.

With deepest love, as always,
your friend, Greta

Dear Margareta,

I'm sorry it's taken so long to write. Every day there seems to be something that needs attending. Now it's the steam generator. We're without power. Michael has promised to come and take a look at it. Between the two of us we may one day discover where the problem lies. The bigger challenge will be to find someone to machine a part for it, if it should come down to that.

Nicholas and Alexandra are now twice the size as when I got them. They're proving to be quite intelligent dogs, and ferocious, too. If we'd had them the night the marauders came and destroyed the Baptists' tent, it's likely nothing would have happened, as the men were cowards. They wore their caps low so we couldn't see their faces, and some even went to the trouble of wearing sacks with eye holes cut in them. We recognized several voices, among them, that of a man who used to work for the Koops in Rosenthal. But what he would be doing so far from home and with a gang of Lubitskoye hoodlums is beyond my reasoning. I'm certain it was Zhinka's brother, brother of the girl who works for your uncle Bernhard.

We heard recently that the Baptists managed to find another tent in Moscow, and that they have set it up near to the village of Eichenfeld. They have invited Tante Helena to join them when they conduct Easter services. Yashka, the old Jew, delivered a crate of bibles on behalf of the bookstore in Nikolaifeld to Tante Helena, and so it appears as though she's considering their invitation. It seems that books, bibles in particular, are about the only item not in short supply these days. I wonder what that means?

Although Papa is quiet when the topic of Tante Helena joining the evangelists comes up, I hardly think he would remain quiet if she should decide to go.

It's occurred to me that you likely don't know what happened to the Baptists. Another reason I haven't written sooner is because I thought I would see you soon, and could tell you in person all about our midnight adventure. Yashka said he would come back when he finished his rounds of the area, and I could go with him as far as Chortitza. But that was not to be. Old Yashka became sick at the Zacharias' and remained there until he recuperated. By then, it was time to go out with the men on the fields. The Baptists' tent was cut to shreds by men who came across country during the night. Papa's Cossacks kept them from harming the preachers. There's no reason for you to worry as I'm sure you especially will now that your family is returning.

Now, what you said about Adam and Eve, friendship and innocence. Well, I suppose God might have kept on making sets of grown people out of clay and rib bones. Eventually he may have got around to making you and me, and we could have been best friends for an eternity. But likely not. The garden may not have been large enough for more than one happy couple. I can't help but wonder why God let the serpent into paradise in the first place. Why did he put the tree there? It seems to me that, from the start, the underlying plan may have been that men and women were supposed to be more than friends (or less than friends, if we go by your argument).

Why do I keep on asking for a kiss? If you would give me just one kiss, then I would know that you feel the same way about me as I do for you. I would be free to speak to Papa and to your father. Time changes things. People change. In any case, when it comes to my parents, I think you're imagining more than you should. If not a kiss, then give me a word. I would, of course, prefer the kiss. (I can imagine your face turning red as you read this.)

At Pentecost we'll both be baptised. We're ready to talk about this. I only wish that you would come to your home church to be baptised. Won't the Krahns find a way for you to come? There are near to twenty girls who will take their place among the member-ship on Pentecost. I wish I would see your face among them.

This extra-long letter should make up for not having written sooner.

With love,
your dearest friend, Deet

$\mathcal{I}$n April they returned to Privol'noye, Katya a changed person. She had written to Greta, "Easter is coming. For the first time I feel joyful when I say the words 'Christos voskres, voistenyu voskres.'" The carriage taking them back to Privol'noye travelled through the countryside, and she drank in the familiar sight of the dun fields patched with the brightness of spring flowers. She had seen cranes, watched their flight across the western sky, their elongated bodies and outstretched necks arrows heading towards a mark. Towards their nesting grounds, the end of their migration from Africa.

The sight of the cranes told her that Privol'noye and Ox Lake couldn't be far away and when she at last came near to the estate she noticed that her father's meadow had been ploughed. Black furrows ran from the road up to that ridge of trees she once called a forest. She was old enough now to see the grove of trees for what it was, nothing more than a weedy leftover park that once belonged to the Orlov family. She would, in a distant time, come across their name in a book of photographs intended to expose the decadence which had precipitated a people's revolt. The Orlovs' lands had been sold to pay off mortgages, the sons' debts, and to keep their houses and apartments in the cities; this was to become a common story.

The elder Orlov and his oldest sons, all officers in the service of the tsar, had gone to Petrograd at the beginning of the war, wrote David Sudermann in a letter to her father. One letter among the many she would take with her to a new country in a small oak box. "I am told that the oldest of Orlov's sons was struck down by a mutinous Volynsky guardsman during the uprisings in Petrograd in February. And another son, instead of responding to the call to help keep order in that city, shed his uniform and went to Odessa. I saw him in a ship-yard office, trying to arrange passage for his family, should the need arrive. The rats smell a sinking ship."

When at last the estate came into sight, it was as though her grand-father had read her mind, as he stopped the horses and said she and the children should get down and enjoy a moment. Gerhard and Johann immediately went in search of frogs and snakes in the damp ditches, while Sara went running down the road, the wind catching at her skirts and carrying her along. Running for the sake of running. To stretch her wiry limbs, which, she complained during their journey, ached with growing pains.

There were circumstances of travellers being robbed by bandits and so they had accompanied three other families in a convoy of car-riages and a wagon. They left the convoy at the junction of the Colony and Chortitza roads to embark on the two-hour trip to Privol'noye on their own. She would write to her sister, *Opa and Uncle Bernhard had a moment of prayer for our safety. I said a prayer of thanks, because I knew we would be safe.*

She looked down the road towards Privol'noye, hoping to see the orchard in flower, to see what always looked like a pink fog, but it was still too early for the blooming of Sheep's Nose and Snow Whites, damsons and morellos. How sad, she thought, that Tante Anna wasn't here to see the waves of wild poppies, crimson and shining as her satin bed-curtains had been. She supposed that Tante Anna, in all her seventy-nine years, hadn't witnessed spring on the steppe. The spinster's dream about Katya's father had come true. Her father had obtained his release and returned home. He, her mother, Peter, and the new baby, Ann, were already at Privol'noye, and no doubt watching for them. The woman had left an impression on Katya's skin which she would feel now and then. It was the feeling of a house cat that had gone missing, but whose presence remained an imperceptible settling at the foot of a bed, paws kneading a lap. The poor dear Tante Anna, whose travels had only taken her as far as one house to another, to care for other people's children, until she became too feeble to even care for herself. A woman alone, whose cherished keepsake was an empty ring box. Oh, if only Tante Anna could see this, she thought, with the arrogance the living possessed when they assumed the departed were somehow deprived because they were unable to experience what had just given them pleasure. Assumed that the dead might be longing for another glimpse of the tricks nature played with colours and light; a bead of rain magnifying pores on a sister's wrist, veins on a leaf.

ODESSA   March 28, 1917

My dear friend Peter Vogt,

I was overjoyed to learn that your medical leave was granted and that Privol'noye is once again in your care. I hope you didn't find the two weeks' bed rest in Kiev too onerous. Being confined to bed and being poked and prodded seems a small price to pay for freedom. I'm hoping when it's my turn, everything will proceed as smoothly. I cannot, however, claim to have a specific ailment such as headaches, but rather a general malaise. Welcome home. I'm certain my dear brother is grateful for your return.

The following is yet another instalment of a Mennonite Teacher's Adventures in the big, wide world.

Lately there hasn't been much for us to do in the office, and so I often go walking on Ekaterininskaia Ploshchad' and say hello to Catherine as I go by, and then down all one hundred and ninety-eight steps of the Richelieu Esplanades to the harbour. Often there are sailors marching off into the city in their formations.

The last time I went down to the harbour, several naval ships were coming in. They were signalling the news of the tsar's abdication to one another with their flags. Within moments the news reached the streets, and people began singing the "Marseillaise," or the "Marsiliuza," as some pronounce it. You hear it being sung everywhere now. The words depend on who's doing the singing, soldiers or workers. I hear that where you are, they're singing, "Who formerly was a nobody shall become the most important." Paradise on earth, yet. Oh well, let them dream. It may come to something. In any case, people need to dream, don't you think? The exuberance and joy in the faces of the people reminds me of the early days of the war. Life has become one long and exhausting party. Neverending band music, speeches of the kind that are so familiar these days, and which I'm sure you get your fill of, even there. *Da zdravst'vooiet svoboda*, long live this and that. Up with and down with about everything under the sun.

Everyone is anxious to learn all they can about the French revolution. The bookstores and stalls are crowded with people hungry to read about the French. You hear the language being spoken on the street, and in the cafés.

Because of a lack of spit and polish in our office, tea time has become almost like *faspa* at home. My co-religionists are very popular with the Russians during tea time, as often one or two of them will have a special tin of goodies from home, and how quickly are they relieved of their contents. There is no place to hide a tin of homemade sausages that a nose won't eventually sniff out. Auguste continues to send me generous amounts of halvah, which unfortunately isn't in demand and can't be bartered with the Russians for an eclair, or even a lowly raisin tart. And all because I made such a fuss when she served halvah when I was courting her, when really, I don't care for halvah all that much. Heat makes a fool of a man sometimes.

Tea time may soon change, however. We have received word from a Revolutionary Committee that we're to elect representatives to a staff soviet who will then collectively determine office procedures, duties, and disciplinary measures when the need for them arises. Ah, democracy rears its head, and will soon touch all of our lives. My own life has already been touched by certain aspects of freedom and equality. I'm frequently being relieved of the burden of my personal belongings. My room has been rifled through, and in the spirit of the day, items such as hair-, shoe- and clothing-brushes are being liberated. Such is the notion of democracy in action. I'm sure this is bound to get worse before it gets better.

Pray that my medical discharge will go smoothly. A fellow co-worker recently appeared before a medical board which consisted of three excellent doctors, and representatives from the

Revolutionary Committee, a sailor, and a nineteen-year-old store clerk. Everyone but the clerk agreed that he should be given a discharge, and so it was granted.

Recently there have been many articles in the newspapers praising the stalwart service of Mennonites on the hospital ships and trains, young men I suspect, unmarried, wanting to prove a Mennonite's worth. Which, I also suspect, will quickly be forgotten by whoever winds up being in power.

I must confess, I felt much admiration and pride for them, when I read the glowing reports.

Until we meet again, your friend as always,
David Sudermann

Dear Greta,

Our little attic room remains the same dear room. But other things have changed. You wouldn't appreciate how the fountain looks. It's become so pitted and grey and stained with rust that it's hard to tell that it was once white. I tried to clean it with lava stone, but I'm afraid I didn't improve it, only added a few more scratches. Also, the rim of the bowl is broken. According to Martha Wiebe it was damaged the night the Baptists were chased off. Helena noticed it the following morning.

When Opa drove onto the estate I also saw that the wall was broken, too. There was a hole in it near to the south entrance large enough for a wagon to pass through. As we came onto the yard it was being repaired. As usual, four men were doing what one could easily have done. They were patching the wall with red bricks, and not stone. More than likely, they were too lazy to go out to the rock pile and get them.

There I go, being Miss Critical. I haven't lived their lives and so I shouldn't pass judgment. It hurts to think of the names I used to have for Helena. I'm not without my blemishes, as you know, one of them being my critical nature.

Mary was quick to tell me about the Baptists, which you already must know about, judging from your last letter to Mama and Papa. Mary said she watched from an upstairs window, where she and Martha had gone to hide in one of the storage rooms. She said she saw sabres and sickles flashing as the men came onto the yard. Somehow they knew what building the Baptists were staying in. The marauders weren't making a point against the gospel being preached, but were showing off what they could do, Mary said. It's more that they were against Abram putting a stop to Helena's soup kettle. That is Martha's opinion. She and Mary had been taking bread and a kettle of soup to the front gate every other day for the beggars and worn-out soldiers.

According to Martha, Helena acted poorly for a Christian when Abram put a stop to their soup kettle. She got hot under the skin and said he should be ashamed of himself. She said that God might have sent angels among the hungry men to see if we were practising what we professed to believe. She was entertaining bandits and hoodlums, not angels, Abram said. While he paid Cossacks to keep them out, his own sister was inviting them in the front gate.

Why wasn't I told that Sophie and Kolya had married? Did you know? I would have made something for her. I hardly recognized our Sophie. She's become so terribly wide. About as wide as the old oak tree. Well, not really. I shouldn't exaggerate. Papa says that Kolya has become a good worker, and has done his best to look after things while Papa was away.

Sara was happy to discover that Mama had already planted the bowls with barley and oats for Easter. The grain is almost a foot tall already. Sara also pointed out that this year the number of eggs for our family has reached fifty-five. Add another eighteen if you were here, then as many eggs as years for Mama and Papa, which would make a grand total of one hundred and forty-two eggs. However, I told her she was not to get her hopes up. We'll colour the usual three dozen. The store in Nikolaifeld didn't have any dye, and so I will have to see what I can do. Beets, Mama says. Onion skins, walnut shells. What else? Lilacs, and leaves, perhaps.

Papa has already hung the swing and after supper Sara is on it until bedtime. I can hear her singing a song she learned in Rosenthal: *Swing, swing, Easter, we eat eggs. Pentecost we eat white bread, and if we don't die, we'll all grow tall.*

Mama says there are lots of memories for her in that song. She says I am to say hello on her behalf, she thinks of you often.

Greetings also to Willy and Frieda and a kiss for their sweet little Erika who, from the sounds of it, more than fills your time.

With love,
your sister, Katya

P.S. The sister cousins, Barbara and Mariechen Sudermann, are coming to stay at Easter. Lydia says she wishes you could be here too. So do I.

Greetings, my dear friend David Sudermann,

I so much appreciate your long and informative letters. I am indeed glad to be restored to my family, and to be back at Privol'noye. There is much to be done to get the place back where it was.

When I read your letters I can't help but wonder if the changes that are taking place so rapidly will brighten our future and the future of all people in this country, as you seem to think they will. I agree that, unlike the Americans and French, little blood has been shed, and it seems a miracle. For a feat of such magnitude to be accomplished and, so far, with little loss of life, is a wonder. We have God to thank for that.

I am hopeful that, now that the laws regarding proselytizing have been lifted, others will risk setting up tents as the Baptists already have. Even if only to prove your prediction wrong, my dear friend, that the status quo will prevail. Business as usual, was what you said. Above all, business. But I do agree that it will be difficult for us to go back to being turtles living in our shells and to remain *die Stillen im Lande*.

I wish that time would allow me to return an equally long and interesting letter, but my poor body is still not used to so much activity, and bedtime comes early. My Marie sends her regards, and we both hope and pray that in due time you will also be restored to your dear family.

With God's grace,
Peter Vogt

The land unfurled beyond the stone fence, viridescent, and the gardens were alive with birdsong. A man working on the roof of the horse barn suddenly broke into singing, and then the shrill call of a falcon hunting near Ox Lake rose above the song. Although Katya's brothers had been to the lake, she hadn't the time to join them. They'd returned hours later caked in mud, but bringing home two small trout. Later, when she was frying the fish for supper, her father came into the kitchen rubbing his hands in anticipation, which redeemed her brothers for the work they'd caused. She'd scraped the clay from their trousers with a knife, hung them near the stove to dry, then brushed them clean.

There were other things now that required her attention. The season brought an abundance of eggs and fresh milk. A bowl of clabbered milk congealed on a shelf in the pantry, and she would use it to make *schmaunstsupp* for tomorrow's supper, ladle the soup over hard-boiled eggs. Scrambled eggs with onions for Wednesday, fried potatoes with eggs for Thursday, beggar's soup with egg noodles and cream on Friday. Her father couldn't get his fill of eggs in spring.

She was fifteen years old and her appearance had changed, her light-brown hair thick and heavy, a sun-streaked coil of braids at the nape of her neck. She preferred dark colours, blue and aubergine skirts and blouses topped by an unadorned white apron that was often longer than her skirt, and skimmed the tops of her shoes. She knew that men, when looking for a wife, judged a woman by the evenness of stitches on an apron patch. That strength and honour were her clothing. A wife looked well to the ways of her household and did not eat the bread of idleness. A young woman's modesty and purity was of equal value to the wisdom of Solomon. She hoped she would one day attain such value, and attract a man who wanted such a woman. Unlike Greta, she had no desire for anything other than that.

Years later she would reread the letters she had sent to Greta and be put off by her own effusive froth of description, and then understand that the letters had been her only means of self-expression. Strong emotions, such as anger, were being contained, and sexual feelings, too. After she married she would hear from women that a woman's desire for sex increased with each child she bore, which she doubted, as much as she doubted there was no passion until the first child came. She'd seen it in her own girls, as young as eight and ten, wanting to touch themselves, being puzzled about what they were feeling down there. And so she, too, must have been of the age for those desires, which, if anyone had noticed, they likely ignored, just as she had tried to ignore what was going on in her own daughters, nursed them with an aspirin, warm milk, a story, because there was nothing else that could be done. And there was nothing her parents could do either, which was why her parents and others still called her a girl, even though at fifteen she'd been of age to marry.

Her shadow travelled with her as she went across the compound, arms swinging, body leaning into the task of visiting Helena Sudermann, as she'd arranged. It's not necessary for you to go, her mother had said. It was enough that she had confessed to Lydia and been forgiven. If you like I'll ask Helena what the cup was worth on your behalf. You don't owe Helena Sudermann an apology.

As she went past the summer kitchen, a tall, thin woman came striding towards her on the path. At least judging from the skirt, Katya believed it to be a woman. The person's features were blunt, a square jaw and heavy brow that hooded deep-set eyes. Her cropped dark hair looked like a tight-fitting cap, a crow's wing hanging across her forehead. Katya saw her coming, and stood still. The air between them seemed to quiver, and Katya knew this was Vera. Let her come, Katya thought. Please let me greet her with true friendliness. She felt her heartbeat quicken as Vera came towards her, a full pail of water knocking against a knee, her stride as long as a man's. And then she stepped from the path and went off towards the cow barns, and Katya was relieved that her desire for true friendliness had not been put to the test.

Someone called, and she turned to see Helena coming out of the greenhouse, carrying potted plants. Helena was going to be a few minutes, Katya should wait for her in the kitchen. She saw Vera join up with two other women at the women's quarters, saw a puff of smoke as the women passed a pipe of tobacco between them.

When she entered the kitchen she didn't at first recognize Sophie for her broad shoulders and the breadth of hips beneath her skirt. She was standing at a table chopping onions, and at the same time staring out the window. Her hands worked by rote as she chopped, cleared the onions aside with the blade of the knife, and reached for another while she looked out across the yard. Vera and the two women came into view, and as they went on their way to the bathhouse, Sophie's shoulders dropped. "God, God," she muttered, and only then did Katya realize who she was.

When Katya spoke Sophie's name, the woman turned, and her face lit with pleasure.

"Oy, stand back so I can see you. You're almost as tall as I am, but not nearly as wide. Too bad for you. Only when you're as wide as I am can you find true happiness. Now turn around. Let me see everything," Sophie said.

When Katya finished turning, Sophie crossed her arms over her hen's bosom. "So, you're married and have ten children, I guess. For all I know. I know what I hear, and what I don't hear, I have to make up for myself. I imagined, she must be married and have ten children, because she doesn't write to me. I can read, you know. As much as you can write, I can read. Or someone would have read it to me. Two letters. Ten children already, and I get two letters saying, Hello Sophie. Life is fine. The roads go east and west and north and south. The sun comes up and goes down. End of story, your friend, Lady-of-the-Town-Who's-Too-Busy-to-Write." Sophie said.

"Five children," Katya said, returning the teasing, wanting Sophie to stop going on about not having written. Sophie's replies, the child-like awkwardness of her large writing, the misspelled words, the simple sentences that made her sound so much less than what she was, were painful to read, and so Katya had stopped writing.

"Five children? Who's the papa?" Sophie asked.

She thought of Bull-Headed Heinrichs. Kornelius Heinrichs was his real name. She thought of his shining eyes as he looked at her. She remembered his smile beginning to grow, just before he saw Trifon about to strike Nela. The memory of his smile hadn't been diluted by what followed. He had come to the house on her grandfather's say-so. Her grandparents had wanted to thank him for his quick thinking and swiftness. She was in the summer room, listening. God put you in the right place at the right time, her grandfather said. Luck, Kornelius countered. In the silence that followed, she'd heard the man cracking open sunflower seeds, the scrape of chair legs as her grandfather got up and came for her. Business, Kornelius called after him. He had gone to the train station on business, that's what had put him in the right place at the right time. Well, no matter what, it's all the same, God put you there, her grandfather said. Thank you, was all she had managed to say to Kornelius, her eyes on the litter of sunflower-seed shells on the floor between his boots, which, she noticed, were freshly blackened, and shone.

She felt Sophie's hard scrutiny. "You must have heard what happened at the train station," Katya said.

"That's all we heard for days, until the mistress said not to keep jabbering about it. We're not supposed to talk about anything that happens around here, either," Sophie said with a touch of her old sullenness.

"About the men who came looking for the Baptists?" Katya asked Sophie as Martha Wiebe entered the room, bringing a pan of bread from the bake kitchen.

"Among other things."

She'd expected sympathy from Sophie, and hadn't got it.

"You were right, Martha, Katya has grown up. But she's not wide enough to be a woman yet," Sophie said and returned to her chore of chopping onions.

Martha rolled the crusty loaves onto the table and began covering the bread with towels. From the far reaches of the house came the sounds of people moving about. Lydia practised minor scales in the parlour, allegro and forte. Katya heard women's voices coming from the sewing room. As the ceiling in the kitchen creaked with footsteps, Sophie glanced up at it.

"The girls still haven't come downstairs yet," she said.

The sister cousins had come for Dietrich's baptism on Pentecost Sunday. "They're staying in a room as far from the stairs as it's possible to get. Mary has been running so hard all morning. Before breakfast, yet. Carrying water for a bath, and then for their hair. Her face is terribly red already from so much lifting and carrying. Couldn't those girls have bathed at home before they came? Poor Mary, she's made to lift far more than she should," Martha said, and then stiffened as footsteps approached in the hall. Moments later, Helena stood in the doorway.

"We'll talk in my room," Helena said to Katya. She saw the woman's tense jaw, her glasses turned to mirrors and impenetrable.

Helena chose to live near the kitchen and servants rather than in one of the large bed-sitting rooms upstairs. Her room was a short distance down the hall, adjacent to the kitchen. A narrow room, with a single window that looked out at the west garden wall. A household account book lay open on the table, a pencil resting in its gutter, and, beside the book, a New Testament with different-coloured ribbon markers. Ivy plants still stood on the shelf above the window next to the empty birdcage.

Sit, sit, Helena said, indicating a chair at a table as she pulled out one across from it and sat down, pushing the account book aside. Katya noticed that for all her neatness, the lace-trimmed collar fastened at her throat with a bronze pin, the metal combs keeping her greying hair smooth, Helena's fingernails were chipped and stained. One was purple with an old injury, its nail flaking. The hands of a field worker, an outside woman, she thought. She didn't know where to look, as Helena was without an apron and so didn't seem completely clothed.

"Now what did you want to talk to me about, Katya?" Helena asked. She eyed the testament almost hungrily, as though she couldn't bear being so near the book without holding it.

When Katya finished confessing to having thrown Lydia's cup in the butter well, Helena sighed. She looked up at the strings of ivy trailing across the window. Sunlight brought out the silver in her pewter hair, making her appear younger, and soft. She plucked a handkerchief from a sleeve, took off her glasses, and began cleaning them. She sighed again as she hooked the glasses onto her ears and pushed them up the bridge of her nose.

"You're just like me. At least, we have something in common. That's what I meant to say. We have something in common. No one is like another person. I shouldn't have said that," Helena said. "It must have been hard for you to carry this around for such a long time and not say anything."

Yes, Katya thought with gratitude, unprepared for Helena's understanding.

"The cup isn't worth risking life and limb to get out of the well. What we should talk about is why you did it. And why, while everyone wondered where the cup stayed, you remained quiet. Yes?"

"Yes," she said.

Then Helena got up from the table, stepped onto a chair and took the birdcage down from the shelf.

"You children were always so curious," she said as she set the cage onto the table between them. "What was *Schnurrbart-Len* keeping this birdcage for?"

Katya winced when she heard the woman use their nickname.

Helena nodded. "I have ears." She ran a finger lightly across the wisps of hair on her face. "I was about your age when it started to grow. Abram would say, 'Lena, go and wash, you have dirt on your face.' Jakob once said he didn't want to go to church with me along. My father thrashed that idea out of him. My mother came with the scissors then, and she said if I wanted, I could cut it off. But I said no. I would just have to keep cutting it off, all my life. God gave it to me for a reason. He meant for me to learn how to take the slings and arrows of men.

"Now I'll tell you about the birdcage. I know you, along with all the other children, always wondered why I had such a cage, and no bird. Well, I'll tell you.

"We were on a vacation in Germany, Karlsbad, at the same inn where I stayed one summer before the war. Another Mennonite family was staying there and they had a girl, Susanna, whose last name I won't say. Susanna was near to my age, the age you are now, and she was always puffed up because she had been to the inn before, and knew everything about it. She even knew the names of the swans swimming in a pond across from the inn. She could hardly keep from mentioning my face hair. Likely, she'd been told not to.

"The innkeeper's wife had recently got a bird, a green-and-blue bird that had a yellow head with a tuft at the back. She'd taught the bird to say 'Good morning, children' whenever anyone would come into the sitting room, where people visited before supper. She kept the bird there, and an aquarium. I had never seen such a bird before, and neither had Susanna. I hadn't seen much of anything, as this was my first trip with Abram and Aganetha. It was Abram's first trip, also. He took all of us to Karlsbad the year our father died. He had to wait for our papa to die before he could travel. Our father was a man who counted the number of potatoes we ate at a meal, and wrote it down. Just by walking across the yard, he knew if a chicken was missing. My mother had to ask his permission to butcher one for Sunday dinner. He refused to pay taxes for the *Forstei*, as he said he didn't believe in the idea of paying men to work for someone else. Until a committee came from the *volost* and threatened to take his livestock. Then he believed. If a traveller stopped at our place wanting to water and rest their animals, he would charge them so-and-so much for each pail of water they drew, and so-and-so much for feed, and so much for the time the horses stood in the barn. That's what kind of man my father was.

"The innkeeper's wife encouraged us to put our hand into the bird's cage, and let the bird sit on it. Susanna was quick to show that she wasn't backwards. Everyone was so taken, and made a large fuss when the bird – Tristan, the woman had named it – walked all the way up Susanna's arm and onto her shoulder, and stroked her ear with its beak. The bird was kissing her, the innkeeper's wife told us. He'd never done such a thing before.

"Well, do you think that bird would come near me? When I put my hand in the cage, it went as far away from me as it could possibly go. Good morning children, it said, but as soon as I came near, all I got was screeching. How this ate at me. I was old enough to marry, and there I was going around thinking, Please love me. Why won't you love me like you love Susanna? I asked God to make the bird take to me. But with Susanna around, it never would, I knew.

"One day I came into the sitting room, and no one was there. As I came near to the cage, the bird looked at me hard, but it didn't screech. And so, very slowly, I put my hand in the cage. I made kissing sounds, like Susanna did. But would it sit on me? No, it would not. Instead, it bit me, and very hard. I saw that two windows near the cage were open. While I nursed my finger, I purposely left the cage door standing open. It was just as I thought. In a blink, that bird came out of the cage and flew out the window. It was as though it had been waiting for such a moment. Immediately I was sorry for what I'd done.

"I heard people coming. I ran back to my room and lay down, my heart going so hard I could hear it in my ears. I hoped, I thought, Lena, just stay put. If you stay put, then the time will somehow go back, and the bird will still be in its cage. But I was old enough to know what nonsense that was, and so I made myself go to the sitting room, to confess. I was sure that by then, the bird would have been missed, and I was ready to own up to what I had done.

"But the bird hadn't been missed. There were women in the room, Aganetha, too, and the cage door was standing open, just as I'd left it. No one had noticed the bird wasn't there. I'm saved, I thought. I don't have to speak up, because no one will suspect me. I sat and waited. Sure enough, when Susanna came into the room not much later, right away she noticed the bird hadn't greeted her. Everyone jumped up and went running outside to look for it.

"At supper that evening, we were all in the dining room, when the innkeeper's wife said she wanted to make an announcement. She said that someone had let her bird loose. Whoever had let the bird out of its cage may as well have wrung its neck. The nights were cold already, and Tristan, who had come from Paraguay, wouldn't last long outdoors.

"Days later, when we were preparing to leave, the woman came to our carriage at the last moment with the birdcage. She wanted me to have it, she said. Why me, and not Susanna, who, when they couldn't find the bird, had cried her eyes out? My brothers didn't wonder, but I did. They only wondered if we had room for it, and encouraged me to throw it out along the way. But I knew why the woman had given the cage to me. She had given it to me as a punishment, a reminder that I had killed her bird."

From the kitchen came the sound of a pot lid clattering against the floor, the smell of sauerkraut soup and smoked sausages cooking. Helena cast an apprehensive look towards the hallway. The bowed metal ribs of the cage made a graceful flaring structure, through which Katya could see Helena's linen blouse, its iridescent shell buttons moving with her breathing. The perch suspended from the domed ceiling, the nicks and gouges the bird's beak and claws had made in its wooden rung must seem a taunt, Katya thought.

Helena got up and put the cage back on the shelf, then stood beside the table leaning on her hands, gazing out the window. "So, you can see how you and I are alike," she said. She smiled and fell into her thoughts, the muscles in her face working. A bird skimmed the surface of the yard, a jittery flutter and glide of dark wings, and then it swerved up and over the garden wall.

"It doesn't matter how old a person gets. Fear still keeps us quiet when we know that we should speak up," she said softly.

She turned back to Katya, becoming brisk and efficient. "Envy, that's what made me do what I did. But you don't have to say why you threw the cup in the well. God knows. No, there's some other business that needs taking care of now. When I heard you wanted to come and see me, I thought, well, Tante Lena, maybe this is the right time for you to mend a hole in the fence."

Helena went to the apron hanging from its hook beside the door and rummaged in its pocket. Katya heard the tinkle of bells.

"Hold open your hand," Helena said.

And there, lying in her palm, were the tiny brass bells Katya had lost so many years ago.

"They made such a racket, I couldn't hear myself think. I thought, one day I'll give them back, when Katherine is old enough to understand." Helena raised her hand as though she would touch Katya's shoulder, and then turned away.

Katya pocketed the bells, her hands trembling with shock and confusion. She remembered how she had retraced her steps over and over, had waited for spring, when the snow melted, to search once again. Helena's intention to one day return the bells didn't lessen the pain of a joy being snatched away. But she'd been a child making a racket and Helena an adult, and so she didn't think now to question the fairness of Helena's act, or to reason that they were now somehow even.

Then all at once she knew she was being dismissed, and as much as she wanted to run from the room, she couldn't leave things so disturbed. "I wanted to be the one to tell you, because you would know how much the cup had cost. I intend to pay for it."

"That was an expensive cup," Helena said.

"I will to pay for it," she said.

"How is that?" Helena asked.

From the kitchen came the sound of happy voices. Sophie called out in surprise, and Martha joined in. Katya thought she heard a third familiar voice. Greta? Was this possible?

"With work." Katya was desperate to leave.

"Work? How much work? As I said, the cup was not cheap."

But the idea had already begun to take root, Katya realized as Helena fell into thought. She heard footsteps coming along the hall.

"Well, yes, you should at least do that. I'll make a list of chores," Helena said.

Katya left the room, almost colliding with Greta. Her sister's scarf dropped to her shoulders, her dark wiry hair flying about her head, a vivacious face bright with windburn, home at last; their family, for a short time at least, was once again complete.

"The Krahns said their conscience wouldn't allow them to keep me away from home on my baptism. And at the same time, I'll have a chance to get to know my new sister," Greta said as they embraced.

"Why did you run off?" Helena asked Katya from the doorway. She held a piece of paper. "You may as well begin paying for the cup now. We can use an extra pair of hands for our Pentecost company." Her rust-coloured skirt swung around her narrow body as she turned and went back down the hall.

She had begun the day's list of chores that morning, and now, as the land turned dusky with twilight, she was in the summer kitchen rubbing shanks of lamb with fat and salt to prepare them for the oven. The buildings had turned pigeon grey in the fading light, gullies of shadows deepening between them. She was nearing the end of the first day of what would be a month of service.

Faint waves of sound travelled through the moisture-laden air, young voices, the coachman's children, she realized, out in the yard in their night clothing. Scampering, ghostlike creatures, the grainy air making them seem indistinct and fleeting, their nightshirts rippling about their legs as they played what looked to be a game of chase-the-goose. Likely they had been sent to relieve themselves behind the house before bed, and had forgotten to return. A light had come on in the kitchen of the Big House, but the windows in her own house were not yet lit with lamplight, the glass in the summer-room windows reflecting the twilight and becoming the colour of mercury.

She would always prefer this time of day, a farmyard in another country bathed in the same light, the land broken here and there by a copse of burr oak, mist rising from a dugout pond as cattle came to drink. Her children coming, wanting to be held at sundown; a cup of tea sweetened with barley honey sipped in the quiet while sitting outside on benches at the back of an old farmhouse. The strong light of day sometimes defined too clearly the business of life, and the hard brilliance of the night sky made a person ache for things beyond their reach. The gloam of twilight softened hard edges, her thoughts about Helena, a woman whose strictness might well be concealing a person hungry for love.

Her mother emerged from the house and came along the path to the summer kitchen. She stood at the screen door looking in, her apron a patch of white, but otherwise she was a silhouette, her features indiscernible.

Moments later she said, "I didn't think when we came here that it meant my children would become servants." To herself, Katya knew, as when she spoke, she'd turned and looked at the Big House.

Katya suddenly wanted to weep. She was chilled; the fire she'd lit when she'd opened up the summer kitchen had long ago gone out; the thought of being left behind tomorrow was almost more than she could bear.

Her mother shivered and hugged herself against the cold, and Katya stifled the desire to cry. "You don't have to do this, Katya. We could somehow find the money. I will not have you miss your own sister's baptism."

"I'm doing this because I want to do this."

"If it's your conscience saying so, then fine. Just be sure you aren't wallowing in your feelings," her mother said.

Then they saw Katya's father and Gerhard coming down the steps of the coachman's house, the coachman and his son Yerik behind them. As they left the yard, the small children filed into the house.

Katya's mother went with her to the storage cellar, its roof a hump of earth overgrown with grass and wild asters. The coolness of the dank interior enveloped them as they went among the carcasses of chickens hanging from the ceiling. They put the shanks of lamb on a shelf. When they came up out of the darkness of the underground room, it seemed lighter outside than it had been, light enough for a walk in the garden, her mother suggested, to see what flowers they could find that might brighten the family room for Pentecost Sunday.

Katya's father and Gerhard had gone to the carriage house with the coachman and Yerik to make arrangements for their trip to church tomorrow, her mother said while they went among the flowers, her mother snipping stems with the scissors she'd brought with her. More than twenty people would be going in three carriages and the coach, washed, its brass and leather polished. Abram preferred to travel to church in the coach. "His back-loader coach hitched to six matching black stallions," her mother said. "He likes to be noticed. Apparently when he came calling on Aganetha, he made the driver go at top speed from one end of Main Street to the other, then return and do it once again just in case someone hadn't seen him."

Her parents had heard stories of Abram's courting of Aganetha, his showy arrival that scattered the chickens and ducks, brought the village children on the run. There was no understanding his choice of bride, Aganetha, daughter of a half-farmer who had caught his eye at a funeral. She was known to burst into giggles whenever anyone looked at her. A person only had to say, Hello Aganetha, and she was caught in a fit of giggling, red-faced and bent over clutching her stomach.

Aganetha was nothing more than a backward girl from backward people whose manners in church offended others, her mother said. They talked during prayers, the men using coarse language and telling crude stories in the churchyard. Aganetha's people were the kind who would fill their pockets with their hosts' baking, and who never knew when to go home, staying on and on waiting to be invited for supper.

Her mother straightened, cradled a bundle of daffodils against her breasts, their pollen streaking her apron bib with gold dust. "She thinks she's become a silk purse," she said softly, her tiny smile inferring that she thought otherwise.

As they went toward the garden gate, Katya thought of her mother's self-knowing smile, the way she now walked, swinging her shoulders slightly, her chin lifted, her step sure. With a haughtiness Katya had once seen before, a self-possessed assurance. She thought she might be seeing her mother as she might have been when she'd been Greta's age, when Katya's father had begun to notice her.

Helena Sudermann was coming towards the garden now, no doubt for a moment of quiet prayer.

"Here," her mother said suddenly, and thrust the daffodils into Katya's arms. She went on ahead to meet Helena, her arms swinging, as though this were a moment she'd been looking for. Katya's mother drew near to Helena, who waited on the path, her shoulders becoming hunched and face jutting forward. Katya heard the low murmur of her mother's voice, a sentence uttered, and then another, her voice growing stronger as she continued to speak, her hands raised at her sides and chopping the air, Helena attempting to interrupt, and being cut off. Helena rose to her full height and stepped back, Katya's mother advancing. Then there was silence while the women looked at each other, Helena then turning away and going back to the house.

When Katya joined her mother, she saw that her eyes were shining, and her chest heaved. As they fell into step, Katya asked her what she had said.

"Never mind. It's said, and that's that. And what's more, you'll be going to church with us tomorrow."

▮▮▮▮

Dampness shaped the smoke pouring from the outside oven, a white column set against the early morning sky. Katya hurried with her family across the compound to the carriage house where Abram's coach and three carriages stood waiting to take them to church in Nikolaifeld. The land beyond the perimeter of the stone fence seemed to be a well of darkness, the birds and insects waiting for the first hint of sunrise to begin sculpting the fields with sound. The lanterns on the vehicles bathed the gathering of people in a warm light, the Sudermann brothers and their puffy-faced wives, the sister cousins, the Wiebe sisters who huddled together. The young people would travel in one *droschke*, Abram said, Mary and Martha in the smallest one. Go, Katya's mother said as Greta joined Dietrich, Lydia, and the sister cousins waiting beside the carriage. Yerik, their driver, was already in place and looking half asleep. You're a young person, no? her mother said. Sara would help her with the little ones. What's keeping Helena, Abram came over and asked Martha gruffly.

Helena, when she at last appeared, stood on the top step for moments, outlined by light shining from the doorway. While she must have known that her oldest brother percolated with impatience, she took her time, standing, to gaze down the avenue, then descended the steps with slow deliberation. Helena ignored her brothers and their wives, went past them where they had come together beside the coach, the women bulky and stolid-looking in fur coats and hats. She went over to the smallest *droschke*, and the Wiebe sisters, then motioned to the driver that he should take her bags, in this way telling everyone that she would not be riding in the coach with her brothers.

194

Once the convoy got underway their voices seemed to overcome the darkness that pooled in the fields beyond the road. The road's surface was sticky from an overnight drizzle, and the animals' hooves made pleasant sucking sounds.

Throughout the following hour, a mist was gradually drawn off by the rising sun, the land appeared, and streaks of magenta emerged in the sky. A rim of fiery liquid simmered on the horizon, and then the sun appeared all at once. Lanterns were extinguished, scarves and hats removed. Greta and Dietrich were seated across from Katya side by side, their arms touching. Dietrich plucked at Greta's cape, and while she didn't look at him, it was obvious her smile was meant for him. Lydia sat on the other side of Dietrich, turned away from him and looking out across the land as though wishing she were somewhere else. When Greta took off her coat in church everyone would see how beautiful she had become, Katya thought. For the baptism, Frieda Krahn had helped Greta sew a dress of fine sateen, a dress that even Katya's brothers couldn't help but admire, were stuck silent by when Greta tried it on. A white dress, a narrow ribbon banding its hem, flounced sleeves trimmed with satin rosettes. Her mother had worried that the dress would draw attention, that they would be accused of trying to stand in the same light as the Sudermanns. Greta's dark eye-lashes fluttered, her eyes turned aside as her mother fussed with the shirred yoke, pressing it flat, her hands crossing the soft swell of Greta's breasts. Greta had become a ruby, a virtuous woman, she had become so aloof and secretive, and for a moment Katya wanted to smack her. She would never possess such a fine dress; she didn't think she would ever want to be as self-satisfied as Greta. Their Gypsy Queen, she thought, her eyes suddenly brimming.

Soon they were near to Lubitskoye, and as they drew closer, the green dome of a church appeared through the trees, and then houses that nested behind wattle fences. Abram's coach travelled ahead, and was already midway through the village as their carriage was entering. A church bell began to toll, but although the bell called the people to prayers, the street lay empty.

Ahead of them, a silver-haired man came out of his yard carrying a hoe, and went to the side of the road and stood there. Several other men followed. Their movements seemed disjointed and odd; they flailed their arms, a cap was doffed, and jammed back on again. They all went off in different directions. Then as suddenly as they'd dispersed, they returned to the side of the road.

Dietrich muttered under his breath, "I see the neighbours are up to their eyebrows in the spirit of Pentecost."

Abram's coach slowed, and stopped when it came alongside the men, who all at once marched single-file across the road, as though someone had given them a command. They stood now in front of Abram's coach, legs spread and arms crossed against their chests.

"Yerik, go and see what's happening," Dietrich told their young driver, and although he seemed reluctant to do so, he climbed down from the carriage, and slouched off the down the road.

Just then someone else came through the gate of the same yard, a man sitting on a wheeled platform, which he propelled over to the side of the road with his hands.

"Simeon Pravda, up to his usual tricks," Dietrich said. He attempted to sound nonchalant, to convey that Pravda was nothing more than a bothersome and unruly child, but Katya heard an edge in his voice.

As Simeon called out, Abram's head emerged from a coach window; Katya recognized Simeon's effusive, sing-song greeting as belonging to the beggar she had seen years ago at Privol'noye.

Yerik stopped in his tracks, and when it appeared he had no intention of going any farther, Dietrich left the carriage. When he met up with Yerik, he, too, did not venture any further.

Abram's voice grew loud in a familiar tone, one Katya knew was meant to convey that he was the boss. The driver of the *droschke* behind them had climbed down and as Katya's father came walking along the road, he joined him. "What is it?" Helena called, but her father didn't stop to answer. As he approached the carriage, his eyes found Katya's, and he nodded. He said they should act normal, try not to appear worried or frightened, and then he walked to Abram's coach.

By then, Jakob and Isaac Sudermann had got out of the coach, and as they were about to go round it, they were encircled by the men, who began shouting and cursing at them. The brothers stood shoulder to shoulder, meeting the flow of the men's abuse with silence, refusing to reply to their taunts.

The sister cousins were stricken with fear, their faces mottled as they held back tears, while Lydia seemed unmoved, as though she thought the commotion wasn't worth the effort to turn and have a look at. Katya's father stood outside the stormy circle, arms crossed over his chest. He must have spoken, as moments later one of the men, and then all of them, noticed he was there. In all the time he'd been overseer, he'd had occasion to hire many men from Lubitskoye, and they knew him to be fair, her mother had said, and both the village and Abram prospered because of it. When her father finished talking to the men, an agreement seemed to have been reached, as they dispersed and went back to the side of the road, and to Simeon Pravda. Now they were laughing and needing to lean into each other in order to stay upright. Her father returned to the convoy with the other driver, meeting up with Dietrich and Yerik along the way.

"They want money," Dietrich explained, as he got back into the carriage. "They won't let us to pass through the village unless we pay them. The beggars are demanding a ruble for each *droschke* – five for the coach."

Lydia snorted. "They should have asked for a hundred and made themselves feel even more important. It doesn't make any difference, because Papa would never pay."

They were going to go around the village, Dietrich said.

"Fine," Lydia said. "As if my body isn't sore enough already."

As Yerik waited for the carriages behind them to turn on the road, he sat chuckling. Dietrich wanted to know what could possibly be amusing him, and Yerik told them what Katya's father had said. Comrades, you have the right to demand money from us, and we, being as equal as you, have the right to refuse to pay it. I know you will recognize the wisdom that every man is free to do as he chooses.

Yerik blew his nose between his fingers and wiped them on the seat of his trousers. "I never heard such a thing."

"But will they allow us to go across the fields?" Mariechen, one of the sister cousins, asked.

"It's Papa's land. They're not so ignorant as to stop us from crossing our own land," Lydia said.

"So, Yerik. As a free man, what do you choose to do now?" Dietrich called, his voice suddenly jovial, trying not to show he was relieved the incident had passed. The men had returned to the yard and crowded around Pravda; a bottle passed between them.

"I freely choose to follow the other carriages," he said.

What they had just experienced was only one incident of many similar incidents, and most of them sparked by Simeon Pravda, Dietrich told them matter-of-factly as they left the village and the road to cross a shallow ditch and go out into a cultivated field. Katya wasn't taken in by his casual manner. She saw that his eyes moved constantly, as though wary that at any moment someone might come riding. They went away from Lubitskoye, and then parallel to it, until the village was a distant smudge on the land. Then their *droschke* rejoined the road, Abram's coach passing them, once more in the lead, and they continued on their way to Nikolaifeld. Moments later she could see their church in the distance, its grey masonry and white arched windows, an abrupt presence on the flat and greening land.

Children sitting on the church wall, the prized vantage point from which to view the arrival of families, grew silent and stiff as Abram's coach approached the gates. The coach passed through, and the children swivelled round to watch it circle the yard beyond, coming to a standstill beside the coach of another estate owner. When Katya entered the walled churchyard, it was as though a storm had passed, the memory of what had happened only a faint rumbling of thunder in the far distance. People were gathered in clusters, visiting, turning to watch their arrival, Abram's black stallions already being unhitched, the animals snorting, heads lifted as they scented the other horses in their stalls. Yerik drove the team to the back of the yard, where a sea of wagons and carriages spread out from the perimeter of the church wall.

As Katya joined up with her family, Sara was begging to be allowed to sit among the girls of her age, but today being Greta's baptism, they would stay together, her mother said, just as Sara's brothers would remain with their father on the men's side of the church. Katya searched among the groups of visiting women for a girl she used to sit with in church, and found her among the young women gathered near the women's entrance. She noticed suddenly that in comparison to women of the same age in the towns of Rosenthal and Chortitza, they were dressed plainly, and were more subdued. The girl nodded shyly as Katya greeted her, her shyness blunt and unappealing.

Katya sat between her mother and Greta, her baby sister Ann asleep in her mother's arms. Somehow a chickadee had got into the church, and the dry scurrying of its feathers against a window stirred the children, who craned their necks, bobbed up and down to try to find the source of the unaccustomed sound. A bird, a bird, a bird, they began to whisper, as though they had never before seen an ordinary chickadee. No bright bead of sound preceded the telltale *dee-dee*; instead, the bird's chirp became shrill and frantic as it battered at the window. Katya wished one of the men would show it the way to an open door. But then it gave up, darted through the air above them, and up to a ceiling beam, whereupon it perched, and gradually the children grew quiet too, their attention, Katya's attention drawn to the front of the church as the names of the baptism candidates were called out. Greta shed her felt cape and draped it across Sara's lap, her dress suddenly looking almost too glorious, which Greta seemed to feel too as she stepped into the aisle, her elbows tight against her sides, hands clenched against her stomach, cheeks flaring.

Each of the baptism candidates was questioned by the elders and gave a short and often hurried testimony of their faith, then came forward to receive a sprinkling of water on their head. But Katya's attention was drawn to the chickadee, a soft pouch of feathers set against the oiled timber. Its presence seemed uncanny and she thought of Helena's empty birdcage, and looked around for Helena in the church. She found her sitting several benches behind, and to the right, her angular face framed by her black bonnet, the fringe of hair under her nose a straight line as she stared at the back of the woman's head in front of her, her expression calm, but unreadable.

After the service, the newly baptised, who were now members of the *Gemeinde* of the Nikolaifeld church, stayed to visit with each other in the churchyard, and so Katya was to return home with her parents. Her father guided the horses among the people who had come to church on foot, some calling out that her parents shouldn't be slow to visit, even though they knew that because of her father's responsibilities, they weren't free to visit. All of a sudden they saw Helena Sudermann going past in a carriage with people they didn't recognize. As the wagon came abreast, Helena turned to them, nodded and smiled, a rather sad smile, Katya thought. And she thought that perhaps Helena was conveying to her mother that she bore no hard feelings for whatever had passed between them the previous evening.

"Where's Tante Lena going?" Sara asked the question that was on Katya's tongue.

"She's going with the Baptists," her mother said without explaining further. As though Helena joining another religious group was something that happened every Sunday.

GRUZNIKIE

Greta gave me this recipe, which she got from Frieda Krahn from Arbusovka, who got it from her Oma Hildebrandt of Neuendorf. Frieda Krahn's Oma baked these Gruznikie to hand out to Russians who came calling at Christmas. When Oma Hildebrandt passed the recipe to Frieda, she advised her that if she was still in bed when callers came, to let them come in anyhow, strangers or not. And if they sang a blessing, to give them a few extra Gruznikie.

1 1/2 glasses sugar
3 small or 2 large eggs
peppermint oil to taste (about 5 to 6 drops from the 15-kopeck bottle at Penner's store. The smaller bottle doesn't drip the same)
2 glasses sweet or sour cream
1 glass hot water
3 kopecks' worth ammonia
Mix ammonia in hot water. Add enough flour to make a not too soft dough (it has to stick a little to the fingers when you touch it, but not overly much).

Katya copied the recipe for *gruznikie* in her notebook on that Pentecost Sunday afternoon as she sat out on the platform, and her parents and young brothers napped. She watched Greta and Sara go walking along the road, their arms outstretched and teetering as they followed narrow ruts. She saw Abram and his brothers come from the Big House and go to the barns. Their dark trousers and shirts made them three black-and-white men, Jakob's hair the colour of mahogany and setting him apart, as did Abram's girth. Abram supported himself on two walking-sticks now, his face scarlet after a short journey across the yard. She thought how comical he looked whenever he talked to anyone. He'd go over to whatever was nearby, a fence, wagon, table, and put the object between himself and the person. He'd rest his arms on it, and lay his chin on his arms, his legs crossed and his body on such a tilt that he appeared in danger of falling onto his stomach. In this way he presented only his huge goat head and shoulders to the listener, most likely thinking that the pounds of lard hanging from his body were invisible. She smiled inwardly at the thought as the three Sudermann men were swallowed up by the dim interior of the horse barn.

Now, as she waited in bed for Greta to come up the ladder to their attic room, she took out the notebook and recorded the circumstances of the day when she had written down the recipe. Years later, whenever she read the entry, she would be reminded of Greta's baptism and would wish they had travelled together as a family to and from church on what had proved to be one of their last outings together.

Today the pink hue of sunset was like a rose petal, soft and sympathetic, as if to ease our memories of what happened in Lubitskoye, an event that still reverberates in my mind.

When we got home there was a big fuss when it was learned that two sacks of flour had mysteriously disappeared from the bake kitchen while we were away at church. And a ham from the storage cellar, even though the cellar door remained locked. Martha, whom Aganetha has put in charge of the female workers now that Helena has left, decided to do an inventory and discovered the missing food. Papa tried to persuade Abram not to whip Kolya, who had been appointed overseer while we were away, and was therefore responsible. But Abram, fired up over what happened on the way to church, Papa explained, wasn't persuaded. He took his brothers with him to the barn in case Kolya decided not to take the beating. I heard the strap as many as six times, others say there were more. But no one heard a sound from Kolya. Not only is stealing ingrained in a Russian, but how to take a beating as well, which is how Dietrich put it.

After church we again went overland to pass by Lubitskoye, and by then my cramps had started. I could hardly keep Daniel on my lap, and the bumpy ride didn't make things any easier. Sara and I went for a walk to Ox Lake at sunset. Sunset was the remedy. All of nature is a remedy for any ailment. It captivates the mind, and the heart is overcome by its beauty. Nothing seems worth fuming about when the sky is lit with a glorious sunset.

Later, she would reread what she had written and recall Greta, her dark hair like unravelled wool tumbling across a pillow; the warmth in their attic room being dispelled by chilly air that billowed the curtain, the brass bells she had pinned to it tinkling noisily. The sound of bells would always make her think of snow blanketing the compound, and banking up its walls. Snow wedged in the tongues of her boots, landing in clumps on the doormat as she loosened the laces. She would remember the feather quilt covering their bodies, a counterpane of white hovering in the shadows, the lamplight falling across Greta's face when she told Katya that she and Dietrich were going to marry.

Katya stood at the window, her sister's news still fresh and startling as first snow. The sound of the bells was like that of harness bells, and she thought, and remembered: I am coming, I am here, I am going. Greta had broken the news, and Katya said, So you're engaged, and got out of bed. She felt that she didn't have the right to be so near to her sister, their legs touching.

"Papa says we should wait, and of course, we agreed," Greta said from across the room.

"And the Sudermanns also?"

"Dietrich hasn't told them yet."

Katya saw her father coming across the compound, heard him enter the house. Greta and Dietrich, living in the Big House. Katya's house connected to Greta's house by a narrow path, a spoke leading to the hub. Greta, mistress of Privol'noye. A moment later her father came to the bottom of the ladder and called up to them. They were to dress and come down, he said, as he had something to show them.

Their father walked behind them, the light of his lantern arcing on the path, lengthening and shortening their shadows as they went towards the greenhouse. To the greenhouse, what for? Sara asked, her boot laces undone and tripping her up. The light tilted suddenly as their father caught Sara before she fell and set her upright on the path. You'll soon see, he said. Now go quietly.

As they went through the potting shed and into the greenhouse, Katya smelled fresh damp earth even before her father lifted the lantern to reveal a mound of dirt where a potting table had once been.

"This is what I want you to see," he said. He stepped around the pile of earth, and they looked down into a large rectangular hole in the greenhouse floor. As he lowered the lantern to the surface of the hole she saw that the dark earth gave way to yellow clay, the marks of his spade, brown threads like hemp rope interwoven in the earth walls.

The hole was to remain a secret, her father said, a secret only he, their mother, and now they, would know. He spoke to all of them, but his eyes turned to Sara. "A secret. Which means no one else should know, understand? You're not to tell your brothers, either," he said.

Sara nodded, her eyes large and solemn. "But what's it for?" she asked.

"For you three girls. To go inside, if need be," he said.

"But I don't want to go inside, what for, anyway?" Sara asked, her lips beginning to tremble.

"Safety," he said. "The hole is for safety."

Greta made a sound as though she'd sipped at air, which made Katya's skin prickle. She hugged herself and looked at the lights shining in a window of their house. Safety for them and not for her brothers, why? she wondered. In a hole deep enough for them to sit in, chins on their knees, arms hugging their legs, heads only inches from the top. Smaller than a grave hole, but nevertheless it was a hole.

"Listen," her father said. "Remember the chicks we saw at Ox

Lake?" The hen had called a warning, and her chicks stayed under the water until the danger passed.

"Should there be trouble, here's where you come," he said. He explained that he would make a slatted cover for the hole, glue straw and peat to it, loosely spread, the space between the slats allowing for air and some daylight to pass through. Once the table went back, no one would see it was there.

"What kind of trouble?" Greta asked.

Trouble such as they had met up with on the road today when the drunk men stopped them from travelling through the village, Katya thought, even before her father said so.

"Today, on the way to church, when those men stopped us, were you scared?" he asked Sara.

Sara nodded.

"Well then, if something should happen that makes you feel like that, if any one of you feels like that," he said to Katya and Greta, "here's where you come. Wherever you are, don't stop to think, just come. Here." He pointed to the hole. "You crawl under the table. You pull the lid to one side, and get into the hole. Then you slide the lid back in place, and stay quiet. Very still and quiet, until someone comes for you."

"Papa, I'm returning to Arbusovka tomorrow," Greta said. "I won't be here."

"You won't be in Arbusovka forever," their father said, and Katya remembered that was so. Greta would be across the compound, living in the Big House.

"And you're not to tell anyone. Anyone at all," he said, his eyes latching onto Greta's with hidden meaning. She was not to tell Dietrich, Katya knew.

They returned to the house and gathered in the family room around the table with the others for hot cocoa and bread. Their mother sprinkled sugar and cinnamon on their bedtime snack, Gerhard's eyes lighting with appreciation, innocent of what had precipitated the treat, unaware of their mother's troubled silence. Katya felt uneasy and hadn't been able to look at her brothers directly until they were all seated at the table and waiting for their mother to bring their bedtime treat. Then they sang an evening hymn and listened to their father read the Twenty-third Psalm amid the loud ticking of the clock in the parlour, the hollow tick-tocking, the words of the psalm putting everything back into place.

Later, the rooms beneath Katya and her sister lay in stillness. The bells tinkled softly as the curtain stirred. Tomorrow Greta would return to Arbusovka, and Katya would again be the oldest, and responsible for the care of her brothers and sisters. She would help her mother look after them. Her brothers could take for granted that she would see to their needs, her mother could assume she would do so, and, she thought, someone greater would be watching over them all.

My dearest, my Dietrich,

I'm sure the news has already reached you that Frieda Krahn has died, and her unborn baby with her. It seems impossible that she's gone. The evening before she died, we sat at the table together, and I read to her from Bettex's *Nature and Law*. It's a book she had read many times, and was fond of, and she wanted me to enjoy it, too. That afternoon we had gone through a bag of fabric pieces, choosing those that would be suitable for a quilt we were going to put together during the winter months. The quilt was going to be for us. For our marriage bed. I have to explain that one night I was overcome by loneliness and I confided to her about you and me, and that we had promised to wait a year. She said the quilt would help the time pass. She was cutting and arranging the pieces on the table while I read to her. And by the next evening, she was no longer with us. I know that childbirth often takes both mother and baby, but when it happens to someone you've grown to love, it makes a person stay awake and wonder why.

This week I had a terrible scare. Little Erika has learned how to undo the latch on the gate and often goes wandering. I went to look for her, and when I got back there was a stranger in the kitchen. He was standing over the *miagrope* and drinking soup from the ladle. I didn't scream or run, I just hung onto Erika and shook. He was a dirty-looking person with awful sores on his face and hands. Just then Willy came into the house. When he saw the situation he invited the man to sit down and join him at dinner, and said I should serve them. The man smelled so bad, it was hard to go near him. When he left, I threw the leftover soup to the pigs and scalded the *miagrope* and dishes he'd touched. The outcome is that Willy has decided that things have become too uncertain for me to stay here any longer. He's sent for a widowed sister to come and do for him and Erika, and I'm coming home.

I can hardly wait to see you, but I must wait until the middle of August when the Heinrichs Pauls Hildebrandt family from Arbusovka will go to Nikolaifeld and take me along. Willy will let Papa know the exact day we are leaving. Then Papa will send someone to come and get me at Nikolaifeld (you?), as more than likely he will be on the fields with harvest by then.

Our first kiss was pleasant. Our second, even more so. I'm looking forward to our walks in the forest, and our third kiss, my dear more-than-a-friend, Dietrich Abramovitch Sudermannchenko.

With love,
your Margareta

PRIVOL'NOYE   June 30, 1917

My friend, my dearest Margareta,

I leave this letter with your mother to give to you.

I wish with all my heart that I could be the one to fetch you from Nikolaifeld, as how wonderful it would be to be alone with you even for a short time. But unfortunately this is not to be. Harvest approaching or not, Father has decided it's time for me to put my commerce education into practice in Uncle Isaac's factory, and I will leave for Ekaterinoslav tomorrow. I know you'll be as down-hearted to discover that I'm not here as I am that I must go. Especially now that your kisses belong to me, my dear one. Privol'noye has not been the same without you, and now just as you're about to return, I must leave.

It's not likely that I'll be home for Christmas, according to Papa. You spoke of making a quilt in winter to help pass the time, and I suppose I must look on my training in Uncle Isaac's factory in the same light. It will help the time pass more quickly until, at last, we never need to be apart again.

My heart goes out to Mr. Krahn and his child, may God comfort both of them.

I will write again soon, and often,
yours with love,
Dietrich

November 5, 1917

My dear Peter Vogt,

I have been wanting to write ever since I returned from Odessa. The recent news of the raids and burnings at Privol'noye compel me to do so now. I am growing concerned for the safety of your family. We, too, are beginning to experience the current unrest, and although you likely don't appreciate how I enjoy hearing myself going on and on, I'll begin with more than a little news, as you have come to expect from me. This writer never imagines that a dreary missive can induce voluminous snoring as readily as a long-winded sermon.

When I arrived home to Chortitza in September, the first thing I took it upon myself to do was break the seal and lock on the school door. As you can imagine, there was much speculation as to how soon I would be arrested. But fortunately that was not to be – or unfortunately, for those who predicted that would be the outcome. It's a puzzle how disappointed some people can be when their dire predictions don't come to pass. But it was just as I expected, the officious *schlorre-kap'tän* of a school inspector didn't show his face at my door. Nor the police, either; further proof that neither rule nor order is being kept these days. As you know, the jails and prisons have been emptied by amnesty, and we in Chortitza and Rosenthal are afforded the experience of rubbing shoulders in the streets with convicted thieves, rabble-rousers, and even murderers. So why would anyone bother to arrest a school-teacher acting in the interests of pedagogy? The sooner all the schools reopen, the better for the children, as the routine gives them a sense of stability.

There were no noticeable changes here in Chortitza after the takeover by the Bolsheviks, not to the extent of what was taking place in the cities. Except for train travel, the revolution didn't affect us directly, at first. But the chaos on the trains was shocking. Ruffians and returning soldiers demand civilians give up their seats, and if they're dimwitted enough to object, they are hastened from the train, sometimes through the windows and always when the train is travelling at optimum speed. During my journey home from Odessa I wore the red ribbon on my lapel – to assure my fellow passengers that I was in step with the times – and, wisely, my old worn boots from forestry camp. Many a man disembarked in sock feet, and minus a topcoat. Other than having to submit to numerous toasts to freedom and equality with the inevitable and vile-tasting *samogon*, I am happy, and can report that my boots and greatcoat remained untouched.

However I'm afraid life in our sleepy villages is beginning to be affected by the winds of change. In Chortitza we have a commissar, a rather agreeable fellow, Chuev, a sailor from the Black Sea fleet. He was appointed to head a village soviet by a Revolutionary Committee in Alexandrovsk. His first task was to divide our belongings equally and fairly among the soldiers who, at the suggestion of the same committee, continue to move into our villages in large numbers. I suppose we should be grateful for Chuev, as I am told that in villages where there is no commissar, the soldiers forcefully and arbitrarily claim their promised rewards for having given up fighting the war. With the arrival of Chuev, I'm sad to say there went all but one of my cows, most of my chickens, and all of my horses. Camels, it appears, are not worth liberating. It's now necessary for me to ask Chuev, who has set up his headquarters in one of Koop's factory houses, for permission to borrow my own horses and wagon in order to fetch supplies. When Chuev decides for some reason that I may not, I travel on foot, as does everyone else except him, I might add.

But on to the reason that compelled me to write.

I am thinking about your girls. I am thinking about all of your children. You must read the same newspapers I do, and yet Marie's father tells me that you're reluctant to let the children out of your sight. Let me add my voice to your father-in-law's. Send Marie and the children back to Rosenthal. Auguste looks over my shoulder as I write this, and she says to tell you that she would welcome any number of your children into our home for as long as it's necessary for things to grow calm and stable, as I'm almost certain will be the case. We are in the early stages of great change, and many people are taking the opportunity of these uncertain times to settle old scores, and to indulge their base and lawless natures. The current unrest is something we must go through before everyday life will improve. In the meantime, why not send your family here?

I'm almost certain that you have already heard the news of the upcoming marriage of Dietrich to Jakob's Barbara. The world may be upside-down, but Abram's will prevails. While it looks as though his brothers may soon become workers in their own mills and factories, Abram still schemes to enlarge his holdings, and this time through matrimony. He refuses to read the writing on the wall.

My dear brother expects us to come home and give the newly-wedded couple a Sudermann family welcome, which I will do for the sake of family harmony, although knowing my nephew's heart, I do not approve of Abram's matchmaking. And so I will likely see you at Privol'noye before the snow flies.

Perhaps by the time I come you may have considered my proposal and agree to send your family back with us, and into our tender care.

With warm regards, as always,
David Sudermann

My friend, David Sudermann,

Greetings, my fellow worker and member of the proletariat, Comrade.

I address you in such a manner to demonstrate that I, too, am keeping in step with the times, which you related so interestingly and well in your previous letter.

However, time will not allow for me to write more than a hasty reply to your long and informative letter. Dietrich and Barbara are still here at Privol'noye, but tomorrow they will travel to Ekaterinoslav on the first leg of their journey, and Dietrich has promised to forward this letter to you.

The early and heavy snowfall that prevented your travel to Privol'noye is a blessing, for it has covered up the ruin. My heart could not bear the sight of such wanton destruction. The burning of grain and slaughtering of animals that are then left to rot is an evilness that will bear its own bitter fruit.

I am grateful for your concern over the wellbeing of my family, and for Auguste's offer for them to stay with you in Chortitza. It would have been a great relief for me if they had been able to go to Rosenthal, but that is not to be. For reasons you may or may not be aware of, Maria is of the mind that staying here will be less of a trial for Greta. I choose to believe that the reason for this is unknown to you, otherwise I would question why we, and Greta in particular, had to learn of Dietrich's engagement during the announcements in church, and not in a more direct way. There are fewer and kinder tongues at Privol'noye than in Rosenthal and Chortitza, which is why my children will remain here with me for the time being. That is all I wish to say about the matter. We wish the married couple God's richest blessings.

I continue to put my trust and hope in the Lord God Almighty, who knows the beginning, the middle, and the end.

Greetings to Auguste, and to Maria's father when you see him.

Until we meet again,
Peter Vogt

S now smothered the sour odour coming off the burned fields beyond the estate walls, and gradually began to conceal their blackness. The meadow – what had been the meadow and was now her father's land – was also black. The rye he'd grown with Dmitri's family, and was about to harvest, hadn't escaped the live torches, the stray dogs, tails dipped in kerosene and lit on fire, that were released to run through the ripened grain. She had stood at the stone wall the night the crops were destroyed, watching the dogs burn a fiery trail through the fields as Abram and her father tried in vain to shoot the animals. Not only had Abram's Cossack guards failed to stop the burning, they hadn't even appeared, although the flames could be seen for miles. Her father had wondered about their absence, about Kolya, who stood before him with the other workers the following morning, his hat off and head bowed. If I know who did this, I'm ashamed to tell you, he said. The fire had spread to the edge of the forest beyond the meadow lands, and the burned trees now stood like black stumps of teeth among the falling snow.

The snow was early but she welcomed it. Slate-grey clouds had pressed close to the earth for days, and now a tension was being released. She had written, *It looks as though His Majesty Winter will soon take possession of the land, and for this I'm glad. It will make everything look and feel so much better.*

She saw the carriage come along the Chortitza road, moving silently and steadily through the falling snow, large airy flakes, pieces of muslin sailing down end-over-end. Tree branches above the avenue dripped with melting snow; the hedges in the rondel and garden looked as though they were loosely draped in cheesecloth. The plants she and her sisters had uprooted lay in a mound beyond the picket fence, their leaves wet and a heightened green. Dahlias, pink and white gladioli, zinnias, their blossoms salvaged and put in a tub of water to bring into the house. Dahlia rhizomes lay in a heap against the fence. Just as Katya used to do, Sara had turned work into play. She found one rhizome that resembled a camel, another, a rabbit. She found two grown together and dunked them into water, and when the tubers emerged shiny brown and ancient-looking, Sara named them Oma and Opa, and set them onto the fence railing to oversee while they cleaned the garden. To oversee Greta going about as though her heart weren't sore.

Katya was fifteen then, but knew she looked younger, younger than she felt. She wore her father's barn jacket, which hung down to her knees. Her ankles were knobs protruding through the softened felt of her boots, whose soles had loosened, and were bound to the boots with twine. She had stuck begonias into the bib of her apron, wanting to warm them near to her breasts. The sight of the blossoms pinched off by the cold and lying on the ground disturbed her, made her feel as though she were somehow responsible for the sudden and early snow.

"They're coming," Sara announced suddenly.

"Yes, we know," Greta said.

Katya saw how Greta's spine went rigid, and she felt a rigidity in her own. She harvested the corms Greta's garden fork turned up, carried them in her apron to a sack already littered with gladioli corms lying at the edge of the garden.

The two dogs, sisal doormats thrown in a heap against the side of the house, jumped up in an instant, running for the road and barking ferociously, as though to make up for having been caught asleep.

The carriage bringing Dietrich and Barbara to Privol'noye emerged from the avenue and stopped at the parade barn. The coachman shook snow from his red hat, and then dusted his shoulders before climbing down from the carriage seat.

"What took you so long?" Abram shouted as he made his way across the yard in his house slippers. "Your mama has been looking out the window for hours, already. Sophie made *varenyky*. Where did you stay?" he shouted, flailing his walking sticks as though the snow were a line of wet laundry he had to get through.

"They're here," Sara said in a subdued voice, stating the obvious. Katya knew that Sara had concluded from their silence that they were not to go running to meet the couple. She sympathized with Sara's bewilderment, knowing what she was feeling. Her parents and Greta had endured the humiliation in silence, her mother stilling the little ones' questions or mentions of Dietrich and Barbara's engagement with a shake of her head. They'd learned of the engagement at church when the minister had read the banns, only days before the couple would be wed. Katya thought the minister was confused and had made an error, until her mother reached for Greta, clutching her knee to prevent her from fleeing. Katya realized then that it was true. It will be worse if you leave, her mother whispered to Greta. But what was worse than staying, pretending not to notice the sideways and backward glances, eyes examining their family for signs of a loose thread, knots in their shoelaces, some indication that they had not measured up?

Her parents and Greta had sat up late each evening, and on the day Dietrich was married she heard her father reading Scripture in the parlour, her mother's consoling murmurs, Greta's silence. She awoke in the night to find Greta, her back turned to her in bed, shaking as though with cold. "We all love you," Katya said, knowing enough not to expect a reply. The wedding had taken place in Einlage, in a machine shed on Jakob Sudermann's factory yard. The wedded couple spent the week following their marriage travelling from village to village to visit relatives and friends near to Barbara's village of Einlage, and had come now to Privol'noye to do the same.

As the dogs barked and circled the carriage, Aganetha and Lydia hurried across the compound from the Big House calling their greetings, and the noise brought Katya's mother out onto the platform.

"Why don't you girls come inside now, you're getting wet," her mother said.

"We'll finish here yet," Greta said, her voice thin but determined.

"Don't go and make it hard for yourself. There's no reward for that."

Katya had been asked to prepare the room for the couple. She had aired new bed linens, was appointed the task of monogramming towels and pillowcases, which she'd done in the sewing room of the Big House, their initials embroidered in white satin stitch over and over again, her chest tight, and eyes growing weary. That morning she filled vases with white chrysanthemums and maidenhair fern and set them on a bureau in the room, avoided the hurt in Greta's eyes when she returned home.

Dietrich came towards them, the fox lining of his overcoat a flash of russet moving through the snow, and before Katya could stop her, Sara was out of the gate and running to meet him, snatching up flowers from the tub. As Dietrich accepted the bouquet, he looked across the yard at Greta. When their eyes met, Greta's features twisted as though she'd been struck in the stomach. She dropped the garden fork and fled round the side of the house.

"Go with her. Stay with her until she has it out with herself," her mother said.

Katya yanked the begonias from her apron bib and threw them down, wanting to trample the blossoms into the ground. Her anger sent her running towards him, her body suddenly tense and shaking. She knew she was clenching her teeth, that she wanted to feel the sting of her palm against his face, even while she knew that she would not strike him, that she didn't know what she would do when she got there. She was vaguely aware of people across the yard, statues standing amid the falling snow, their faces turned towards her, and then she realized that she was shouting. What she wanted to say became *you, you, you.* You hard and cruel people. You self-loving and selfish people. You fat people.

She stood before him, her heart knocking against her breastbone, recognizing his longing as he looked back at the Big House, where his parents and new wife stood waiting, then to where Greta had gone round the side of the house. Rivulets of melted snow ran down his cheeks and dripped off his nose and chin. He was like a dog caught between two masters, fearing one and loving the other, the pull between them equally strong. She tore Sara's flowers from his arms and threw them to the ground.

Greta's weeping upstairs in the attic room overcame the sound of the wall clock ticking in the parlour. The family Bible lay open on its stand beneath the clock, at what would be the reading at the end of the day. *A continual dropping in a very rainy day and a contentious woman are alike. Whosoever hideth her, hideth the wind.* Her mother entered the room and stood before her. Katya felt something hit her lap, and saw the square of sheepskin, grey and grimy-looking against her apron.

"You're like your father," her mother said.

Katya sat with her mother, waiting in silence while Greta's weeping grew muffled and the metronomic ticking of the Kroeger clock took over the room.

"You should apologize to Dietrich," her mother said.

"Dietrich is the one who should apologize," Katya said.

"To Greta, yes. And more than likely he has," her mother said, referring to a letter Dietrich had begged Katya to give to Greta. "But that isn't your concern." Her hand moved across the space between their chairs and descended, warm, on Katya's thigh. "Your father had such a temper, too. But he tamed it, and gradually I never saw it raised any more."

Katya held the square of sheepskin to her nose, smelled her youth in it, remembered when she had carried it wherever she went, traipsing back and forth across the compound, going in and out of the Big House at will, her world seemingly larger than it was now.

"Greta will survive," her mother said.

Throughout the following week, the snow fell intermittently, white strings slanting across the compound, joining the sky to earth. The land was covered in a wet blanket of snow that muffled the cries of geese congregating on Ox Lake. The temperature hadn't fallen enough for the water to freeze, and the geese preened and fed all day. Their wild, harsh cries, sounding on edge, would quicken Katya's step, but as the snow lay thicker on the land, the birds' calls became indistinct, and less intrusive.

When the day arrived for Dietrich and Barbara to leave Privol'noye and travel to Ekaterinoslav, the clouds thinned, and here and there sunlight lit the land. Katya had been awakened by the hardy voices of the Cossack guards who would accompany their carriage, and she could see that Greta was already up and watching at the window. She got out of bed and went to the other window, and saw that the lake had been wiped clean of birds. A beam of sunlight shone through an opening in clouds above the lake, and the lake's glassy surface reflected the colour of lemon, and she could see in the distance a mist hovering between the thinning clouds.

The more she looked, the more it seemed to her that the mist concealed something. Grey creatures trickled across the earth from the north and south, and met at the centre of the horizon. There they piled up, became a bulge, a wobbling grey eye sitting on the land. Then the eye disintegrated as the grey creatures drifted off in opposite directions, only to return moments later to the centre of the horizon where they melded, and flattened into a gelatinous grey band. She saw Dietrich and Barbara's carriage going down the road, the Cossacks' coats spots of scarlet moving against the unmarked snow beyond the carriage. Their horses' hooves threw up crescents of snow as the riders and carriage went on and far away to where the Chortitza road would meet up with Colony Road, on towards the grey band on the horizon, their dark trail marking where they had been. They would turn and disappear into the horizon.

She realized that her eyes were wet, that she was weeping.

Her hair had become a cloud of white and too soft to hold combs when, for the first time, she told what happened that day. Her stilled hands, their enlarged knuckles and translucent skin, were strangers.

She could see through the backs of them to all the tiny bones and veins. Like branches of a winter tree, she thought. She had known all along that she would one day tell what happened, but had delayed telling it until she'd become a widow, until her children settled into middle age and had satisfying lives, not wanting to chance harming anyone lest the spirits of the story pollute the air.

The moment to tell it had arrived, a young stranger coming with his recording machine, wanting her to speak into it. She would let the story tell itself, let it wander just as she had often permitted an exploring child the freedom to wander while she watched from a distance.

When she told him the story of what happened that day, she began by saying that when Dietrich and his wife left the estate, the rest of the day passed slowly. That's the way time went, more slowly, when people left the estate. As with the geese departing so suddenly in the night, it took time to become used to their absence, for the clock to return to normal speed.

She said to him, "After the noon meal my father went to the carpentry shop to repair a chair whose leg rungs had come loose. He had been promising my mother he would do so when harvest was over. I remember that he was also looking forward to finishing a bureau. The previous spring he'd cut and planed the pieces and stored them in the rafters. Dmitri was supposed to come and help him assemble the pieces when he had finished sanding. Greta and I went to the classroom in the Big House looking for lesson books; my mother had sent us there. Greta should keep busy, she said. Keeping busy was the best thing a person could do while waiting to feel better. Since we'd returned from Rosenthal in spring, the little ones had gone without schooling. Abram had hired a tutor as promised, a young Polish woman, but she wasn't able to begin until the new year, and so my mother said Greta should tutor the little ones."

Their footsteps echoed in the empty room as they walked around it, Greta noting that not much had changed. The same diorama depicting the biosphere of their eutrophic Ox Lake hung on the wall, as did the alphabet cards whose black ink letters had faded. The chart Katya and Gerhard had drawn, of the leeches in their various states of prognostication, was pinned to the wall beside the window. Imagine, Greta said, when Franz Pauls was our teacher he was only seventeen, younger than I am now.

That evening, as usual, they gathered around the table in the family room, listening while Sara and her brothers read, Peter only five and already reading, and much quicker than Johann, who was always more interested in what was going on around him than an open book. She finished a cutwork piece of embroidery, a bureau runner to present to Sophie and Kolya as a belated wedding present. She completed the delicate task of snipping open its embroidered pattern, although daylight would have better served the intricate work.

It was November, the killing had been done, and so there were fresh smoked sausages. Her mother made sausage *bobbat* and *plumemooss* for the noon meal – but not with *kjielkje*, as some would do; they didn't prefer noodles in *plumemooss*, but dried apricots and apples. She used damsons – that, and anise, made the *mooss* special. Because killing day had taken place recently, they had been allotted a proportionate amount of hams and sausages. The sausages were already smoked, and so her mother had put a ring of sausage into the *bobbat* for their noon meal. They didn't do their curing and smoking in the chimney the way most people did, as Abram's estate had a smokehouse. Otherwise, they would have hung hams and rings of sausages in the chimney chamber in the attic. It happened sometimes that someone would allow a fire in a stove to get too hot, or forget to watch it. She'd heard people in villages tell how it could happen, how a fire would get up too much, and the smoke and heat of it would send a ham flying out a chimney to land in a neighbour's yard.

She and her sisters had spent several days cooking blue plums in the outside oven, hovering over them until the skins swelled to the point of splitting, the exact moment to take them from the oven to dry into prunes. Then they brought in the melons, a hill of muskmelons, cantaloupes, and sugar melons beside the front gate. She wrote down the instructions for pickled watermelons that her mother told her, and which, later in her life, she would come across and pass on to her oldest daughter without telling her the circumstances of the day when she entered it into the recipe notebook.

This is my Mama's receipt

Cut up some melons into pieces. Grind them to a pulp in the grinder. Put a layer of whole melons (small, 2 – 3 pound size) in a wine barrel, then some pulp, dill and salt (so-and-so many saucers of salt, depending on how much the melons weigh). Continue to layer the pulp, dill, salt and melons until the barrel is full. Cover with cheesecloth. Put a wooden bar over the cloth and weigh it down with a scrubbed stone. It takes a suitable amount of time before the melons are ready to be eaten.

Greta and I boiled down melons for syrup today. We got three buckets, one for us, two for the Big House. This year it took twelve buckets of melons boiled down for one. The syrup is thick, and will go far to sweeten winter.

The cheesecloth would accumulate scum as the watermelons fermented, and she'd rinsed the cloth out every morning since the melons were set for pickling. The barrel of melons sat in the cellar under the kitchen, along with two barrels of sauerkraut, and crocks of eggs in waterglass. Like the King of Egypt, like everyone around them, her family heeded Joseph's interpretation of the king's dream, and lay up provisions for times of need. The granaries and cellars in the Mennonite commonwealth burgeoned with the record harvest; in the boys' room there were muskmelons under the beds, sacks of roasted sunflower and pumpkin seeds on shelves above their windows. She and her sisters had already dried apples and apricots on the roof during the heat of autumn, and the dried fruit now hung in sacks from rafters above their bed, filling the room with its fragrance. She and Greta went to bed that night surrounded by the musky fragrance of dried fruit, their attic room seeming like a cradle. It seemed as though the house breathed, its walls expanding with the energy the fruits and vegetables gave off, the sun's energy and the goodness of the earth held inside them.

She awoke to the darkness of early morning, the sound of pounding on the door downstairs, Greta already awake, halfway across the room. The coachman and his son hadn't returned from taking Dietrich and Barbara to Ekaterinoslav the previous evening as expected, and her father had worried – this was what came to her mind as she followed Greta down the ladder. She thought, something has happened to the coachman and his son, there's been an accident, and she began to pray. Her father had already left the house with one of two men who came for him. The other man stayed behind. When she entered the outer room, her brothers were already there, in their night clothing, lined up against the oven wall. Her mother stood in front of the open door holding the baby, Ann, and Katya could see her father going across the compound with a man, heard the voices of other men, and saw a wagon standing beside the Big House. Then there was a glow of light just beyond the open door, a man smoking. His shoulders were so broad that at first she thought he must be Kolya, and was going to call him to come inside, but something stopped her.

She would remember her mother's bare feet against the splintered floorboards, her toes crooking to grip the floor as she rocked Ann, who slept. They were all in their nightclothes, her brothers in their long nightshirts that were so white they gleamed in the semi-darkness as the boys pressed their backs to the oven tiles for warmth. She went to close the door and her mother spoke for the first time, her eyes hollow-looking in the light cast by a lantern on the table, its wick turned low. The man outside had said to leave it open. Why? She didn't know. I just don't know, they wouldn't say why your father should go, either, just that he should go, and that the one out there should stay.

"Are we supposed to stand here freezing?" Greta said. When she left the room, the man outside on the platform came over to the door and watched until she returned. She had gone through the rooms gathering up shawls, coats, and sweaters. She draped a garment around their mother's shoulders, tucking it about the sleeping Ann, or Njuta, as her brothers had named their newest sister; and as the clock chimed the hour in the parlour, Greta went to each of her brothers doing the same, draping them with sweaters, with shawls, the melancholic sound of the clock's chimes like a benediction. Her mother went over to the window and looked out, still rocking.

Katya put on the shawl Greta gave her, and the clock stopped chiming; the fifth hour, she thought, grateful for the warmth of the woolly garment as she stood to one side of the open door, the cold air scuttling around her ankles and up her nightgown to her knees. She wondered if Greta was asking the same question as she was: why had the man been told to stay? She looked out across the yard. The stars and moonlight had faded and the sky was beginning to lighten, so perhaps the clock had marked the sixth hour and not the fifth; she couldn't be sure. The sky was cloudless and so why then was it snowing? What looked like snow funnelled out from the upstairs windows of the Big House and billowed across the yard. There were men out there, grey figures threading among wagons that stood on the compound near to the Big House. She felt the warmth and softness of Greta's breasts against her arm as her sister leaned into her to look out at the yard.

"It's bedding. Those are feathers," Greta said.

"*Ja*, that's what it looks like to me. They're spoiling the bedding," her mother said.

"Who is?" Gerhard's loud question made the man on the platform shift and adjust his cap. Then he left the platform and went over to the gate, and she thought he would leave, but moments later he returned, his cigarette butt dropping to the ground, its glow ground out under his heel as he muttered to himself.

Her mother must have forgotten about the little ones when she'd spoken, as she turned to them and said softly, "It's not important. Your papa will tell you about it when he comes."

Thieves breaking in, moths and rust corrupting; Katya thought of the Scripture warning against putting too much store in earthly treasures when she saw the feathers swirling in the air. Pillow feathers, down feathers from quilts and mattresses, Lydia's dowry likely taken from trunks in an upstairs storage room, cut open and emptied to the wind.

The man outside swore suddenly and once again went to the gate as though wanting to join the others. He came pounding back up the steps to the doorway, breathing heavily. They should follow him, he said.

She went across the yard with her sisters and brothers to the Big House, their mother hurrying them along. Katya was certain her father had taken the time to pull on trousers before answering the door. She didn't know why this had become so important to her. She didn't want him to be out there like they were, in their night clothing. The dark had dissolved to shadows that were set against the sides of buildings, the summer kitchen and washhouse, and she sensed bones creaking, sinew humming, that someone might be standing in the shadows between the two buildings, watching as they came by.

She remembered seeing a light flickering across a window in the women's quarters beyond the parade barn, and thinking that although the outside women were awake and moving about, they hadn't gone to do the milking, judging from the lowing and bellowing coming from the cow barn. When she would go over and over this moment, she would realize there had been sounds, the cows, the voices of the men; she had seen a light in the women's quarters. But then, it was as though she was seeing the world from underwater, voices and movements muted and slow. A man came across the compound from the genera-tor house, suddenly becoming a huge bird about to lift off from the ground as a gust of wind filled a cape he wore and flung it out and around him. As she came closer, she recognized the gold cape as the velvet tablecloth which covered the dining-room table in the Big House. The same gust of wind wrapped her nightgown around her body, and for the first time she felt the cold go through her.

Her father stood beside the wagon fully clothed, she was relieved to discover, and on the wagon was a man reclining in an armchair. Even before they arrived, the man's long hair told her he must be the half-man from Lubitskoye, Simeon Pravda. She saw he was surrounded by furniture, the oval cherrywood table from Abram's study, his plush sofa and sagging armchair; his smokestand lay across the arms of another chair. There were other wagons also piled with furniture, and she vaguely recognized the plank table from the bake kitchen, a wash-stand, a bureau.

Her father saw them coming, his concern quickly masked, and he gave his attention to Pravda. The men moved between the house and the wagons as though they were in a race, throwing what they had brought onto the piles of furniture, and hurrying back inside, the man who had led them across the yard quickly joining them. Pravda talked to her father rapidly, gesticulating with a small whip, pointing out the men whose families, he had decided, would move into the Big House once they were finished rummaging through it. The house was large enough for as many as five families, Pravda told her father. Dmitri's family would be given two rooms, it was only right, he said, and for the first time Katya wondered, where were the Sudermanns? Lights shone in all the windows but there was no sign of them.

"Will you also live there?" her father asked.

"Me? No, perhaps I'll live over there," Pravda said, and with his whip, pointed to their house.

"Live where you please," her father said.

When Pravda talked, he rolled his head from side to side. His hair, brilliant with grease, had feathers stuck to it, a corona of white fluff that was being tugged and riffled by a breeze.

"He looks like a chicken," Sara whispered, and clamped a hand over her mouth to stifle a nervous giggle.

Her comment caught the attention of Pravda. "Are these your children? Why are they here?" he asked, frowned, and looked about the yard. When he saw the man who had brought them, he shouted at him in Ukrainian and received a string of curses in reply. "Please forgive him," Pravda said to her mother in a contrite voice.

This was how they should call him, he said: Little Father, Father Pravda, Bat'ko Pravda. They would see much of him now. Her mother's question, Peta, what is it? had been stilled by a look from the Little Father. It was for him to ask questions, he said.

"Yes, all these children are mine," her father said, after he had explained to them who Pravda was, and how they were to address him. Simeon Panteleimon Pravda was a patriot, an anarchist. He was a bandit, his voice told them.

They were his basket of apples, her father said. Four daughters and four sons, one of whom was almost a man, could work as hard as a man. At the mention of himself, Gerhard covered his lap with his hands to conceal his member, stiff and poking against his nightshirt.

"The Queen of Heaven has blessed you," Pravda said. Katya felt his eyes pass across her, saw that when he looked at Greta, his eyes stayed on her for moments before going on to the others. Greta was looking away, hard, at the Big House, at the lit-up windows. What had happened to the Sudermanns, the Wiebe sisters?

"Now you've met them, and now they're going home and back to bed," her father said.

"You're afraid for them," Pravda said. "You don't need to fear," he said when her father didn't reply.

"I'm sure that's true. I believe you," her father said, and folded his hands across his chest.

"Then why not let them stay? They may learn something useful," Pravda said, his eyes once again coming to rest on Greta.

The locksmith's house where Sophie and Kolya had a room was dark, which she'd noticed when they'd come across the compound, and she had wondered where Sophie might be. She hadn't recognized any of the men, except for Dmitri. She saw his grave and grey old face as he stood, back to the garden wall, cap held to his chest, as they'd gone by, a quick nod in their direction. When the man had told them to come with him, they had all scrambled for their shoes, which were lined in a row beside the door. Her mother had for some reason stepped into a pair of their father's boots, and Katya had thought, well, he must be wearing his scuffs then, and hoped he had taken the time to pull on socks.

The boots her mother wore had clomped against the ground, her gait childlike, made more awkward by the lolling tongues of the boots and trailing laces. "'Tis So Sweet to Trust in Jesus." Katya thought of the hymn they'd sung the night before. She and her sisters and brothers walked behind the man and smelled the pig manure caked on his rubber boots and trouser legs. *Jesus, Jesus, how I trust Him, How I've proved Him o'er and o'er.* They reached the wagon, stood grouped together beside the horses. "Are these your children?" the man called Bat'ko Pravda had asked her father.

She saw Vera come from the garden toolshed now, followed by Kolya. Vera was wearing a black leather coat which flapped about the tops of her high leather boots as she moved through a swirl of feather snow.

Pravda's eyes followed Vera and Kolya now too, as the two of them, Kolya carrying a spade, went off into the east gardens.

He then turned to Katya's father. "Do you own a gun?" he asked.

"Yes, of course I have a gun," her father said.

Pravda nodded approvingly and then leaned down and spat over the wagon wheel. "It's good you said so, because I know you do have one. You said the truth, that is good. But tell the truth now, would you use it against me?" he asked.

"Why do you ask this question?"

"Because I've heard all about what you people believe," Pravda said.

"Well, so, then you know the answer. But why would I use a gun when I have nothing to fear?" he added, his eyes looking at him steadily. "You said so yourself."

Pravda laughed, and Katya saw her father send her mother a look meant to reassure, and her mother's little nod in return. She rocked the sleeping baby, her eyes riveted to her husband's face, while little Peter clung to her leg, his face turned sideways against her thigh.

Katya could describe Pravda in every detail, this man who, despite his leather tunic and the two pistols stuck into his wide belt, still looked like a common beggar. Feathers lifted from his shoulders and drifted away across the yard.

"So you think it's wrong for us to do this," Pravda said. He was a man baiting a dog, waving a stick and wanting it to jump and latch on.

"That is not for me to say," her father said.

"But you must have an opinion. You think something, isn't that right?" Pravda said.

"Yes, I do. I think that whatever you want, you'll take. I have not tried to stop you," he said.

"And what if I should take what belongs to you?" Pravda asked.

"I will help you carry it," her father said.

Pravda laughed again, and her father, who had been so rigidly planted in one spot, relaxed and shifted his shoulders. By reasoning with Pravda, he was preventing anger from erupting all around them, and she felt his wisdom, a light shining out from his body, and they, her mother, sisters, and brothers were bathed in his light. He stepped closer to the wagon and rested a hand against its side, looking like a man who had stopped another to talk about the weather.

Beyond him she saw two buff-coloured heaps lying on the ground, the dogs, Nicholas and Alexandra, she realized, lying dead in a patchwork of muddied footprints and bloodied snow.

"Papa," she said quietly, and pointed.

"Be still, my girl," he said.

She was sorry that she'd pointed, as Daniel and Johann, when they saw the dogs, began to whimper. Greta went over to her brothers, drew their bodies into her own.

They all turned at the sound of glass breaking, as the kitchen windows shattered, one after the other. Men had gone down to the cellar and were coming up with jars of food. They were throwing the jars out the windows, and as a mound of pickled beets, crabapples, cucumbers, pears, grew higher among the broken glass, Katya's stomach turned, and there was a strange metallic taste on her tongue. She didn't know yet that they had urinated in the flour and sugar bins in the bake kitchen, its shelves emptied and food scattered and trampled underfoot.

Each time a jar smashed, her father winced. "I must say something," he said to Pravda.

"Bat'ko Pravda will always be willing to listen," Pravda said.

"You asked me if I thought what you were doing was wrong. I have to say this, here, is wrong. Take the food, but don't spoil it. You could eat well this winter," he said.

"We could eat cow dung this winter if we wanted to, and it would be our business. We're in charge now. It's not for anyone to tell us what to do," Pravda said.

Katya saw fear rise in her father's face, which suddenly made him look haggard. He stared at Pravda as though seeing him for the first time. The man was not what he'd taken him to be – simple, part fool, a posturing beggar – but someone to be feared. Then her father turned and looked at her, and she understood his message, and took Sara in hand to show him that she had. Her scalp began to tighten, and sounds suddenly became sharper. She heard glass breaking inside the house, a burst of maniacal laughter. She didn't know if she could move. Her father's eyes then sought out Greta, but she was again turned towards the Big House.

"Greta." He'd spoken through his teeth, but fiercely, the sound instantly catching her attention.

Greta nodded almost imperceptibly, the grey light washing all colour from her face; all of them shades of grey and darkness, like people in a photograph. Greta clasped Daniel and Johann more tightly against her body. Katya saw the tips of the boots her mother was wearing sticking out from under her nightdress, its hem trembling.

"They say you're a good man, is that so?" Pravda indicated with his whip to the workers' quarters.

"God knows whether I am or not," her father said.

"They have no reason to say it, and so it must be true. Why don't you choose something from the wagons? Go ahead, working for King Turd, there must be something. Take, choose, whatever you want, you can have," he said. "Why not take that?" He pointed with the whip to Abram's sofa at the back of the wagon, the gramophone resting on its cushions, a lacquered box of player discs beside it.

"I have all I need," her father said, his eyes taking them in, his sons, his daughters, his wife with a child in her arms.

"Yes, you have your little apples," Pravda said.

"Let them go home now. Their mother will make a meal. I would be happy if you would come and be our guest. She's a fine cook," her father said, his voice even.

His invitation went unanswered, as several men came round from the front of the house, struggling beneath the weight and bulk of Lydia's piano. One of them slipped on the snow-covered grass and, losing his grip, dropped the piano to the ground, its strings vibrating in a thrum of sound.

Now Katya saw Vera was coming back from the garden, coming through the arched gate, her black coat shining, and behind her was Kolya. She carried what looked to be a strongbox, and when Pravda saw it, he shouted at a man inside the house who was standing at a broken kitchen window to go and tell the others to come.

The man wearing the table covering came from the front of the house, wandered over to the piano, and began fingering its keys. He poked up and down the scale until Pravda shouted for him to leave it be. Feathers swirled up and around the feet of the men as they walked, carried up and away by a sudden gust of wind, over the wall, vanishing into sunlight, mixing with what snow remained on the fields. Where patches of snow had melted, the burned vegetation spotted the land. Someone might come by on the road. They would see the wagons, the commotion in the yard. Orlov might hear the cows complaining and send someone to investigate.

She heard an inside door slam in the Big House, Abram's voice rise in anger. Moments later she saw Kolya again, this time coming from the front of the house; behind him was Abram leaning heavily into Aganetha for support, and several men coming with Lydia, and the Wiebe sisters, who walked stooped and slow, clutching one another. Abram's nose was off-kilter, his nostrils black with clotted blood; rivulets of blood ran over his mouth and into his beard. They came near, and her father turned to Abram, his hand raised then lowered as if to say, Go slowly, be quiet. But when Abram saw Vera, he began to shout. She should go and milk the cows. She should go immediately, and tell the others to do likewise. What was he paying them for? he demanded, as though the men who had gathered around him were not carrying guns, revolvers tucked into their tunic fronts and belts, others with their *nagaikas*, such as the small whip Pravda played with constantly, or sabres hanging at their sides. Abram's voice was bubbly and nasal, and his Russian at the best of times was almost unintelligible.

"Abram Abramovitch asks that the women go milk the cows," her father repeated. "If you like, let me send my girls. They can do it." The animals' moans rose in waves and broke apart in hoarse screeches as they bawled for relief.

"King Turd wants his cows tended to, does he? Well, my men are happy to carry out his wishes. Go and look after them," Pravda said to two men.

The Wiebe sisters, who had begun to weep when they'd come upon the battered dogs and the broken glass and food, continued to sob. Lydia went to her father, whose nightshirt was spattered with blood. She was the only one who was fully clothed, her hair freed of its combs and flowing across her shoulders.

When the first shot came from the cow barn, Katya's whole body began to shake. She hadn't understood that Pravda meant the men were to shoot the cows. The sound reverberated in the loft, and then came another shot, followed quickly by another, the horses in the horse barns beginning to whinny. Njuta awoke and began to fuss; their mother jostled her and made shushing noises.

Abram sputtered, his massive head quivering as he stared at the barn in disbelief. Then he tore himself away from Aganetha, spreading his legs as he stood upright, his mountain of flesh jiggling beneath his nightshirt. The men around him moved back and fell silent.

They were all swine, they were pieces of dog dirt, snakes, sons of the devil, sons of immoral women, Abram shouted in Low German, and what more he called them, Katya would not say. Then, as if put off-balance by the velocity of his own swearing, he slipped and fell backwards, his body thudding against the ground. Aganetha cried out and was about to go to him, but Kolya pushed her aside and went to stand over Abram as he struggled to rise to his knees, his lard swaying, hanging close to the ground. His nightshirt rode up, exposing the shame of his enormous buttocks, and Kolya laughed.

Lydia muttered something, and looked as though she would say more, but Kolya turned and glared at her and she fell silent. Abram grunted and wheezed, his nose bubbling with blood, and the man draped in velvet cloth took it off and threw it over his exposed flanks.

Kolya cursed and tore the covering off of him. Another man approached and, with the butt of his gun, prodded Abram between the legs, causing laughter, a release of whatever fear and awe they might have still had for him. One after the other they touched Abram with a toe of a boot, in his belly, his flanks, his ribs; another with a sabre, pricking the skin of his neck, tentative nudges that ended when Pravda called for them to bring Abram to the wagon. The strongbox Vera had given to Pravda lay open on his lap.

"You said there was nothing. You said the girl wasn't telling the truth," Pravda said to Abram. He lifted out a blue leather case, and took out a silver tiara.

Katya recognized the tiara; she had seen it on Aganetha's head in a family photograph taken on the day of their silver wedding anniversary. A picture that she would see lying on the floor in the parlour, its convex glass smashed and ground underfoot, obliterating the image of Aganetha and the silver tiara that glinted out from her pewter crown of braids. There was a silence now, and moments later, the two men who had been sent to shoot the cows came towards them, their guns at their sides.

"There are other things hidden. Look in the well," Vera said to Pravda.

Abram protested this wasn't so. They wouldn't find anything in the well.

"In what they call the butter well," Vera said, and pointed to it.

"Yes, yes. I know. Once again, the girl is lying," Pravda said to the now subdued Abram, who stood swaying back and forth beside Katya's father at the wagon.

When Pravda sent several men to search the well, Abram lifted his hands to indicate the futility of it.

But there *was* something in the well, Katya knew, and Vera seemed to know it too, as her eyes became hard beads of light shining across the distance between them. There is something in the well, Vera's eyes told her. Yes, she thought, there *is* something there, but how can Vera know that?

They stood frozen in place, Njuta beginning to cry now, and, desperate to quiet her, their mother rocked her harder and harder, shushing, jiggling, appealing to their father with frightened eyes.

"Who here can make music?" Pravda asked, and gestured at the piano.

Her father's eyes found Lydia, and then it seemed as though an idea had come to him. "Why not play something for us," he said to Lydia; and, turning towards Pravda, "she plays well."

Lydia stood with an arm about her mother's shoulders, and Aganetha, whose lips had been moving with silent prayer, whimpered, "Don't leave me."

"Come now, Aganetha, a little music is good for the soul, yes?" Katya's father said with a false lightness, which Lydia seemed to

234

understand. "Something everyone will enjoy," he called after her as she walked slowly over to the piano and stood before it, hands splayed above the keys. Her hands then descended, and the melody of a Russian folk song rose up and carried across the yard, drawing the men who had not gone to the well over to the piano, and they stood around it, their blunt faces softening with pleasure at the sound of a favourite song rising from beneath Lydia's touch. They began to sing, first one, and then the others took up the song, their voices harmonizing naturally, full with longing. Pravda gripped the arm of the chair, his head rolling from side to side.

The men who had gone to the well returned, the trousers of the smallest one among them soaked to the knees. He began emptying his pockets. Three long-handled dessert spoons fell to the ground, one after the other, then a small silver tray, and finally, Lydia's two-eared cup. Abram backed away from the objects lying on the ground, shaking his head in disbelief. Katya could almost feel the weight of the cup in her hand. Her teeth began to chatter; she wanted to hold her jaw to make it stop, but she couldn't move.

Pravda took the cup as it was handed to him, spat on it, and rubbed it against his sleeve. His face opened in a smile of triumph as he lifted it and turned its engraved initials out for all to see.

It was then that Kolya swung the shovel, silencing Abram's sputtering with a blow to the side of his head. As Abram fell, the men descended on him, and Katya heard the solid thud of their fists and feet pounding his body. Someone cried out, Aganetha, or one of the Wiebe sisters, a high-pitched sound that came from the back of a throat, becoming a scream as the first sabre slashed through Abram's nightshirt, parting the flesh of his shoulder. Katya saw how white and shiny was his bone.

Sara was yanking her hand, but Katya couldn't move. The sounds burst forth, Sara's whine of fear, her father's sharp gasp as he moved towards them now and was stopped suddenly by a rifle butt rammed against his chest. Greta, silent while she backed away from the men, their sabres hacking and fists and boots pounding at Abram. Daniel and Johann whimpering, turning their faces into her stomach, still clinging to her nightdress. She was inching them away from the sight of blood splattering pant legs, from the sound of Aganetha's sobbing, which became a shriek as one of the men struck her with an axe. Gerhard bolted away from their mother's side, gone suddenly from sight. Greta kept inching away, as if hoping she might back into a deep shadow with her brothers and disappear, until one of the little ones stumbled and fell against her, sending her sprawling to the ground.

"*Schnell*," her father shouted as he pushed the man's gun aside, his fists tight and shaking in the air beside his head, his features swollen and contorted. Hurry, hurry, he screamed at them. She saw his mouth shape the words, saw Greta rise to her knees, saw someone come up behind her and force her back down. "Oh God, God in heaven," her mother cried out, while Katya felt the ground moving beneath her feet as she began to run, Sara before her pulling her along. She saw Lydia, across the yard at the piano, begin to run at the same time.

When she finished telling the story that day, she ended it by saying, After they killed Abram they thought they had to keep on killing until no one was left. They didn't want to leave a witness. They didn't know that the times were such that they could kill without fear of punishment. They hadn't known yet that they could have chosen who to shoot and hack to death and who to leave standing.

Well, yes. *Na ja*. And so they killed them all, she said, and noticed that the young man's hand had begun to shake, that he had to turn off his machine and go over to the window for a moment and look out at the parking lot, where cars were beginning to arrive for the Sunday-afternoon visiting. Children were emerging from the vehicles with their parents, were being urged to button up against the cold, promised a trip to somewhere more interesting afterwards. Had they remembered to bring nail clippers, yet? Oma likes to have her nails, just so, filed and shining with clear nail polish. How had she got to be so vain?

III

SURELY GOODNESS AND MERCY

And I said, Oh that I had wings like a dove!

for then would I fly away and be at rest.

– PSALM 55:6

S he had wanted to run farther than the hole in a greenhouse floor, to run away from her thoughts, from waking each morning to the absence of voices; escape to another country. But that wasn't possible, not yet. In any case, escape where, and to what, she didn't have the will to imagine. She hadn't known that men of influence were beginning to sound out the possibilities for a mass migration to Canada, the United States, Mexico, and South America. Perhaps it was just as well that she hadn't known. Because she would have held her breath, waited too long for her life to begin. By the time she left, a rigor mortis might have set in. She had no choice except to go on breathing, and she wound up escaping into the heart of a man who always seemed to be there when she needed him.

She had wanted to go away, she would tell the earnest young interviewer, who was accustomed to a warmer winter than what was experienced in Manitoba, judging from the way he was dressed. But she couldn't go away, and so for a time she went away in her mind from the place of the accident. Yes, that's what it was, an accident. When she grew old, she came to understand that life was a series of accidents. Since she'd come to live at Bethania, she'd heard of other people's accidents, told to her by the onlookers, and survivors such as she was, people who, like her, had come to end their days in identical cubicle-size rooms of a personal-care home. Rooms with a single window; rooms about the size of one where a doctor might instruct, Put your feet into the stirrups, here, and here. Where a doctor once told her – a Mennonite with a self-satisfied smile, offspring of one of the wealthy ones, a man so satisfied with his own plain face that she was always relieved to see the back of him when he went out the door – he had said: The uterus, yes, there it is. The cause of most of the world's problems. He would leave her shaking because she'd been enraged, and so intensely.

All right, then. She would come to need personal care, and to live among other survivors of that time in Russia, women mostly, who had stories to tell, but no words to tell them. Just as their recipes had lacked concise instructions and measures, their Plautdietsch language lacked the necessary words to give shape to the colours, describe the nuances, the interior shadows of their stories. Perhaps they would have been better off trying to sing them, a hymn with stanzas and a rousing chorus to inflame the heart with a desire to be better at things. Better at loving, at being, or, at least, better at doing. In their time, the road to eternity had been crowded with everyday things, chickens, children and men that required constant tending, the earth in the garden crying out to be subdued, and so they were used to singing hymns to remind them that heaven was their ultimate goal, and joy was the best vehicle to get them from here to there.

The people she would come to live with near the end of her life were octogenarians and older, several within grasp of their hundredth year, as she was. Doddering people who were half the size they'd once been, could not see the numbers on the telephone, or work the button on the elevator. Some of them slobbered when they ate, their dentures caked with bits of food while they told nonsensical stories such as the one about a child who had been born without a bone in her nose because her mother had looked upon the cruel beating of a dog. Who would give credence to their stories?

The tall young man would smile sadly when she said it was an accident. Something that happens without being expected, which could mean almost everything that came to a person in life. But perhaps there was no such thing as an accident, for a person could easily make a list of known causes, point fingers, find fault and intention for every small and large misfortune. One cause would lead to another and another, and finally come down to this: If only God hadn't created Adam and Eve, then such-and-such would not have happened.

Six months following the massacre of her family she was still far-away, the word *far-away* coming from Nela Siemens. She's not here yet. She's far-away and doesn't have much to say, which is to be expected, Nela told a neighbour who stopped at her gate to enquire.

She's far-away. Katya heard Nela say on an afternoon when the windowpanes in the house buzzed with a concussion of sound, the Soviets having dynamited a section of the Einlage bridge while fleeing the city of Alexandrovsk. The Bolsheviks had captured Kharkov, Kiev, and Ekaterinoslav, and now they were retreating, blowing up the bridge behind them. Petrograd was now Leningrad. Kerensky had been replaced by the Bolsheviks. The Old Style calendar had given way to the New Style, the Julian; and as with all the other changes, it was as if something had passed away while she'd been asleep and something had arrived, without it making much difference to what she was thinking or feeling. She was far-away, which was to be expected; that she would endure was prayed for, and also expected. She had lifted up her mother's hand mirror to see what a far-away expression was, and for a fleeting moment caught herself unaware, a stranger looking at a stranger.

"It's time to lengthen your clothes," her grandmother said one morning soon after Katya had heard Nela say she was far-away. She had returned from walking Sara to school to find Tina Funk in her grandmother's kitchen. Her grandmother had made the announcement as though she were saying that something had passed, and something had arrived. That it was time to lengthen Katya's skirts, and get on with being alive.

"A girl from Neuenburg ran away with a Russian bricklayer," Tina Funk said. She had finished unpacking her supplies, fabric ends of various materials and colours, and seated herself at the table. Now the real purpose of her visit, gossip, could begin. She was a middle-aged bespectacled woman who lived across the backyard from them, across the Chortitza creek.

"A Kasdorf girl. Green-Thursday Kasdorf's daughter. You remember he was given the Green Thursday twice for working on a Sunday. His daughter, just like him, is rebellious. What you plant, you harvest," Tina said. "Show me the skirts."

"Everyone knows about the girl," her grandmother said, pointing out that the news was old news, and Tina shouldn't bother embellishing.

"You look good," Tina Funk said to Katya as she sorted through the skirts Oma had draped across her knees, and apparently didn't expect a reply, as she went on to say, "Your oma is right, there's not much to let down." Her voice had become less animated, and she didn't look directly at Katya, which was what many people did, turned their heads as though not wanting to breathe the same air, as though she might have something contagious.

"Your grandfather took Njuta along to the barn to give us a moment," Oma said to Katya, as she'd seen the girl was puzzled by the sight of the empty high chair.

"False hems won't do," Tina Funk said.

"I've already considered that," Oma said. What they should consider was adding a band of fabric and concealing the seam with trim. She rummaged through the woman's basket and came up with packages of trim, which she spread almost lovingly across the table and stepped back to admire.

"*Na, ja*," Oma said and turned away from the table, the pleasure in her eyes fading. What would it look like, so fancy, and so soon after. She anticipated gossip.

Well then, what she could do was make a tape of the same material, the seamstress said. She could cut a strip of fabric on the bias, and although it was time-consuming work, she could make such a tape, use invisible stitching, and from a distance the seam would resemble a tuck. And what about the petticoats, would Mrs. Schroeder be wanting to lengthen them, too?

"No, no, not the petticoats," Oma said. There were still some petticoats from Greta yet, which should be put to good use.

Katya knew her grandmother's words were meant for her. She was referring to Katya's refusal to wear Greta's clothes. Greta's blouses and skirts, the dress she had worn the day she was baptised, her undervests, waists, and petticoats lay in a bureau drawer, still holding her scent, a scent which was released bit by bit each time Katya opened the drawer. Wearing the clothing would mean washing it, would mean the scent would disappear.

Tina Funk went on to say that ordinarily she would be only too glad to take on the work of lengthening the clothing. As it was, she would not charge Mrs. Schroeder the full price for the supplies. She'd like to be able to do more, however, she said, and fell silent.

"No, no, Katya can do it," her grandmother declared vehemently. Katya should do it. She must do it, her tone implied. "She's very good with her hands," she added in a gentler tone, to soften what had sounded like peevishness.

"Even so, I'd like to be able to contribute something. But it's just not possible right now," the seamstress said, and sighed deeply.

Katya knew the woman wanted to be asked why it wasn't possible. Her grandmother more than likely knew the answer, she realized as Oma got up from the table and rushed to the stove, returning with a pitcher of steaming *prips*. Then, with an impatient wave of her hand, she sent Katya to the pantry for a plate of buns and a saucer of thinly sliced cheese, which had been prepared earlier.

"*Nanu*. So." Oma said firmly as Katya returned with the food, and she knew that her grandmother intended to change the topic of conversation entirely. They were going to have a small bite to eat now, rather than later, Oma said. Otherwise they might be interrupted by Opa bringing Njuta back. They would say grace, yes? and then Tina should say what news she had of her daughter living so far away in the new Arkadak Colony.

"There's very little to tell," Tina said.

Katya could see that Tina Funk wasn't pleased with the change of conversation, and so she asked, "Why isn't it possible for you to hem my skirts?"

She was overwhelmed with sewing now, the seamstress said, eagerly taking up the invitation to explain. Her work had fallen off terribly much, almost to nothing, but now she had more sewing than she could handle. She had been occupied with nothing else all winter, and the work was not from our own, either, she told Oma, lowering her voice.

"Yes, yes, I know," Oma said. Her shoulders dropped in a slouch as she surveyed the saucer of cheese, the plate of buns, as though regretting this courtesy.

She didn't like going close to them, Tina Funk confided. She didn't like taking their measurements. She made her sewing student do it. "She has to learn," she said defensively as Oma shook her head in disapproval that she would make a young unmarried girl take the measurements of men.

Oma glanced at Katya across the table, as if hoping that what the seamstress said had somehow passed her by. Everyone in Rosenthal knew everyone else's business, who the seamstress was sewing for, that the rebellious girl had eloped with a Russian bricklayer, just as everyone now likely knew that Katya's skirts required lengthening.

And everyone knew Tina Funk's new customers were men, men of a certain kind, Makhnovites, who took their name from their leader who had formed a new party, a union of peasants. They had undermined the authority of Kerensky's community committees, and were now challenging the authority of the Soviet councils and the Ukrainian nationalists. They called themselves anarchists, a word most of them had likely never heard, Katya's grandfather had said, until a man called Nestor Makhno was freed from Butyrki prison, and returned to his village of Gulyai-Polye to become a big fish in a little pond. Within months, Makhno, a pimply-faced dandy, had attracted a large following, as he accomplished more quickly what the community committees had been set up to do and what the Bolsheviks were promising. What they had accomplished so far was robbery, her grandfather said.

They demanded that inventories be drawn up, herded Russian families into villages to squat on land owned by Mennonites, designated which rooms in a house they should occupy. The Schroeders' sixty-five *desiatini* of land amounted to no more than wormwood and thistles under their new plan, and would fare just as badly under the Soviet plan as under Makhno's union of peasants.

Like others in Rosenthal, her uncle Wilhelm had schemed ways to avoid the redistribution of their possessions, "redistribution" being the name given for robbery. He made a bargain with several less well-to-do Mennonites. These families, who had fewer than the number of livestock allowed, agreed to add his animals to their inventories in exchange for money to purchase the necessary fodder and for the use of the animals and their produce, until life returned to normal. He also took in a widow with six children, just as David Sudermann in Chortitza had done – the same widow. The men registered the woman and children as living under their roof. Cornelia Fast Wiebe became Nela Fast on Wilhelm's account; Cornelia Wiebe on David Sudermann's. Meanwhile the widow continued to live with her six children in a tidy small house near to the bazaar grounds in Rosenthal. But should it become necessary that she move in with one of them, a house crowded with their own was more endurable than a house filled with strangers, who would make demands and threaten reprisals if the wind didn't blow from the right direction. We're the true workers, her uncle would say to justify his actions. The German and Mennonite colonists had worked the country up to where it was today with their sweat, their bodies sometimes broken, and by the grace of God. They had been made stewards of the land, and a good steward had to scheme and bargain, or risk losing what God had put into his charge.

The seamstress Funk said that, so far, her son had always been home when the Makhnovites came to the house with their bundles of velvet cloth, wanting her to make jackets for them. But what would she do if one day they came when he wasn't home?

"Has *he* come?" Katya's grandmother whispered, her hand involuntarily flying up to her throat. When she realized she had done it, she quickly straightened the collar of her dress as though that had been her intention.

"No, not him. Not Kootzy." Tina lowered her voice as she spoke the code name for Pravda, "Kootzy" a reference to his shortened legs. She then went on to say that if a certain man should come, wanting her to sew for him, she'd tell him her machine wasn't working. Which would be the truth, because if she didn't work, the machine wasn't working, was it? She would send him and his men to a seamstress in Chortitza who was almost as good as she was. Or they could find their own. But she doubted that their own could work with such fabric, or make the patterns up out of their heads, which, she added, was what she'd had to do.

"Do they ever think to pay?" her grandmother asked, caught up by the woman's story and by her own sense of curiosity. There had been speculation about whether or not this was the case.

The bandits always travelled with their banker, Tina Funk said, a man designated to carry the money bags, which he tied to his saddle, grain sacks bulging with *kerenkii* and *chervontsy*, and the tsar's rubles. Her customers made a show of saying they recognized the value of her labour, Tina Funk said. In the bandits' opinion what she did was honest work. But then they paid her mostly in the tsar's rubles, she said, which were next to being worthless, and so she wasn't sure if this meant she was being paid or not. At least, not in the currency everyone preferred now – a window glazed in exchange for butter, a pair of trousers sewn for a load of ice hauled from the river. What did those ruffians have to offer other than stolen notes? Wherever they went, a dirty tail followed them, women and children, cows, goats and dogs. Sometimes the women and children rode the cows and hitched them to carts, butchering them when their stomachs rumbled. When the cows and goats dwindled, the ruffians came knocking at the door. The last time they came to her house, they went off with a dozen chickens and a fur coat she had been repairing for Tobacco-Chewing Klassen.

To demonstrate that they were for the people, the so-called anarchists made a show of scattering a few notes and coins in a street when they left a village. Katya and her grandparents had seen this in Rosenthal. This was after the anarchists had gone from house to house, comparing the contents of one against their inventories, extorting contributions, *kontributsia*, they'd say, whether or not they had found a discrepancy. Like most of the people in Rosenthal and Chortitza, her grandparents and uncle had been called upon to make the necessary contributions, and so had reason to dread the sound of unexpected footsteps on the stairs, a family shuffling across the platform, the ensuing rap on the door. It did no good to keep the shutters closed and hope they'd go on by, as a person risked being reported to the nearest Makhno Little Father, a sometimes self-appointed leader of a hundred or so men, such as Simeon Pravda had become.

If a knock on the door was ignored, the black flag would soon appear, fluttering from a troika or an automobile, or a carriage with a machine gun mounted on the back. The anarchists came riding through town at a gallop, the men in their nightmarish garb, satin capes and silk top hats stolen from a Jew's haberdashery; hats which, as they rode, they held fast to keep from flying away. Some of the men wore *Gymnasium* uniforms, preferring those whose crests identified them as law students and engineers, their chests criss-crossed with bandoliers of ammunition, and grenades hanging from wide leather belts. Those who claimed to have status wore the prized jackets of scarlet, blue, or gold velvet that had been made by Tina Funk and other Mennonite seamstresses. Velvet cloth that had once covered a dining-room table or draped a window was fashioned by the seamstresses into *tuzhurka* jackets in the French style, which, to the bandits, reflected their high status.

Peasant families had knocked twice on her grandparents' door. A crowd standing on the platform one wintry day peering into the house, the children among them – some with lips bubbling with cold sores, others with eyelids thick with festering sties – inching through the door, soon wandering about the room, pulling open drawers, fingering the lace doily covering the sewing machine. What are you doing, Sara was bold enough to ask a girl the first time the beggars came calling. *Poshariu*, the girl replied. Rummaging, she said, parroting what she'd heard others say. Sara should mind her own business, or she would tell her name to Makhno, who would come and cut off her ears and tongue. That day, her grandmother gave the beggars a set of agateware pans and a new crock. On the way to the door, they helped themselves to various cooking utensils and an enamelled dipper. As soon as the door closed behind them, her grandmother put a dent in a remaining dipper to make it less appealing and wired it to the handle of the water pail. Then she took her china dishes from the cupboard and hid them in the attic.

The second time the beggars came straggling up the sidewalk, her grandmother saw them coming and sent Katya with Sara to the attic to wait for them to leave. Katya cleared frost from the window, welcoming the bite of cold against her fist, the meltwater trickling down her arm a brief respite from a constant numbness. Then she set her eye against the cleared glass and looked out at the village, ignoring Sara's whispered pleas to let her have a look, while downstairs objects were fondled and pilfered. Her grandfather's low voice beat against the attic floor as he followed the intruders through the house, her grandmother's voice sharp. Katya would see later that they dared to venture as far as the bedrooms at the back of the house. They had opened the door of the washstand in her grandparents' room, taken out the chamber pot to see what might be hidden behind it. They'd gone through Katya's and Sara's bureau drawers and stuffed their sleeves, Oma said, with bloomers, collars, and Greta's undervests. They tore open bundles of dried roses in the drawers, thinking there was other than scent inside them. They went into the summer room, with its large corner windows, where Katya had left her mother's hand mirror lying out on the windowsill. But her grandmother had rushed in before them, quickly hiding the mirror between pillows before they could see it.

She saw that in the village, the streets and yards were empty; roof tiles pressed through melting snow, and smoke lifted from chimneys all across the village, drifted through the clear sky and up the side of the snow-covered valley, where tree branches knit their stark winter patterns. She took in the grey-and-white landscape, the empty street marked with footprints, heard the heavy, dimmed voices of the thieves in the downstairs rooms, and felt the emptiness around her vibrating. She'd been told what a blessing it was that she'd run and hidden, and been spared sights that would have stayed with her for life. But it was her father, mother, Greta and brothers who were hiding, she thought. She could see where they had been, in the perfect footprints in the snow, the smoke rising from chimneys. They could choose to come out from wherever they were hiding, if only they wanted to. Their silence seemed a back turned against her, a door remaining closed, elongated colourless spots of sun-bleached sky that followed her wherever she went.

The beggars came that day prepared to take more than they could carry, she realized when wagons and carts began filling the empty street. The wagons followed them to houses they'd entered, waiting for them to emerge carrying a table, a butter churn, a washing machine. At the Siemens' house, three men struggled beneath the weight of a cream separator. Moments later she recognized her grandparents' sofa, their bed, still made up with its blankets, on a wagon going down the street.

The thieves had also taken her grandmother's bread-kneading pan, a wide two-handled shallow tin pan that Oma later saw out in the yard of a brick factory, lying on the urine-sprayed snow. It was being used to feed dogs, she said. They could afford to give food to dogs, yet, she said indignantly. But the next time she went looking for it at the brickyard, it was gone. Days later, she saw it again. She saw her bread-kneading pan come flying down a snowbank on the other side of the Chortitza creek, a small child riding inside it. It wouldn't hurt as much if the pan was being used for its intended purpose, she said. Her grandmother could forgive murderers, but she grieved and nursed grudges against waste and thievery.

"Go and get a stool and stand on it so we can measure," her grandmother said even before the seamstress finished drinking the glass of *prips* and eating the bun which she tore apart bit by bit, as though to make it last longer. "There's been enough talk to cause nightmares already."

As Katya stood on the stool, the women knelt on the floor, her grandmother scampering about on her hands and knees, as agile and quick as Njuta. Tina Funk calculated the number of inches the skirt needed to be lengthened in order to touch the tops of Katya's shoes, if that was the length Mrs. Schroeder thought the skirts should be. Yes, yes, that's what I think. Not above the ankle, Oma said. Not from this house. She didn't care if others were wearing their skirts that short.

Katya smiled inwardly, thinking that while her grandmother went about the day whistling hymns, and would sooner find something good rather than bad to say about a person, she judged women by the length of their skirts, and only one length was proper. Most of her growth must have happened when she was at Privol'noye, where not as much attention had been paid to the length of a skirt. But her new slenderness, the evidence of it in the buttons she'd moved on the waist of her petticoat and skirts, had come about, she knew, since she'd come to Rosenthal. She could feel her hip bones now, plates that she set her splayed fingers across as she stood on the stool.

When, later that day, Katya went about the village on errands, she was aware of her new height, and walked as though her centre of gravity had shifted, with the cautionary gait of a person about to venture across a patch of ice. She went up Main Street into Chortitza, counting the number of steps it took her to reach the *volost* offices, and turned there onto Hospital Street, going up to the post office, to collect the mail for her grandparents. A bell tinkled above the door when she entered what was the front room of a house belonging to a Little Russian family, one of few who had always resided in Chortitza. A chair creaked in a closet-sized room off the main room, which housed a telephone central operated by Valentina, the postmaster's daughter. As the young woman tilted her chair to see who had come in, her face appeared in the doorway.

Her grandmother commented that in the past Valentina would at least have made a show of going behind the wicket to peer into the appropriate letter slot, pretending that she hadn't already snooped to see who had received mail, and from whom. But now, apparently, the postmaster's daughter no longer bothered with pretense. It's as though they suddenly think they're better than us, her grandmother said to explain the change of attitudes of the few non-Mennonites who lived in the two villages.

She knew her grandmother would be disappointed that there hadn't been any mail, but she was relieved. She didn't want to receive yet another letter from Franz Pauls. Soon after the massacre at Privol'noye, he began to write to her, her former tutor assuming a brotherly role that she found offensive, as if he could even come near to filling in one of the spaces. His letters came to her from the Red Cross train, where he'd seen more than he could remember, he'd written to her, his tone world-wise and condescending. Then his train received orders to go to Warsaw to collect the wounded, and he obeyed his instincts when it stopped at a remote station to take on water. All day he had seen columns of infantry, children and women going in the opposite direction. Something told him the train would likely meet more than the wounded in Warsaw, and so he joined a soldier-nurse who had ostensibly stepped out onto the platform for a cigarette. He and the other man began to talk, and arrived at the same conclusion. They traded their uniforms for rags and joined the stream of people going east. Now his letters came to her from a village in the colony of Ignatyevo, where he had gone to join Helena Sudermann and the Baptists in their mission to evangelize the enemy. His letters became pious-sounding and full of reports of conversions and baptisms, the lost becoming found.

Sometimes she found herself hoping for a letter from Lydia, though she had no real expectation of receiving one. More and more she'd begun to wonder about her, and over the weeks had composed several letters, which she'd never sent.

Dear Lydia,

While I was in the hole in the ground the darkness was like coal and it was as though I had disappeared. I hugged Sara, but didn't feel anything, not her body, or mine. However, I did feel the cold air seeping through the straw, and in this way I knew I was in the hole and alive. I listened for sounds that would tell me what was happening outside, but it was as though that world had ceased to be. The dampness and darkness were overwhelming but I didn't want to be discovered because I feared the moment when the cover would be drawn aside, and I would see my father or the face of a murderer.

Dear Lydia,

They tell me that you were found wandering nearby Orlov's place. Did you see what happened? After they killed your mother, who was next? And then who?

Dear Lydia,

Can you tell me how it came about that Njuta was found in your father's office? She was blue with cold and her legs cut from crawling through broken glass.

Dear Lydia,
How are you?

With the exception of David, who, being a teacher and not considered bourgeois, the Sudermann brothers had fled to Ekaterinoslav, and when the Bolsheviks took over that city, they had gone to Spat, taking Lydia, Dietrich, and Barbara with them. Katya had heard that Privol'noye was going to ruin, as were other estates, had heard of a *gutsbesitzer* in the Second Colony who'd been robbed of ninety-five shirts and forty-seven pairs of shoes. His bake kitchen had been raided, cakes gulped down on the run, along with rings of sausages children had first wound about their necks. While the estate of Privol'noye had been taken over by peasant families, others had been abandoned, disappeared entirely when houses and barns were dismantled brick by brick and carted away to become dwellings in the new Russian villages that were beginning to spring up around the countryside.

She returned to Rosenthal on Main Street, once again counting her steps, how many it took for her to reach her grandparents' house. When viewed from across the street, the Schroeder house looked small. Pots of African violets and gloxinia lined the windowsills, their blossoms magenta and pink jewels. Her grandmother was known to have a hand with gloxinia, and hers were always in bloom. She knew her grandmother would have mourned the loss of a gloxinia plant more than she had the bread pan, and the loss of her bed. On losing the bed, she had pronounced that it was better to have no beds at all, God would only bless them more. She had replaced the bed with a sleeping bench, its wood groaning loudly when they climbed onto its unforgiving hardness.

A crisp wind tugged at Katya's skirt, and she felt the bite of it at her ankles. She wouldn't be able to tell her grandmother who'd been in the Penner store; when she'd gone by and looked in the window, what she'd seen was herself, shoulders bunched and arms slightly extended as though for balance, as though she expected to fall. A wagon went by in the street, going towards two dark figures, boys standing at the side of the road, watching the wagon approach. When she returned home she also would not be able to say who had called a greeting from the passing wagon. She remembered seeing a brown leather coat, a sheepskin hand rising.

The wagon was approaching the two boys who waited at the side of the street for it to pass. Or so she thought, because no sooner was the wagon upon them, when first one and then the other dashed in front of it – Johann and Peter, two fists slamming her in the chest. The wagon didn't hesitate in its forward movement; her brothers did not appear on the opposite side of the road, but had vanished. She realized water was seeping through her shoes, she was standing in a puddle of slush, holding her chest and gulping for air.

Her feet crunched through frozen puddles as she approached the Kanserovka creek and the community gardens beyond. She couldn't say if the weather was fitting for the end of April, or not. If the greyness was what they'd always experienced this time of year, the snowbanks along the Kanserovka creek caving in, chunks of snow pulled into the black water to become islands carried away by the spring current to the Dnieper. Already she had forgotten what to expect; the end of April in the New Style seemed the same as the old one had been.

When she stepped inside a large room at the front of Dr. Warkentine's house, she was aware of people seemingly piled up on the benches. A fetid odour billowed up and escaped out the door behind her, the odour of their unwashed bodies, illnesses and lethargy. Peasant children lay on the floor at their mothers' feet; older ones crouched like wild animals about to spring at her. She couldn't look at them directly, but she felt they regarded her with suspicion. Lensch Warkentine emerged from the pharmacy, the starched apron and skirt of her nurse's uniform as stiff as paper. When she explained to the people in the waiting room that Katya was a friend who had come on a visit, and not a patient, their suspicion changed to malevolent glares as Katya followed the doctor's wife into the pharmacy.

She had come for her monthly supply of iron pills, but she was not to be given them outright this time. Lensch Warkentine said she couldn't dispense the pills until Katya had seen either Dr. Hamm or her husband, agreed? She indicated that Katya should go sit on a stool beside a window and wait.

The two closed doors on either side of the pharmacy led to the examination rooms. Katya heard Dr. Warkentine talking behind one of the doors, and a man's halting reply, as though he were speaking with his mouth open. Eucalyptus oil burned in a metal dish which was suspended on chains above an alcohol burner that rested on a counter, its medicinal scent hardly dispelling the odour of the patients emanating from the waiting room. Lensch Warkentine and Auguste Sudermann were sisters, and the resemblance was strong in the woman's small sinewy body; in her hair, which she wore in a topknot; in her economy of expression. She was as stiff as her starched uniform, some said, unbending in her opinions, which she dispensed as efficiently as she did the ointments and liquid medicines to the "people of darkness" in the outer waiting room beyond, with succinct instructions that they were not to eat the salves, or smear the liquids on their lesions and boils.

As Katya waited, Lensch began to polish the glass doors of an almost empty wall cabinet behind the counter. She worked with a furious energy, her hand moving in quick tight circles as though she were angry. Like most women in the villages, Dr. Warkentine's wife had come to depend on the labour of Russian servants to lighten their household load, and suddenly they were without help.

Documents hung in frames on the wall beside the medicine cabinets, Dr. Warkentine's degrees, one from a university in Kharkov and another from Berlin. There was also a photograph of students sitting at tables in a classroom, a younger Warkentine among them. An inscription that said this was at the Feodosia Gymnasium, Feodosia being the largest city near the village of Ogus-Tobe, where the doctor had grown up beside the Black Sea. The story was well known of how one day he had been snatched by soldiers from a Chortitza street and made to serve in the Japanese war. Eventually he'd been taken prisoner, and during the experience had become bald, which made his bushy eyebrows and walrus moustache seem even blacker.

She hoped it would be him and not Dr. Hamm she would see, because Dr. Warkentine exuded a kindness; things had happened to him which he preferred not to talk about. On one of her monthly visits she'd seen Dr. Hamm, and had got bound up inside when he'd asked questions that had to do with the reason she required the iron tablets.

She suddenly became aware of a whining sound coming from outside, and growing louder. She pushed aside the curtain, and saw a man beyond the fence gazing skyward. Lensch set her cloth on the counter and came over to her. All at once, people in the waiting room got up and fled out the door. She watched them over Lensch's shoulder, the children running through the mud of the community gardens, followed by the adults, all of them struggling through the black pudding, going towards the reed beds along the Kanserovka creek.

She now saw what had frightened them, an airplane swooping low over Main Street, its wings tilting back and forth, looking as though they might brush against the treetops. As it passed overhead, its engine was like a hive of hornets, and then the sound flattened and gradually faded, and a quiet descended so that she could hear the hiss of the alcohol burner across the room. The people had stopped running now, and were turned towards the street as the silence was overtaken by a faint wash of sound that quickly grew louder. She saw metal flashing as a column of uniformed soldiers came riding, four abreast, their steel helmets bobbing. Behind them was a row of automobiles, the flag of Germany fluttering above gleaming fenders. Yet another momentous event was taking place. A treaty had been signed at Brest-Litovsk, and she would one day hear of it and of its far-reaching implications, remember that for a brief time life in the village had returned to near normal while she stood in the middle of the event, unmoved, the elongated spots of bleached sky hovering beyond the leafless trees more tangible than what was unfolding in the street.

Dr. Warkentine emerged from the examination room, the muscles in his face working as he came to the window and put an arm about his wife's shoulder; she had begun to weep. People were already hurrying to meet the German cavalry. Women still wearing their washday aprons, men in their barn overalls, came from yards, their children lining up along the street, Sara among them. Women had filled baskets with baking, and were offering it to the riders going by in the street. Others, like Lensch Warkentine, were weeping, aprons held to their faces. There was a noise behind them, and they turned to see the man Katya had heard in Dr. Warkentine's office, standing in the doorway looking on in bewilderment.

"Hans, come and see this – the Germans are here. I never thought I would say this, but I have to admit I'm glad to see them. Maybe those fellows will bring us some peace and order," Dr. Warkentine said.

The peasants hadn't returned to the waiting room, but had trudged up the valley and gone out across the windswept plateau, going back to wherever it was they had come from, poor souls, Dr. Warkentine later said to Katya. She sat on a chair as he drew down the skin beneath her eye, exposing the tissues to look for signs of her anemia.

"Are you still flowing as much?" he asked.

"The same." She wanted to tell him, they cut open the bedding, and feathers covered the ground like snow.

"Can you describe how much?" he asked.

No, she couldn't. She was shy to admit to the heat of it, the sodden cloths that needed to be changed hourly. She was aware of Lensch hovering in the background, her stiffness intact, her face closed; listening, she knew.

It was snowing. That's what I at first thought. Then Greta said it was the bedding. It's the bedding, Greta said. She had gone over and over the events of that early morning, and had realized that those had been her sister's last words.

He turned from her and went over to a basin, holding his hands over it, while Lensch trickled carbolic-smelling water from a jug over them.

"Do you pray often?" he asked as he washed his hands.

Did she ever pray? Did she pray, *forgive them*, as her oma had done? Did she pray, *let me not harbour anger, or entertain thoughts of vengeance. Help me to love my enemy*? She wondered if that was what lay behind Dr. Warkentine's question. "No," she said.

As she got up to leave, he lifted her hand and wrapped her fingers around a bottle of iron pills. "Try to pray. One word, that's all. Then next time, say two words, and so on, until your prayer is at least three minutes long. Sometimes prayer can be the best cure of all," he said.

When she returned along Main Street, she saw a wagon parked in front of her grandparents' gate. She saw it intermittently, through the passing of other wagons and carriages going by, people hurrying off to Chortitza, where the German cavalry had gone.

Sara came out of the Siemens' veranda, and Katya held her breath when she saw her crouch down, then propel herself through the air, jumping to the bottom of the steps. Only once had Sara asked, where are they? She'd looked up at the lip of the valley, and the dome of the Orthodox church, likely thinking of the cemetery lying beyond that church. They aren't there, Oma explained. Even though they had seen her mother, father, and brothers all in a row in their wooden cradles, seen them being lowered into the ground, they were somewhere else, above, alive, and waiting for a glorious family reunion.

Think of them as just being in another room, someone had said. Katya in one, and they in another. She thought of hearing the clank of a spoon against a bowl, a rustling of voices, on the other side of a wall. But the idea of them being in another room wasn't a comforting thought. Eternal happiness and hymn-singing in the presence of God and the angels while the living grieved amounted to callous indifference.

As Sara came through the Siemens' gate, she saw Katya and quickly pulled a scarf up onto her head. She had only just recovered from an ear infection, and knew better than to go outdoors without her ears protected against the wind. A scolding rose to Katya's tongue as her sister came running to meet her, but as Sara took her hand and began to chatter, Katya forgave her for being who she was, brave and eager, a puppy on the end of a tether, pulling Katya off in several directions at once.

Had she seen the Germans? Sara asked.

Ja, she'd seen them.

Weren't their helmets funny looking? Ohm Siemens said that the Germans and Austrians would make the bandits bring back their cream separator. They would order them to return Opa and Oma's bed, and the sofa, also. Young boys in the street had told her the Germans would whip the thieves and teach them a lesson not to steal, Sara said.

As they came near to her grandparents' house, Katya noticed that whoever the wagon belonged to had left his coat behind on its seat. Already the presence of the Germans made people feel safer, she thought. The brown leather coat looked familiar, and then she realized she'd seen it on the driver of the wagon that had gone by when she was on the way to the doctor's house.

Bull-Headed Heinrichs ducked as he came out the door of her grandparents' house, as though he thought himself tall and not a middle-sized man, which was what he was. A strong and sturdy-limbed man, whose broad hands were freckled, his knuckles scuffed and enlarged. It was his long face, bristly with gold whiskers, that had presented itself to Katya as the slatted covering of their hole in the greenhouse was lifted. She remembered how the insides of her thighs had stung as her bladder emptied with relief to be looking in the eyes of a Mennonite face. Sunlight shot through the glass roof, obliterating the darkness and the fumes of the mouldering earth, and she heard herself say *Danke, danke*, as he drew her up and out of the hole into clean air. She wept with the release of fear and held her stomach to contain her retching. As her eyes grew accustomed to the light, she saw him up to his hips in the hole, gathering a sleeping Sara into his arms.

Don't thank me, Bull-Headed said, his voice clotted and strange-sounding as he stood before her, Sara held against his chest. She was thanking God, she said. Don't thank anyone, he said, and as she looked across the yard he tried to block her view. She stepped around him and saw the Big House beyond, its shattered windows, a tattered strip of window curtain pulled through the shards of glass and trailing in a breeze. She saw the bodies of the dogs, their legs crooked as though they'd been struck down while on the run.

There were people, men, standing in a huddle near the back door of the Big House. One of them left the group and stooped over a mound lying on the ground, lifted the blanket covering it, and let it fall. Then she saw all of them, the large and small mounds beneath blankets, lined in a row. She ran to the far wall of the greenhouse, pressing her hands against the glass, wanting to see if anything under the blankets would move. Then she was running between tables of flats and potted plants, knocking them to the floor in her panic to find the door to the potting shed and outside, the way she had come when she had known exactly where that door was, her hands undoing the latch in the dark while Sara stood panting. But now, in daylight, she couldn't find it.

You don't want to go out there, Bull-Headed said. Sara began to wail, and Katya thought then that all of them might be gone. Her father the last to breathe, Bull-Headed would later tell her. Still alive when Bull-Headed had arrived at Privol'noye early that morning at Abram's request to sell him draft horses. Then he'd found them. Katya's father alive for long enough to say where she and Sara might be hiding, in a hole in the ground, but where it was, he hadn't the breath to say. There's a baby crying, she was inside the house, whose is it? Bull-Headed had asked Katya, and she knew then for certain that, of her family, only Njuta, Sara, and she had survived.

Now, as Katya waited beside the gate for Bull-Headed Heinrichs to come down the stairs of her grandparents' house and out the gate, Sara let go of her hand, and stared after him as he climbed up onto his wagon, her eyes becoming glittering blue agates, remembering, Katya thought.

When Katya came into the house, her grandparents were sitting on a bench in the parlour, silent, studying their hands, which rested in their laps. They looked up as she came past the door, and she knew immediately that Bull-Headed Heinrichs's visit had something to do with her.

That evening, she stood at a window peering through a veil of fog that had settled on the valley, thinking, This is the man who, twice now, has saved my life. Kornelius was his real name. Bull-Headed, he'd been called, because he refused to go to church following the death of his young wife. He'd asked her grandparents if he might come calling. What made him think Katya was the one for him, Opa had asked. Not everything needs an explanation, Kornelius said. Not everything, and not to everyone, her Opa agreed. But your desire requires an explanation, as Katya is ours, and so we're entitled to hear it. They wanted to hear that he'd reconciled his mind to God, but he refused to give them even the hope that he might do so in the future.

There will be others, Oma had said to Katya, as if Katya had set her mind on Kornelius and was in need of consoling. And in any case, it was too soon after, there would be gossip. Streetlamps and lights in windows were yellow smears of colour barely illuminating the snow in the street and yards as she stood looking out through the fog, emotionless, thinking that the man wanted her for his wife. She did not remember what she'd felt the day Kornelius Heinrichs had smiled at her at the train station. She thought of him wanting to marry her, though she didn't yet know what the act was that consummated a marriage.

The next morning the fog had lifted, and as she walked with her grandparents and sisters to church, it was through a world hung with lace. Ice crystals sparked iridescent fires, a brilliance that made her squint. The hoarfrosted trees and underbrush spread across the valley slopes like orchards in bloom.

The church service was at the halfway point when Katya heard a name being whispered, and then a rustle of clothing and creak of benches as people shifted in their seats. As the singing gradually faded, she turned and saw Kornelius striding down the centre aisle, his hat in place. In the moment of silence that followed, the air bristled. Then the *Ältester* stood up and went to the pulpit. Did Kornelius wish to speak? he asked.

No, he did not. He had come to listen, Kornelius said, and made a motion as though to sit down with the other men, but although there was space on the bench, those on the outside did not move over to make room for him.

There was a proper way for this to be done, the *Ältester* said. In order to be among them and to listen, Kornelius first had to come before the ministers and speak.

At that, Kornelius laughed and shook his head. I have twenty thousand rubles, he said. Will that be enough?

Katya heard gasps of shock, a rising murmur of voices; saw looks being passed around. The ministers, sitting on the front bench, Nela's old father among them, stood. Kornelius didn't wait to be escorted to the door, but left using the centre aisle, his hat still in place on his head. Separated from the church, and therefore separated from God. Trying to buy his way into heaven, Katya heard when she walked outside after the service, and then down the street, not wanting to linger, fearful that people might have made a connection between Kornelius's visit at her grandparents' house and his sudden appearance at church.

She was at the gate when a sleigh stopped in front of the house. Her grandparents and sisters had accepted a ride home with Olga

Penner and her father, and with them was Nela Siemens. They were about to go riding in the country – would Katya like to come? Nela asked. Her grandmother suddenly fussed with Njuta's bonnet, pretending that she wasn't praying that Katya would begin to take in some of the world around her and agree to go, while Njuta gazed into the empty air as though something had caught her attention. Who had taken her to Abram's office? Had it been an act of kindness, or a whim? Could she remember? Perhaps she was attuned to the invisible, hearing voices, a clink of a spoon against glass.

They left the village of Rosenthal, then Chortitza, the land still snow-bound from a late and recent storm that muted the sounds of the sleigh and harness bells and the sing of runners against the packed trail. She sat beside Olga, warm beneath a sheepskin. Nela faced them, her hands buried inside a muff, her sharp features softened by a fur muffler that covered her chin and met the edge of a muskrat-trimmed hat, her pale eyes shining as she looked down at Olga's black mongrel curled around her feet.

Katya had forgotten how satisfying it was to ride through the countryside. Their breath escaped in white puffs, which were pulled sideways and shredded by the wind. Barbara and Dietrich were going to have a baby, she learned from Olga. They would all change, grow older, while Greta remained the same. Beyond them, there was movement in a field, white moving on white, a rabbit bounding away, and then another. The dog got up onto its haunches and sniffed the air.

Rabbits, Olga shouted, and her father stopped the horses. The dog leapt out of the sleigh and ran across the field, going in one direction and then another, barely able to keep track of the rabbits that sprang out of a thicket of bushes, their ears pricked. Soon the dog became a black spot moving against white, until Olga called and the animal returned to them, its tongue bright red and mouth steaming. Laughing, Katya thought.

The sleigh followed a well-worn trail, which soon dipped into a shallow valley and curved round a pond, its surface stippled with the footprints of birds. Then they left the pond behind, and as they neared a group of houses, Olga's father urged the horses into a gallop. The houses were the beginning of a new Russian settlement, he told them.

Haystacks stood behind twig fences; there were goats in a yard, and a dog that yapped frantically as they approached. Then the sleigh emerged from the shallow bowl of land, and beyond them the countryside spread out flat and broad, the sky dropping to meet the tufts of yellow grass where the wind had skimmed the crests off snowbanks, flattened drifts, and exposed the frozen earth.

They were going to Arbusovka, Olga said. They would drive to the end of the village, where there had been a soap factory which had been shut down. Her father heard there were moulds stacked out on the yard. If there were any left, the boards and iron rods might prove to be useful.

As they went round a bend in the trail a broad street opened up, Main Street of Arbusovka, lined with the familiar red-brick houses with their arched attic windows and grey roof tiles. When they neared the centre of the village, Nela pointed out a buff-coloured stone house, a rambling low house partially covered in vines and trimmed dark green. That was Willy Krahn's place, where Greta stayed, she said. A wagon and sleigh were parked outside stone gate posts which flanked the entrance to a barnyard. As they approached the house, the door opened and Willy stepped out onto the platform. As though he'd been expecting them and watching, Katya thought as the man waved and called that they should come and stay a while. Olga's father pulled the horses back and as the sleigh slowed down, the dog jumped out and bounded over to the gate – deciding for them, Olga said, laughing.

The man's window curtains were plain white cotton, and not hand-painted with pictures, *a bright border of sunflowers; the next time he might surprise us with a geometric pattern, or vines*, Greta had written. Standing behind Willy in the doorway was David Sudermann, looking as hollow-eyed and worn-out as he had in church that morning. He pushed past the man and came down the stairs.

"There you are Heinz Penner, a toad among the roses," David called to Olga's father.

When he saw Katya, David's grin collapsed and he averted his eyes. Behind him came a greying stout woman – the widowed sister of Willy, Nela explained. Hanging onto her skirt was Frieda and Willy's child, a curly-haired girl with saucer eyes. Auguste and David's three daughters came skipping down the steps. They grabbed Olga by the hands and escorted her into the house, ignoring Nela, who looked on in bewilderment, her eyes pained.

When Katya went into the parlour, Auguste Sudermann rose to greet her with a dry peck against a cheek. There were several other women present. An elderly woman peered nearsightedly at a coat she was snipping apart at the seams, while others were mending and knitting. They nodded hello without missing a beat of their lively, intense conversation. Olga and Nela went from chair to chair, greeting each of the women in turn. They were putting together a box of clothing for refugees, Auguste explained. The circumstances were such that it was necessary they meet on a Sunday to do so. Across a hallway, the men had gathered in another room and as Olga's father and David Sudermann entered, the men's voices rose.

From the far reaches of the house came the muted sound of chirpings, what could be children's voices scratching against the walls, Katya thought as Auguste explained that a village near Arbusovka had been routed and women and children had come on foot across country, bringing only what they'd had on their backs. The women had arrived wet and shivering in their washday aprons and thin house dresses, their children without shoes and frostbitten. Several families whose houses were burned down or occupied had been taken into homes in Arbusovka until other arrangements could be made.

"Aren't you going say who this girl is?" Willy's sister asked Auguste moments later.

"Katherine Vogt. From Privol'noye," Auguste said, her cheeks flushing.

Katya felt the women's immediate stillness.

"Margareta's sister?" the woman asked, and when Auguste nodded, she set aside her handiwork and came across the room to engulf Katya in an embrace. Katya felt the heat of the woman's breasts and stomach, felt her own legs begin to shake, and she didn't want to let go of the woman for fear the others would see the tremble of her skirt. But the longer she allowed herself to be held, the worse the shaking became, until her entire body was caught in spasms of shivers.

"Would you like to see where your sister stayed while she was here?" the woman asked in a whisper.

She followed the woman out to the hall. The men looked up as she came past their door, their voices stopping in mid-sentence, smiles frozen, a brow becoming heavy, or, like David Sudermann, their eyes turning away as they became lost in a thought, a scene, a discomfort her presence aroused in them.

They went deeper into the house and she heard the clinking sound of glass being set down on glass, the tinkle of a spoon in a cup, a woman's voice, a child's reply coming from behind a wall. As they approached a closed door, Willy's sister stepped aside so Katya would be the first to enter the room. She turned the knob and pushed open the door. A woman sat at a table with children, their white faces turning to meet her. Her mother, sitting at the table, Gerhard, Johann, Peter, and Daniel with her. From somewhere far away she heard herself screaming, felt the floor hard against her back and her skull rocking against it. She heard the screams become cries, and then sobbing. Willy's sister knelt beside her, and then she felt the woman's weight against her body, her hands pressing against the sides of her head to keep it still, her arms holding and rocking her.

The people in the room where Greta had once stayed were refugees from the ransacked village near to Arbusovka, and not an apparition. Their presence had brought a release, and the feeling she'd had of being a stick of wood vanished. Her limbs became liquid, and too long for her body, and for a time she walked crookedly, bumped into door jambs and tripped on stairs. The sound of laughter in a street brought tears, as did sunlight touching a snow-covered roof, sparks of frost cartwheeling around her when she went walking.

In summer she would take her place among women hoeing in the community gardens, crouch to notice how weeds growing near to the carrots resembled carrots; potatoes, in the potato patch. She saw how vine weeds threatened to choke out the lentils, the grasp of their tendrils so strong she had to cut the vine rather than pull it and risk uprooting a bean. She stopped weeding to listen to the coo of a mourning dove in an evergreen tree, warblers singing in an oak grove on the slope of the valley. When summer arrived she was sixteen, and although she sometimes appeared to be far-away, it was because she chose to be. She had begun writing in her notebook once again.

KREJKELMOOSS

My mother's recipe, as given to me by Oma Schroeder

damsons plums or prunes (if using prunes, add a few handfuls of raisins)
water to cover
enough starch to thicken
sugar to taste
cream if you have it

If using fresh fruit, scald and remove skins and stones. Boil with water and sugar. Be patient when you add the starch mixed with cream, or there will be lumps. If you use red plums, it will turn out differently.

The primroses are blooming.

My dear nephew Dietrich, and brother Isaac,

Jakob Klassen arrived safely yesterday and immediately delivered your parcel. I received it in good condition, and with thanks. It is indeed a blessing to find ourselves the benefactors of Abram's foresight, and thanks to the presence of the Whites in Spat, the funds are still intact. But for how much longer, I wonder?

At first we were told that cheques would be accepted, and then not. Those of us who had already sent cheques to Alexandrovsk also learned that they wouldn't be returned. Which is how I suddenly found my funds depleted and myself facing our delegation who expected yet another donation to take to the extortionists. What a scandal if a Sudermann was seen to have failed to contribute to the rescue of our Chortitza *Ältester*. On top of it, Mary and Martha Wiebe's father came to see me, looking rather the worse for wear. According to his account, Abram owed his daughters a year's wages. I had no way of knowing if that were the case or not, but I gave him what little I had and he went away satisfied.

The two million rubles has finally been scraped together, thanks to the efforts of the delegation who travelled throughout the entire colony asking for donations. The delegation will go to Alexandrovsk tomorrow with the last instalment, and should return the same day bringing our *Ältester* with them. I'm grateful for your generous response, as I wouldn't want the demise of our pope laid on my conscience (as the extortionists pointed out when they took him away).

If anyone else from our colony were held for ransom, we'd be hard-pressed to meet the extortionists' demands, as we've been bled dry. The Reds don't believe this; the bandits, either. They think our resources are unlimited. First the Bolsheviks came demanding a quota of guns. Some people went out and purchased guns in order to fill that quota. Now taxes, requisition, redistribution, outright extortion, whether coming from the hand of the Reds, Whites, Petliurists or Makhnovite bandits, has taken all of our cash, and most of our belongings and resources. In this way they force us to our knees and will keep us there.

When Klassen delivered your parcel he came with a story which has brought home a truth. In Einlage, bandits lined a father and his sons up against a wall, and were threatening to shoot them. Present in the room was a girl – I should say a young woman – and she, naively thinking she could save her family, carried an infant in her arms and walked back and forth between her family and the bandits. The noble young woman thought that as long as she did so, the bandits wouldn't risk firing. She, in her purity of spirit, which our young women so endearingly possess, was appealing to their higher nature. She thought she perceived in them a spark of decency; that they were not yet immune to pity. But they proved to be the animals they really are, and shot her dead. We're in danger when we regard these men as being human. If they are, then they're possessed by evil spirits.

More and more, my sense of humour fails me. But here is a recent incident: the other day the soviet called a meeting. All men between the ages of eighteen and fifty-five years were required to attend. The leader of the soviet, Fedor Sawchuck, a man who used to sweep floors in Koop's factory, said we were to divide into two groups. The bourgeoisie should go to one side of the auditorium, the proletariat to the other. When no one made a move to divide, he kept pleading over and over, Comrades, comrades, won't you please cooperate. Who among you are bourgeoisie? Of course no one ventured to raise his hand. You see, the soviet had decided that there should be some ditch-digging. What the ditch was needed for wasn't clear. It appeared that they wanted the so-called bourgeois to dig for the sake of digging.

A discussion began over the exact meaning of the words proletariat and bourgeois. Someone pointed out that the workers now owned as much, and in some cases had more possessions, than the people they once worked for. The workers had become the bourgeoisie, not? The poor befuddled Fedor couldn't keep order. In desperation he went to the telephone central to call headquarters in Ekaterinoslav to get the meaning of the two words.

In the meantime we waited in the *Mädchenschule* auditorium as instructed. We could hear the girls in a classroom below us reciting Maikov's poem "The Hay Harvest." Someone began mimicking their recitation, and then another took it up in earnest, ". . . The poor old horse who draws the cart stands rooted in the heat, with sagging knees and ears apart, asleep upon his feet." Many in the room knew the poem, and we recited the final verse, proletariat and bourgeoisie alike, half-singing the words, "But little Zhuchka speeds away in barking brave commotion, to dip and flounder in the hay as in a grassy ocean."

When Fedor returned, we got down to business. It was decided that although I was a school worker, because my brothers owned factories I was a bourgeois. Just as I went to pick up a shovel, it was noted that I had been in military service, and so my name was struck from the list. So my dear nephew Dietrich, and brother Isaac, at the end of the day I found that I was neither one nor the other. You see what madness we must endure, and on a daily basis.

As to your enquiry about the Vogt girls, I see them from time to time, mostly at church. Whenever I have the occasion I speak to Katya, she seems well enough, but rather withdrawn, which, given the circumstances, is understandable. We can only continue to hope that one day she'll be whole again. In my opinion that would be a miracle. Auguste and the other women have been trying to draw her out of her shell.

Please give my greetings to Jakob. Tell him that while I agree that we must put our trust in God, I also put my trust in that which I failed to surrender, quota or not. You would be wise to do the same. If the times should dictate that we join you in Spat, then we will do so. In the meantime, the education of our children is of utmost importance. When this madness ends, they, at least, will be ready to take their place in this world.

Auguste sends her warmest regards to you, Dietrich, and to your dear wife, Barbara. I understand that you will soon be blessed with one of your own. A fifth grandchild for my dear brother Jakob, which should please him well.

Your uncle, and brother,
David Sudermann

*K*atya came up the stairs to the attic, and knew by the stillness that the silkworms had reached the end of their fourth period of feeding. The worms would be reared up, their glossy black heads fixed in a trance as they dreamed their new skins. One more week of feeding and their silk glands would be ready to produce. As she stepped up into the room, the sound of band music coming from the town of Chortitza grew stronger. The windows in the attic were open at either end of the room to clear the air, and had been ever since her grandfather had set the eggs to hatch on the feeding bed. However, the days had been too heavy with humidity to allow for a crossdraft to clear the odour, which was both sweet and sour. The smell had seeped into the rooms below the attic, prompting her grandmother to say that, had she remembered what a strong smell the worms gave off, she might have had second thoughts about revisiting such a venture. But thread was scarce; out of necessity, old skills were being revitalised.

Her grandfather had constructed the feeding bed, a rectangular wood frame set on legs, with a wire grid bottom which allowed the worms' refuse to drop onto paper spread across the floor. Refuse which she took away, twice a day. He'd bought clusters of minuscule pearly eggs from Penner's store, and set them on mulberry leaves to incubate in the heat of the attic. Within a week, the bed was crawling with what looked like bristly pieces of black wire with large heads.

Katya had brought fresh mulberry leaves for the silkworms and now began spreading them overtop the old leaves, which glistened with the threads the worms secreted when they'd made their short journeys from leaf to leaf. She knew that tomorrow the worms would be released from their trance and wearing their new skins like wrinkled stockings, the attic filled with the sound of their feeding, a sound like rain against the roof. Over the weeks the worms had become beautiful, their pleated bodies thick and cream-coloured, and holding a sheen. The sound of band music rose above the rustle of fresh leaves as she emptied the sacks, the scuffle of paper as she gathered it from the floor.

All the hot summer of 1918 there had been weekly military band concerts, and the sound of brass instruments made her throat constrict; the hollow thump of a bass drum seemed to mark her steps as she moved through the rooms of the house. The entire summer had the air of a celebration – the band music; victims of thievery riding with the troops to reclaim what had been stolen from them, returning in a high mood, their wagons filled, trailing livestock that raised a cloud of dust and bawled when familiar barnyards came into sight. The concerts always began with the hymn "Groszer Gott, Wir Loben Dich," and in her mind she could see the band assembled under the old oak tree on chairs arranged in a semi-circle by people living near to the tree, young women whose fairness entranced the German and Austrian men.

The soldiers were billeted in homes in both towns. The seamstress Tina Funk had several staying with her, and she had reported that they were taken by the immaculate gardens and swept paths, the wholesome cleanliness of the houses and barns, which made them nostalgic. Such a sight they never imagined possible, German villages in Little Russia similar to their own. The Mennonite women reminded them of their mothers and sisters. They'd held a Ludendorf festival, which proved to be a day of picnics, music, and games of soccer. All were invited to attend, bringing a warning from the *Ältester* in church, that young women must not be allowed to go. But several had attended the festivities, and took part in an evening of dancing, and the following day, rumours abounded that couples had gone walking in the oak grove after dark, which brought an upset to the streets as great as that of the previous spring, when cannons had shelled them from Alexandrovsk, across the river.

During the festival, she'd sat with Nela on the Siemens' veranda after dark, listening as the band played Viennese waltzes, the music faint until carried to them by a gust of wind in brief flares of sound. The war had brought the outside world into the centre of the colony, German and Austrian men in their spotless, tailored uniforms, shoulders squared as they strolled along the streets of the towns, stopping to bow over the hand of a woman. She suspected that in comparison to these bright, shiny soldiers, their own boys and men had begun to look homespun to the women who were recipients of the soldiers' compliments.

Moths had buffeted the veranda screens trying to get in, and she thought they were smelling the odour of the silkworms on her clothing. She would one day see photographs of the silkworm moths, their feathery antennae, their bow-tie wings that were powerless to lift their velvet body. She would learn about pheromones, an odourless perfume that signalled the female moth was ready to mate, and brought the males to her in a fluttering frenzy. What if Kornelius were not separated from the brethren, and her grandparents gave him permission to approach her, she suddenly wondered. And she in turn gave him permission to come calling. She was expected to bestow a kiss at such a moment, but she didn't know what lay beyond the kiss. When she thought of Kornelius Heinrichs, his strong and stocky body, fair skin, the red curly hair at his wrists, she felt nothing more than gratitude. She sat out on the veranda with Nela Siemens, listening to the dry flutter of wings against the window screens, and, as though her heart-soft friend had read her mind out of nowhere, Nela said that she'd noticed a certain person had come calling in spring, and she hadn't seen him since.

"*Ja*, that's so," Katya said. Everyone in the village knew as much, and likely more than she, about Kornelius's visit.

"They say that when Kornelius's wife died, his heart was bent,"

Nela said. Everyone knew the sad story. Kornelius, while on a trip to Switzerland, had been smitten by love and returned home with his bride. He had built a house for her on a hill outside the village of Arbusovka, a two-story wood house in the style of the Swiss. They'd been married less than a year when his young wife went visiting in a nearby village. On the way home, she met up with a band of hooligans, and, frightened, she foolishly turned her horses from the road to go across land. One of the horses stumbled into a rabbit hole, and the carriage tipped.

She knew Nela hoped for a reply that would give her a clue to what she was thinking.

"Some are saying that Kornelius Heinrichs believes because he was close by when you were in danger, you and he are meant to be. In my opinion, when he came to church, he should have been allowed to stay."

In the silence that followed, Katya mulled over Nela's startling words, *you and he*.

"I was there that day, too. I was in danger, too," Nela said softly.

She realized Nela was referring to the day at the train station when the madman Trifon had attacked them. She was relieved now to learn that not everyone knew Kornelius had found her and Sara, and taken them out of the hole. That he had found Lydia wandering in a field beyond the Orlov estate. She reached for Nela's hand, and held it.

Now, as she cleared away the soiled papers from under the silk-worm-feeding table, she heard the military band playing "Ich hatt' einen Kameraden," and knew that the concert was about to end. The band would leave the semi-circle of chairs and march back to the churchyard, where they had earlier mustered. She stood still, listened as, through the marching song, voices rose from a room below. Moments later Oma's voice filled the stairwell as she called for Katya to come downstairs. She should fix herself, and then come to the parlour, as they had visitors.

When she went down the stairs, Sara was waiting for her. She held up a doll she'd been reverently cradling. The doll's features were scratched and mottled where its paint had peeled, but Katya recognized the dress and bonnet as one she'd sewn.

"Franz Pauls brought it to me. Tante Lena is here, also." Sara said.

Katya went to her bedroom and poured water into a basin. Her hands shook as she cupped the tepid water and dipped her face into it, cooling her cheeks. When she went to the bureau for a fresh blouse and apron, she was stopped at the sight of the middle drawer, which had been left open when she was certain it had been closed, a crumple of silk stockings, a heel scuffed and rounded, still holding the shape of Greta's foot. Sara, she thought. Like her, wanting the scent of Greta, tangible proof that Greta had not been a dream.

She stood before the window in her room as she tied her apron strings and watched her aunt Susa at the water pump, her children standing and waiting for the pail to fill so they might carry it for her. In the distance the ridge of the valley met the sky, wild roses growing up its gentle slope a smudge of pink among variegated green. Rosenthal was home now, the other had been put far enough away that it didn't often come back to her, except in her dreams. She dreaded having to face part of it now.

When she entered the parlour, her grandparents turned towards her simultaneously, their faces brightening as if to say, Here she is at last. There was Franz Pauls across the room sitting on a sofa, and Helena Sudermann beside him with Njuta on her lap, turning the pages of a storybook.

She could see at once how Helena had aged, and that she was dressed all in black, as though in mourning. She had become a Baptist, but still wore the Mennonite *haube*, and, she noticed, Helena was without her moustache. The skin of her upper lip was smooth and shiny, as though the hairs had only just been soaped and scraped off with a razor. Katya tried not to stare, thinking that the woman's face looked bland without it, her jaw longer and heavy, eyes more deeply set in her head.

"Katya," Helena said.

Her voice was filled with sorrow that seemed to demand a response of tenderness. Once upon a time Helena had said, You and I are alike. Helena had let a bird out of a cage, and Katya had thrown a cup in a well. The consequence of Helena's act was a bird killed by the weather. Katya had confessed before God and man, and still, she'd been punished. She'd been punished with silence.

"Katherine," Franz said to Helena, correcting her.

Her grandmother nodded as if to say, You see, I told them. They're to call you Katherine, and not Katya.

Yes, Katherine, she thought. She had emerged from the hole fully grown.

Franz got up from the bench and came to greet her, his hand extended. Then his foot caught on a curled edge of a runner in the centre of the floor, and he flew across the room, and beyond her. He landed on his hands and knees in the parlour doorway, which Sara was about to enter. When Sara recovered from her astonishment, she stooped to peer into his face.

"He doesn't have cow eyes," she pronounced to the room.

Helena's hand flew up to cover her mouth, and her shoulders began shaking with suppressed laughter.

Laughter bubbled up from Katya's stomach, huge sounds breaking at the back of her throat, her body caught in spasms, and she had to hold her stomach while Franz got up from the floor, dusted his knees and returned to the sofa. When at last she was able to stop laughing, her knees were shaking, and she had to sit down.

"Well now, let me see what I can find," her grandfather said loudly, filling the ensuing silence. "Now that everyone is here at last, let's see what old Opa can find, eh? I think I must have something – do I, Oma?" he asked, turning to her and winking.

Njuta's storybook dropped to the floor as she slid from Helena's lap and ran to him.

Katya's sisters went with her grandfather to a corner cupboard, where he took a key from his waist pocket and fitted it into a keyhole on a cabinet door. He took down a sack of roasted pumpkin seeds. Then, reaching far into the recesses of the cupboard, he brought out a cube wrapped in brown paper that was slick with oil.

"Halvah," Sara said with a sigh of pleasure.

"Go to the kitchen," their grandmother began to say, but before she could finish, Sara and Njuta had left the room to fetch a knife and a plate. She went over to the curled-up spot in the sisal runner, muttering as she stamped on it, as if to punish it for having curled, while the red-faced Franz looked on.

"So, Katherine, why don't you tell us what you've been doing," Franz said, his voice brisk, Sara's comment no doubt still lingering in his mind.

When she told him about the silkworms, he was eager to see them.

As they went up the stairs to the attic, she dreaded each step that took them farther away from the others. She feared he would have a message, that he might use this opportunity to assume his teacher's role and come alongside her with words of encouragement, which she didn't require, or want.

Because she had just put down fresh mulberry leaves, the worms were covered, and there was little for him to see. She explained why the silkworms were motionless, and he nodded enthusiastically and made noises of interest, but she knew his mind was somewhere else.

The thick heat of the attic made him sweat, and beads of perspiration broke and ran down the side of his neck over the red swellings he had there. The beginnings of boils, she thought. He removed his jacket and tucked it under an arm, pulled a handkerchief from his trouser pocket and began dabbing at his forehead.

When she had finished explaining the silkworms' cycle, their voracious feeding, growth and shedding of skin, she started to leave the room, but Franz went over to the window and the crate of china dishes on the floor.

He squatted and picked up a plate, and with his handkerchief wiped dust from it. Sara's doll had been given to him by Sophie, he said. She had begun to attend their tent services, and seemed to have a hunger for the gospel.

Sophie's conscience had caught up to her, Franz Pauls said. And went on to tell Katya what she already knew, that Sophie, along with the other wives, the children of the workers, had run off to Lubitskoye at the appearance of Pravda and his men.

"At first she said they were afraid. Then she admitted that they'd gone there to wait for word that they could come and move into the Big House. But she never once thought . . ." Franz Pauls said, letting the sentence go unfinished. "Apparently she was inconsolable, and couldn't eat or sleep for days."

"So then she's at Privol'noye," Katya said, wanting to keep her voice flat, but her eyes had grown moist with tears. Her grandparents had kept gossip from reaching her, she knew.

"Sophie? No, but her family's there. Sophie refused. And Kolya went off to join the Makhnovites," Franz Pauls said. Rumour had it that he'd been seen in Ekaterinoslav in a hotel that had become Makhno's headquarters.

And Vera? Katya wondered.

Franz set the dinner plate back into the crate. Some people were burying china in their gardens, he went on to say. Winter clothing, silver, bedding. They thought burying was safer than hiding things in the attic and hayloft. "But the brutes seem to possess a devilish instinct that tells them where to dig for the buried treasure," he said.

She studied him, took in his apparent satisfaction at knowing these things, as though the knowledge increased his stature, and she realized that his comment had been made without thinking about her, that he hadn't been referring to the buried treasure in Abram Sudermann's garden.

"Well, Katherine, won't you at last tell us what happened?" he asked after a moment of silence.

He, along with everyone else, knew more about what happened that day than she did, she would one day come to learn. Most people would have read the account of the massacre in the *Odessaer Zeitung* that her grandparents had kept from her, a vivid description which she later read in archives, *All of the victims had either been shot or had their throats cut. Gerhard Vogt was found slain on a field near a haystack, where it is believed the bandits caught up with him as he attempted to escape.*

And yet, when her father's brothers had come to see her after the funeral, they had expected she would tell them more. When later she recalled the questions they had put to her, their questions seemed, in the light of the present day, almost preposterous. Had her father raised his hand against the men? Did he defend himself, or anyone else? She couldn't reassure them that this had not been the case. She couldn't ease their minds, tell them that her father had turned the other cheek while his wife and children were struck down. And so she had told them what little she knew. He'd tried to defend them with words. Tried to get them away from the scene by saying they would milk the cows. He'd tried to defuse Pravda with an invitation to come for a meal.

"Katherine, won't you tell me about Lydia? Was Lydia laid on the ground, too?" Franz asked, his voice lowered and cajoling.

She was confused, rooted by the phrase he'd used, and couldn't repeat it. She could only ask, "Too?"

At her question, he drew inward and stuffed his handkerchief into his pocket. Then he went over to the feeding table, becoming lively and jovial, rocking on his heels, his teacher's enthusiasm for the silk-worm venture taking over. As though he hadn't asked her about Lydia, and left her muddled and worrying over the phrase he'd used.

When they returned to the parlour the table had been set for *faspa*, the samovar was heating water, and on the table were plates of buns and ham, a dish of apricot jam. The halvah was sliced and arranged on a plate.

As they talked, Katya only half-listened, thinking, *laid on the ground*, a phrase she'd heard whispered between women, its connotation ugly and something to be feared. She heard Franz tell her grandparents that Tsar Nicholas, the tsarina, and all their children had been murdered. She felt the room go still, heard water simmering in the samovar, saw steam curl from the spout of the teapot. If they can kill the tsar, then who is safe? Helena said, repeating a question that, wherever she went, she said, people were asking.

"There's the new Mennonite look," Franz later said with a wry-ness, as he and Helena were about to leave. Young men no older than Gerhard would have been came marching down the street. They were being drilled by a German officer in the rudiments of marching before going off to the Second Colony to join the *Selbstschutz*, a self-defence unit of young men. Her grandfather looked on, shaking his head. "Those who live by the sword," he said, and turned away.

"Some of those fellows are going around boasting how they're going to knock out teeth. Maim and pulverize, which doesn't sound like self-defence to me," Franz Pauls said.

"Violence begets violence," her grandfather said. "Wait and see."

Katya waited until evening, after she had set a basin of water on the floor and sponged her sisters' bodies clean and washed their feet. When she was sure they were asleep, she went to the family room where her grandmother sat at the table mending, and Opa across from her, a wooden box set before him, its lid open, and what looked to be letters and photographs spread around him on the table.

"What does it mean when a woman is laid on the ground?" She knew if she had taken the time to sit down, her courage would have left.

Her grandmother's eyes darted from one thing to another, and her jaw began to work. She set aside the shirt she'd been mending as though she suddenly didn't have the stomach for darning. Opa glanced at her sharply overtop his reading glasses, got up, and left the room.

"I pray you'll never know," her grandmother said.

"Franz Pauls asked if Lydia had been laid on the ground," she said. Familiar faces looked up at her from the photographs spread across the table.

"Oh, I see. Franz Pauls wants to know. He's snooping around. He's still trying to catch a big fish, and he wants to make sure that Lydia is good enough," her grandmother said, her chest heaving with a sudden anger.

"He asked me if Lydia had been laid on the ground, too. What did he mean by 'too'? Did he mean Greta?" she asked. The Wiebe sisters, her mother? She didn't ask.

Her grandmother closed her eyes, and then cradled her forehead with her hands, motionless for moments. She got up and left the room then, and Katya heard the pantry door close behind her.

She picked up a photograph, and held it to the light of the lamp. Greta, Lydia, Barbara and Mariechen Sudermann in their school uniforms, gathered around a pedestal and an open book. Greta's chin was lifted, her gaze direct with a self-assurance that she had only just gained. The more Katya studied the photograph, the more difficult it became to picture the Greta she remembered, the tilt of her head just before she would ask a question, the light shining from her eyes.

She was awakened in the night by the creak of footsteps as her grandfather went down the hall. She heard him pleading softly for her grandmother to come out of the pantry, and to bed. He returned to his room alone, a ghostly figure in a long nightshirt going past her open door with a heavy sigh. In the morning when she came into the family room her grandmother emerged from the pantry, haggard and pale, but whistling a hymn. Without glancing in her granddaughter's direction, she stopped whistling to say, "There are some things we don't talk about," and went to the stove to set water to boil.

∎∥∎∥∎

In autumn the silkworms began to spin, their heads moving in patterns of figure eights as they threw off loops of silk, an iridescent stream flowing from their spinnerets, hardening like glass as it met the air and became the ribs of their sleeping chambers. Within two days the silkworms' encasements were too thick for her to see the shadowy figures inside, the gradual and final shedding of their skins, the nutshell pupae emerging. While she knew it was necessary, she was reluctant to harvest the cocoons, set them into bake pans and into the oven to roast like seeds. It took her and her grandfather several days to soak the baked cocoons in pails of soapy water, to find where to begin to pick at a string, and unravel a mile of silk thread, leaving behind the shrivelled pupae, brown debris floating in the water.

Throughout the late autumn, crickets chirped beneath the platforms of the houses and under the doormats. She heard the clap of beans in the watchman's rattle as he came down the street and went past the house. The sound was meant to relay the message: I am here, all is well. Lo, I am with you. She might have taken up that thought and asked, Where was the night watchman when the knock came at our door? For her to question the existence of God was unthinkable. If she had been a man, calloused by the killing of beasts, the unforgiving hardness of the earth and heat of the sun, she might have thought to blame God for being uncaring, or asleep. She'd been born a female, been given a soft body and hands, born to be a helper, a representative on earth of God's gentler side.

*I*n mid-November, her grandfather brought the news home, following a meeting at David Sudermann's house, that armistice had been declared. A date when, years later, she would see a poppy pin on a lapel and realize why her body felt heavy, why the list of chores she had given herself to do that day would not be completed. A day that had brought cautious hope to the people around her, but that, to her, had little meaning.

Her grandfather had attended a meeting for prayer and a discussion, mediated by Nela's father, Ohm Siemens. When Katya went to hang Opa's coat in a cupboard she saw the elderly Ohm Siemens across the street climbing down from his wagon and going over to the barn gate to open it. She saw Nela on the veranda step. She sensed that Nela was watching her as she had been watching Ohm Siemens; all of them watching and waiting for what would happen next.

The time had come for meetings while they could still meet safely, as now that the armistice had been declared, the retreat of the Austrian and German armies would soon be complete, her grandfather said. "Did we think that they were going to stay here forever?" he asked himself aloud. Throughout the war they had denied being German sympathizers, and then had welcomed the Germans as long-lost relatives, a fact that hadn't gone unnoticed. He had brought the wooden box of letters and photographs into the family room with him and set it on the table. He wanted to write a letter to a cousin living in Manitoba, Canada, a relative who had left Russia with the Bergthal villagers over forty years ago. But he was too agitated, his shaking hands wouldn't allow it, and so he asked Katya to write it in his stead.

"Greetings to all my cousins and what other relations who may still remember my dear father with kindness. Many thanks for the photograph you sent. Sincere greetings, in love.

"Now you are wondering I'm sure, why it has taken me so long to answer your letter. You are correct in assuming that the turmoil of the past year has taken up most of our anxieties and thoughts. Our grandchildren continue to live with us as you surmised. How long we will be able to provide safety and comfort for them is a question that lies heavy on my heart. For this reason I am writing to ask you to pray for us."

Most of the German and Austrian troops had left the colonies in early autumn, and the remainder retreated before the first snowfall, a three-day blizzard which buffeted the house. It was as though the storm had swept their protectors away, leaving in its wake knee-deep waves of snow that looked solid, as if sculpted from marble, and made the streets impassable.

Katya went outside and began shovelling a path across the barnyard. Her aunt Susa was due to deliver a third child, and she reasoned that the way to the house should be cleared. Her uncle Bernhard must have seen her, as he came now from his house with a shovel. The path they carved through the snow merged halfway across the yard, and he smiled, his eyes softening in appreciation. She stood on the cleared path leaning on her shovel, a slender and tall figure in dark grey, the snowbanks on either side of her as high as her thighs. A scarf covered her head and the bottom of her face, ice particles matting the wool around her mouth and nose. When she had played in winter with Greta and Lydia, they would sometimes inhale deeply and pinch their nostrils to see who could hold their breath the longest, a spurt of white frost coming from a mouth betraying the cheater. She learned that it was better not to cheat; it was better to be still, to think of something other than breathing.

She leaned on the handle of the shovel, glad to have remembered a happy moment, realizing that she had stopped telling God that enough time had passed. The departed had played their trick long enough, and it was time they returned home. She followed her uncle Bernhard's gaze to the slope of the valley where children were mounting a hill to go sliding, Sara and Njuta among them, their footholes in the snow holding blue shadows.

"It's good that the children still know how to laugh," her uncle said. His words surprised her, as he had spoken to her as an equal. What he said was true. Everyone went out of their way to shield the children from fear and worry. Olga Penner's parents had almost perished while journeying to Alexandrovsk during the blizzard in order to buy the Christmas toys and fare children would expect to see in their store before the holiday.

All of winter the children spent hours sliding down the hill, and skating on a patch of ice Tina Funk's husband kept cleared on the Chortitza creek. Katya watched them from a pantry window, a small window that had recently been set into the back wall of the house. Her grandmother had requested the window. She didn't want to chance being surprised by a stranger coming to the house through the backyard when she was working in the pantry. She wanted to be able to see the children at play.

A table stood before the window, and one day Katya was at the table about to mix a batch of biscuits for their supper. She spooned fat from the jar and shook it onto the flour in the bowl. Beyond the window the children skated and slid on the creek, Sara, Njuta, and their cousins among them. They were dark stick figures set against the snowy creek bank, their arms and feet propelling them across the ice and away from the footbridge. They would round a curve of red willows and disappear from sight, moments later reappearing as they returned to the bridge to circle, and to warm themselves beside a bonfire that Funk, the train crossing guard, kept going beside the footbridge. That the man had found the necessary energy to do so had come as a surprise to everyone.

She picked up a spoon that was so light, it almost flew from her hand. The utensil reminded her of the tin spoons which had been chained to the tables in the workers' quarters in Privol'noye. She thought of her grandmother sitting on a chair in the family room, her feet hooked through its rungs to anchor herself to it, as though she were as inconsequential as the spoon and in danger of flying away.

She heard a door opening at the front of the house, feet stamping on the mat, Nela calling, "Where are the children?"

The children's voices had come to Katya in fragments while they played on the creek, as had the chirping of sparrows clustered in a bush beyond the window. She saw the sparrows lift up from the bush and flitter away, heard a sharpness in Nela's voice as she came through the hall calling, "Are the children outside?" She stood in the doorway of the pantry looking in at Katya, panting, her face constricted. "Papa said to warn you there are men, riders, coming towards the town."

Katya looked across the creek and saw that the children were gone. My biscuits, she thought, and then dropped the spoon. She raced down the hall, grabbing a cloak on the run, and out the back door, flinging the cloak about her shoulders as she ran across the yard towards the creek, Nela behind her. She neared the bridge and began to hear the sound of the riders, an echo skating along the ice, then turned and saw them coming down the hill into town, a hoard of insects in an array of colours, on horseback, in *tachankas*, *droschkes* and farm wagons, light glancing off the riders' bayonets and swords as they rode alongside the telegraph and telephone lines. She thought she would remember for as long as she lived that flash of wire, a silver arc as tension was suddenly released and the wires whipped up as if they too were blades, slashing at the air before coming down, one by one. This was a story she would tell her children, to keep from telling the other. Although she had been much too far away to be able to see, she knew how the wires had arced and flashed silver.

The children must be hiding, she said breathlessly as Nela came up beside her on the bridge. She pointed to their footprints along the bank, going up into the willow bushes where the snow was deep. She saw her grandfather appear in the entrance of the barn door, his frantic gesturing that they should stay away. There was no movement among the willows, no indication that the children were there; the footprints, the scarred ice, the remains of the smouldering bonfire would look as though the children had finished playing, and all gone home. She reluctantly gave into Nela's urging that they should hide under the bridge.

She felt as though they had spent hours under the footbridge, but it must have been less than an hour, otherwise they would have been frostbitten. The sun hadn't set when she saw her uncle Bernhard come running from the barn in his limping, uneven gait across the barnyard to his house. Moments later two men appeared with her grandfather at the barn door. Then the men, carrying guns, set off towards her uncle Bernhard and aunt Susa's house. A window at the back of the house opened and Bernhard pushed himself through it and dropped to the ground. He ran across the frozen creek, up its bank and into the bushes.

Soon after the sun waned, and the creek was cast in shadows that she and Nela crept through, they went to the children. When she called, their faces appeared above the willows. Njuta's round face, and the cheeks of several other children, were streaked with wet.

Within moments she saw someone hurrying along the creek towards them. Nela, recognizing the stooped figure of her father, went to meet him. They should come home now, he called, and Katya saw his relief and surprise to see so many of the town's children with her as they came through the willows down to the creek.

She couldn't stop the children from running to the stout old man and clustering about him. He cautioned silence, and they grew silent. He touched their shoulders and heads as though counting and blessing them at the same time. He and Nela would lead the other children back into the village, taking a circuitous route to avoid Main Street, believing what later proved to be true, that the best they could do when their town was occupied was try and stay out of sight.

Katya lay on the floor, Njuta curled into the curve of her body and Sara spooned into her back, both of them sleeping. In the bed across the room, her aunt Susa wept silently as the new baby nursed, and her two children slept on either side of her. A *schlaf* bench had been made up in the room for her grandparents, but although the night was almost ending, they were still playing host to the men who now occupied all the rooms of the house except for the one they were in, a small room beside the pantry.

She lay rigid, listening. Gradually the men grew quieter; some were already asleep, judging from the sounds of snoring that came through the walls. She heard voices in the family room suddenly rising in an expletive, a demand, a taunt. All night there had been sounds of glass breaking as stores and houses were pillaged. Demands had been made for hot meals and music. The two men who had gone looking for her uncle had brought Dr. Warkentine to come and treat a man's festering wound, and now as she thought of his visit, she remembered that he had once told her that she should try to pray.

The Lord is my shepherd. Yea, though I walk, she breathed, while across the room her aunt's muffled weeping shook the bed. She wondered what had happened to her uncle, and the other men who, now fearing reprisal for having demanded the return of their stolen goods, had fled. At daybreak the bandits could track the men by their footprints in the snow, and bring them to their leader for his judgment. She heard a thump against a wall and uneven footsteps in the hall approaching the door to their room, felt a welling of hot air when the door opened and someone stood in the doorway holding a lantern.

"What are you keeping in here?" the man asked whoever was with him. His breathing was laboured as though from exertion, and drink.

Katya knew by his voice it was Simeon Pravda. It must have been Pravda who Dr. Warkentine had come to treat. Their leader, Opa had said, without saying who he was. A festering leg, one of his stumps, she thought. Would he recognize her? she wondered, her bowels suddenly churning as she thought of the crate of china dishes hidden in the attic.

"You said you wanted chicken. Well, the chicken is ready. I didn't cook a meal for you to let it sit and get cold." Her grandmother was the person who had come with him, Katya realized.

"Little Mother, what are you hiding in here, eh?" Pravda asked.

"Nothing. My grandchildren, my daughter-in-law. But if you don't believe me, then go and see for yourself," her grandmother said.

Katya heard him grunt and suck air, like someone who had just experienced a jolt of pain. His stump, she thought. He lifted the lantern and flooded the room with light. She kept her eyes closed, her breathing still.

"A nest of birds," he said. "God bless them." He laughed, and the light swung round towards the door, the room going dark as he went out into the hall, and the door closed behind him. The sound of his mirthless laughter hung in the room. She waited for as long as she could. She counted the minutes and held her breath as her intestines gurgled and ran with water. Then she got up and squatted over the chamber pot, remembering the grey light, the early-morning chill. The deep shadows lying between the summer kitchen and washhouse. That she had sensed bones creaking, a person concealed between the two buildings, watching as she had come by with her family. She remembered a light moving across a window in the women's quarters beyond the parade barn.

After the funeral she had tried to grab hold of what others had repeated, that if Abram had led the bandits to the strongbox buried in the garden instead of denying its existence, the outcome of that day might have been different. Now, with her heart racing and bowels rumbling, she closed her eyes and saw the silver cup in Pravda's small puffy hands. The presence of the cup had wiped out the memory of the dessert spoons and the silver tray that had gone missing so long ago, and so she hadn't yet wondered how these items had come to be in the well. She squatted over the chamber pot, fearing the men would hear the noises she was making, the small explosions coming from her body. She remembered Vera's crooked painted mouth, a crow's wing of black hair set against her brow, the glitter in her eyes when she'd said, There's something in the well.

Her grandparents came to bed without acknowledging that she was still awake, and Aunt Susa was weeping. They didn't undress, nor had she. They had all gone to bed fully clothed. Her grandparents knelt beside the bench, their voices hives of whispers as they prayed.

How she managed to fall asleep, she didn't know. But she must have, as some time later she awakened to the sound of moaning, and for a moment she thought, Aunt Susa's baby is about to be born, forgetting that the baby was already three months old and at its mother's breast in the bed across the room. The sound was coming from another room, the moan of someone in pain. She saw that her grandmother was awake, sitting on the edge of the bed and listening.

"It's Kootzy," her grandfather whispered.

Moonlight shone through the slats of the shutters, casting bars of light across her grandmother's white apron, her hands clasped in her lap. From somewhere in town a dog began to bark. "I know," Oma said. "Warkentine said hot poultices. Brandy for the pain."

"One of his own can do it," Opa said.

"Yes," Oma said. The bars of light seemed to move as her hands unclenched and her knees shifted as though she might turn and lie down on the sleeping bench beside him. She sighed, and then began to mutter Scripture, or a prayer, the sound of *s* becoming sharp tiny hisses. She grew silent. "But do unto others," she said, moments later.

"*Na*, Anna, don't you go to him," her grandfather said.

No, don't go, Katya thought, her teeth clenched and jaw beginning to ache. Don't dirty your hands by touching him.

Her grandmother went around the mattress on the floor, and Katya felt the air move against her face. The thought of her touching Pravda filled her with revulsion.

In the morning she told her grandfather that she wanted to leave and, surprisingly, he agreed that she should go. He sat on the edge of the sleeping bench, his long hands dangling between his knees, his face tinged yellow, and haggard. She shouldn't stay in the same house as Pravda, but take her sisters and go away. How and where, he did not know, but he would try and make some arrangements. Sara and Njuta, their hair uncombed and clothing wrinkled, sat on the floor staring at the door as though they expected at any moment it might burst open. Their grandmother prepared breakfast for the men in the family room, her voice occasionally rising above theirs, surprisingly bright and cheerful sounding. They had become mice in a house of hungry cats, listening, eyes turning to the slightest sound, a voice rising in the street.

When Pravda and his men had eaten and gone outside, Katya took the opportunity to go to her room and gather up a bundle of clothing.

Drawers were open and half-empty, and soiled clothing lay in heaps on the floor among broken bottles and the stubs of cigarettes, which had been ground into the floor. The room smelled of cow dung, unwashed hair and bodies, of vomit, she realized when she stepped into a sticky grey puddle near the wardrobe.

She went into the family room, where her grandparents were at the window, peering between the shutter slats. As at their house, as at all the houses across the street, the Siemens' window shutters were closed. And, like them, people stood behind their shutters watching the street where Pravda's hooligans had gathered. Their Bat'ko sat in a troika which she recognized as having belonged to David Sudermann. The men were looking down the street and seemed to be waiting. Soon a wagon came in sight, and as it came nearer she recognized her uncle Bernhard, his dark beard matted with blood; David, his head bowed and wrists bound behind his back; and Olga's father. The man driving the wagon was Kornelius Heinrichs, hatless, without a coat or jacket, his shirt bloodied.

Just then Ohm Siemens came from his house and down the steps, wearing nothing but boots with his winter underwear and a greatcoat draped across one shoulder. Nela and her mother stood at the door watching as he went down the steps to the gate, carrying an auger. He called out to Pravda and his men, and immediately gained their attention. Within moments, like children in a high state of excitement, they swarmed around Ohm Siemens and followed him down the street, all of them, turning at the crossroads leading to the Chortitza creek, their prisoners on the wagon forgotten, and unguarded.

That was how she found herself on the wagon bench beside Kornelius Bull-Headed Heinrichs; once again he was exactly where she needed him to be, and would always be throughout their more than half a century together. Her grandfather urged him to go quickly, to take her and her sisters to Arbusovka and Willy Krahn. Kornelius waited only as long as it took for her grandmother to come from the house with blankets, one to cover his bleeding back, one for Sara and Njuta to hide under, and then they were gone.

They left Rosenthal then, a place which she would not see again for almost four years, and then she would barely recognize it. She would think of this day as being the final leave-taking, although in the near future she and her grandparents and her sisters would board a train and leave Russia forever. They would be among the first group to go, among seven hundred and twenty-three people gathered at the train station on June 22, 1923, the place where, years before, Kornelius had saved her from Trifon's ice chisel. They would sing a hymn of parting, their voices swelling and rising above the town, a silence descending as the last note faded away, a silence in which they could hear the stirring of the wind in the trees, hear their memories of loved ones, buried in the cemetery beyond the Orthodox church, whose gravestones would soon be carted away to become the foundation stones of future houses.

While they took their leave of those who would follow in the months and years to come, and of those who would choose to remain, Kornelius packed their belongings in a boxcar hitched right behind the engine. When the train passed through the gates at the Lithuanian border, some people shouted hurrah and others wept for sadness, while Kornelius was busy scribbling figures on paper, rubles to dollars, determining how much farm equipment would cost in the new country.

They left Rosenthal, Kornelius driving the horses hard, and entered Chortitza along Old Row Street, the iron-banded runners scraping harshly where the cobblestones were bared of snow. The windows there were shuttered, too. No one came out to investigate their passing. Yards were empty and the town was motionless, as though, like the icicles hanging from the gutters, it was suspended in time. By then, the winter of 1918, the children had learned to hide at the sound of horses approaching, to get out of sight the moment anything unusual happened, and it became a game to them, an adventure, a chance to climb onto the roof of barns to keep watch, to huddle like mice in the grass and send word if strangers were coming. It became a diversion from their stomachs, which by then were often empty. They were hungry, yes, often. And later, more than hungry. She would say to her own children, and to their children, don't you ever let me hear you say the word *starving*. Be careful how you use words. She was not ashamed to admit that she had once slapped the mouth of one of her boys when he said in a fit of anger that he would like to kill someone.

The silver dome of the Orthodox church had receded behind her, and the voices of the men rising from the creek where they had gathered around Ohm Siemens to cheer him on as he sang "Gott Ist Die Liebe." He had been boring a hole in the ice for his winter bath, just as he had done every winter, an event that never failed to cause excitement and laughter. This time Pravda's hooligans were excited, too.

God is love, He makes me safe, He loves me, too. Let me say it over again. God is love, Ohm Siemens had said, repeating the words of the song in Russian, likely hoping that its message would somehow change them. Not realizing that they had only said, Tell us once again, old father, what does your song mean? just to see how long his patience would last.

*T*hey're half frozen," Willy Krahn's sister Irma said to the onlookers crowding around the doorway of the family room. Sara and Njuta's hands and feet were like ice, she told them. She was the female version of her brother, a round-shouldered, soft-looking woman.

Blankets appeared, several pairs of thick socks were passed down the hall and into the room for Irma to put in the oven, and moments later, Katya and her sisters were ensconced in warmth.

"It's cold, but not nearly as cold as it was yesterday," a woman said. "I went to the store yesterday, and it was colder and no one made a fuss."

She stood at the table, bent over a pot of steaming water, a towel draped over her head. When Katya first entered the family room, she had lifted the towel to peer at her and inform her that she had sinusitis. As Willy and another man came by the door carrying Kornelius between them, she asked, And what's the matter with that one? When no one answered, the woman lowered the towel and bent over the pot, but not before Katya saw that the front of her dress was fastened from waist to neck with large safety pins. There soon won't be enough chairs in this house, the woman had said moments later, loud enough for everyone to hear, and Katya sensed that the comment was directed her.

The windows in the room fronted the street, and were misted with steam. Near to the windowsill the curtains were stuck to the wet glass. A design had been painted on the curtains, and the moist windowpane had made the paint bleed and run. Katya sat holding Njuta, Sara pressed up against her on the bench at a long table in the centre of the room, waiting for Irma, who had gone to the stove to heat some milk. The large number of pots and pans, washboards and pitchers hanging on the walls made the room look to Katya almost like a store. Hooks held a clutter of pantry paraphernalia, egg beaters, rolling pins, flour sifters. She guessed that the items came from the households of the people who lived with Willy and his sister. Boarders, Irma called them when Katya expressed her surprise at the number of people who'd come to watch.

"And here's our Erika," Irma called from the stove as a curly-haired little girl with ruddy cheeks came into the room. "Erika, come and see, you now have a little sister," Irma said, in this way telling Katya that she and her sisters were welcome to stay. Irma returned to them, bringing cups of milk and a spoon of honey for Erika to give to Njuta to lick, but Njuta had already fallen asleep in Katya's lap.

Within moments her sisters were asleep in the bed Greta had slept in; in a room with a square table set before a window, where her sister must have sat to write letters. A groove was worn in its soft wood, and Katya rubbed the indentation, believing that oil from her sister's fingers came off on her skin. The refugees had sat around the same table, the mother and children turning all at once to look at her. After she had rubbed the indentation in the wood and felt her fingertips becoming cool, tingling, as though peppermint oil were on her skin, she crawled under a quilt beside Sara and Njuta. She knew from an apron hooked onto the door, the soft, greying folds of a petticoat draped over a chair back, that someone had recently occupied the room.

Then, although it was only noon, she fell asleep instantly, waking only once during the long afternoon, when from across the hall came the sound of male voices. As the voices dimmed, she again sank into the heat of her sisters' bodies, and sleep; the comforting thickness of the plaster walls surrounding her, the satisfying deepness of the window casements where geranium plants bloomed, their winter blossoms delicate flames burning at the ends of spindly stems. Stems that reached for the daylight seeping through the shutters, a light that faded to darkness while she slept.

The woman who'd had the towel over her head was Liese Peters, Katya learned at the supper table. Liese was the daughter of the man who had contributed the socks that were now warming her feet, a small man who sat beside Sara. When they had arrived at Willy's house and Kornelius brought the wagon and horses to a halt, he had slumped over on the bench, and Sara grabbed the back of his shirt to keep him from falling. Papa, come and help me, Sara had cried out, her face dark with frustration. Katya noticed the paleness of Sara's skin, the shadows under her eyes. Now, she seemed intent on watching Liese Peters, her angry appeal to their father to come and help apparently forgotten. Liese had changed her dress for a blouse and skirt, and wore a necklace of safety pins. She had stuck pencils into her hair on either side of her head. Katya feared Sara would ask about the strange necklace and the pencils, but she seemed mesmerized by the way the woman ate, her arms hugging the bowl, the necklace of pins clanking against its rim as spoonful after spoonful of soup disappeared into her mouth. Katherine, Sara, and Njuta Vogt, Irma had said by way of introduction when they'd gathered around the table for supper. From Rosenthal.

"From Privol'noye," Katya said, and felt Liese study her as though she were trying to remember something.

"From the Abram Sudermanns," Liese said moments later, as if to say, I should have known. Her statement had been a quiet declaration. Abram Sudermann's overseer. Someone less than herself, Katya heard in the woman's words.

There were two families living in Willy Krahn's house besides Liese Peters and her father. There was Willy, his sister Irma, and rosy-cheeked Erika, who preferred the outdoors to the indoors, no matter the season. Even before she could walk, Willy told them at supper. In winter Frieda would put baby Erika in a box on a sleigh and cover it with a blanket, and there she would sleep for hours of an afternoon. When she was brought inside, her cheeks would be as red as –

Snow White apples, Katya thought.

"As beets," Erika finished jubilantly.

"*Ja, ja*, those were the days," Willy said. "We had some good days," he said to himself as he rolled a piece of bread into a ball and dropped it into his soup.

A daughter from Willy's first wife also lived in the house; Willy's middle-aged daughter, her husband, and their son shared a room. The son was their youngest child, a lanky boy with pimples, whose shyness was so intense he kept his head down during the entire supper and slipped away before the meal was finished without anyone seeming to have noticed he was gone.

They had other sons, the husband said. One son had been taken by the Whites and was somewhere fighting with Wrangel in the Crimea.

"He's driving a wagon," his wife said, to clarify her husband's account.

Their son had met and spoken to Wrangel. Once, when he'd had the chance, when the general was going by on a horse and he stood nearby, he called out to Wrangel, could he please speak? And Wrangel said, Go ahead, feel free to talk. Their son said to the general that if he had the power to rule, he would see to it that all the Jews were sent out of the country. He said that to assure the general of his loyalty, and was rewarded with a thousand-ruble note, and the compliment that he had the soul of a true Russian. Another son had the soul of a German, apparently, as he accepted an invitation to travel with the soldiers when, following amnesty, they retreated to Germany. Most of the men who had been conscripted, or had volunteered, like his son, preferred to wear their farmers' clothing and not a uniform, and in this way, they would blend in with whatever army wanted to claim them next.

Kornelius Heinrichs had been taken to the room of Liese's father and put to bed. The voice that had roused Katya when she'd been asleep had belonged to a doctor coming to tend to Kornelius's back, which had been cut open to the bone by a whip, Irma told them. At that, their storytelling ended and everyone around the table grew quiet and introspective, Katya seeing in her mind Abram Sudermann's shoulder bone laid bare, how white it was, how it shone.

The boarders in Willy's house were people whose homes had been taken over by peasants and left in such a state that they were uninhabitable. As soon as the Germans and Austrians had left, Makhno's men returned. They went from house to house until they ran out of houses to dirty and ruin, and then they went on to the next untouched village, sometimes fighting among themselves over who had more right to a certain house. Whoever had less in the old life, it seemed, was entitled to have more in the new one, Willy Krahn said.

"Yes, those with less brains and less industry. The vodka drinkers," Liese Peters's father said, tapping the side of his bowl with a spoon. His body curled inward, and he had a large swelling at his throat. Katya tried not to look at the swelling, how it moved when he talked, as though the pouch of skin held an egg.

Willy Krahn sat at the head of the table, his beard shining silver in the light of a lantern hanging above them, the skin of his plump hands and cheeks as pink as his scalp shining through his thinning hair.

When Liese finished eating her soup, she got up and went around the table peering into their bowls to see whose was empty, and could be cleared away. When she asked Irma how many potatoes she should peel for tomorrow, Katya heard the true question behind the words, which was, would Katya and her sisters be staying, and it was clear that she hoped that would not be the case.

After the meal, the men disappeared, Willy and his son-in-law to the barn to milk the cows and continue a game of chess. Katya expected that she would help milk the cows, but when she offered, Irma said, "There are only three cows, and little enough for the men to do in winter as it is."

As Katya was about to leave the table, Liese came with a basin of potatoes and plunked it down in front of her. "Seeing as how you're so anxious to help," Liese said.

Just as swiftly, Irma took the bowl away. "Don't be so quick," she scolded.

Katya knew from Liese's abrupt movements as she scrubbed and then peeled the potatoes that she was fired up with resentment over her presence. The pencils the woman had stuck into her hair resembled insect antennae as she hunched over the bowl, and Sara kept glancing at them as she helped clear the table.

When they finished washing up, Irma set a ham bone to boil, and then measured flour into a bowl and set it aside to be leavened in the morning and pummelled into elastic loaves of dough that would be peppered with the leftover grounds of *prips*, or the potato peelings Liese would put through the meat grinder when she finished peeling them, Irma explained to Sara. Sara's eyes went round with a question, which made Irma laugh. "Yes, Miss Big-Eyes. Potato peelings, beet skins, too. Carrot and apple peels. You'd be surprised what Tante Irma can put into bread and still make it taste good."

By the time the clock in the parlour chimed the eighth hour, Willy's boarders had gone to their rooms, and the house grew quiet. As Katya sat beside the bed waiting for her sisters to fall asleep, she thought of Kornelius, and realized that she stopped thinking of him as Bull-Headed. She liked the cracked skin of his knuckles, the broadness of the backs of his hands, the orange woolly hair in his ears. The door to his room was ajar, and when she'd gone past, she'd seen the heel of his foot sticking out from the blankets, its skin worn smooth and shining. The image was something new for her to think about. That, and his inert form, a hill of a man whose body would warm her own. She didn't know where the thought came from, or why her feeling for him had changed from gratitude to desire. She recognized a longing to lie beside him, to curl around his hard body.

She heard movement in the room next to their room, the scraping of chair legs against the floor. A man clearing his throat, and Liese's voice; for some reason their near presence made her anxious. She sorted through the bundle of clothing she had brought, and when she began to put them in the cupboard, Sara asked, "Are we going to live here now?"

"Yes," she said. But she didn't know for how long.

"It's not right that we have to be here while Papa and Mama are in heaven doing nothing except being happy," Sara said, and Katya was shocked at hearing her own earlier thoughts come from her little sister.

She felt empty as she sat watching her sisters sleep, taking in their crooked fingers resting on a pillow, the sweep of their lashes against pale cheeks. People talked about heaven as though it were a country they had visited and returned from with stories of their adventures. Heaven: a city of shining houses, flowers made of glass, a fiery choir of angels suspended in clouds, the music indescribable. Heaven: a wooden room with rows and rows of narrow cots neatly made up, and everyone arriving being handed a broom and put to work. She wondered if the stories of heaven gleaned from dreams and fevers were wishes, ghostly birds in search of a home. She left her sisters and went to join Willy and Irma in the family room.

Irma looked up from her mending and greeted Katya with a smile, and then nodded in the direction of the rocking chair in the corner. Willy stood at the table smoothing wrinkles from a cloth spread across it. A paint box lay open beside the cloth, and beside it stood a glass of water. The window curtains had been taken down, washed, and were now hanging on a line near the stove, Katya noted. Willy was about to decorate another pair. His step was springy as he went to a cupboard and took down a jar that held pencils and paintbrushes. He sat at the table, the cloth spread out before him, and Irma, with a smile pulling at her mouth, said, "*Na*, Willy. You're sure you haven't borrowed someone else's pencil by mistake?"

Willy grinned, and held up the pencil to show Irma that it was notched. "There's only one rule in this house, Katherine," he said, and winked. "Make sure the pencil you use is your own."

"And safety pins, also?" Katya asked, which brought laughter.

"*Ja*, pins. I wonder how you could know? Needles, too. And thread," Irma said.

"And you'll discover that she likes to pull backwards. She would argue against blue being blue. If you want blue to be blue, say it's green," Willy said.

"She's had a hard life," Irma said in defence of Liese Peters.

And she doesn't want us to be here, Katya thought. She wanted to do something to help earn their keep. An idea had come to her while waiting for her sisters to fall asleep. "I could teach kindergarten," she said. Three days a week, she went on to say in a rush. There must be other children like Erika, of kindergarten age.

"Not many people could afford to pay," Irma said.

"Butter and eggs, whatever their parents could manage," she said.

"You're welcome to try, if you like. See what happens," Irma said, but she didn't sound convinced. You don't have to do it on our account, she went on to say. The miracle of the loaves and fishes happened over and over again. No matter how many people sat down at the table, they always went away fed, if not satisfied.

"So when will you two marry, tell me?" Irma asked. She nodded in the direction of the room down the hall where Kornelius stayed.

Katya's expression was one of shock.

"But you *are* engaged, yes?" Her eyes turned to her brother for help.

Katya knew too well how rumours like that were spread. From church to church, from a wagon passing another wagon on a road. Before she could deny being engaged to Kornelius, Willy and Irma broke into soft laughter. "He told Willy the two of you were engaged," Irma said.

Katya felt a rush of emotions, tears; a hunger. "It's not possible, and anyway he doesn't go to church," she said, and felt her face grow hot with embarrassment.

"*Ja*, we know. People around here think they know all there is to know about Kornelius. But I've known him since he was a boy. He was always hot-tempered, but just as quick to be sorry for showing his temper. Sooner or later Kornelius will grow tired from being so angry. Wait and see. Anger is poor fuel to keep a man warm the way a man needs to be kept warm. Especially one who has already sat by the fire," Willy said.

$\mathcal{A}$ ll through those first winter months in Arbusovka, I waited to hear that Pravda had died," she told the young man. Ernest Unger was his name, he'd said, and while he insisted they might be related, she doubted it, as the Ungers were mostly from the Second Colony, and it wasn't all that common that someone would marry across the river.

"I didn't pray that he would die, but I hoped he would. From cholera, gangrene. Or at the hand of one of his enemies. In the end he was being chased by the Reds; with him was Yerik, the coachman's son, and Kolya. A wheel on their carriage broke, and they had to run for it, but of course Pravda, with his cut-off legs, couldn't run. He begged them not to abandon him, but they said he had whipped them with his *nagaika* for the last time. Pravda knew what he would face when the Reds came, and so he shot himself dead. The story goes, when the Reds found him, they were so angry they cut him into pieces with their sabres."

The so-called anarchists with their black flags had slunk off, their tails between their legs. Many disappeared back into their families, shamed or unbowed; their leaders were hunted by the Red Army, Nestor Makhno eventually ending up living in exile in Paris.

"I don't know what happened to Yerik, but Kolya, I heard, found refuge with the Baptists," she said. "Apparently he was converted and became a good Christian. And so I suppose one day I'll see him in heaven."

She kept her voice even, but she saw Ernest Unger glance at her feet, which were resting on a hassock, at the way she'd begun to move a red-slippered foot rapidly back and forth. She made it be still. Then she told him that the slippers were from Indonesia, a gift from a granddaughter who had bought them at the Mennonite Self-Help store. When he didn't reply, she thought to offer him a peppermint from a bowl sitting on the table beside her chair, but then decided not to, for he might take the tremble of her hand to mean more than the shakiness of old age.

"Well, yes. My father used to say, one day we'll be surprised to find out who all will be in heaven, just as we'll be surprised to find out who isn't," she said moments later.

She saw the faint hint of a smile rise in his narrow face – of agreement? She couldn't tell. But more than likely, like her grandchildren, he was amused by her old-fashioned way of speaking.

"That first winter in Arbusovka, all we heard about was the killings. After the Germans left, Makhno and his Little Fathers, Pravda included, went rampaging through the colonies, killing our people," she said.

"Two hundred souls in the colony of Zagradovka died in a single weekend. Thirty-seven in the village of Number Seven were herded into a church basement and blown to bits by grenades," Ernest Unger said, breaking in suddenly, his voice strong and rising. "Rosenthal," he said, "one thousand three hundred and fifty inhabitants, one thousand and ninety sick with typhoid. In Chortitza, another six hundred and sixty were stricken." He ticked off the numbers on his fingers – wearing a school ring, she noticed, but not one that she recognized from her own children.

He had been to the archives, she supposed, had read the stories which, in the end, all sounded the same, and which had made her own stomach rumble with gas, a taste on her tongue as though she'd just eaten blood sausage. He must have read her translations of the Sudermann diaries and letters, done so many years ago when her eyesight still permitted, when she was one of the few remaining Russländers in Winnipeg, it seemed, who could read German Gothic script.

Across the room, a tiny wooden door on a clock opened, and a cuckoo bird sprung out. They waited in silence until the mechanical bird had stopped chirping. Ernest Unger rewound the audio tape in the machine, to record over the cuckoo-bird sounds, she thought. Then he pressed a button and the wheels began turning slowly once again, with, she noticed, a slight grinding sound. His wrists were chapped from the cold, and the cuffs of his plaid shirt looked worn. He seemed only half grown, not having completely filled in his skin yet, she thought. He was not well-off, she gathered this from the look of his cuffs, and likely he didn't have a car, as when he'd arrived at her door, his pant legs were wet from the slushy snow, and he'd complained about how long it had taken him to reach Bethania because of the poor Sunday service of the metro transit.

"Just what do you hope to get from my story?" she asked, and saw a brief flare of surprise in his face, that she would be one who would want to know something about him, too.

Moments later, he said he had just come from Saskatchewan, where he had been doing the same thing, collecting stories which he intended to give to the Mennonite Heritage Centre. The stories of the Russländers, told in their own voices, for future generations to come and listen to. "It's important they know what happened. All in all, disease and violence took nearly three thousand lives," he said.

Then he told her that he had once come across a Russian proverb, which was what had started him on his journey. "Dwell on the past and you'll lose an eye," he recited; "ignore the past and you'll lose both of them."

She laughed, which sounded to her more like a sharp little bark than laughter. As if the past could be ignored. She listened every Saturday to news broadcasts from the Mennonite radio station. To the community news following the news, which included birthday announcements. *Our best wishes go out to Mrs. Mary Klassen of Niverville, who reached her one-hundredth year on February 12;*

Mrs. Sara Neufeld of Mordon, who today is ninety-two years old; Mrs. Margaret Funk of Altona will celebrate her ninety-fifth birthday on February 27. Despite the hunger, disease and what they had gone through, the Russländer women lived to be very old. They had taken on the responsibility to live long lives, to remember, she believed, and so those who had not come through were resurrected to continue their lives – Well hello, Katya, there you are, coming to visit me again.

"You have heard, I'm sure, about Eichenfeld-Dubovka," Ernest Unger said. His father as a young boy had witnessed his own father being killed there, along with eighty-two people.

Yes, she knew about Eichenfeld-Dubovka. Most of the men had been whisked quietly away, and their jugulars were severed before the women knew they were gone. A grandfather had been decapitated in the presence of his grandchildren. She had learned about Eichenfeld-Dubovka, and other atrocities, from the women she lived with. When there were no children, no men around to consider, they sometimes spoke with a bluntness that Plautdietsch afforded. A sentence coming out of the blue during a moment of conversation in the vestibule; chairs lined up on either side of the entrance and windows that looked out on a busy street, a street of tall city buildings; a square of grass enclosed by a perimeter of new trees, and in the centre of it, the brightly coloured tunnels and climbing structures of a playground. *They fried her breasts in a frying pan. They did it to her with the barrel of a gun. A man was swinging from a tree by a leg, naked, with a walking cane hanging out of his rear.* There was no point in telling Ernest Unger those kinds of things. The majority of the women kept the more vivid details to themselves. They were like her grandparents had been, they had no desire to draw pictures. God knew what had happened and, for them, that was enough.

Soon after she came to Arbusovka, she learned of the death of Nela Siemens's father. Ohm Siemens had used the occasion of his winter bath to divert the Makhnovite bandits, but instead they used it to place wagers on how long it would take for him to freeze to death. They'd put rifles across the hole in the ice and stood on them, pinning his shoulders while they counted the number of minutes it took for him to give up the ghost. She'd heard that in a village near to

Nikolaifeld, Helena Sudermann and Franz Pauls and others had been conducting a religious service in a school when they were interrupted by Nestor Makhno and his men. The worshippers fled. But God did not intervene, and in spite of Helena Sudermann's and Franz Pauls's prayers, the shutters and doors were nailed closed, and the building set on fire. Helena Sudermann, Franz Pauls, and three lay preachers were burned alive. She remembered the day Kornelius came to tell them, how her joy at seeing him had evaporated, and her mind numbed into its old woodenness by the horrible news.

Months later, her grandfather brought the news that she'd already learned from Kornelius. He also brought with him a bundle of spring and summer clothing and a sack of potatoes. He brought the recipe notebook, her mother's hand mirror, and Sara's doll. She and her sisters should remain in Arbusovka for a longer time, he said. The front sometimes passed through Rosenthal and Chortitza twice in a day. With it came the demands of the Red Army, the Whites, the Makhnovites, for food, shelter, and horses, paying for the items in the exchange of the day: lice and hunger. Fifteen soldiers had been killed by shelling from across the river, and were buried in a grave in the yard of the Teachers' Seminary. He'd heard of such cruelty: Red soldiers nailing the epaulets of White officers to their shoulders. That the Whites sometimes buried their enemies alive. Three of their town boys had been challenged to denounce God or be thrown off the Einlage bridge. When they refused, two were thrown and drowned, and the other jumped, rather than be pushed, and saved himself.

She watched her grandfather and uncle Bernhard go off down the road, and within moments they were obliterated by snowfall, as though a curtain had been drawn behind them. A curtain that gave her a feeling of safety, that a vast distance lay between the village of Arbusovka and the town of Rosenthal, and not just an hour's ride.

The following spring and summer she grew used to the stillness that radiated above the land like heat shimmer, a stillness punctuated by the twittering of tomtits nesting in a tree outside her window, a rooster's solitary crowing as the town's only street began to emerge from a grey light. The stillness had been interrupted several times by what sounded like thunder reverberating in the distant sky, a trail of smoke calling attention to that far border and the people who lived beyond it, her grandparents, her uncle and his wife who, in her mind, had become featureless, and as small as clothes pegs.

One street divided the settlement; nothing in the village was far from Willy Krahn's house: a small church, school, the village's only store. She grew frustrated by the short distance she could walk up and down that single street, until Irma reminded her that the smallness of Arbusovka was a blessing. There was little to attract men intent on mayhem. There had been several instances of riders coming to Arbusovka, but after they and their horses were fed and watered, they quickly moved on to a village or town that offered more in the way of spoils.

Near to the end of autumn, a woman whose family had travelled to visit relatives returned to Arbusovka with the news that many of the women in the towns of Rosenthal and Chortitza had been laid on the ground. Katya stood in the hallway, her body gone rigid with fear as she heard Liese tell Irma. The traveller and her companions had come upon wagons carrying the women, and girls as young as twelve. They were being taken to a doctor to be rid of disease and what was growing behind their aprons. Who they were, the woman couldn't say, as they had covered their faces. She said the poor dears were being taken to a far-away place to prevent their terrible secret from being known. She also brought news of the typhus that had felled as many as a hundred people in the colony of Chortitza. Not long afterwards, the woman herself succumbed to spotted fever, and then there was a small outbreak of typhus in Arbusovka, which claimed several members of one family.

Living with Willy Krahn and Irma, being surrounded on all sides by people in the house, was like wearing an extra coat or layer of fat. Katya felt removed from innuendo and rumour; she felt watched over and protected. Every day she sat down to meals with people who might, at any time, have broken out in a quarrel had it not been for Willy and Irma's mitigation, and their sense of humour. One such Sunday afternoon in the spring of 1921, she entered the parlour where

Irma was visiting with several other women, and knew from their expressions that Irma was about to say something amusing.

"I heard a story recently about a woman who was worn out from having children," Irma was saying. "And so the doctor thought it was time to have a talk to the husband. He was concerned for the wife's health. Apparently her womb had fallen, and he couldn't get her blood up," she said.

It was the word *womb* that had caught Katya's attention. She'd come into the parlour to add water to a pan set on a windowsill, which held jars. The clay-coated jars were to become table centrepieces, a project she and her kindergarten children had completed only the day before. She felt Liese's eyes on her as she touched each of the cloth-wrapped jars, feeling them for moisture. She had begun to suspect that any reference to the affairs between men and women was directed at her. That the women could read her mind. When she was thinking about Kornelius, her body secreted an odour which they recognized. They knew about the strange constrictions, the sweet pain, the release.

"Come and sit," Willy's daughter called, patting an empty chair beside her, and because Katya didn't know how to refuse, she joined them.

"I think I know which woman you're talking about," a neighbour woman said to Irma.

The parlour where they sat was the only room not taken over by boarders. It was a large room with potted herbs, and now with jars wrapped in dampened cheesecloth lining the windowsills. A room with a wall clock whose minute hand was missing, and where Katya held her kindergarten class. The time was near to Easter, 1921, and she had taken her kindergarten children to a pit near a brickyard to gather clay, which they'd plastered onto the jars. She endured Liese Peters's criticism when she explained the project: the seeds of grain gleaned from nooks and crannies in the barn would be pressed into the slip. The jars would be kept moist and the seeds would sprout and grow, and become a table decoration which the children would take home for Easter. A waste of time, and seeds, Liese had said.

"That would be the P.P. Janzen family you're talking about," Liese

Peters said now, without missing a twist or loop of her crochet yarn and hook.

"It's more than likely Mary Dyck," Willy's daughter said.

"The Janzen's fifteen children outdo the Dycks' by three," Liese said.

"Yes, but don't forget, the Janzens' fifteen come from two wives," the neighbour woman pointed out.

Katya had two of the Janzen children attending her kindergarten. Listless and white-faced children whose worried eyes often betrayed their hunger. Children whose eyes she'd had to bathe to soften a crust of mucous; she then boiled the cloths to prevent the infection from spreading to others. They always arrived early, knowing that a cup of soup awaited them. Soup she made with water, dill, a tablespoon of fat and a few egg noodles to give the children some nourishment. Famine fare, she would later call the soup when she began to add dandelions and strips of calf hide to it. Her kindergarten had not become a source of income for her, as she'd hoped, but rather a place for the children to come expecting to be fed a piece of bread, a single wafer of apple doled out from a bag of dried apples.

"It doesn't matter who the woman is. Tante Irma was going to tell us a joke," Willy's daughter reminded them.

"Yes, let her say it. We can use a laugh, too," the neighbour said when the sound of merriment rose outside where Willy and several men, Kornelius Heinrichs among them, were talking together on the platform.

"The doctor came to talk to the husband. He told him that his wife shouldn't have any more children, as her health was too poor. 'Well, what am I supposed to do about it?' the husband asked. The doctor suggested that the husband should start sleeping in the barn. 'Oh,' said the wife. 'Do you think that would work? If so, then I should sleep in the barn, too,'" Irma said.

Their laughter filled the room while Katya stared at her hands in her lap, and felt herself blush.

When last week she'd gone to the barn in search of stray kernels of grain for the kindergarten project, she hadn't known Kornelius had come looking for Willy. She couldn't understand how she missed seeing his cart on the barnyard, the single emaciated nag hitched to it. Where once he'd had a barn filled with riding horses, this sway-backed mare was his one remaining animal. She heard someone step up behind her, turned, and found herself being held in his arms.

"Oh Katya, I have such a need for you," he said. She thought her ribs would crack as he squeezed her suddenly and hard. Then he released her.

It happened so quickly she might have blamed her imagination, if it weren't for his odour and heat lingering as he turned and went towards the open doors and the sunlit barnyard. Daylight framed his body, accentuated the slight bow of his legs, his stiff-legged way of walking. Once he stepped from the barn into the light, he would disappear.

"I haven't thanked you for bringing us here," she said. "It's true, what my opa said. God put you in the right place at the right moment. Twice now," she added, after a pause.

Did he ever ask himself why that hadn't been the case when his wife met the hooligans on the road? She had heard about Kornelius's part-Arabian horse which he rode at top speed across open fields. He carried a pole, a hammer tied to the end of it, yelling at the top of his voice as he chased a rabbit down and killed it.

He turned to face her, and for moments they looked at each other, her words hanging in the space between them.

"People can read into things what they want. If you believe what your grandfather said, then thank God, and not me," he said.

"They say . . . I've heard it said that you blame God for what happened to your wife. That it's the reason why you don't go to church," she said.

"I don't go to church because there are enough hypocrites occupying the benches as it is," he said.

A longing drew her to him, across the distance towards the light beyond the open door. When they stood face to face, she still felt the impression of his body against her own.

"If I blamed anyone, I blamed myself for being alive. But that was long ago. I don't any longer. Not since the day I saw you at the train station. I had said to myself, Kornelius you need something to hope for. And when I saw you, I thought, there it is. Don't lose it."

She felt the heat of tears, his hand come to rest on her shoulder, his bristly cheek, and then his mouth brushing against her own.

"It's not your fault that you're alive, and they're not. Put the blame where it belongs, on the shoulders of evil men," he had said.

"Someone here doesn't care for your joke," Liese said to Irma.

Katya felt the women's careful scrutiny, and was relieved when their conversation went off in another direction.

A wild woman had been seen running about the countryside, the neighbour woman told them, repeating what they'd already heard.

She had been seen among cows put out to pasture early one morning, on her hands and knees eating dandelions. A group of boys were out playing at dusk, and kicked a ball into the churchyard. When they climbed the wall to get it, they came upon the woman at the water pump. Her face was terrible to look at, scratched and streaked with dirt. When she spat at them, they threw stones at her, and she in turn flung liquid at them from a cup, which caused two of the boys to immediately become drowsy.

"Those were P.P. Janzen boys. Liars, all of them. And if you ask me, they're always half asleep," Liese said. Her chain of safety pins had grown, a double loop that now reached her waist.

Katya had heard the story about the wild woman from Sara, who brought it home from the *Dorfschule*. She'd heard Kornelius telling Willy he'd seen the woman early one morning sneaking out of his barn, where he suspected she'd spent the night. People were saying that the woman was from Moscow, or Leningrad. That she was a distant relative of the Romanovs. She had come on the train along with the bagmen, and the thousands of beggars who believed the streets in the villages were paved with butter and liverwurst. Kornelius had laughed at his own joke, the sound of his laughter a note hanging in the air above the yard, holding her breathless, her knees quaking.

"Katherine is preparing for baptism," Willy's daughter said when they'd exhausted the topic of the wild woman.

"Good," the neighbour woman said and nodded, and Katya wasn't sure whether she meant it was good that she would publicly proclaim her faith and become a member of the church, or good because they recognized the feelings rising in her body, and baptism prepared the way for marriage.

If she'd grown up in a village she would have attended choir festivals and travelled to other villages and caught the attention of a man, not for what she'd said, but for how little she had spoken. He would have noticed her preference for dark colours, how neatly her apron was patched, and assume that she would look after his interests well. And after enquiries were made about the man's family, within a week or two, they'd be married and sharing a bed. And then what? She didn't exactly know, as she had neither mother or older married sister to tell her, but when she pondered over it, the sweet clear pain came in waves.

"What is the church of God?" Irma asked, looking up from the catechism book to peer at Katya overtop her rimless glasses. She had come to Katya's room later that evening to drill her in the questions she would need to answer to be baptised. If you like, we can do it, Irma said. And although they usually did not study on Sunday, Katya invited Irma to stay, her intuition telling her that there was another reason for her visit.

"Those who believe in Jesus Christ," she replied.

"Who are to be baptised?"

"Those who believe in him."

"What should the believer's conduct in his daily walk and life be?"

"We should love one another."

"Our enemies also?" Irma asked.

When Katya's grandmother had gone to attend to Pravda's ulcerated stump that night, she had been showing love for the enemy. Katya knew she wouldn't be able to do the same; that instead she waited for news of the man's death.

"There is no reason for you to worry. You know the answers," Irma said and closed the catechism book, not realizing – or choosing to ignore – that Katya hadn't responded to the last question.

Yes, she knew the answers. But if she stood before the congregation and said that she would bless and do good to those who hated her, she would become one of those hypocrites Kornelius had referred to.

"You weren't . . . you didn't like the little story I told this afternoon? Am I right?" Irma asked.

When Katya didn't reply, Irma tapped her knee with the book and said, "Maybe you didn't find it funny because you didn't understand."

Katya confessed she hadn't understood entirely.

"But you were honest enough not to pretend that you had," Irma said. "Look here. I'm going to show you something."

She put the book on the table and made a fist of her large hand and set it on her knee. Then she spread open two fingers. "These are a woman's legs."

Then she extended the index finger of her other hand. "This is what a man has between his legs," she said, and wiggled it.

Yes, his stick, Katya thought, and suppressed a smile. Her little brothers, pointing their sticks at the pee-pot.

Then Irma slid her index finger between the spread fingers. "He moves it around inside the woman, and by and by, honey comes out of it. The honey stays inside the woman. The honey mixes with seeds you carry, here," she said, and poked Katya in the abdomen.

"And that's how children are made. So you see, if the woman had gone and joined her man to sleep in the barn, well, it still would have happened. It takes two people to make a baby," she said. "A man and a woman. His honey, her seeds."

For shame, Katya thought, and felt herself blushing. So then, in spite of love and tender feelings, it *was* just like horses, like pigs, goats. She'd always been told, we're not animals.

"Sometimes he groans and moans, and sometimes he says, 'I love you.' But usually he's too busy to think. While the woman? The woman says, Come on in. And along the way some of us begin to want to do it as much as he does," Irma said, as she got up. "Even though it could mean having another child, and the woman is already worn out from child-bearing. That's what the real joke was. The woman was playing with the doctor at being simple. She didn't want to stop sleeping with her husband."

Kornelius, putting himself inside her. The heat of her face had spread throughout her body and her stomach tingled with it. For shame, she had thought, but at the same time, the idea of it gave her pleasure. If she got up to see Irma to the door she would betray herself, the sudden dampness at her underarms, its pungent odour.

"Don't be afraid to ask." Irma said as she left the room.

Katya stood at the window looking out and saw that Sara was coming down the street. With her wind-burned cheeks, and darkening hair, she was beginning to resemble Greta. She noticed the buttons on her sister's dress were strained, that her breasts were forming. At twelve, she thought in amazement and fear, and wondered about the rusty-looking spots she had come across in their bed linen now and again, when it hadn't been her time for it. The time would come too soon when she would need to explain to Sara. The street and yards were sprinkled with the petals of apple and cherry blossoms; ridges of what looked like pink snow had gathered against the edges of sidewalks, and in the fenced corners of freshly tilled gardens. She remembered a time when she was acutely aware of nature unfolding around her, its daily drama played out in the changing sky, the air in the garden hanging with mist, shimmering with heat. She remembered the acacia trees in bloom at Privol'noye, how the roof would be covered with their petals; a wind carrying a curtain of white rain across the steppes, as far away as Lubitskoye.

She'd been Sara's age when she'd written: "His Majesty King Winter is upon us and has covered the world outside my little attic window in a cloak of ermine. Soft as fur from a distance, light as feathers when I walk through it, and if I should ever see a diamond, the stone would not shine as brightly as the diamonds found in deep winter snow. The jewels King Winter sometimes sprinkles onto the earth to make up for the cruel cold. Cruel winter cold, Lydia used to say when it was winter. Cruel heat, she said in the summer. Cruel weather that, when I sometimes run between the Big House and home, makes my chest hurt from the cold, my feet burn with its heat."

She ran her finger across Lydia's name now as if to draw her essence from the ink. She remembered Lydia at Justina's wedding, a mauve taper set on a tapestry of grass beside the west garden wall. Lydia in a dress the colour of lilacs. Lydia standing at a piano one grey morning with feathers drifting in the air around her. What are you making, Lydia? What are you making with your life, Katya wondered. Then she wrote:

APRIL 1921   FAMINE FARE

Given to me by Irma.

When mixing bread, substitute half the flour for clay. Use beet water, skins, and the leftover grounds from prips if you have it. Milled thistle seed can also be used in place of some of the flour.

Liese P. is a headache to do without.
Tomorrow I will plant some beans and potatoes.
Still no rain.

he following morning Katya went along the broad main street of Arbusovka, thinking that the sudden absence of bloom on the fruit trees made it seem as though spring had taken a step backwards. Sara pulled the wagon, and Njuta rode inside it, cuddling Sara's doll, which had become her doll now, against her neck. They would go out to Willy Krahn's land, a strip of earth he'd ploughed in autumn and allocated for his boarders' use, should they have anything to plant come spring. The wagon wheels ground against stones and cinders, setting her teeth on edge. A solemn young boy sat on a step, his watchful eyes made large by the gauntness of his face. He was hungry, she knew by his stillness, from the way his attention remained fixed on the wagon, and the bowl Njuta cradled between her legs. As they passed by the gate, he got up abruptly and went into the house without greeting them, the door closing behind him with a decisive clap.

In the street beyond she saw women gathered in the yard of the village store, Liese Peters among them. They all looked to be the same age. They were all old, she thought, even though she had discovered Liese was not much older than she was. Hunger had turned the women into babushka gossips. Their pinched and suspicious-looking pusses were set off by the dark headscarves they constantly wore because they were chilled from lack of food, because they didn't have the energy to fix their hair. She hadn't looked in her mother's hand mirror lately, or she would have known that her hair had thinned, too. Her skin was dry, and she had the same lines puckering her mouth.

"Where are you going?" a woman called out from the store yard. All the women, their expressions careful, swivelled their heads to watch Katya and her sisters approach.

"We're going to plant beans and potatoes," Sara called out. Then Njuta held up the doll. "Look. My baby has a new dress," she said, a declaration from a child who had learned to trust that the women around her were always benevolent, and interested in her world.

Katya was aware that Liese had come over to the gate with another woman, both of them craning their necks to peer into the bowl between Njuta's legs that held chunks of seed potatoes, and beans swollen from an overnight soaking.

"You won't get much from that, even if it should rain," the woman with Liese said.

"One can always hope," Katya said, knowing that the woman was suggesting she would be better served eating the seed potatoes and beans than sticking them in the parched earth.

"*Ja, ja.* We can hope for snow in July too," the woman said. There was a craftiness in her, a sharpness that said she was looking out for herself.

"Look here, Njuta, why don't you show me your dolly's new dress," Liese Peters said. She had come out of the gate and was marching towards the wagon, and for a moment Katya thought she meant to snatch the bowl from between Njuta's legs. That like the young boy, the sarcastic woman, she coveted the potatoes and beans, and wasn't really interested in the doll.

She was aware from Sara's expression that something was wrong, even before Liese had taken the doll from Njuta, flipped it over, and pointed triumphantly to a safety pin fastening the dress closed at the back.

"Well, well." Liese said and expelled her breath as though she had been holding it for a long time. She unfastened the pin, and dropped the doll into Njuta's outstretched hands. Her hands shook as she added the safety pin to her necklace, and then turned her angry gaze on Sara. "I had a feeling it was you."

"What will you do about this?" Liese asked, turning her attention from Sara to Katya.

"We didn't have any hooks. Or a spare button," Sara said.

"That's neither here nor there," Katya said, speaking what was expected of her, while her heart remained detached. "You must apologize." She was aware that the women standing in the yard had come to the gate to watch.

"I'm sorry," Sara said.

Which was a lie, Katya knew from Sara's defiant pout, but she was relieved to hear it.

"People who steal should be punished," Liese called after them as they went down the street.

For borrowing a safety pin, she should punish a child for that? For throwing a cup into a butter well? She had turned back without thinking, she was striding towards the woman, going faster and faster, her breath rising, her arms swinging and body pulsing with heat. She had been punished with a neverending silence; with a void every time she had asked for a voice; had turned back to a room expecting to find her mother at the table, a brother going out a door. She had been punished with memories that came unbidden, such as a time spent sponging and ironing her brothers trousers when they'd come back from Ox Lake, the heat and damp cloth releasing the mushroom scent of Gerhard; Johann, a wet-animal smell; Peter, the earth after a lightning storm; Daniel. Daniel still too young for wandering, and attached to the immediate yard, and his mother's skirts. All of them having the smell of motion, arms and legs churning through a day, the heat of ideas and plans. She'd been told she had been fortunate to have been spared images that would stay with her forever, but her imagination was hers forever, and it gave her pictures that snatched away her breath.

"What do you know about being punished?" she shouted. "Be still. Go home, and shut your mouth for once, you're nothing but a small-minded puddle of cow shit."

She felt their silence, a force that pressed against her body. When Liese scurried back through the gate and rejoined the others, Katya was relieved, as she was angry enough to have struck her.

Within moments they were at the garden, a strip of tilled earth Willy had prepared for whoever wished to use it. She found release as she hacked apart clods of earth with a hoe, and felt the impact in her elbows. She carved out a furrow, while Sara came behind dropping beans into it, Njuta behind Sara, filling in the trough with loose earth and then tamping it down with her feet. The village lay far beyond them, a single dusty street with houses on either side of it, the picket fences in need of repair and whitewash.

The wind that had carried away the fruit-tree blossoms swept across the open land, raining dirt against their faces, flipping the leaves of a grove of poplars which had been planted as a windbreak beyond Willy's fields. The lack of rain and uncommon spring heat, the wind, would bring drought; another punishment, she thought. *He turns rivers into a wilderness, a fruitful land into barrenness for the wickedness of them that dwell therein.* She was beginning to sound like everyone around her, those in church who nodded in agreement when the psalm had been read.

She didn't know that the villagers of Arbusovka were like many others in the colonies, like people in the Second Colony, and in Arkadak, Alt Samar, and Ufa in the north. In Kuban, Suvorka, and Terek beside the Caspian Sea. People who wanted to point fingers, to find reasons, to take the blame for having brought on the end of their world. They had somehow caused the Russian Revolution and the ensuing Civil War with their piety, their high-mindedness, greed, a worldliness. They had either been too arrogant, or too timid. They had eaten too much crackle and fatted calves. They were guilty of harbouring unkind thoughts, resentments, and had failed to make things right before taking communion.

When she finished planting she sat in the wagon with Njuta on her lap, Sara sitting on the ground beside them, squinting as she stared out across the land. Katya thought of Kornelius, imagined his hands circling her wrists, his hands pressing against the small of her back, her breasts giving in to the boniness of his ribs and warming him, warming herself. Warming herself with his words: *It's not your fault. Put the blame on the shoulders of evil men*. She was afraid of coming too close to him, of not being able to pull away in time to think her own thoughts and draw her own conclusions.

Sara yanked at the hem of Katya's skirt, disturbing her thoughts, and then pointed to a grove of poplar trees.

A woman stood among the trees watching them, a dark figure, her face a white oval framed by a scarf that covered her head and shoulders.

Katya held Njuta tighter and looked at the woman, at the wind rippling the woman's skirt and the fringed edge of her headscarf. Katya knew they weren't imagining her. They were looking at the wild woman. A hunger-crazed woman. A woman forced to live outdoors, and because of this, she had likely seen and heard things that disturbed her mind.

"It's Vera," Sara said moments later.

"*Nanu*, don't be addled. That's an old woman," Katya replied.

She had never heard what had happened to Vera, and didn't want to know whether or not she lived at the estate with her family, was no longer sure that the world beyond the border of her night-mare had ever existed. That oasis – moths fluttering in the gardens on nainsook wings, the echo of cattle lowing from distant green pastures – was gone. Vera had crossed the border into the nightmare that was the present world. She had chosen to stand with the enemy in the biting morning chill, a sparse grey light, feathers trampled into the mud. Pravda had found his way to Rosenthal, and so Vera could have, too. She could be among the women travelling with the horde of anarchists, and perhaps by chance, or by design, she had found them here.

The thought of Vera being the wild woman made her stomach lurch. She had given Njuta a piece of string from a ball of string used to mark out the row of beans, and her little sister was now binding it around the doll's chest to keep the back of its dress closed. Sara had got up, and stood hugging herself and staring at the woman among the poplar trees, the woman unmoving, too, the oval of her face turned towards them.

For days after, she went about thinking of the woman, thinking that whenever she turned, the dark figure had just stepped out of sight. She abandoned thoughts half formed – Njuta had been found in the Big House in Abram's office, who put her there? Sentences went unfinished – Do you think? she asked herself aloud, bringing a quizzical look from Irma. She kept her sisters within sight, and at night held them more tightly while they slept.

■ ▮ ▮ ■

Within days there were strangers coming through the gate and up the walk to the house. Katya was in her room when she heard them mount the steps to the platform as though they had a right to be there. She went out into the hallway and saw them standing at the door, and Irma coming to greet them.

"They're asking for Willy," Irma said as Willy's son-in-law came up behind her at the door, a bulky and bearded man becoming smaller as his shoulders dropped in a slouch. He stepped in front of Irma to face the trio at the door.

"Hello, Chaim," he said, a limp attempt at joviality directed at the man who seemed to be in charge. He opened the door, his offer of a handshake ignored as the men pushed past him and into the house.

"Yes, yes, come in comrades, you're welcome, you're welcome," he said. Katya heard movement behind her, and turned to see his young son standing in a doorway, the eruptions on his face brightening as he blushed and nodded at the man named Chaim, who appeared to be his age.

Katya stepped back into her room and moments later, they came past the door, three self-important men wearing dark jackets and trousers, their boots polished and shining. Willy's son-in-law came shuffling behind them in his slippers, saying Yes, yes, the parlour, it's the last room on the right. She heard Chaim say they had come from the *volost* of Belenkoye, a nearby Russian town. The Revolutionary Committee there had received a complaint. An anonymous complaint had been dropped into the *zhalobny yashtshik* hanging on a wall outside the door of the store in Arbusovka. The complaint was that Katherine Vogt, kindergarten teacher, had wasted food.

She heard her name mentioned, saw Njuta look up from where she sat on the floor, playing. Sara got up from her chair and stood rooted, listening. Katya heard the young man go on to say that although she had been accused of wasting grain for the making of table decorations, it was Willy they wanted. They wanted him on a charge more serious than wasting food. The kindergarten project marked Easter, and therefore constituted teaching religion in a school, which was prohibited. Because the kindergarten was in Willy Krahn's house, he was to be held responsible.

The men left soon after, taking the clay-covered jars with them, and Willy, his hands tied at his back. Katya listened as the sound of their horses and carriage faded, and in an ensuing silence went to the family room where Irma comforted Willy's children.

"No one could have foreseen this. Imagine, someone making a complaint out of such an innocent thing," Irma said.

"That someone was Liese," Sara said as she came into the room, her voice implying that they should have known as much.

"You don't know what you're saying," Willy's daughter scolded.

One of the Janzen boys had seen Liese Peters at the store putting something into the complaint box, Sara told them. "She was angry because I borrowed one of her pins."

Irma cast a troubled glance in the direction of Liese's closed door across the hall, and then she turned from them and went to the window, head bowed and her clasped hands tucked beneath her chin. "If it hadn't been this, they would have found some other excuse to take Willy," she said moments later. She sighed and slowly undid her apron strings. Then she left the house, going from door to door to let people know what had happened, and to ask for prayers on her brother's behalf.

When she returned hours later, Katya was taken by her sense of accomplishment. Her step was light as she went about preparing the evening meal, her chin lifted with determination not to appear to be worried. She had left Willy in God's hands, Irma said almost matter-of-factly. She had done the best anyone could do for him, which was to pray, and now, it was up to God. Then Irma's attention was drawn to the window, and lit with pleasure. Katya saw the source of it, Kornelius Heinrichs coming into the yard.

The moment news reached him, he had gone to Belenkoye, Kornelius told them. He had snooped around and discovered that Willy was being held there along with nine others, in a small hut. Sit, sit, Irma urged him, and he accepted a place at the supper table in Willy's chair, a glass of tea, his hand touching Katya's as he took it from her. She felt his eyes follow her as she went about setting the table and Irma explained what had happened. Before they took him away she had gone to Willy in the barn while the men were examining the evidence in the parlour, she told Kornelius. She brought him his wooden scuffs to wear in place of boots, and insisted he change his clothing for a pair of worn coveralls hanging in the barn because she'd heard that prisoners chosen for execution first were those whose apparel the guards coveted.

"After supper, some of us are going to meet and pray for Willy. You'll come, too, yes?" Irma said to Kornelius.

Katya saw Kornelius shake his head and grin wryly at Irma's manoeuvring. But when Irma went on to say that there was a reason why God had allowed Willy to be arrested, her meaning clear in the way her eyes moved between him and Katya, Kornelius winced in irritation.

"Reason or not, that doesn't excuse the person whose actions caused Willy's arrest," he said. "Everyone knows." He had brought a sack of sugar with him and set it on the table, and he reached for it now. "Divide this up into small bundles and take them with you when you go to pray for Willy. See what you can sell. Money still talks," he said. Meanwhile, he would find which authority he would need to bribe in Belenkoye.

"Chaim," Willy's grandson said. He had slipped into the room unnoticed. He and Chaim once shared a bench at the *Gymnasium*, he said. Throughout the years Willy hired Chaim for the harvest. "Surely . . ." the grandson said, but left what he had begun to say unfinished.

Just then, Willy's middle-aged daughter and husband joined them, their faces knotted with worry. Then, as Liese Peters entered the room, they fell silent, averting their eyes as she went over to the table and sat down at her usual place. Kornelius cleared his throat before he spoke. Send the children out of the room, he said. When Sara, Njuta and Erika were gone he began to speak, and although he didn't look directly at Liese, it was apparent that what he had to say was intended for her.

There were always at least ten men kept as prisoners in the hut at Belenkoye, he said. Every morning one of those men was taken before a tribunal to answer for the complaint that had been made against him. And every morning the guards drew lots to see who would perform the execution. Who among them would be lucky enough to wear the clothes of the man they were about to kill. After the man undressed, they would escort him from the hut to a shed, where he was made to kneel and put his head against an anvil. Sometimes they delayed shooting him to see if he would begin to hope. To hear how loudly he might pray, see how badly he would soil his underwear.

At this, Willy's daughter gasped.

"Be still," Irma said sharply.

Liese covered her face with her hands, and her shoulders began shaking as she wept.

"Yes, cry your crocodile tears," Willy's daughter said.

At that Liese began to howl, her head thrown back and face twisted grotesquely, causing Irma to become alarmed. She went to Liese and put her hands on her shoulders, held her against the swell of her stomach until she grew quiet.

That evening while the others met to pray for Willy, Katya filled pails with water. She hadn't asked God for anything since she'd stopped asking him to bring her family back, and she didn't think she had the right to do so now. Instead, she would water the row of beans and the potato hills. She wanted to encourage the seeds to sprout. While the others prayed, she would try and coax life out of Willy Krahn's land.

She carried a pail of water from the wagon across a ditch and up onto the land but even before she reached her strip of garden she knew that something was wrong. The earth was disturbed, holes had been poked into the ground.

She dropped to her knees and began digging in the dirt, certain that what she already suspected was true, someone had come behind her and hooked the beans out of the ground. No, not someone, several people, she realized, as the ground was patterned with footprints both large and small. She remembered the boy's look of hunger as he stared at the bowl, the women's veiled interest in it. She could see herself soon doing the same, becoming as watchful, looking for the opportunity to get something extra for herself and her sisters. She thought of Willy locked up, fearfully waiting to find out if he would be the one to be called up before the tribunal in the morning, and she was suddenly flooded with relief, realizing for the first time that it could have been her. That she could have been the one to be arrested. And then she was ashamed. The impulse to think of herself and her sisters above all else was beginning to set in, she thought. After all, her footprints were there, too, overlapping those of whoever had stolen the potatoes and beans she had planted. She knew she could not stay in Arbusovka any longer. She would not be able to forgive Liese's treachery, which had made her thankful that someone else had been arrested, and not her.

She went north across open country with Njuta on her back, Sara carrying a bundle of their belongings. At sunrise she had awakened her sisters and made them dress quickly and silently. They were going back to Opa and Oma's, to Rosenthal, she assured Njuta. She left a note for Irma, not wanting to answer questions, or be persuaded against her will to stay. They went across land that was soft underfoot, their feet cushioned by wintered grass and weeds.

"How do you know we're going in the right direction?" Sara asked.

"The trees," she said. They would keep heading towards a brown smudge on the horizon beyond them, which more than likely were trees near to Rosenthal and Chortitza. And along the way they might encounter a Baba stone, she said to keep their minds occupied. They might see an old stone woman whose features would point the way to Rosenthal. If only she understood how to read them, she thought.

The first house they came to in Chortitza was abandoned, its interior blackened as though with soot. She and her sisters stood on the doorsill, peering in, not wanting to go farther because of a sour smell emanating from the rooms, the dampness. Her call of greeting echoed. When she stepped inside, she saw there was filth everywhere. Heaps of refuse, shredded cloth, eggshells, broken bottles, mixed together with rotting vegetation and excrement. A fire had been built in the middle of the floor and eaten its way through the boards, its smoke blackening the walls and ceiling. Katya saw a rat's tail disappear into a dark corner.

She heard the sound of hammering from the adjacent house, and went outside. The gate hung askew on its hinges, and the yard was tall with weeds. She made Sara wait near the gate with Njuta. As she entered the house, the hammering stopped. She noticed that a room off the hall was completely bare of furniture; there were shards of glass scattered across the floor. An emaciated cat stopped prowling to stare at her. She turned and looked into the room across from it. There was a dead woman in a nightdress lying on a tabletop set on two chairs. Just then a man came into the room carrying a hammer, a man whose overgrown beard and long uncombed hair made him look wild. He was wearing a woman's underslip. As their eyes met, his face caved in, and she thought he would weep. He looked down at himself, as though seeing himself through her eyes. He looked at his bare feet, the obvious fact that he was without underwear. "This is all the clothing I have," he said.

The dead woman's lips were rimmed with black, her face sunken and yellow, mouth turned down as though in disappointment.

"Go away from here. There's sickness," he said.

She heard moaning come from yet another room, and then a woman called out for a drink; she was hot. "Papa, come, the fire is burning up the wall," she called.

It was the fever, the man said. He was the last one standing.

"Your grandparents likely know by now that you're here," David Sudermann said. "The telephones aren't working, but the word gets through; even better, without having to go through Valentina. And without becoming everyone else's business in the process."

"Don't talk so loud," Auguste said sharply.

Katya had been surprised to come upon the telephone operator, Valentina, at the clothesline in the Sudermann's yard, just as the woman was surprised to see her. The town's former postmaster and his family lived in the front room of the Sudermann's house now, while another family occupied the remainder of it. She learned that, like many of the previously affluent in the towns of Chortitza and Rosenthal, David and Auguste were consigned to living in a single room in their own house.

As Auguste poured tea into glasses, Katya saw that her hand shook. In the room was a table, a sleeping couch, sleeping bench and two chairs. Also a cupboard whose doors were missing, its shelves holding dishes and cooking pots; also a pile of bedding on a sewing machine. Sara and Njuta had joined Auguste and David's three girls where they sat on the bench, leaning into the wall. Their girls seemed placid and withdrawn, Katya thought as she accepted the glass of tea from Auguste's trembling hand.

"Pretend it's cocoa," David said with a short laugh. "It pays to have a good imagination during these times. Some people are actually putting on fat using their imaginations. They go to bed imagining they've eaten cheese, meat, bread, and in the morning their stomachs are full," he said and patted his midriff. "They keep their shutters closed so others can't see them using their imaginations. *Ja, ja.* Just trust in God. He will satisfy your every need, even hunger. Those who wish to see us starve make us even more religious," he said with a sardonic laugh.

Once again Auguste reminded him to be quiet, and their voices dropped to a whisper. Katya noticed how Auguste hovered near the perimeter of the room. When she had finished serving them she went to a chair in a corner and sat there, eyes cast down and arms folded against her chest as though she were suddenly chilled.

David fell into thought. He stared at his hands circling the glass of tea, into whatever darkness he was contemplating. Katya thought about her father then, and was almost grateful that he wasn't there. It would be a terrible thing to see him as wounded as David. She wondered if the reason his daughters were so watchful and silent was because their father seemed to be defeated.

David Sudermann had been among the men digging a trench on a factory yard, and when he saw her coming he'd straightened, and put aside his spade. He'd come towards them slowly, and she had wondered, who was this old, stooped-shouldered man? And then when he was certain it was them, and broke into a run, she realized this was David. She thought he would embrace her, but he stopped short of doing so, expressing concern that Njuta was too heavy for her to carry, and taking her sister from her arms.

When he had told her that her grandparents no longer lived in their house, he spoke without looking directly at her, and she wondered if he ever would look directly at her. She wondered how long she would have to endure the certain looks, and avoidance. As if she needed to be reminded that her family had been murdered. David went on to tell her that her Opa and Oma Schroeder had moved across the street and were living in the little house at the back of the Siemens' property. Her uncle Bernhard and aunt Susa and their family continued to live in their own house, however. Who was in the grandparents' house? You will see. You will be surprised to see, he said, without explaining why. As soon as they had something hot to drink and had rested, he would take them to their grandparents.

She didn't want to take the time to rest, she told him now as she sipped at her imaginary glass of cocoa. She was impatient to see her grandfather and grandmother. After being in the cluttered and noisy Krahn house, she was hungry for the dignity of their silences. Unlike Irma, they didn't have a need for self-examination, a need to find meaning behind every occurrence. And she would be free, too, to think about Kornelius without his presence interfering with her thoughts. David said he would accompany them to Rosenthal, of course.

As they neared the *Mädchenschule*, they heard the sound of children in the courtyard, and, except for the sounds of their play, Main Street of Rosenthal lay before her empty and silent. She noticed the absence of smoke in factory chimneys along the way, of the sound of iron striking iron; she noticed the deserted coalyards.

As they passed by the school she saw that its brick façade was pocked with bullet holes; the wrought-iron railing on top of the stone wall was twisted, and sections of it were missing. The Reds had declared that the school was for both boys and girls now, David informed her. And it was closed more often than not for lack of heating fuel. When the Makhnovites had left the town months earlier, David and others cleaned the school to prepare it for classes. They found mounds of discarded clothing that seemed to be alive. What moved were the lice, he said. The lice were ankle deep in all the rooms, and in whatever house or building the Makhnovites had stayed. The lice spread from house to house, columns of insects coming in under the doorsills and through cracks in the walls and floors. People resorted to burying their infested clothing, baking them, hammering the seams before retiring at night. "The two-headed offspring of anarchists. Lice and typhus," David said, speaking more to himself than to her.

The burnt shell of a house pressed through the trees beyond the school. Many of the trees around the Teachers' Seminary had been cut down. There were tree stumps in the yards of houses along the street, and up the sides of the valley. Fences were pulled down for firewood, David explained, barn boards stolen during the night, furniture broken up for the sake of heat.

As they grew near to her grandparents' house, David let them go on ahead, and moments later when she turned to look, he was going back down the street. He'd been rather mysterious about the inhabitants of her grandparents' house, she thought.

There were gloxinia plants on the windowsills, and the curtains appeared to be freshly starched. She saw movement beyond the windows in the summer room; it had been her mother's room at the onset of the war, when her father served at the *Lazarett*. While she knew it was impossible, as she came near to her grandparents' house she thought she could recall a time when her mother had been a child as young as Njuta. She imagined her mother in a white dress, squinting into the sun as she sat out on the platform on a hot summer afternoon, surrounded by aunts, uncles, cousins seated in rows on the steps and on chairs in the garden below. Her mother, a small girl, her hand rising to shield her eyes against a burning sun, watching her daughters coming down the street.

Whoever lived in the house now took good care of it, she thought, vaguely aware that a woman had come out onto the platform. She was followed by another woman, and then she recognized Dietrich Sudermann as he came from the house, holding a child in his arms. Although his hairline had receded, he looked much the same as when she'd last seen him.

"Katya, yes?" the woman said as she came down the steps. "I'm Barbara," she said. Behind her was Justina, whose queenly demeanour was intact, as was her shiny blond hair twisted in its usual skein at the back of her head. But it was Lydia Katya wanted and waited for as Dietrich thrust his child into Barbara's arms and hauled Katya into an embrace. His arms tightened, and she felt the quick thud of his heartbeat.

"And comes Lydia," Dietrich said, and released her.

Katya turned to see Lydia hurrying along the sidewalk towards them, her hair darkened now, the colour of old straw. Katya realized that her knees were shaking. *Lydia, what have you been making of your life? Can you tell me, after your mother, who was next, and then who? Can you tell me how Njuta came to be in the house?*

She felt Lydia's narrow body against her own, felt her shudder as they embraced. Then Lydia stepped quickly back. She'd been at the Seminary, helping care for the orphans, when she'd heard of their arrival, she explained as she tugged at the sleeves of her blouse, as though the cotton were chafing her skin.

"Lydia has psoriasis," Justina said.

"Yes, I'm covered with it, from head to foot," Lydia said with a sad small laugh, her eyes briefly meeting Katya's and then flickering away. "Sara, how big you are," she said, and Sara drew her shoulders up to try and make herself look even taller, causing the women to laugh. Dietrich stood rooted, his eyes clouding as they rested on Sara.

"But I wouldn't have recognized Njuta," Lydia said.

"Well, how could you? She was the age of this one when you last saw her," Barbara said, indicating the child she held in her arms. She had spoken in an off-hand manner to fill an awkward silence, without realizing the tactlessness of referring to that day. Dietrich, his features strained and troubled, left them and went into the house.

Katya felt rough in their presence, made so by their appearance, the women's lawn skirts and crisp linen blouses, a string of amethyst beads at Justina's neck.

"How *are* you?" Lydia asked softly, the question meaning so much more than what it usually did. I am doing as well as expected, Katya thought. What about you? When their eyes met, Lydia looked as if she were in search of something.

"We're a little worn out from our walk," Katya said.

"I know your grandparents are impatient to see you, otherwise I would invite you to come inside," Justina said, and Katya felt that she was being told to go.

"I'll walk with you the rest of the way," Lydia said.

They went across the street, Sara and Njuta between them, and Katya realized that she and Lydia were now the same height, both of them tall for young women, and like most everyone else, rather thin. Lydia would rub the sleeve of her blouse, touch a shoulder, move her body as if to ease the itch of psoriasis against the fabric of her clothing. Again their eyes met, and Lydia was the first to turn away, spots of colour rising in her cheeks. As they neared the gate to the Siemens house, Lydia took a step back, allowing for Sara and Njuta to enter first, and then she took Katya by the arm, indicating that she should stay. Katya felt the sudden dry heat of Lydia's palm against her own, a slight pressure, as she squeezed. "It was horrible," Lydia half-whispered, and closed her eyes for a moment. When she opened them, they were wet.

"They made you play the piano," Katya said, her lips tingling suddenly, her face gone stiff.

"Yes," Lydia said.

"And then the men came from the well."

"Katya, do you know about me?" she asked, her pale eyes widening. "Do people know, did Kornelius Heinrichs say?"

"Kornelius only said that he found you, just as he found me, and Sara, too," Katya said.

Katya saw Lydia with Greta, sitting together in the classroom, their heads joined, their eyes shining with concentration. Lydia's small hands washing creases in baby's legs, soaping its tiny head, threading its limbs through arm holes and leggings. She was still rescuing children, apparently, although larger and more needy ones.

Lydia looked at her sharply. "And were you and Sara. . . . Are you and Sara . . . Are you all right, then?" she asked, sounding like an older and caring sister.

Katya remembered Franz Pauls's question, Was Lydia laid on the ground, too? Had men done unspeakable things to Lydia while laying her out on the ground? Kornelius hadn't said any more than that he had come upon all of them struck down where they had stood, all except Lydia, who had been left for dead but was resurrected in Orlov's hayfield not knowing day from night, or who she was. "Yes, we're all right," Katya said, and found herself being embraced, felt Lydia's breath on her neck, heard her say, "Oh, how I prayed that would be the case." Then she smiled, her features softening for a brief moment.

"What about you?" Katya asked.

As they walked through the orchard at the back of the Siemens' yard, Lydia linked her arm through Katya's, and they walked just as Greta and Lydia had once walked, Katya feeling the heat of Lydia's skin, a wiry strength. "Well, I have the orphans to care for. It's something that needs to be done," Lydia said. Sara and Njuta were being joyfully received by their grandparents, judging from the noise. Lydia went on to explain that the Teachers' Seminary had now become an orphanage, a temporary place to house homeless children until people could be found who were willing to take them in. The orphans brought pieces of amber, she said, rings, silver they'd stolen at the thieves' bazaar in Alexandrovsk, copper pots. They came with their swollen stomachs, and stick-thin legs, wanting to exchange what they had stolen for food.

"Opa, come look, here's Katherine, she's coming," Katya heard her grandmother call, and she felt Lydia's lips brush her cheek before Lydia turned away.

Katya barely recognized the stooped figure who came towards them on the path, the round tanned face now pallid and hollow-cheeked, her mouth collapsed into her jaw. She reached for her grandmother, and in holding her felt she was cupping a wounded bird, and feeling its weak flutter against her palms.

S he sat with her grandparents in the semi-darkness, while across the room her sisters slept on a makeshift bed on the floor. She recalled the last time she'd been in the room, imagined the air still held the scent of ammonia and old cheese, remembered that her father had appeared to Tante Anna in a dream and told her that he was going home.

They didn't have any kerosene, her grandmother had explained, and so, like most, they usually went to bed at sundown. In order for them to sit and visit for a while this night, she had made a *pracher*, and the grease-soaked rag now burned in a saucer on the table between them, giving off the odour of animal fat and singed wool. The twist of flame illuminated the surface of the table and the space immediately around them, and the photographs of the Schroeder ancestors seemed to dissolve into the wall where they hung. She felt their sombre gazes penetrate the darkness, imagined that they'd heard the hoot of a barn owl coming from beyond a sandpit behind the house, listened now as her grandfather read aloud from a letter he'd received in reply to one of his own. "We think it's best you stay where you are, as even here in Canada, there are hardships. English may soon become the language of our children's schools. It seems everywhere in the world there is trouble. It may be best for you and yours if you remain where things are at least familiar."

There was much talk about going to Canada, her grandfather said with a sigh. The loudest voices in favour of it were those of the well-to-do, while others were willing to wait and see what changes the Soviets might bring. Contacts had been made in the United States, too, and food parcels were beginning to arrive from there, he told her. People were being given vouchers, which they were supposed to take to a central office in order to claim the parcel. But the office was nearly a hundred miles away, how would they get there?

With some difficulty he refolded the letter, and when his shaking hands made it impossible for him to slide it back into the sleeve of the envelope, she did it for him. The foreign-looking script, the red-and-blue stamp holding the likeness of the king of England made her feel the letter was heavy with importance.

"Speaking English yet," he said and shifted his body away from her as though he did not want her to see his bitterness, as though she hadn't heard it in his voice.

"We wrote to them that we would be willing to learn Chinese, if we had to," her grandmother said. "They don't know hardship. Here, if we were fortunate enough to own a cow, we'd have to pay the government eleven million rubles in tax, eighty million for a horse." She had heard of several cases of animals committing suicide, she said. A cow's head had been stuck on a fence post, and a sign saying that life before the Communists had meant lots of hay and grain to eat, and now the cow was only given straw and had to deliver so much milk as a tax to the government that life was not worth living. A hen had done the same thing, complained of her owner's demands for more eggs in order to pay the taxes.

Her grandfather's face lit up with a smile that quickly faded. "It's funny, but would be very dangerous for the person who made the sign if they were ever found out."

It was no wonder so many wanted to emigrate, he said. He had put their names on a list along with the names of over seventeen thousand Mennonites who wished to emigrate. Countries such as Mexico, Paraguay, South Africa and the United States had been visited by a committee. But after two years of travelling and negotiations, they learned it was Canada, in the end, that agreed to take them in. The final arrangements were now being made with the Canadian Pacific Railway, for payment of transportation costs. Some people had already begun to sell their belongings in anticipation of needing to pay for their passports.

He sounded breathless, and any physical exertion made him wheeze. Katya had noticed his laboured breathing when earlier, to ward off dampness, he'd lit a small fire in the stove. With great effort he had kept the fire stoked, and seemed almost relieved when the fuel, a sack of twigs and wood chips, was depleted. The stove had barely warmed the room when the meagre fire died. The sun had now set; the chill returned and dampness was seeping like smoke through the floorboards.

Her grandmother got up and went over to a bench beside the door, returning with several pieces of leather, which she held out. "Look, your opa has become a shoemaker," she said, and went on to tell Katya that he had been hired by a *kulak*, supplied with the necessary leather, and promised a hundred rubles to fashion a pair of boots. "An application for immigration costs twelve hundred rubles. Twelve pairs of boots. There aren't that many people in town who can afford new boots." She shrugged in resignation and returned the leather pieces to the bench.

Bernhard had taken the china dishes they'd stored in the attic to Alexandrovsk and sold them, her grandfather said, which had provided them with enough flour to get through the previous winter, and now they were without. What little money came their way went to buy food, if and when food staples could be found. A person did what he could. Her grandfather had been forced to acquire new skills, as had most of the men, David Sudermann included. He had made a window frame from scavenged wood, and sold it in the market across the river. He had even sold a fish or two he'd managed to catch in the creek.

Across the room, her sisters were dark shapes on the floor, their breathing shallow and even. The owl hooted, an eerie sound that seemed to come from the bottom of a barrel, and not across the sandpit behind the house, from the yard of Teacher Friesen, a man who had answered a knock on his door one night and been killed by the blast of a gun.

At least Friesen doesn't have to see this, her grandfather said. He didn't have to witness people meeting on street corners and trying not to say the words *hungry*, *food*, *eat*. Her grandparents had told what happened as though they were reading the event from a newspaper, as though they lacked energy for strong emotions and had become immune to grief. They had seized this opportunity to voice their worries, though in better times they would have waited until Katya, like Sara and Njuta, had fallen asleep. In the silence that followed, she became aware of the dampness, her feet and legs sweating and chilled, the feeble light barely illuminating her grandparents' aged and colourless faces. They had become like animals huddled in a cave, she thought.

Nela Siemens and her mother had joined them for supper, the latter bringing an unsweetened rhubarb *mooss*, her grandmother dividing half a loaf of bread among them, black unsalted bread made with more clay powder than flour, and which stuck to Katya's teeth and the roof of her mouth. She had been relieved at the appearance of Nela, whose soft heart had somehow remained soft, and seemed reinforced with a determination that was surprising.

She had gone with Nela to the room across the hall where the school boarders had once stayed. Its windows were now covered with sacking and the walls hung with horse blankets and carpet to keep out the cold. She wanted to show her the clothes she was making, various items of baby apparel, which, Nela said, she had cut from old garments, and planned to sell at the market in Alexandrovsk. Clothing hung from lines strung across one end of the room.

"And these? You're not using this?" Katya said, tugging at a shirt which seemed like new. She thought of the man she had come upon, reduced to wearing his dead wife's underslip.

"No, no. That belongs to Dietrich," Nela said.

The damp blouses, pillow casings, towels and various pieces of undergarments and nightdresses pinned to the lines belonged to Dietrich Sudermann, his wife, and his sisters. It was their laundry, which Nela had scrubbed only that morning, she explained. She had taken on the chore of doing their wash and cleaning their house, she said. As though the house had always belonged to the Sudermanns, and not the Schroeders.

"They're not used to that kind of work. And I don't mind doing what I can. A piece of ham now and then makes a lot of soup," Nela had said when she saw Katya's reaction.

"So are the Sudermanns paying you rent for the house?" Katya asked her grandparents now. Her grandmother's face disappeared into the darkness as she turned away from the light, while her grandfather looked down at his hands, folded across his stomach.

"*Ja, ja*. At first they did," he said. "But now all their money is gone."

"Justina's man is being kept in prison in Sevastopol. Their money went towards bribing the officials to keep him alive," her grandmother said.

"And Dietrich's child isn't well, either," her grandfather added. "I suppose they have their own kind of troubles."

Some things remained the same, Katya thought. Dietrich and his sisters living in her grandparents' house, and although their wealth was gone they were still exalted, so much so that people were expected, and willing, to give way to them.

She stood and carried the *pracher* across the room to the cupboard. She lifted the light and saw a coat that had once been hers, and that would now fit Sara. Instinctively, she dug into the pocket's flannel pouch, half expecting her hand would meet a soft, balled piece of sheepskin. The memory of it made her smile and want to weep. She went through the other clothing hanging there for something she could fashion into a child's trousers, a tunic, a nightshirt, or a baby's dress she might trim with a bit of old lace and embroidery, but there was little in the cupboard to choose from. She touched Greta's baptism dress, and then lifted it from the cupboard and held the light up to it. The dress was yellowing but unstained; the satin ribbons and rosettes were still intact. Then she decided. She would cut it apart, wash the pieces and iron them, make two, perhaps three infant dresses and sell them at the thieves' market.

"*Nanu*, you haven't said about yourself and Bull-Headed Heinrichs," her grandmother said.

Katya had known from her grandmother's studying looks all evening that she had wanted to ask this question. She used the darkness now, the opportunity of Sara and Njuta being asleep, to at last speak it.

Katya crossed the room, thinking of the sack of sugar Kornelius had given to Irma to sell, regretting that she hadn't brought them something, a loaf of Irma's famine-fare bread. As she set the *pracher* on the table, her grandparents' faces emerged from the gloom, their eyes reflecting the flicker of amber light.

"So you've heard, then, that Kornelius Heinrichs still wants to marry me," she said moments later.

"*Ja*, we heard," her grandfather said. Then he smiled and shook his head in wonder. "Imagine, love in these times."

Yes, imagine. Love, she thought. If this ache to hear his voice was love, then, yes, she had come to love Kornelius.

Her grandmother's features had grown pinched and stern. "Yes, we heard, but I thought likely it was just gossip. Katya, you know that no minister would agree to marry you and Bull-Headed," she said.

"Kornelius," Katya said.

"And you know very well what your parents would have said about this," her grandmother added with a note of finality.

Her parents. She had come to think of them as stones worn smooth by the elements. Stones polished by a flow of water. She accepted that they had been where they were supposed to be in life, in a stream whose water had flowed over, around, and under them, and swept them away. There, at Privol'noye where her father had worked as an overseer on the Sudermann estate during a time of contentment. When a house cat could sleep for hours undisturbed in a bureau drawer.

"Yes." She knew what they would say, but while they had taught her who she was and what she'd been born into, they had also led her to expect that they would always be near to answer for her.

The next morning her grandmother brought out what remained of the loaf of bread and tore it into three pieces. She set the chunks of bread on plates and slid the plates across the table in front of them.

Then she turned away from the questions forming in Sara's and Njuta's eyes.

"Eat it slowly," Katya told her sisters, believing that her grandmother would open the shutters and let the sunlight warm the room, but she went over to the bed where Katya's grandfather lay facing the wall and, fully clothed, climbed in beside him. Going back to bed to conserve energy. Because hunger made her cold, constantly.

Katya's sisters had already devoured their bread, and now they looked at her as though expecting there would be something more. She divided her portion in half and gave it to them. Somehow, from somewhere, she would need to find more, or the money to buy it. She left the room and went out into the hall without knowing what she would do, and seeing that the door to the other room was open, she stepped into it.

Her eyes grew accustomed to the dim light, and the clothing hanging from two lines at the far end of the room emerged like ghostly apparitions. Nela had worn her knuckles raw scrubbing for the Sudermanns and counted herself fortunate to be rewarded with a piece of ham for soup. Well, she, Katya, couldn't wait for such rewards. She strode across the room and yanked a shirt from the line, an underslip pinned beside it, and then a pillow casing, a towel. She went down one line and up the other one, wooden pegs flying across the floor as she tore free a nightshirt, a blouse, piece after piece of clothing. Clothing which she took with her back to her grandparents' room.

When she opened the shutters, sunlight streamed across the floor on which she had spread the apparel. Her sisters looked on in amazement as she carefully cut the clothing into pieces, her grandmother pacing and wringing her hands, no doubt expecting that at any moment lightning would strike the chimney, the roof would come crashing down.

▮▯▮▯▮

The next day, she stood beside the table in the family room of what had been her grandparents' house while Dietrich paced back and forth, his brow furrowed. She had been summoned by Justina to explain her action, and she had done so, strengthened by Lydia's absence, believing that she hadn't wanted to be part of her family's tribunal. For a long moment there was a silence, during which she observed Justina sitting at the table, staring at the scraps of material scattered across it. Dietrich went over to a bookshelf and ran his hand along it as though feeling the grain of its wood, or inspecting it for dust. Dietrich the Dust Inspector, she thought. The Dietrich she had known was almost unrecognizable behind an affected, officious manner of speaking, his shoulders squared and his back straight.

When her eyes met Justina's, she was surprised to see her look away.

"We understand. Of course you want to help your grandparents," Justina said, the unspoken word *however* reverberating in the air between them.

She thought of how Justina had become so much like Aganetha. She had inherited her mother's manner of plucking at her skirt, her way of speaking, and she had inherited her mother's girth too, a body that had begun to rise around its frame of bones. Justina hadn't been blessed with children, and so there was no accounting for the flesh welling up around the wide gold band on her finger, the swelling of her stomach and hips.

"Everyone is in the same position. What if we all resorted to such means?" Barbara said as she bustled into the room.

They were waiting for her to apologize. To say that she realized the error of her act. From the summer room came the loud ticking of a wall clock – her grandparents'? she wondered. The summer room, which offered its view of Main Street, Rosenthal, and the changing world beyond. Where she had seen children caught in the orchard by Ohm Siemens just as they were about to help themselves to his pears, and then were made to stand in a row and recite a poem while Ohm clapped out the beat of their choral presentation. Students going to and from school, their navy wool capes undone, the crimson lining flashing as the young women bounded down the steps and over to the gate. And she had seen the *podvodchiki* going to the train station, their wagons stacked with cannons and shell casings, which had been tooled in the factory of a pacifist. Teams of horses arriving from

Jakob Sudermann's factory in Einlage, drawing a chain of wagons to be shipped for use at the front.

She would not apologize. That the first would be last and the last first in the kingdom of heaven seemed a hollow promise when her grandparents had to stay in bed to conserve energy because they were starving.

"Katherine, you're not alone. There are many like you and your grandparents," Dietrich said, speaking softly, as though what he wanted to say was meant for her ears only. "Somehow the money to emigrate will be found. Already in the United States, and Canada too, our people are responding. We won't be left behind. If need be," he added, chin lifted, voice raised, "I will put your names on our applications."

She heard Barbara's sharp intake of breath, saw the quick glance she sent to Justina. Justina went over to Dietrich and put her hand on his arm. He turned away from her questioning gaze. "Papa would have done the same," he muttered. And Katya, seeing this, wondered if it would really come to pass, or if Dietrich would, once again, go against his heart and do what he was told to do. The three of them now looked at her.

They had expected her to apologize, and she hadn't. Now they anticipated gratefulness, tears of joy, perhaps. Justina might be moved by such a display, Barbara gratified. Canada, a word on a map, a place to escape to, providing her grandparents would be able to sell their house and what furniture hadn't already been sold. She didn't know anything at the time about Canada except the little she had learned from the letters her grandparents received from distant relatives in Manitoba. Letters complaining about too much or too little rain, about infestations of grasshoppers, about their children being forced to learn English in school.

Their attention was drawn towards the window at the sound of hoofbeats. The appearance of a horse in those days was infrequent, and worthy of notice. She heard the rattling of wooden planks, the grind of ironed-banded wheels against the road, and then she saw Kornelius. He's changed, she thought. His hair is shorter. Kornelius stood up before the horse had stopped moving. There goes an uncomplicated man, David Sudermann had said. Someone who says there is no God, and so there isn't one. Her father's question – Is that what he says, or is that what people say about him? – had gone unanswered.

Then the horse came to a halt, and Kornelius leapt down from the cart and strode up to the gate. Kornelius, bringing a gift, she would discover – a hedgehog that he had snared on the way and skinned – and the joyous news that Irma's prayers had been answered: Willy Krahn had been set free.

∎ ∎ ∎ ∎

Each day, throughout the spring, she thought she saw Kornelius in every man who came walking down the street. Remembered the moment in the orchard when she had said yes, she would marry him. Then closed her eyes and accepted his kiss. He then told her of his desire to go to Canada, that he would take her there, take her sisters and grandparents too, if they wished to go. Her grandmother's opposition had been dampened by his generosity, and she now remained silent whenever Katya mentioned his name. Her grandfather had placed his hand on Katya's head, saying that, above all, he knew Kornelius to be an honest man, and gave her his blessing.

The next time Kornelius returned to Rosenthal, it was in the heat of the dry summer that followed, land turned as hard as stone from the lack of rain, and from the sucking thirst of hot winds. She had expected him, as he had sent a message with Willy Krahn: A Lutheran minister in a village near to Arbusovka had agreed to marry them, and he would come for her within a week. When Willy delivered the message, and a small sack of rye flour, his happiness for her and Kornelius was evident in his beaming, round face. Sara and Njuta looked on solemnly, their eyes moving from Katya to their grandmother, who, upon hearing the news, shook her head.

Katya listened for Kornelius's arrival in the middle of the night, heard the constant swish of wind in the trees along the street, her eyes itching with dryness as she stared into the darkness, mouth dry too, its skin chapped and rough. When she put her hand against her lips, she thought, this is what he felt with his mouth when he kissed me, and she couldn't tell whether her lips or fingertips were tingling. The sensation passed between them, and then she was feeling it in her breasts, and then *there*. Stop, she told herself, you will soon know. And although Kornelius wouldn't come for her during the night, she imagined she heard the faint rumble of wheels against the earth, but it proved to be a distant roll of thunder as, once again, rain clouds skirted around the valley and emptied far out on the scorched steppe.

During the week, while she waited, she believed that the women watched her as she went past their houses, believed that they, too, were holding their breath and waiting. Nela, perhaps, had spoken for them when she had said, At last, Katya. At last some happiness, yes? I wish you and Kornelius all of God's best.

When Kornelius came for her it was in his cart, pulled by his worn-out horse, and not in the old custom, with a team of matched horses, the groom wearing black serge and a white shirt, a passenger in his own flower-garlanded *federwoage*. The way he had likely come calling for his first wife on their wedding day. Her Kornelius wore the only clothes he had, a twill jacket and patched trousers, and with a belief that their union had been ordained.

When he arrived, Katya was in the community garden with other women. They had gone there to weed and irrigate what vegetables had managed to survive. She was washing dust from her ankles in the Kanserovka creek, which, now, in the heat of summer, was just a narrow ribbon of water. He brought his horse to a stop, stood up and shielded his eyes against the sun as he tried to find her among the women, who had by now gone silent.

Kornelius waited for her beside the cart as she struggled to slip her wet feet into her shoes, not taking the time to tie the laces, the soles of her feet squeaking inside the shoes as she hurried to meet him. When she approached, he held out a package tied with a frayed red ribbon.

"Lydia Sudermann said I should give this to you," he said in answer to her questioning look. Lydia had seen him coming down the street and hailed him over. "She said she'd been saving this to give to you yourself." Then she had asked him to wait and went back into the house. Nela Siemens had come over to her gate and told him where he would find Katya, and before Lydia had returned with the parcel, Sara and Njuta appeared from the back of the Siemens' yard and told him the same thing. "It must be hard to get lost here," he said, with a sharp bit of laughter. "Big eyes, your sisters," he said. "Both of them."

The parcel was light and soft, and the paper crackled as Kornelius helped her climb up into the cart. He then stood for a moment, the muscles in his face working. "For sure, your sisters would like to come with us," he said. "And you would like that too, yes?"

But it wasn't possible, she knew. The distance they needed to go meant that they would have to stay overnight with the Lutheran pastor and his family before returning the following day. Her sisters would soon have her back, as she and Kornelius had agreed she would remain in Rosenthal and he in Arbusovka after they married, until the time came for them to leave Russia.

They went away from the community gardens, towards the outskirts of the town, where the road wound up the hill to the ridge of the plateau and beyond. Katya felt as if the women in the garden were still watching, felt the heat of Kornelius's thigh against her own. I don't know him, she thought, and she never would come to know him, not unless they began to talk. They had barely passed more than a few sentences between them. Sitting by his side, she grew tense, daring to glance at him only now and then, and at the horse, its mangy tail switching flies from its hindquarters. She looked down at the parcel on her lap, at the knot of the ribbon bow, then pulled it loose. The brown paper began to unfold and she spread it open. Lydia had given her a green cashmere dress, to be married in, she supposed. Tucked into its bodice were a pair of silk stockings, along with a note, which she opened and quickly read.

Dear Katya,
I found this verse in the Song of Solomon, and I thought it could fit any occasion, and especially yours today.
"Many waters cannot quench love, neither can the floods drown it."
Love prevails, yes? And it can never be taken from us. We have that promise.

In the name of our Father who has saved us, and keeps us strong,

your sister, Lydia.

Katya's eyes swam with tears. She looked back at the town. What fences remained were grey from lack of paint, but sunlight glinted in the all the windows, and the slate roof tiles held a sheen.

"Devil," Kornelius suddenly exclaimed, and Katya heard a soft thud as the cart lurched to a stop. She saw that the horse had stumbled and fallen to its knees. Kornelius jumped down from the cart and, gripping Katya around the waist, lifted her to the ground. He went over to the animal and stood for a moment looking at it, then whistled softly. A gust of wind swept over the crest of the hill, raining particles of dirt against the cart, against Katya's body.

He looked at her, a wry grin twisting his features as he straightened. "Well, well. This is bound to entertain people for years to come." He laughed ruefully and pushed his cap to the back of his head. "Bull-Headed's horse struck dead while taking him and his bride to their wedding. Can't you just hear what will be made of this?" Then he pushed at the animal with his foot, toppling it onto its side. "She's lasted longer than I ever thought she would. The horse was tired out, underfed; old age finally got her," he said as he began to free the animal from its traces.

Yes. Exhaustion, old age, she thought. The horse has died of those things, just as he said. But why now? Just then, a boy appeared at the crest of the hill, coming at a run, and then slowing to a walk when he saw the horse lying on its side in the middle of the road. He stood for a moment, his inquisitive eyes fixing on the animal, and then on them, and back again to the horse.

Kornelius returned to her side, and they watched the child scoot past them and down the grade of the hill, arms pumping and feet raising puffs of dust in the powdery earth. Kornelius took out his pocket watch. "I wonder how long it's going to take." She began to shake as he put his hands on the small of her back and drew her to him.

She let herself go, sank into his lean, hard body, her breasts flattening against his chest, felt his heat and smelled the sun, the wool in his jacket, a clean smell, she thought, while the hot wind buffeted them, and her skirt fluttered about the calves of his legs.

The boy had now reached the first of the houses in town, and she saw him stop briefly in front of a gate before continuing on. A man emerged from the yard and stood with his legs astride as he looked up in their direction. He quickly returned to the yard and went into the house. Moments later he reappeared, a woman with him.

Again, Kornelius glanced at his watch. "Maybe three minutes, if that," he said, and tucked the watch back into the breast pocket of his jacket.

Several other people came from a neighbouring house, and then a woman with a child in hand from a house across from it. The young boy had now begun to shout as he went through the town, a high voice calling out, and then its faint echo came from the other side of the valley, a valley made so much greener by distance, by the quavering waves of heat. The rose bushes spreading across the far slope, the clutch of houses sheltered by the leafy crowns of trees, were already being translated into the green paradise of future memories.

People were hurrying down Main Street now, one passing another, and being overtaken again. As though a signal had been given, they began to run all at the same time, up the hill, the women coming first, and then their more energetic children breaking free and passing them. The men soon fell behind, several of them stumbling along the way; the stiff-legged gait of others was proof that when there was not enough food, they chose to go without. As the townspeople drew near, she could hear their panting, see that they had brought basins with them, and gunny sacks. One of the women she had been working with in the gardens carried a hacksaw. They came to stop, a crowd of nearly twenty people, she guessed as they spread out in a single line, while still others were mounting the hill behind them. They stared at the horse lying on the road, its legs bent at the knees, wind riffling through its dusty mane.

Kornelius released her and stepped between the crowd of people and the animal, crossing his arms over his chest. Everyone grew quiet and wary. A moment passed, and then one of the women made a move towards the horse, stopping suddenly when a woman raised her hand.

"See here. Don't you think it's only right that the bride and groom should have the first choice of meat? Yes?" she said, when the other woman didn't answer.

"*Ja*, that's so. That's the way it usually goes," another woman replied. "The bride and groom are served first," she said, and handed Kornelius the butcher knife she was carrying.

The woman who had first spoken smiled shyly at Katya. "*Ja, ja*, at the wedding the bride comes first, but not afterwards," she said with a gaunt smile, and offered Kornelius the hacksaw. The women around her smiled faintly, and looked at one another, nodding in agreement, yes, that's the way it was in life. Forever after, the men and children would come first.

Kornelius looked at Katya and then back at the horse. Meat, she thought. The last time her grandparents and sisters had eaten meat was when he'd brought the hedgehog. Her mouth filled with saliva. She nodded and he went over to the horse, dropped to his haunches and began slicing into its front quarter. Moments later Katya heard the saw cutting through bone. Soon after, he walked towards her holding a chunk of meat away from his body, blood dripping from it onto the earth, and trickling across the bed of the cart as he set it down.

Katya stood mesmerized as the crowd surged forward all at once, obliterating the animal from view. They began cutting it into pieces, their voices rising in excitement, a man advising on how best to free the entrails, what might be made of the animal's hide. And there, wedged in among them, was a woman in faded black, her tattered shawl framing an angular face the colour of an old pearl. Katya saw the look of starvation in her face, the skin stretched tautly across her cheekbones, the terrible concentration that seemed to make her oblivious to those around her. Turned inward by the slow cold burning of her insides. Vera, she thought. This is Vera. Her breath rose, grew quick and shallow. How did you know the cup was in the butter well? she thought.

"Vera," she said.

The woman's eyes met Katya's, briefly.

"Vera," Katya said, once again, and the woman's grey eyebrows arched in a question. Njuta. How did Njuta come to be in Abram's office? The woman stood up, holding a leg bone, her hands slick with blood. Strands of hair the colour of iron had escaped her headscarf and were trailing across her forehead. She was mistaken, this old woman couldn't be Vera, Katya told herself, and felt Kornelius's presence at her side, his arm slip around her waist.

The woman turned, and with her spine stiff, she walked down the hill as slowly as the incline would allow her to go. *Haulftän*, Katya thought. Grudge-bearer. Walking as though she carried a chip on her shoulder. Katya's legs began to tremble as she watched the woman descend the hill, as the woman became a small dark figure, and then, smaller still. She reached the first of the houses in the town below, came near to a hedge, and then, one, two, and three, she was out of sight forever.

When she had finished speaking her story into the tape machine, she felt as though she had been talking all day, when really Ernest Unger had been present for no more than two hours. He had photographs he'd taken on a recent trip to Ukraine, and began spreading them now across the hassock in front of her: the Schroeder house, a house that had been built in the design of the canal builders' houses in the Vistula Delta. Although the picture had been taken nearly eighty years after she left Russia, the house looked the same. The Teachers' Seminary had gained a statue of Lenin, his arm raised, and a finger indicating eleven o'clock, Ernest Unger said. Lenin was pointing out the time when the liquor stores would open for the day, his guide had dared to joke. The seminary itself had been divided into small rooms to house a kindergarten and nursery.

Chortitza and Rosenthal had remained intact, he told her, just as many other of their villages remained whole all over Ukraine, the names of them changed first to Russian names, and then Ukrainian. The surviving schools, houses, the factories had become monuments for the relatives of the original owners to visit on yearly pilgrimages, to make gravestone rubbings, uncover the name of a Mennonite brick maker on a doorstep. They came to pay homage to the stories their grandparents and parents had told them, and to refurbish the operating room in the Chortitza hospital with more modern equipment. In another village Mennonites had rebuilt an Orthodox church which had lapsed into ruin. They brought suitcases filled with antibiotics and aspirin, clothing, hard currency, and forgiveness.

Ernest Unger had seen the tourists disembark from the tour bus at a field of sunflowers and go in search of the foundations of houses, the site of a well they'd been told about, others content just to stand beside the road in silence. They fixed such importance on the smallest of things, he said, a ladder nailed over a doorway of a falling-down barn, full of meaning for a man who had once used it to climb up into the loft. The Mennonite tour had taken them near to the mighty Dneproges dam, and out in boats on the Dnieper to drift for moments over the place where the village of Einlage had been, submerged now since the building of the dam. Looking down through the water, they could see the roof of the church, a wavering dark behemoth, and what appeared to be a row of spires, but which were tree trunks marking out where the streets had been. Below the spires were rectangular shapes, the walls of houses, broken shells where water plants now grew from the river silt, a refuge for fish.

"Completely covered over, flooded," he said, and made a cutting motion with his hands. "Gone."

"Yes, I heard that," she said.

Flooded, but not drowned, she thought suddenly. Across the room in a bureau drawer was a chocolate box, and Lydia's note inside it, along with a packet of letters tied with the frayed ribbon Lydia had used to fasten her wedding-gift parcel. And neither can the floods quench it, Katya thought, and saw herself floating on the river, looking into the depths. What she saw was her family lying there. They were all in a row in their wooden coffins, their heads bound, as though they were wearing turbans. Their throats banded too with the soft white cotton, because of injury. They looked tucked in, safe, she thought.

In the drawer there was a photograph of her parents, Katya a babe in her father's arms. A plump doughy child who had once gone to and fro, believing that she was strong enough to blow the world down. There was also a cluster of ceramic violets, a brooch Kornelius had given to her on the birth of their first child. By the grace of God, she and Kornelius had raised seven good children, and they, their own children, who were now raising their own. At the last count, seventy-three people had come from her and Kornelius's union, healthy people, and no accidents or heartbreak had yet to touch them.

"Yes, and so it goes," she said.

And then she told him that when their journey ended in Manitoba she was amazed at how similar the countryside was to the steppe. She had written this in a letter to Lydia, hoping to change her mind, hoping that while it was still possible, she would come to Canada. But this was not to be. What did Canada have to offer her, Lydia had asked, except pity, and she, like many Mennonite young women, like Sara, would likely end up working as a servant for a wealthy family until she had paid for her passage. At least she was doing some good where she was, caring for the orphans. Her letters grew less frequent as the years passed, and ceased all together during the Second World War. Katya had heard a story that she had been among the Mennonites who fled with the German army at the end of the war, but had been captured and returned to Russia. She'd been exiled to Siberia where, during a particularly hard winter, she had died of starvation. Others said they'd heard that she had eventually married a Russian, and that her children were all Communists. Katya preferred to believe that Lydia did have children and grandchildren, even if they were Communist, because they, too, were God's children, whether or not they wanted to be taken as such.

"Close to our destination the train came to a stop to take on water," she said, "and Kornelius and I got off to stretch our legs. A farming village lay far beyond, a settlement of about ten houses or so and, like us, the people there were mostly Mennonites, the conductor told us. Living there was our man, a man named Harder who had agreed to take us in for a year. The conductor said we should stay on the train until the next stop, which was a large town; it was more than likely Harder would be waiting for us there. Kornelius said he wanted to feel the land under his feet, and so my grandparents and sisters remained on the train while we began to walk. The sound of the wind in the grass was so loud that I had to shout to make myself heard."

As she was likely shouting now, even though, to her own ears, her voice seemed to come from a great distance. Which was to be expected, at her age, that her hearing would go, and eyesight dim. But not her mind, oh no, not yet, she still had all of her mind, and she could imagine herself now, swimming through the grass towards her new life, through the sound of the wind driving waves to a far-away shore. She was the wind, and she was the vibrating drone of insects. Like the gold face her father had once cupped in his hand and returned to the earth, she, too, was about to disappear into the past. But one day, someone will come. Someone will stop to take a pebble from a horse's shoe, and discover her burial mound, her name, Katherine Vogt Heinrichs. Her name chiselled in a stone. Her gravestone will become a Baba stone, her features defined by shadows cast by the sun.

ACKNOWLEDGEMENTS

I am indebted to my late, great uncle, Gerhard P. Schroeder, for his book of memoirs *Miracles of Grace and Judgment*, and his journals *Swing High, Swing Low*. I am also grateful for *The Diaries of Anna Baerg* and *Wintergreen* by Helena Goosen, and *Hope Springs Eternal* by John P. Nickel. With thanks to Norma Jost Voth for *Mennonite Foods and Folkways*.

The novel could not have been written without the wonderful account of Mennonites in Russia, *None But Saints: The Transformation of Mennonite Life in Russia 1789–1889* by James Urry. His advice and encouragement have been most valuable.

Many books proved helpful, and I would especially like to acknowledge *First Mennonite Villages in Russia* by N. J. Kroeker, *In Her Own Voice*, edited by Katherine Martens and Heidi Harms, *The Russian Century* by Brian Moynahan, *A People's Tragedy* by Orlando Figes, and *Rites of Spring* by Modris Eksteins, to name only a few.

Thanks to the Mennonite Heritage Centre, and the Canadian Mennonite Brethren archives in Winnipeg for making their archival material available to me.

While I have used the actual names of Mennonite towns, villages, and colonies that existed in Russia, I have taken some liberties with their geographical locations.

The Scripture epigrams are from the King James Version of the Bible.

Finally, I am grateful to readers of early drafts of the manuscript, Jan Nowina Zarzycki, Byrna Barclay, Hildi Froese Tiessen, and especially Irmgard Wiebe. Their suggestions and comments have been exceedingly helpful.

I reserve my deepest gratitude for Ellen Seligman, my editor, for her unwavering dedication to the story I wished to tell.